She found hersel... smelled of books. W... hind the drapes, she ... ..., as many as the Sysbaet had. Megan wanted to take one, thinking surely the Wizard wouldn't miss just one, then thought better of it. A book was too expensive; all she needed was a little thing.

On the shelf above was a bell shining in a ray of light from the window. She picked it up to read the writing on the rim but couldn't make it out. As she lifted it, it rang and she grabbed the clapper, wrapping her mitten around the bell and stuffing it in her shirt. Jorge'd believe her now. As she turned away from the shelf, something hissed at her from the near corner.

She ran, wiggling out the window but getting stuck halfway because of the bell. Frantically she squirmed, trying to worm free. She wiggled loose just as a light bloomed behind her.

She looked back over her shoulder. The Wizard stood in the door, with a light shining around her hand. Megan almost fell through, and clung to the windowsill roof.

The Wizard, a woman with long, curly black hair and eyes the same yellow as the statue in the garden, wore blue trousers and a shirt gleaming rainbow colors under a black vest. Her hand whipped down, as if throwing something, and Megan ducked, slipping, feeling an ice wind graze her head as she slid down the roof and rolled into the snow. She jumped over the fence and ran and ran and ran.

Novels of the Fifth Millennium:

SHADOW'S DAUGHTER

Shirley Meier

BAEN FANTASY

SHADOW'S DAUGHTER

This is a work of fiction. All the characters and events portrayed in this book are fictional, and any resemblance to real people or incidents is purely coincidental.

A Baen Books Original.

Baen Publishing Enterprises
P.O. Box 1403
Riverdale, N.Y. 10471

ISBN: 0-671-72096-1

Cover art by Larry Elmore

First printing, November 1991

Distributed by
SIMON & SCHUSTER
1230 Avenue of the Americas
New York, N.Y. 10020

Printed in the United States of America

Dedication

To my Great Grandmother who was one tough lady. To my father who encourages my imagination and my mother who always listens despite the weird names.

To Richard Hall, Maureen Walsh and Nino Basacco who all took extra time to give me honest critique and keep saying "But I *know* you can do better." To Professor Don McKay who saw Megan first.

To Bill Chong, Robert Hayes and Way Lem. To Robert Lombardo (R.I.P) and Thom Gardner. Thank you to everyone who ever went through the karate class and taught me something . . . sometimes by *not* teaching . . . or learning.

I'd like to say thank you to members of the Legion of Super Davids for the loan of Point Ariel and Hephalump repair. Also Margaret and Edwin Layton (Marg for support, Ed for history of technology information).

To everyone in the Bunch of Seven, members past and present, (Tanya Huff, Fi Patton, S.M. Stirling, Michael Wallis, Louise Hypher, Karen Wehrstein, Terri Neal, Marian Hughes, Julie Fountain, Mandy Slater, Jan Stirling, Julie Czerneda, Stephanie Rendino) who critiqued it.

But most of all, love and galleys, to my love,

Karen

Chapter One

It was spring in F'talezon, and the *Blutrosh*, the Blood-roses, bloomed. The hand-sized blossoms nodded in the breeze over the head of a four-year-old child sitting on the white stone steps in the sunshine, pulling her tunic over her knees. The house was set into the ground, with only the windows, the door and the roof showing, like most of the other old houses in the Middle Quarter of the city. Her mother called the flowers her sisters because the newly planted bushes had first bloomed on the child's birthday.

Megan Lixandashkya sat with her arms clasped around her knees, knowing she wasn't supposed to pull her tunic so far. She scrunched her knees up high; it wouldn't stretch so much that way. Her father had woven it new. Down the street one of the drover's husbands laughed with the *roheji* seller as he bought some of her pastries hot out of the oil.

Around the corner she could hear the Old Brewery Gate rumbling open onto Brewer's Street; the horses snorting and stamping, harness jingling as they hauled

1

the barrels out. She didn't like horses much, though she didn't mind their smell mixed with the bread-rising smell of the beer.

Downstairs, inside, she could hear her mother singing, her hands flying over the lace-frame like the *Veysneya*, the Silverwings, in Koru's Temple. They flew in the light of the rose window, and the painted faces of the Goddess, hundreds of years old, gazed down from the smooth-polished rock walls. The Ladyshrine down the street in the park was a tiny shrine compared to the temple, but Megan liked the statue of Koru there much better. Her father would take her there sometimes, holding her hand because she was too little to walk alone and might be lost, or stolen by those whose market was children.

Lixand Mikhailovych, called Weaver, whistled as he opened the yard gate with one hand, balancing a sack of *'maranth* flour on one shoulder. He was average height for a Zak, four and a half feet tall, with dark brown hair, and green eyes set in a lightly tanned round face that smiled more easily than it frowned. "Ness! Megan! I'm home . . ." He laughed and caught Megan's hand when she ran and hugged his legs. "Come on, *bylashka*, little princess, help me put this in the cupboard and come for a walk with me."

Megan would stretch her legs and trot to keep up to her papa whenever they went on these walks, while he told her stories. Mama always said that if he weren't a *Gospozhyn*, a Great Master in the Weaver's Guild, he'd be a storyteller. Megan always liked listening, though she didn't always understand.

They walked past the lawyer's house, with its red brick and worn black gargoyles. It leaned and always looked like it wanted to fall on their house, but never did; past the baker's house, that smelled so good, past the drovers' houses and the empty space that had nothing in it but broken, burned stones and grass taller than Megan; past the brewers' houses and the high grey wall of the *Sysbaet* School.

They were good teachers as well as healers, almost as good as Haians, and she might be able to go to the school and learn to read. Megan wanted to learn, but her parents said that it cost a lot of Dragonclaws and they didn't have time to teach her more, though they tried. She knew her letters already because Papa said that it was a good thing to know. He knew because his family had had enough money for schooling before the Great Fire took most of his family, and Ness had learned from her mother, Grandma-who-was-with-Koru. If you couldn't read, you couldn't be apprenticed in the Guild and would have to be a beggar or a thief.

The cobblestones were old; worn by the tread of generations of people. Because the year had been dry so far the sewer in mid-street was cracking mud and didn't smell, which to Megan's mind was almost as nice as when the fall rains came and washed the mud and odor away. Her papa nodded hello to the neighbors who sat on their front steps or walked along Szyzka Lane.

The bare trees' branches reminded Megan of old people's gap-teeth. The buds were just big enough to make small shadows to step in. She skipped from shadow to shadow, pretending the sunny spaces were the rat pits in the *Va Zalstva*, the Arena, where she mustn't step or she'd be devoured. Her papa got ahead of her a little and she gave up her game, running to catch up. Even this far down the street she could still hear the vats in the brewery groaning and sighing, like sleeping men snoring.

"Megan, you mustn't let go my hand until you're bigger," Papa said and stroked her hair back out of her face. "Bylashka, my little shadow, in a crowd, anyone can get lost. I want you to be careful, even when you walk with me."

"I will, Papa." She held tight to his hand and walked onto the dusty grass of the park as if she were grown up, instead of running ahead like she wanted to.

The park was a small patch of grass with a few trees along the streets and the stream, and lilacs around the Shrine. Across the park the Sneykh tributary gurgled to itself, on its way down to Chas Lake. It was a shallow creek cascading from the Dark Lord's Temple in the northern cliff wall of the City. The Sneykh was usually dirty because the Dark Lord's priests sacrificed into the water. The other stream, the Byeliey, ran out of the Ladyshrine on the south cliff wall, and was carefully kept clean.

"Tell me the best story again, please," Megan said. Papa sat down on one of the wood benches of the shrine and took her on his lap, and Megan hugged him looking over his shoulder at the white fountain with the statue of Koru. *She's so beautiful,* she thought.

"Szyzka Lane," Papa began, "is a street with Middle Quarter ways of thinking, hanging on to the First Quarter's skirts with its fingernails so it doesn't slide any farther down the rift. It's the sort of street that, every morning, blinks its shutters, looks around, and wonders vaguely where its grandeur has disappeared to overnight. It's the sort of place where quiet people live quiet lives, away from the notice of the *Prafetatla* above and the thieves below. We have nothing that either of them wish to steal and when the riots come, we pull in our heads and wait until they're gone. We didn't always have riots, Megan-mi."

"Tell me, Papa." She didn't understand it all, but she liked sitting on his lap, hugging him when he had time like this, on a rest-day at Hand'send. She loved feeling his big arms around her so she'd be safe and cozy.

"The *Zarizan*, the Young DragonLord, Ranion, is the only Heir. His father the Dragon, the *Woyvode*, was harsh, ruthless, the very spirit of Prafetatla before he grew old and weak, but he cared what happened to us, here and in the other lands. The *Kievir* nearest the young Lord, Dark One notice him, cares for himself and his own *zight*, or pride, and nothing else. When the Old Dragon fell ill the first time, the Four-days War happened with the Thanes. No protection was offered us, no retaliation for people persecuted. That was when pogrom began along the Thanish border—"

"Which is why Mama-came-to-the-city-you-met-and-fell-in-love-andhadme!" Megan finished in a rush, glad to get to the best part. Her papa laughed, all crinkly laugh-lines that she liked better than the frown ones, then he stood up and swung her around, off the bench high like a bird, before setting her down and taking her hand.

"Yes, yes, little bylashka. We had you." Then he poked her cheek gently with one finger. "Nice to see a smile there, little solemn face!" They walked all the way around the park, from the fountain past the path through to Svinina Street where the Guildhall was. Then Megan let go and ran and ran in big circles, arms wide, pretending she was a bird, flying high, always staying in sight and coming back to her papa.

Someone had made a swing out of an old bell rope and a board, and her father pushed her so she swung high, laughing.

Then he took her down and said, "We'd better go back or your mother will wonder what happened to us." He always said that before they left, every time. She pouted, then tickled him, and he put her on his shoulders to "keep you out of trouble" and carried her up the street that way, higher than the world.

She was high enough to see the sun shining in the bits of broken glass set along the tops of the garden walls. People looked different enough from this angle that she felt shy about waving to them, but did anyway; it was neighborly.

Everyone's yard was different within the stone and brick walls; plots of dirt for vegetables later in the year, grass, covered flowerbeds or stone and sand gardens. As Papa opened their wooden gate, they could hear voices inside the house. "Hello," Papa called, and stepped inside as Megan ducked her head under the lintel.

The inside door was still open, along with the shutters around the top of the house. From the landing, ten steps led down into the house proper, where the stone floor was covered with bright carpets. Sitting cushions were scattered here and there. In the kitchen corner a red-tiled stove sat and a small brazier helped keep the floor warm. Across from the stairs, the wallbed was open to air out and the feather tick, pillows and blankets hung outside to get the winter's mustiness out of them. Near the stairs stood a wooden chest with Megan's bed tucked in behind it like a miniature wallbed. The sun shone in through the shutters, cutting the room in half slantwise from top corner to bottom opposite, bright and dim light, dust dancing in the breeze from the outside.

"Lixand, Marte's come to visit." Mama's voice was cheerful as she called from her cushion by the table, but Megan could hear tears in it. Beside her, Megan's aunt Marte put down her *kahfe* cup with a click. *Mama cries sometimes when Aunt comes*, Megan thought. When Papa put her down and went to greet his sister, Megan hid in her bed.

She crawled in under the feather tick and pillow, all her own. Her mama had traded at the Big Market for the feathers and sewed the patchwork cover with pieces of Papa's old green coat and bits of felt from her worn-out boots. The tick wasn't like her parents' that had a red cover all of a piece and two pillows each as big as Megan. Some mornings when Mama opened the carved doors of the bed, Megan would run across the cold floor and climb into the wallbed with them. She wasn't a baby any longer, needing her parents to keep her warm, and had a bed all her own, but she liked those mornings.

It smelled wonderfully of cedar in the dark, but she poked her head out since it was getting too hot and her braids were coming undone. Then she moved to the top of her tick, hugging her stuffed bear Brunsc, listening to the adults' voices and the click of Ness's good cups. They sat on the cushions by the brazier, drinking kahfe, though Megan didn't understand why her mother would serve it; kahfe was only for special company.

"Lixand, you have your position to consider," Aunt Marte said. "As next in line for the Guildmastership, you should at least live in a more prosperous neighborhood. Somewhere in the First Quarter, where you can associate with people of your own station, people of—quality." She always looked sideways at Mama when she said things like that.

"We like it here," Lixand said quietly.

Megan peeked over the edge of the trunk for a second before ducking down again. Like Lixand, Marte had dark brown hair and very fair skin that burned easily. Next to her husband, Ness was tiny with raven black hair and slanted eyes almost dark enough to be called black. Megan tended to favor her mother which, for some reason Megan couldn't understand, angered Marte. Aunt wrinkled her nose as if there were a foul odor in the room, and Megan pretended that Brunsc had teeth and could bite her.

"Of course, I understand your tastes, brother," Marte said and smiled, but she kept looking at Ness. "Never quite refined enough."

"Marta Mikhailashkya, my tastes are none of your business." Megan remembered one time when he'd almost hit her; she was kin so he restrained himself. He was starting to sound that angry again.

"Oh, certainly. Ness, dear, the kahfe is lovely." Megan lay down again and started to play with Brunsc. He only had one ear left because she'd chewed the other one off when she was a little baby. Her mama said she was a big girl now. She lifted him up over her head, pretending she was old enough to have access to the *manrauq*, the power of mind that all adult Zak had, and could make him float without holding him in her hands. Her mother could do that, but it would tire her out.

Megan didn't want to listen to Aunt Marte. She didn't understand how Aunt could make Mama sad and Papa angry all at the same time without raising her voice.

"Megan," Papa called to her. She pushed Brunsc out to see if it was safe, and when the toy just lay there dribbling sawdust from a little hole under his arm, she looked around the corner of the trunk.

"There's the child! Megan, come here," Aunt Marte

said, and held out her thin hands, beckoning. Megan didn't move. "Willful, isn't she? Just like western stock."

"Megan, come out and be polite." Papa's voice was like his flint and steel scraping to start a fire. "Your aunt is just *leaving*."

Marte had a peevish, annoyed look, entirely unlike her younger brother. She was taller than he was and her hair was streaky with grey. Lixand's face was flushed and if Ness held her cup any tighter she was going to break it. Megan crawled out dragging Brunsc to protect her and Marte held out her hands again. Those hands never felt like what her voice said, usually holding too hard or pinching. Megan shook her head and stayed by her papa, hiding her eyes on his leg. She thought that her aunt smelled like the medicines she made. "Such a sweet little grig! Such a child, Ness! With her looks you'd think that *both* her parents were City Zak of the purest sort," Marte said. Ness looked away, silent. Megan wanted to spit on her aunt's feet, but wouldn't; she was kin.

Lixand looked tired. "Marte," he said, "she looks like her mother and I am proud of my family." He took a deep breath and tried to be civil. "Tell me, have you made a connection with the Haian?"

"No, but I've made some other good contacts, nonetheless. The Haian isn't likely to be here long, ever since the Woyvode started showing his disfavor towards them." She got up as she spoke, brushing her sleeves hard as if to slap the dust of the house off. "Good Blossoming to you."

Lixand only said, "Shall I see you home? One can't be too careful in the City nowadays. . . ."

She laughed as she walked over to the stairs and her shadow, as she walked by, was cold. "Oh, no. I'm quite safe." She looked happy, which made Megan feel both small and scared. "No," she said again. "*I* don't have to worry. Especially with the new contract I have. Just think on my advice, little brother." He took her by one elbow and walked her up the steps as if to make sure that she left quickly. Ness was shivering. Megan stood a moment clutching her bear, then ran to hug Mama.

"Your poor little cousin," her mama said, rocking her. "Poor Rilla."

"Poor Rilla," Megan parroted. "Can she come t'stay again? She's a funny baby."

"Maybe soon, Megan-mi. Your aunt says that she's too little to be away from her mother." Ness's face was closed as she repeated the words, and Megan could tell that her mother didn't feel them to be true. The door clicked upstairs and Papa came down, his feet making soft scuffing noises on the mat.

"Ach, she's venomous today." He sighed, then kissed Ness. She shushed him and nodded down at Megan in her lap. *That means I'm not supposed to hear that.* Papa hugged them both. "Don't worry, love," he said to his wife. "She's been like that as long as I can remember, thinking I'm living below my status. She knows I don't play the cutthroat games for position and I won't let her pour poison in my ear. It's not as if I'm the only candidate for Head of Guild, and it's safer if I keep out of the way till the dust settles. There are rumors of murder; we'll be safer keeping our heads down."

Ness was silent, holding onto her family.

"I'm four. I'm four." Megan skipped and sang beside her mother, holding her hand as they went down to the school. Four was important because that was when school could start. It was important enough for Ness to take time off from her work at the Guildhall, though they could ill afford the loss of her work time. Megan would normally have been with her parents in the baby's hall at the Guild.

Instead, she was being very careful not to wrinkle her good black tunic and Ness had spent a bit of time brushing Megan's hair, braiding it up neatly out of the way. She took one long stretching step and three little running ones to keep up with her mother, humming.

They stopped before the *Sysbaet*'s gate, and Megan

craned her neck up at the phoenix carved in inlaid light and dark wood. Ness sighed and Megan looked to see what was the matter.

"Someone's stolen the bellpull again," Ness explained. The bell was too high to reach, being metal and very precious.

Megan's eyes filled with sudden tears. "If they don't hear us knock we won't get in and I won't start school and I'll be a beggar . . ." She bit her lip, trying not to cry.

"Hush. They'll hear the bell." Ness took a deep breath and put one hand on the gate to steady herself, closing her eyes. The clapper of the bell started to swing to the Zak woman's thought. She wasn't strong enough to swing the whole bell, so she started it swinging then pushed at the right time. In a minute it rang, once, a tiny ring—then louder, a jangle. Ness was breathing a little hard. "There," she said. "They'll hear that."

"Thank you, Mama." Megan knew her mama was good at magic, manrauq, even if she was only barely a red witch.

The Sysbaet was older than the Weaver's house and dug further under the ground, perhaps the oldest place in the Middle Quarter. It was hard to dig so deep now with handtools. The old buildings had been dug out of the mountain with metal monsters before the Fire, when the sky burned. Some of the oldest tunnels were dangerous, full of the sickness that the Flames had burned away.

"Yes?" The monk who answered the door had his brown robe tucked up into his belt, his sleeves rolled back, hands wet. Megan wondered what he was washing. "How may we help?"

"One for the school, *Sysbat*." Megan looked up at him and hung onto her mama's hand. Suddenly she was afraid. What if they didn't take her? Or what would happen if they did? She'd be in a strange place where everyone knew lots more things than she did. Maybe she couldn't learn how to read or figure.

"Isn't she a bit young, *Teik*?" Megan grabbed onto Mama's hand with both of hers.

"She was four this spring. We understood that that was the minimum age for your scholars."

"Four?" The monk looked away in apology for his tone. He was more used to laborers and their children, who were taller, almost like naZak.

"She's beautifully tiny, Teik. Will you come this way?"

"Thank you." They followed him down the grey and black stone stairs. The walls were smooth, as smooth and polished as manrauq could make it. The monk had been using his power to smooth chisel marks in a newly carved niche in the wall, dipping his hands into a bucket of water to cool them.

The light came in from the bluish glass in the roof, glass out of the mountain where the metal was. Any glass now was brought up the river, from Bjornholm or the Empire of Arko. The sun hit the mirrors along the corridors, and where a mirror wouldn't do the light came from *kraumak*, the glowing rocks as big as Megan's fist. There were quite a few in the halls, probably more than any naZak had ever seen. The first kraumak had been lit five hundred years ago. The manrauq made most naZak nervous. *They call us witches,* Megan thought, *and burn people*. The kraumak were in places where torches had been, from the soot marking the ceilings.

They passed rooms filled with books—old books hung on pegs, new books on shelves and scrolls. Their musty leather and paper smell was everywhere, as if it were part of the rock. There were maps on the walls, showing the known seas, or the lands by country. There was a whole wall covered in feathers of different birds and near them . . . Megan hid behind Ness as they walked by. A stuffed Ri with black-on-black stripes. It was a horse-like creature with a carnivore's fangs bared in a snarl, silver mane falling down into mean, crazy green eyes. It held one leg up with all claws extended.

A live gold squirrel chucked and flicked his tail at them

then whisked into a crack in the wall, Megan craning to see where it went.

They passed a hall where a choir was practicing, as the conductor tapped sharply on her music stand. "No, no. *Don't* breathe after that word. I want the sound to be seamless . . ." Her voice echoed off red columns, carved with herons and fish. Megan stretched back, trying to see as they passed the open doors, but all she could see was a mass of brown habits at the other end of the hall under one of the skylights. Mama squeezed her hand to warn her not to drag her feet too much.

The monk stopped and bowed them into a waiting room. "Wait here, please," he said. "I will inform the K'mizar of Children that you are here." They sat down on the blue cushions and Megan looked at the green tapestry of the river valley across from her. *I'm bored, being good,* she thought.

She kicked her heels against the floor and her sandals pushed up till they were balanced on her big toes by their straps. "Megan . . ." Mama said quietly. "This is very important." Megan sat up straight and tried not to fidget. There was a glass case with the skeleton of a bird in it by the door and Megan wanted to get up and look at it, but she sat still. *I'll see it, when I'm here, learning.* The rich folk, the Prafetatla, *their* children had their own teachers, but Megan was lucky that she had access to some schooling.

The door clicked and a woman with grey and red hair looked in and said, "Come along to my office, if you please. I'm Hanya, K'mizar of Children."

"Certainly. We are Ness, called Weaver, and Megan," Ness answered, holding out her hand to Megan as she got up. "Come along, Megan." The K'mizar was a little taller than Megan's mother and very thin. She looked to Megan as if she were made of milkweed fluff, and sniffled as she walked. She wore a brown robe like everyone else, but her belt was red and white and pinned by a metal pin in the shape of a heron holding a candle in its curved beak. She was wearing fleece in her sandals, tucked around the leather, to keep her feet warm.

Once in her office it only took a bit of talk, after they'd shared the salt, to admit Megan to the first class.

A week or two later, Megan sat at the brazier with Brunsc, warming her hands, listening to the rain splash on the shutters. It was cold this morning and her Mama had already gone to the Guildhall. After she went in the student's gate, Papa would walk through the park, then along Svart Road up to Reyeka, to work. In the summer it wouldn't be too dark for her to walk to school by herself in the morning. *When summer comes and I'm bigger, I'll be able to go to the park by myself, too.*

And then she could help Mama by shopping at the market on Svenina, as long as she didn't talk to strangers. Papa said that slavers preferred younger children, and she'd be old enough to be fairly safe by summer. The Watch patrolled regularly out of the First Quarter and came as far south as two streets up so the neighborhood was safer than either of the Quarters farther down toward the Lake. It had been quieter since most naZak had been chased out of the city by the Woyvode's decree; at least that's what the corner-criers had said.

Ness had a special project at the Guild. She'd left the house so early, to start a lace cloth for *Zingas* Xvan's wedding.

"Eat your porridge before it gets cold," Papa said.

"Yes, Papa." She didn't like porridge, even when they bought tree-sugar for it. She slapped the spoon in it, splashing.

"Megan!" he warned. She shoveled it into her mouth, telling herself there was milk in it, which she liked. *It's good for me. If I threw it on the wall, would it stick?* She tried not to taste it, making faces at the gruel as she ate.

Then she hurried because she liked school. She didn't understand why the other kids complained, but didn't say anything because they'd think she was strange. She looked over to the stairs where her boots were waiting. If she had real boots it meant she was old enough to play outside by herself, since only babies ran barefoot. *Her* boots were red and blue and black stripes with a fringe on top, fallen over on top of her slate and waxboard waiting on the stairs.

She put her bowl in the bucket, hugged Brunsc goodbye, and ran to get ready. *Papa's slow.* She jumped up on the bottom step and her boot fringes swished. Her braids thumped on her back when she jumped down again. Up. And down. Up. And down.

"Papa, come on!"

"Don't be impatient, bylashka. I'm coming." Like a grownup with always one more thing to do or put away. The bed was made, its doors closed, the bucket was full of water for the dishes to soak until Papa or Mama got home, whoever was first. He put the window pole down after he finished closing the shutters and pulled his coat on.

It had stopped pouring but was still wet, cold enough to make her nose prickle inside, the air full of water; a heavy fog, almost a light drizzle. Ice coated every brown grass blade in the yard, slicking black on the wall. Most of the roses were protected under the overhang but some of the leaves and branches, coated with ice, hung down rattling as if made of stone.

She hung onto Papa as they slid down the street and he showed her how to keep her balance by sliding purposely instead of trying to walk and slipping. Her slate and waxboard banged on her back, bouncing on the leather strap as he slid her around him, laughing.

They slid around the corner into the colonnade of Student's Walk and saw Vyaroslaf and his children ahead of them at the gate. Lixand went quiet because he didn't like his co-worker and would have to be polite and walk to work with him. Then tonight, when he came home, he'd be unhappy and tell Ness how much trouble there was at the Gospozhyn's Hall in the Guild. Since she was busy doing something special she'd have been in one of the quiet rooms and wouldn't have heard any of it. Megan thought that if Teik Vyaroslaf Vritaskovych ever smiled his face would break.

"Good morning, Teik," he said to Lixand. Rosziviy, behind her papa, stuck her tongue out at Megan. She had pushed Megan yesterday and almost made her drop her slate. Her brother, Leonid, had stepped on Megan's foot because his big sister told him to, but Megan had stuck him with a pin later and he'd gotten in trouble for yelling in class. Megan smiled to herself, remembering. They were mean because she was smarter than they were. She was already in their reading group and Sysbat Karlovna had said she was quick. Leonid was the littlest in the class, next to Megan, but she knew her words quicker.

"Good morning, Vyaroslaf. The spring is late this year, is it not? Study hard, Megan." Papa patted her and she went in the gate with Rosziviy and Leonid.

"Megan eats worms, baby Megan eats worms!" Leonid hopped both feet together down the steps in time with his chant.

"She's gotta because her daddy's got lower zight than our daddy," Rosziviy said, and giggled. "He's gotta be po—li—ite!"

"He does not! I do not! He isn't. He's lots better than your papa. He's a better weaver 'n anybody! You're lying!" They were all on the lower stairs by this time, and the other kids had stopped playing around in the waiting hall and stood around watching.

"I'm telling!" Rosziviy said. "I'm not a liar!"

"Eats worms," Leonid squealed and jumped down from the bottom step onto the floor. Megan jumped on him and the other kids gathered around them. He fell down and didn't fight back, just yelling, "TEACHER!"

Megan was picked off him by her tunic and shaken. "Megan!" It was Sysbat Karlovna, frowning. "Fighting? I'm disappointed." Leonid was sitting on the steps blubbering, even though he was bigger than Megan and last week had blackened her eye in a fight outside the school.

"He's just trying to get me in trouble! He . . . he said—"

"He didn't say anything, Sysbat." Rosziviy's best friend Danacia interrupted. "She just hit him." Rosziviy was whispering in her ear and they both laughed.

"I did not!"

"Megan, that's enough!" Karlovna angrily shook her again before thumping her down on the steps. "One more word and you'll go speak to the K'mizar. We were worried at letting you in so young, but we've apparently let a vixen into our midst."

It wasn't fair. She looked at their blank-paper faces and Rosziviy's smug one.

"Leonid, stop sniffling and wipe your face. Come to order, children." Sysbat Karlovna let go of her and swept into the classroom followed by the other children, leaving Megan alone on the stairs. "Megan, come!" She looked at the open door, not understanding how it could have gone so wrong, so quickly.

She dragged her feet down the steps, thump, thump. Her fringe swished but she didn't like it anymore. Everyone sat in the circle on their cushions by the big slateboard. She walked all the way across the room to her box and opened it. The hinge squeaked and everyone watched in silence. She put her slate and waxboard away, pulled her boots off, and sat down on her cushion. Sysbat started the Icicle Song, but Megan didn't try very hard to remember the words.

Leonid stopped singing when Sysbat Karlovna turned to help Elexiy and whispered, "Just wait, Megan *Vixen*, we're gonna get you."

Her waxboard was cold as she hugged it. The Assembly Hall seemed much bigger and full of frightening echoes with no one in it but her. The herons stared down from the pillars as if she were a frog, and because they took the extra lights away when not needed, the hall was shadowed around the edges.

The K'mizar had said she needed extra help with numbers from Sysbat Tenara in the library and although Megan knew the Hall now, and the classrooms, she'd never been in *there*.

She hid in the shadow of one of the pillars, away from the heron on it, peeking around at the library door. Rosziviy said that the librarian was a naZak who stuffed stupid little kids and put them in the museum. *Rosziviy's dumb.* Then Leonid said that the little kids weren't supposed to go in the library or the museum or the *oscasa*— the bone museum—and if they were caught, the librarian put their bones in the oscasa with the other skeletons and then stuffed them for the museum. *He's dumb too. They're both lying.* But Vika said they had people's bones in there and he wouldn't lie.

The library door stood in the shadows, closed. Was she supposed to knock or just go in? She tried to comfort herself with the knowledge of all the books behind that door, and that thought kept her from running away; that and the hope that the Sysbat wouldn't be there.

Megan looked down and counted the black tiles between her and the door as she stepped on them. *One. And one is Two.* She could put both feet on one tile. *And one is Three.* She was far away from the pillar now and hugged her waxboard tighter to her middle, wishing she had Brunsc there; or Mama or Papa.

Somebody slammed a door in the upper gallery and it echoed around against the walls; Megan ran back to the pillar, telling herself she wasn't scared, but waiting until the echoes had quieted before coming out again. *One. And one is Two. And one is Three. I did those already.* The other kids were just being dumb, just trying to scare her. *And one is Four.* The door looked very heavy. *Maybe it's locked and I'll just go home before it gets dark. And one is Five.*

Rosziviy couldn't laugh at her for being a scaredy-mouse if no one were there. *And one is Six. And one is Seven.* She could try to open it, then go home. *And one is Eight, and one is Nine, and one is Ten.* She scratched

her neck. *And one is Eleven.* She looked up at the big
rosewood door, shivering. *I'm there.*

She put down her board, reached up to the black glass
doorknob that was slippery but turned; click. The door
hinges gave a tiny mouse's squeak and it stopped, open
just a crack. She picked up her waxboard and wiggled
through the narrow opening.

On one side there stood a desk with a shaded kraumak
on, making a blue puddle of light on all the papers. In
the dim light she could see cabinets on either side and
the bony tail of a skeleton poking out behind them. It
was quiet, except for a big clock that sounded like the
one in the Guildhall that was taller than Papa and had
brass gears and a brass pine cone on the bottom swinging
in time with the tick. Her papa had told her that it was
one of the only ones in the city.

This tick sounded like something big breathing. In the
back Megan could see low desks and sitting cushions.
One of the cabinets was open.

It smelled of books, of leather and thick pages, glue
and dust. There was a sharp odor, high and thin and
acidic from the museum she guessed, and the oscasa.
Encouraged by the silence, she slid along the wall,
peeked around the corner of the open cabinet. Someone
getting up from putting a book away on a low shelf
almost bumped into her. "Oh!" Megan squeaked and
dropped her waxboard.

The person getting up hadn't touched her, but both
were startled. Megan turned to run but the woman put
a hand on her shoulder and stopped her.

Sysbat Tenara was a giant, taller than her parents,
taller than anyone, with long blond hair and blue eyes,
and a long nose and a square-shaped face. The Arkan
spectacles she wore made her eyes look like blue marbles
in jelly pudding. "What are you doing in here, sneaking
around?" She spoke with a strange accent that clipped
and slid around some sounds. Her voice was deep and
as firm as if she hammered nails with it.

Megan tried to explain. "I'mmm not sn—sneaking. Th-the K'mmmizar s-s-sent . . ."

Sysbat frowned down at her. "Megan, yes, that's the name," she said. "I recall. Humph. Well." Then she squinted down at Megan. "You're shaking, child. Are you all right?"

Megan couldn't say anything, couldn't answer, looking up at the Sysbat who looked down at her. *Is she deciding where to put me?*

Then the teacher sighed and shook her head. "I don't eat children. I don't stuff them and put them in the museum. I don't boil them up and put their bones in the oscasa. I don't even snarl at people unless they hurt my books, despite any stories the other children will have told you." She half-smiled with one corner of her mouth. "Even if I am from Arko, I'm not a barbarian." Megan sniffled.

"Here," Tenara said, and directed the child over to the desk. "The K'mizar said you needed extra help with your numbers." She wiped Megan's eyes and nose with a big white handkerchief. "Blow your nose. Today I'll just show you the library, tomorrow we'll worry about arithmetic."

I suppose she needs a kerchief that big because her nose is big, too. I'm ashamed that I cried. Only little kids cried, Vikoria said, and she was in the third class above Megan's, almost halfway to being apprenticed. Megan bit her lip and tried to smile and the librarian smiled back.

1 is a smithy, a steel-maker's hoard.

Megan tried to make her letters as neat and tidy as Sysbat Tenara's. She'd been the librarian for a long time and said that Megan should try to put the numbers with words to help her remember them.

If she copied the verse out neatly tonight, then she could use the sheet of new paper Sysbat gave her, write it in ink and it would get put up on the children's board. Megan had taken the precious sheet of paper and put it away in her box at school, between the pages of the counting book, so it wouldn't get crinkled or dirty.

2 is a two-fang instead of a sword.

Her hand hurt, so she put her stylus down for a while. She was lying on her stomach on the rug and traced the outline of a green flower in it with her finger. When she did her homework she got to use her Papa's lap desk. She pretended her finger was a pink caterpillar trying to crawl up one of the short legs.

"Megan, are you doing your homework?"

"Yes, Mama, just resting."

"Well, don't rest too long, you have—" Ness looked over her daughter's shoulder, her hands wet and soapy "—eight more numbers to go, and two extra lines."

"Yes, Mama." Ness had come home early today, mad at someone, she said, but not at Megan. The child picked up her stylus again and chewed on the flat bone end, though she shouldn't because it was the end she used to smooth out mistakes in the wax. It already had teeth marks.

Ness dried her hands and trimmed the wick on the lamp, then went to her cushion, picking up the laceframe, though she didn't want to work on it, Megan could tell.

3 is a laceframe whose teeth are all broken.

Something had happened at the Guildhall, Megan thought. *Something loud and with lots of shouting.*

The front door banged and Lixand stamped the mud off before opening the inside door. Papa must have come through the park; there was thick mud on his boots. Megan ran to help with his packages because that was one of her jobs. The parcels were bulging string bags full of 'maranth tubers and potatoes, rye bread, milk in a clay jug. There was even a wrapped sausage for the barley soup Ness was making out of beef bones, but there was no butter to be had at the market unless you could pay in silver. He'd been lucky to get almost everything because there were many things you couldn't get in spring. Megan had never liked the feel of the damp bag of tubers and the burlap smelled musty, but she helped carry one corner anyway.

Ness hugged him, though he was wet through. Once he had his coat and boots off he came to help her get dinner ready.

4 is a chain that we shw as a token.

That was the broken chain on the altar in Koru's Temple. She couldn't remember the first time she'd seen it because it was always there, but she knew her papa had showed it to her. It was important because the Goddess freed everybody from chains.

"Ness, how could it have happened?" Papa was pacing. "You set the tension yourself. I convinced the acting Guildmaster that you'd be the best weaver for the commission, because you are. What could have happened?"

Mama slammed a cupboard door. "I couldn't say this there. It would have done more harm than good, Lixand. The teeth and pegs were worn, set in a new frame, so they slipped. Even with Koru's hands on the frame, it couldn't have held the tension. And you know who has jurisdiction over equipment."

"Vyaroslaf." Papa sounded tired. He tasted the soup, sprinkled in a bit of salt, and put the lid back on.

Five are the Silverwings, silver that flies.

They were in the Ladyshrine, too—the Veysneya. They sipped the nectar from the Blutrosh around the fountain.

"Ness, all we can do is for both of us to go in tonight."

"And replace an iron-cycle's work?" Mama looked partly angry and partly as if she wanted to cry. "I was half done. Zingas Xvan's wedding is less than fifteen days away. It's impossible."

Papa sighed so deeply that Megan looked up from her waxboard. "Both of us working together can do it. It's your design, and that was what took the time."

She stopped and looked at him. "You mean secretly?"

"I have to salvage something out of this mess. I've lost zight in this fiasco." He walked away, put his hands on the edges of the wallbed. "Vyaroslaf and I were about equal before. I have to do *something*!" he said voice rising. Megan ducked. Mama went over and put her arms around his shoulders, leaned her head into his back.

"I'm sorry Ness," he said quietly. "It's just so close. The vote for the Guildmastership is this summer and I don't have room for mistakes, but I won't sink to his level. Vyaroslaf drives me mad. The man is so corrupt he—"

He'd turned around and Mama put her fingers over his mouth and nodded at Megan. He looked at her for a minute, then relaxed, smiled, and pretended to bite her finger. *Mushy stuff,* Megan thought and went back to writing.

Six is the Dragon that holds up the skis.

"No, no, Megan," Mama said, looking over her shoulder. "You've forgotten the 'e' in skies." Megan looked but couldn't see where the "e" should go. Ness pointed and she squeezed it between the "i" and the "s." She put her tongue between her teeth and dug the stylus into the wax for the next line.

Seven is the Goddess of loving and living.

Koru. All-Mother. The Lady. She saved the Zak when the world burned, everyone—even Thanes and Arkans—though Megan couldn't understand why the Goddess would want to do that. Her statues were always white or red stone.

"We'll eat first. Then we have to take Megan along to my sis—"

"Lixand, I *don't* like leaving her with that woman, even for an evening. Leaving her own daughter in her care is bad enough!" Megan looked up again. She didn't want to go to Aunt Marte's even if she did get to see Rilla.

"She's kin. Megan will be safer with her than leaving her alone."

Ness thought for a bit and sighed. "I know, love. It's just that she enjoys hurting people so much, especially me."

"She's reliable, even if sharp-tongued. She's just like that. What would she do? She's my sister."

"Well, she can look in later rather than us taking her over there. Megan, are you done?"

"No, Mama."

"Well, hurry, bylashka. Dinner's almost ready."

Eight, Elder Brther, his heart always giving.

He was the Goddess's boy, who fought the Dark One and was almost lost in Halya. Megan liked hearing that story from her papa nearly as much as Heart of Coal. The soup bubbled on the shelf of the stove and the lid banged, letting good-smelling steam out. She didn't want Aunt Marte to come to look in on her.

Nine is the Dark One whose laughter is death.

Megan shivered as she wrote that. The Dark One had white hair, iron claws, and wings like an eagle. All his demons were black eagles as well, with white heads and arrows in their claws. She hugged Brunsc to make herself feel better and chewed on her stylus again, almost finished.

Ten is our Power, our Life and our Breath.

Manrauq, that manifested around puberty. Lixand was a red witch, able to cast illusions, just as Ness could move objects with her mind. Megan wanted to have a very strong Gift, but her mother had explained there was a price; the more manrauq a Zak used, the sooner they died.

Ness pulled out the cutting board for the bread. It made a crusty noise, then a crunch and a thump when the knife hit the wood. *Papa just wiped off the table. I'd better hurry.*

Thes are the numbers we hld in two hands

We think, we creat and we cherish our lands.

She didn't understand all of that, but Sysbat Karlovna said she would when she was older. There. She pushed the stylus into the wax till she heard it tap the wood, to make a finishing mark. Then she put it away through the leather loop and the cover closed with a clap, and she called her mother to help her tie it shut.

Then she pushed the desk over to make room and ran to get everyone's pillows; another one of her jobs. She'd plump them up and put them around the table. The blue one for Papa. The green one for Mama, and the red one for her. The wind whistled against the shutters upstairs.

"Megan, we have to go out so I want you to be a good girl until Aunt Marte comes. I don't know if she'll bring Rilla."

"Yes, Papa."

They closed their eyes and raised their hands for Ness and Megan to pray. Lixand hummed the deep bass note while mother and daughter sang:

"We've lived yet another day, been blessed with wholesome food.
Lady grant our children life, air and water good.
Shelter us from naZak fires, steel and sword of fear,
and as the day draws to its close, Goddess, please draw near."

The next day Megan played skip rope in the children's playhall. Her numbers would go up on the children's board and Rosziviy would bite her tongue because she didn't have anything up.

Megan sang the words to a jump rope song under her breath, hearing other kids jumping to it too, but they were playing with five instead of just one.

"Price for magic paid in size.
Twice a sin in naZak eyes.
Haysa, Hosa 1,2,3
I change you and you change me!

There's a naZak without sense
Make him think that he's a fence.
I don't care he's twice our size
He thinks it's all tricks and lies.

Here comes anger, here comes fear.
Here comes fire on our ear.
You'll get caught here if you stay
Haysa, Hosa run away!"

Last night had been spooky. Before they left, her parents had banked the stove and put the brazier out so it wouldn't tip. It was serious or they wouldn't have gone and left her and Brunsc. Aunt Marte had put Rilla in bed with Megan, and they'd told each other stories under her feather tick until they'd fallen asleep. The wind had been howling at the shutters and Aunt Marte sat by the lamp with some wine that she brought to drink, because it was chilly outside, she said. She'd fallen asleep, too. Megan thought her papa was angry about that when they came home, but she'd only woken up when they took Rilla.

"Hi, Megan," Ursella said. She was six whole iron-cycles older than Megan, but she was born on the same day the younger girl was, so they were best friends.

"Hi!" She wasn't like Danacia, who showed off her finger rings with the blue ribbons between each finger. Ursella jumped in with Megan, who passed her the rope and jumped out. That was one trick Rosziviy and Danacia couldn't do.

They played jump and change a few more times before Leonid came over to watch and stick his tongue out. They ignored him and he went away for a while, then his ball rolled into the rope under Megan's feet and she fell and skinned her knee. It hurt like a pulled tooth, sudden and sharp, and she sat looking at the hole in her pants where the scrape oozed. Ursella picked up the ball and stared at Leonid, then held it up out of his reach when he grabbed for it.

"Hey!" she said loudly, holding it up over her head. "Look at what *I* found!" Leonid shouted and jumped, but she just held it higher. Megan stood up. Seeing Leonid jump made her feel better.

"It's mine! You didn't find it. It's my ball!" he sniveled.

"Ursella, give that back," Rosziviy yelled from across the hall. "It's his!" She ran over and tried to push Megan out of the way.

"Yeah?" Megan said, refusing to move. Rosziviy poked

a finger into her shoulder. Megan slapped her hand away. "He shouldn'ta lost it."

"Mine! Is mine! Gimme, gimme!"

"Crybaby! You're crying over a stupid ball!" Ursella threw it across the children's hall where it rolled into the corner.

Leonid ran after it with Elixey shouting after him. "Crybaby! Crybaby!"

Ursella and Megan stood next to each other, staring at Rosziviy.

"That was his ball," Rosziviy said, but more uncertainly.

"So? You wanna fight about it?" Ursella laughed at her and Rosziviy went red. *She pokes me with her finger one more time I'm gonna hit her.*

"Children! Children!" Sysbat Karlovna clapped her hands for them all to come to order.

"What's wrong, here?" She looked around at all of them, particularly at Megan.

"Nothing, Sysbat," Ursella cut in. "Leonid thought he lost his ball and was crying about it."

"All right then. You all play nicely now."

"Yes, Sysbat," they chorused.

Ursella waited for Megan to get her skip rope and they went behind the ramp to sit down in the narrow place underneath.

There they inspected Megan's scraped knee and swore to be best friends forever. Ursella gave Megan her Baba doll and Megan gave her her red Glassy, a glass marble as big as an eye, and second-best stylus.

"Children! Lessons! Children!" Sysbat Karlovna called, and they scrambled out from under the ramp, running to line up.

When they were allowed into the classroom, Megan went to her box to get her counting book with the precious blank page.

But it wasn't white and clean and flat like it was supposed to be. Somebody had dripped ink on it, big splashes and scribble marks and dribbles all over, then crinkled it. But . . .

"Megan!" Sysbat Karlovna grabbed the page. "What did you do, wicked child! Look at it! Ruined. Wasted!" She waved the piece of paper at Megan. Everyone else in the room looked up at the commotion and went quiet. "Your parents are spending quite a bit of money to send you to school and this is how you show your appreciation? Fighting, ruining expensive paper?"

Megan couldn't see she was crying so hard, then grabbed the paper out of Sysbat's hand and ran, heedless of Karlovna's call behind her.

Sysbat Tenara looked up from her desk as Megan burst in, trying to explain, trying to get in her lap and show the page all at once. The librarian let her cry for a little then sat her up.

"Show me the page. Well, they were pretty thorough about it weren't they? Humph. I'll see to it, Megan. Don't worry. One ruined sheet of paper, even good paper, isn't the Fire that burned the world. I'll speak to Karlovna, even if she's not likely to listen to me, and the K'mizar, who is." She wiped away tears with big naZak fingers. "You look at this book for a while. I'll get this straightened out." She left Megan safe in a nest of cushions with some books and the clock for company.

Chapter Two

Rosziviy didn't talk to her anymore, probably because her papa told her not to. She walked around pretending Megan wasn't there, even if she stepped on her toes. Leonid still teased, but Megan could easily pretend he wasn't there.

A few weeks later, Megan took Brunsc in to school, to show Sysbat Tenara, and she let him sit on her desk. Megan had forgotten to get him back before the holiday and missed having him.

It was going to be a good holiday—sunny. Midsummer. Megan sang the words and swung on their gate, waiting outside, for Mama and Papa to come. It was after the midday meal and she wore her new tunic—yellow with a green and blue edge—and she had green ribbons in her hair.

They'd be going to the Ladyshrine, and then to the Big Market, because today the Year Kievir would be chosen. The priest who won would be the Woyvode's advisor and the tenor of the City would change. The Dark Lord's years were times of decay and death, the Lady's of charity and cleansing.

28

Teik Vyaroslaf and his wife walked by, with Rosziviy and Leonid behind them. Leonid's tunic was smudged and he already had dirt on his face. Rosziviy wasn't looking at him, trying to be like her mama with her nose in the air, being careful not to get her boots dirty. She looked at Megan out of the corner of her eye when they went by and stopped long enough to whisper, "My papa's better'n your papa."

Megan had promised not to get dirty today. "He is not," she said back.

Teik Vyaroslaf looked back and frowned. "Rosziviy, come away from that child."

He wasn't any more polite than his daughter. "Greetings of the day, Teik," Megan said.

"Humph. Well. Yes, child. Rosziviy, come!" Leonid's mama had him by the arm and brushed him off, hard, scolding. He squealed just like a baby pig at the market.

Rosziviy said, "Yes, Papa dear." He turned around to speak to Leonid. *"My papa's going to get your papa,"* Rosziviy hissed, and went to stand with her parents while Vyaroslaf scolded his son. Megan spat on Rosziviy's shadow when she turned her back wondering why they had to keep walking up this street instead of Vyetryena.

When they went away Megan leaned against the gate and made it swing again and stood on the bottom until it closed with a bang. Bang. Bang. Then she opened it and did it again. It was almost as much fun as the swing in the park. Someone had taken it down some time ago and given the bellpull back to the Sysbaet. Grownups were no fun.

The birds squeaked in the ivy on the wall outside where the leaves were big enough now to hide them. Brown sparrows and yellow Soltsniy birds chattered and scolded the lawyer's grey cat on his windowsill. They all sounded like Rosziviy's mama to Megan.

"Come along Megan-mi, stop swinging on the gate. You'll be big enough to break it soon," Papa said, and held out his hand.

Megan put one hand in his and her other hand in

Mama's. Mama's tunic was like Megan's, but green with
yellow and blue, while Papa's was black. Lixand stopped
to lock the gate and they went up the street with all the
other people, Megan swinging between Mama and Papa's
hands. Then Papa lifted Megan up on his shoulders and
put an arm around Mama. *Mushy stuff.*

Megan was almost high enough to bump her head on
some of the overhangs on Brewer's Street. The cobbles
there were pink and the walls were higher than her head,
even on her papa's shoulders. There was room on the
street for flower baskets and potted trees, but most of
them were bare and the pots full of muck.

The tops of everyone's head looked like a brown and
black bobbing sea, and Megan pretended that she rode
a ship over those waves.

Some ladies wore bright scarves on their hair, and up
ahead she saw a blue hat and a group wearing sailor's
wool caps. There were many people wearing bright red,
and almost as many people wearing dark green. "I hope
the Woyvode has many years left to him," Papa said.
"The struggle for the regency if he dies soon will tear
the city apart; whoever wins gets to try and control young
Ranion."

"Surely the Old Dragon is getting better, Lixand.
That's what the reports out of the Nest have been saying,
and he's making a public appearance today," Ness
answered. Megan couldn't reach down far enough to
touch her mama's head, though she tried and started to
slip. "Megan, don't," Lixand said absently.

"That's true. I suppose he thinks it's important to
appear strong. Kievir Mikail's faction has the upper hand,
but Kievir Khovorbod has a gained quite a few of the
young Prafetatla on our side," Papa said, reaching up to
steady Megan. "Notice most of those wearing green are
quite young." Megan, looking down over his bangs
thought he was smiling because she could feel his face
muscles bunching. "Megan, sit still."

It was noisy. People talked to each other and little

babies cried and a kidpack ran around people's legs, chasing a dog with a blood-sausage in its mouth.

The whole City was out today: River Quarter, Lake Quarter, even the handlers of the dead from around the Lake. Someone close was wearing too much musk perfume, and one woman's hair was so black and shiny it looked like the Dark Lord's Temple after a rain. Megan twisted around to look at the temple behind them. In the sun the grey cliff stones sparkled, except the black square that was the Dark Lord's Temple.

Today the Year Kievir would be chosen. Megan turned to look ahead but she couldn't see the Ladyshrine because the Gazhtinizia Garden was in front of them. The playhouse was large because Nuov-Kievir Kostonavic was a good patron.

"We should have gone the other way," Papa said. He was looking at Market Street. There were so many people there that you couldn't see the cobbles, and above the noise of the people Megan heard an ox lowing.

On the corner a flower-seller on the corner shouted, "White flowers! White flowers for the Goddess! Buy Koru's roses! Show support for her Son!" The roses were wilting a little.

Megan banged her heels against Papa's chest. "Megan, don't do that." She leaned over his head and looked down at his nose.

At a new odor she looked around and spotted the pie-seller and a cookie-maker. "Papa, may I have a cookie?"

"Not now, Megan. We have to get to the shrine first." He looked and then said, "Megan, if I hold you up, can you see how crowded Market Street is, over the wall?"

"I think so."

"Tell me how many people are up ahead."

"Careful, love," Ness said. Papa sat Megan on his hand and lifted her straight up.

"There's so many people there, it looks like a mat, Papa, and a cart stuck in front." He let her down, swinging, and she laughed when he caught her and put her back on his shoulders. "Come on, Ness," he said to

Mama. "If we can get to Avenue Street, we can cut across Piva and down to Reyeka. It's the long way, but we'll get there without standing in the sun all day and have to see the choosing from here."

"All right."

Papa had to turn sideways to get past a man with a basket of pots on his head and Mama followed, hanging on to his arm, but they got to the corner and went down that way, through an older section. "Megan-mi, don't pull my hair."

Reyeka Road skirted the edge of the River Quarter. The houses were sooty and dark, as if dirt crept out onto the road from them. Even the grass looked dirty.

Megan looked at a broken fountain as they passed. It had been a bear cub playing in the water, but its face had been smashed. It smelled of piss and shit and Megan wrinkled her nose, old enough to know that you were supposed to use the bucket and put the lid back on. Even Leonid didn't piss his pants or anywhere he wasn't supposed to.

She tried to read the words scratched or painted on the bricks, but Ness saw her lips moving and told her they were words she didn't need to know.

"We're late, Lixand," Ness said. "The priests are already beginning the rites. We'll never get into the temple and out again in time. We'll have to wait until after."

"We'll be able to see from here then, love."

They were just off the Stairs bridge and Megan looked toward the Dark Lord's Temple. Across the city she could see a sparkle at the big black doors. She could see the priests on the steps of the Lady's Shrine with their hands raised, surrounding the priest who was playing the Elder Brother this year. He raised his two-fang over his head. Mama whispered, "It's Beyis the Sage. I know his mother."

His hair was very black and he was wearing the red and silver armor that the Elder Brother always wore when he fought the Dark Lord. The priests and priestesses around him began singing, the Veysneya circling all around them, shining like copper-washed coins.

Across the rift Megan could hear horns and drums and screams, and she tried to stretch higher on her father's shoulders to see the Dark Lord's priests. They stood, surrounding their lord, who wore red and blue armor. The whole City, watching from the steeply sloping lanes and alleys and streets went quiet. In the Piatyacha Tower by the Market, the Woyvode's banner unfurled, snapping slowly in the breeze. Megan looked around, puzzled as the whole world went tight and strange around her. All the adults had a set, tense look of concentration on their faces.

The Elder Brother stepped away from the other priests, out to the farthest point toward the Dark Lord and shook the two-fang over his head. "COME OUT! I BEAR JUSTICE IN MY HANDS! SLAYER OF CHILDREN! ALL DEVOURER! ENSLAVER! MINION OF THE EAGLES OF WAR, COME OUT AND FACE ME!"

A dog barked across the city. Megan couldn't hear the Dark One's answer but knew it, had learned it in school. He wouldn't answer right away. He'd wait until the Elder Brother called again. Then he'd say, "CHILD! FOOL! CHAMPION OF RABBLE! YOU LACKWITTED MOTHER'S BOY! HOW DARE YOU SNIVEL AT MY DOOR? FACE ME IF YOU HAVE THE SPINE! FACE *ME*!"

A priestess struck a tiny bell in front of her and the chime rang through the whole City, echoing. The Elder Brother stepped out onto clear air, nothing under his feet. She'd never seen that much manrauq before. Sysbat Karlovna had told them about the invisible bridge created out of a united thought, but seeing it was different.

The priest walked out and then started trotting to the middle by the Piatyacha Tower where the Woyvode could witness their contest. The Dark One came out to meet him there, two-fang held like a lance. Megan clenched her hands in her papa's hair, praying for the Elder Brother.

The wind howled and tried to pull him sideways. He slipped, caught himself; she gasped and held her breath. Neither priest could see the edge of the bridge, both of them in the hands of the Gods fighting for primacy.

Elder Brother's two-fang flashed in the sun. The Dark One's hair was bright white, as if he were old, but he ducked, quick as a ferret, and slashed back. Elder Brother jumped over the cut and they changed places twice. The Dark One's black-painted two-fang wouldn't flash.

Behind them, at the Dark One's Temple his banner in blue and red stripes flapped, flashing white stars. Their two-fangs whirled and jabbed, ringing off armor and scraping blades together like tinging Mama's kitchen knife with a fingernail.

The Elder Brother was winning; he was driving the Dark One back to his temple. The setting sun shone on the two priests, shining with the Elder Brother's color: red. *He'll win. I know he'll win. He has to.*

Then something happened that Megan didn't understand. Someone screamed, "The Woyvode, he's ill. He's down!" People were starting to shake their heads, the City's will faltering. A man nearby fell, holding his head. Lixand shuddered as the spell ripped, fell to his knees, weeping, trying to stand, trying to keep the bridge whole.

"Hold on," he whispered. "Hold the bridge. Enough of us have to hold . . ."

The Dark One and the Elder Brother stopped fighting and both turned to run for the Dark One's Temple as the City's concentration broke as the manrauq that maintained the bridge began to come apart. There were more yells and suddenly the two priests were falling. Someone had to catch them, Megan thought. They fell like leaves blowing, arms and legs waving. Someone had to catch them, Megan thought. But no one did.

People were yelling all around them. Lixand dragged Megan down off his shoulders and took hold of Ness's shoulder, pulling her into a corner between the steps and a wall. Megan heard someone shout, "The Woyvode! The Woyvode!" *Why didn't anyone catch them?*

"RED! RED! MIKAIL! MIKAIL! . . . GREEN! KHOVORBOD! GREEN!" Two women in red pulled down another in a green tunic and struck her. She wasn't fighting them, just rolling as they hit and kicked.

Lixand tugged at Ness's shoulder and they ran, carrying Megan. She held tight to his neck and cried. Glass smashed somewhere near. Someone wearing red swung a length of board at Ness, but she ducked and Lixand punched him. Ness grabbed Megan away from Lixand and the two men fought. Ness got a tight look on her face and a brick fell off the wall and hit the stranger on the head.

They ran. The sun turned the scene around them red. Something was on fire. Ness stopped in a doorway.

"Lixand! Take Megan." Ness pulled off her green tunic, left it lying in a heap in the shadow of the door; pulled off Megan's green hair ribbons.

There was a roar up ahead and a mob surged into the street. Megan could see rocks clenched in fists and sticks waving, the flash of a knife. Their faces were bloodied and sometimes when they fell they didn't get up and were trampled as the fight surged back and forth.

Papa looked up and shouted, "Ness!" He grabbed Mama, yanked her under an overhang as a hod of bricks smashed down from the roof, dust swirling everywhere. Lixand called, "Here!" and squeezed between two buildings. It was too tight to breathe; Megan was squished against him and the bricks scraped her back. He pulled her hands loose and made her look at him. "We'll be all right, Megan. I've got to put you down now because it's too narrow, but I don't want you to let go of Mama's hand. You have to keep up. You *have to.* Understand?" He shook her a little. *"Understand?"* He had to say it loudly because of all the people on the other side of the pile of bricks in the street.

She nodded. She didn't have any breath because she

was crying so hard. The sound of the riot was loud enough that Megan couldn't hear herself crying. Someone outside the alley was screaming. Papa put her down and started sliding along between the two buildings.

Megan took Mama's hand in both of hers. It was dark in here, the ground was all slimy and it smelled bad. Papa was too big for some spots and had to scrape sideways. At one point he stopped and kicked a rotten, two-board fence out of the way. Mama's hand was slippery and the walls scraped her, too.

Megan looked up at a sky that was still red from the sun. Above, someone ran along the edge of the roof, then jumped across, almost over them. Papa waved a hand at Mama and she held Megan still. "Shh," she whispered. If someone noticed them, they could drop things.

There were flies buzzing, crawling on the wall in front of Megan. She looked way up at the roof and at Papa. He was big against the sky and black, and by his stillness he was using the manrauq. Someone looked down and Mama's hands tightened on Megan's shoulder. They jumped across and went on. *Papa hid us*.

Lixand leaned against the wall gasping. "Ness, we have to wait. I'm too tired to go on immediately.

"It'll be safer getting Megan home when it's darker." She reached over Megan's head and brushed his hair out of his face. "Are you all right?"

He nodded. "I'm fine, love. Though I don't know how anyone can fight after the bridge spell broke." It was getting dark fast. "You must have a headache like mine."

"A little one." Then Mama went down on one knee sideways and hugged Megan. "Are you all right, bylashka?" She wiped the child's face with her fingers and Megan hugged her. There was dust all over them, gritty between their teeth and in their eyes. Megan pressed her face into Mama's chest and nodded. *I'm not hurt. It's getting dark. I'm tired. I want to go home*.

"I think it's all right, Ness." Papa slid down to the other end of the alley. "Come on."

It was a little brighter outside the alley, but Papa hid

them in the shadows as they made their way home, slowly. They spent a lot of time standing still while people ran past with torches. There were buildings burning and sometimes they had to go back or around.

Megan hid her face in Papa's neck, hearing things, not wanting to look. *Fire. There's smoke all around.* He passed her to Ness and checked the street ahead. He was coughing and Ness's voice was hoarse. *My eyes hurt.*

They were near Teik Khitza's toy shop, but Megan couldn't see the yellow and blue stripes of its shutters. The whole street was full of smoke like a cloud and there was only an empty hole where the store had been, with broken shutters and shelves and soot on the walls around. Broken pieces of toys lay scattered in the street.

It was dark and past supper and Megan couldn't cry anymore, she was so tired. All three of them were covered in soot and Papa had a tear across the back of his tunic while Ness was still bare from the waist up. There were goose bumps all over her arms because of the cool wind blowing. They had gotten as far as the park and Megan could hear the Sneykh gurgle in the dark. Up ahead there was a small fire where somebody had dropped a lamp and the grass was oily and burning. Papa said, "Don't look, love. Or Megan." Before Mama's hand covered her eyes she saw the people lying in the grass. *I didn't think that dead looked like that,* Megan thought.

We're almost home. We're almost safe. We can close the shutters and nobody'll try to hurt us. She held tight to Mama.

Their gate swung open in the breeze.

"Lixand," someone said. Megan pulled her head up and looked. Teik Vyaroslaf stood in front of their house, several people behind him. The gate swung shut: bang. On Market Street Megan could hear a roar as if a monster were loose in the city, and the sound of glass breaking, wood smashing.

"Ness." Lixand stood in front of his wife and child. He whispered, "Go." Megan saw that he was sweating. The air went tight again, and when Ness stepped closer to the wall she left a copy of herself and Megan behind, standing by Lixand. "You don't need to lay hands on us, Vyaroslaf, we'll come," he said. "You've sunk to this now rather than letting the Guild choose?" One of the men with Teik Vyaroslaf raised a hand as if to strike, but Lixand didn't flinch: Vyaroslaf stopped his man with an upraised hand, gesturing Lixand and his "family" into the garden.

Mama pressed herself against the wall, her hand over Megan's mouth, and everyone passed them by as if they weren't there. The gate swung open again and she slid backwards along the wall, trying not to rustle the leaves. *They took Papa. He went with them so we could hide.*

Ness ran, carrying Megan to the empty lot in the street and put her in a hiding place near some stones. Megan clung to her and cried. Ness pulled her arms loose and said, "Stay here. I'm going to help Papa. Stay here!" And left her alone in the dark.

It's all broken. It's all red and sticky and fire and all smokey. Why did this happen? Someone was screaming like a bird the cat had caught. Megan scrunched herself down small and peeked through the long grass over the heap of stones, but couldn't see anything. Her eyes hurt, and she coughed and cried though she didn't have any tears left. There were people running in the street. It was quiet for a while. *Mama, come back. Papa, please come.*

Then something blew up in the Brewery and there were more fires. She put her hands over her ears and closed her eyes tightly. The fire burned so bright, licking the sky, that she could see it through her eyelids. The brewery horses screamed and screamed even through her blocking hands.

She looked and saw the fire on the other side of the lawyer's house. Their house was on fire. The wallbed and her bed and their cushions and cedar chest and lapdesk and the rugs and Mama's good kahfe set and everything was burning. *Mama, come, please come back. Papa, come to get me.*

The fire roared up so hot she could feel it on her face. All the houses around were burning. The lawyer's house was full of fire, wings and teeth flaring out of the windows, chewing the walls above. *It's eating his house. It's eating our house.* A cracking rumble and the lawyer's house fell over onto their house as she'd always imagined it wanted to.

It was so bright she couldn't see. *Another Fire's come. The world's burning. It's all broken.* Her lungs hurt. If she closed her eyes tight enough, if she put her hands over her ears hard enough, she wouldn't see or hear it—it wouldn't be happening. It wouldn't be real. *Papa. Mama. Brunsc. Koru. Please, pretty please, put it back. Please.*

Papa Mama, Pa-pa Ma-ma, Pa-pa come. Please come. Please come.

Chapter Three

Some one touched her and she jumped, afraid to look. *If I open my eyes it'll be the same,* but she did anyway. Her eyes had been closed so tightly that all she could see at first were green and white trails in the dark.

Her mama stood holding her papa up with her shoulder under his arm. Lixand, his hair scorched short, slumped over his wife, barely conscious, one arm so badly burned it was black. Ness ignored the burns on her skin. They were both covered in soot and dust and wood splinters, with bits of leaves and grass stuck on them. Megan leaped up to hug their legs, though they smelled of fire.

"Megan, don't knock us over," Ness said hoarsely. "You'll have to carry the bundle, I have to help your papa."

"Mama, Mama, I want to go home. I want to go home. Can we go home, pleeeese?"

Ness shifted, to keep Lixand from falling as his knees gave. "Megan, pick up the bundle. We have to go to Aunt Marte's to stay for a while."

Megan stood and held onto her mother's leg, trying to

see in the dark. The fire wasn't bright any longer and black smoke swirled around them. "No! I don't want to," she cried. "I want to go home—"

"MEGAN!" Ness shouted. Megan wiped her nose with her sleeve, and sniffed, letting go of her mother's leg.

"Megan, I'll explain later. Pick up the bundle and come on. I need you, child." Megan hesitated, then went to the bundle, a blanket heavy enough that she had to drag it as she followed her parents. It was sticky and black and smelly and there were splinters and bits of wood all over it. She shifted her hands to avoid a couple of damp spots. In the distance she could hear voices raised, a rumble like the waterfall, but couldn't make out words, or even if it was still a fight. Lixand stumbled on the cobbles and almost fell. Ness grabbed and tried to get him up, tried to get him to hold on with his good arm over her shoulder, but he kept letting go and almost falling again.

People around the neighborhood were staying inside if they could, though some ran with buckets of water passed hand to hand from the Sneyekh and the splashes of water fell into the fires with no other effect than to hiss. *Nothing's going to stop it.*

The three stopped to rest, and Ness let Lixand lie down. He didn't look like Megan's papa to her with his face grey and sweaty. Ness got Megan to put his feet up on the bundle while she pulled out a tunic to put on.

As she did, a man came up, saying something so low that Megan, who was at her father's head, patting his cheek, couldn't hear. Ness shook her head. "No. Go away." The stranger waved at Lixand with a dismissive gesture. Papa moaned and his face was sticky and Megan wanted him to get up and tell the stranger to leave them alone.

Ness straightened and a quick move put her knife in her hand. She didn't look tired anymore. "Pickings are easier somewhere else, 'Rhokatzk. We have nothing we wish to sell." He backed away, both hands up. Ness kept her head up and the knife in sight until he'd gone.

The going was slow, walking all the way to Pisznychiy Street at Lixand's pace. He was trying to keep going but his knees would give, and every time he jarred his arm a faint whine forced itself out of his throat. In the light of a street torch Megan could see that his face was covered with tears.

There weren't many people around now because it was so late, and near Pisznychiy Lixand couldn't go any further. His foot caught on a raised cobble and he fell, dragging Ness down with him. Megan dropped the bundle and ran back to them. Was her papa dead?

"It's all right, Megan. Papa just tripped and fell." He was unconscious, lying as limp as Brunsc without any sawdust in him. "We'll be all right, Megan." Mama got up slowly. "We just have to get to Marte, then we can rest."

"I'm tired, Mama."

Papa groaned. Megan touched his hand and his skin crackled. He didn't twitch. "Get the bundle Megan," Mama said. "I have to try and carry him."

They were just across Reyeka Road and Pisznychiy was only two streets away. Ness managed to get him up on her shoulders somehow, straightened her legs and stood up, breathing through her clenched teeth. Then she took a half step, then a full one. She sounded as if she sobbed every time her foot came down.

It was dark because the moon had set behind the City ridge, and though Shamballah was bright it wasn't enough to see by in the narrow streets. *Maybe the Goddess could help us if I pray hard. She'd help and we wouldn't have to go to Aunt Marte's.* Lixand's head and hands dangled loosely. *He can't be dead. Mama wouldn't let him be dead.*

The cobbles here were like Megan's back teeth, smooth in the middle, jagged on the edges, and the bundle kept catching on them. "Mama, is Papa going to be all right?"

Ness didn't answer right away. "Ye . . . es, Megan. He just needs to heal." She stumbled, fell on her knees, and just caught Lixand from sliding off with one hand, holding herself up with the other.

"I'm here, Mama. I'm here." Megan tried to help her mother up.

"N . . . o Megan. I'm all . . . all right. It's just . . . just a bit further. Run ahead and get Marte. Get her to come and help."

Megan didn't want to go in the dark by herself. She could just make out her mama's face. Ness's eyes were squeezed shut and a thin red line of blood trickled on her chin from where she'd bitten her lip.

It's just Pisznychiy Street. I've been here before, but I don't remember it really well. It's just Pisznychiy Street. She put her hands behind her back. "Megan . . ." Mama didn't say anything else. *I have to.* She left the bundle and ran.

It was dark and the buildings looming around her were black and tall, the gargoyles on the walls staring down at her out of their shadows. She ran, her heart beating in her ears. There was the faint smell of smoke here, too, and Megan ran, imagining the fire looking for them, following them down the streets like a hound following a blood-trail.

There were echoes everywhere, as if someone were pacing her running steps before and behind her, the light of fires in the First Quarter flickering from the low clouds just rolling in over the stars. Megan tripped and fell, scraping her knee.

There were no torches in the brackets on the walls, and something ran along the wall and hissed at her. A big cat, she thought. Just a big old cat. Her imagination filled the dark with slavers and monsters. Koru's statue in the shrine on the corner shone bright white in the dark like a promise of salvation. Megan hid in the shadow of the statue and hugged it, but Koru was just an old statue and didn't hear her crying. Megan looked to where Aunt Marte's house was. It was dark between here and there.

Papa was hurt and maybe Mama, too. Aunt Marte was

kin. Even if she didn't like Mama or Megan, she'd still help. She had to.

Three houses. That's all. Koru, help me. Even if you are just a crumbly old statue with pigeon poop on you. She bit her lip, let go of the statue, and ran. Two houses. One house. Here.

She pushed the gate open, glad it wasn't locked. Lights from inside shone around the edges of the closed shutters. She could hear Aunt Marte singing, in a high, wavery voice:

> "Red roses for my love, dragon's blood in plenty,
>   red blood to fight for, lest we be drained empty.
>   Red is the setting sun, red the victory color,
>   red roses for my love, red blood for my lover . . ."

Her voice stopped suddenly, then she laughed and Megan heard a man's voice when she knocked. There was a rustle from the room below and she knocked louder. "Aunt Marte! Aunt Marte, open the door please!" She knocked harder. Someone was climbing the steps. "Aunt Marte, Papa's hurt, Mama's so tired. Aunt, please help."

"Marte, what is it?" The man's voice again. "A problem?"

Marte laughed, shortly. "No, Varik. Nothing I can't handle. M'kin, showin' up on t'is stormy n-night."

"Hrmmm." The man sounded big. Aunt Marte shot the bolts and opened the door.

"Megan. Where's my brother? He's hurt?" She was dressed in red like all the rioters supporting Mikail, with her tunic unlaced down the front and her hair loose around her shoulders. She didn't look particularly happy to see Megan. She smelled of wine and incense and spices. "Wh—ere's Lixand? Not come t' help me cel'-brate, hmm?" She swayed a little, clutching drunkenly at the doorpost.

"Mama carried him, everything's all burned up, Mama

sent me and can't carry him anymore and he's not awake and . . ."

"Shhhush. Hush. Slow down," she said, waving Megan silent. "You mean my little brother got himself caught in the thresher today?" She hiccuped, not moving from the door.

The man whose voice Megan had heard came up the stairs behind her. He looked like a brewery horse with a long black mane, a lot of old scars on his chest and right hand. He wore pants and boots, and on his shoulder was a blue tatoo that looked like an open-work diamond. He grinned at Megan, a gap-toothed grin where he was missing one of his eye-teeth.

"Your papa's hurt and your mama carried him here out of the riots?"

"Almost here, she can't anymore and . . . and . . ." Megan's voice stopped as if she had a ladle full of porridge stuck in her throat. Her eyes felt full and hot, but she didn't want to cry anymore. *Aunt Marte's shaking her head, no. She can't say no. She can't.*

"That woman, won't hav'er . . ."

"Come on Martie, my dearling," the man said. "You're too drunk to know what you're saying lovey. They're your kin and you're not the kind to slough them off." He turned her around and patted her behind. "I'll help the kid. Go on then and fix up your spare room like a good girl." She wobbled downstairs, still muttering. He looked down at Megan and she felt scared, but he was helping more than Aunt Marte so she tried not to show it. "Show me where your folks are, kid."

He got a torch and came with her, and as they went down the street Megan heard Aunt's voice rising behind her, complaining: "Tha' dam' wo—woman. Get m' lil' brother in tr'bl. SHIT! B'chy whore. Won' hav't. C'nt. Lixand'll be *fine* once *I* help . . . *Unlicensed whore!*" But they got further away and Megan couldn't hear what she was saying even when she shouted.

"How far have you folks come?" the man asked her. Megan ran to keep up with him as he walked.

"Szyzka Lane," was all she had breath for. He whistled through the gap in his teeth but didn't say anything else.

In the time Megan had been gone, Ness had managed to get up somehow, still carrying her husband, and come a few more steps. She stood with her knees bent and her head down, shaking.

The horsey man, Varik, stopped and put the torch in an empty holder on the wall. "Here, Teik," he said, and took Papa off Mama's shoulders. "I have him." As he was shifted, Lixand woke, struggling weakly, then lay still again.

Ness stumbled when the weight came off her back, almost not believing that it was gone. Megan went to hold her hand. *I'm so tired. I want to go to bed, but my bed's all burnt up.*

They got to Aunt Marte's and stumbled downstairs, back into her spare room. "H—ic—ere! You're slobbing soot 'n my rugs," was all she said. Varik put Papa down in the bed and Ness thanked him. Rilla cried in the front room and Aunt Marte took the baby up on her shoulder, not saying anything to them now, just patting Rilla until she fell asleep.

Ness undressed her husband as if she were a sleep-walker, washing and binding up his arm. Megan undressed herself. She used the bucket and put the lid on, like you were supposed to. Ness called her and lifted her up on her lap and held her close.

"Megan. We're going to have to stay here until your Papa's better. You've been a good, brave girl and I'm proud of you. I love you."

"I love you, too." Papa was asleep and everything would be all right again. In the front room, from the wallbed, Megan could hear the rumble of Varik's voice and Aunt Marte's higher one. She sounded nicer when he talked to her, Megan thought, falling asleep on her mama's lap.

Megan didn't go to school next day. They slept late and Ness slept all night in the chair, tending Lixand. He was fevered and his arm puffed up, burned patches peeling off with the bandages when Ness changed them. Bruises came up on his face; his eyes black and purple, swollen shut.

Megan held Rilla, who was two years younger, and told her all about it. *I don't like Teik Vyaroslaf. He hurt Papa. He burnt our house down. He hurt Papa. I hate Teik Vyaroslaf. I hate him.* The distillery hissed and bubbled to itself in the corner like a sleeping dragon. The two children had been told not to touch the clear fluid dripping into the flask; it wasn't water. Marte's herbs hung from the ceiling, the drying plants making it look like a dusty, dark green carpet because she'd adjusted the shutters so the ceiling stayed shadowed. Megan looked up at the sound of voices in the back room where her father was. Aunt had gone in to speak to Ness after she'd vomited up the worst of her hangover.

"He's badly hurt," Marte said. "If he dies—"

"He won't!" Ness interrupted firmly. "He won't." They came out, closing the door behind them so they wouldn't bother Lixand. Ness looked over at Marte. "You hate me, I know, but I don't care about that. Hate me all you like, but don't stint him in any way. He's your younger brother."

"I'll get one of the Brown brothers."

"We'll need a Haian. If you won't pay, I will." They glared at each other until Marte shrugged and looked away. Ness waited until Marte left to fetch the Haian before she went back to look after her husband, leaving Megan to look after Rilla.

The two girls played inside mostly because of the wet weather, and because Megan didn't want to go very far away from her parents. She was careful that they played quietly so they didn't disturb her father. Once they brought more water from the water bucket and cloths to Ness in the back room. Lixand muttered, fumbling at the covers, pushing them off, dreaming. *Mama won't let him die. He'll get better. Aunt Marte's helping, even if she doesn't want to.*

The Haian came later that morning. She was dark brown all over her face and hands as if she worked in the sun, and Megan tried not to stare because Haians were supposed to be brown. The healer's accent was musical, stretching "i's" to "e's" and the other way around. Megan felt better just seeing her. Haians were the best healers in the world.

Rilla played with her rag doll, while Megan sat watching the closed door. The Haian was in there for quite awhile and Megan strained to make out words as the healer talked to Ness. When the Haian came out carrying her bag in strong brown hands, she looked unhappy.

"I will come agin," she said to Ness. "Tomorrow. Kip eet covered and eef the Spirit of Life is weeth heem, hee will recover somewhat. I hold out leetle hope of saveeng hees arm but one never knows. I will do my bist."

"Thank you," Ness said, her eyes reddened with unshed tears. Marte looked up from the corner where she was putting stoppers in glass jars, snorted and went back to her bottles.

Rilla hit Megan on the head with her rag doll. Megan pushed her away and Rilla sat down hard but didn't cry— just sat sniffling a little, looking first at Megan then at Marte. "You're mean," she said, but not "I'm telling."

The Haian went upstairs to the door. "Unteel tomorrow. Spirit be weeth you."

"And with you."

When Mama came back down, Aunt Marte said, "If you waste all your money on a Haian, you'll be destitute."

"I'm a weaver, I still have my skills."

Aunt laughed. "Oh, yes, and who is the Guildmaster now? Or will be, very shortly? Vyaroslaf. Do you think that he'll acknowledge your status as a weaver? And my little brother. If he recovers? He'll be a one-handed weaver."

"We have our friends still." Mama stood at the bottom of the stairs looking suddenly small.

"Friends. Where were they last night?" Aunt hummed

a snatch of "Red Roses." "All green supporters. Even if the Woyvode isn't dead, only ill, Mikail's won because Khovorbod had an 'accident' in the confusion. They won't dare help you."

"I don't believe it." Mama stood up straighter. "I don't believe that people are so weak that they wouldn't help their friends." She walked over to Megan, picked her up and hugged her. "I don't believe the world is what you think it is."

"Ha! Romantic peasant shit! You'll find out. It'll chew you up and spit you out in little pieces. I'll help you because of my brother, but don't you *ever* try to come crawling to *me* for your own sake." Aunt Marte tied a bundle of weeds together and cut the thread with her teeth. Ness set Megan down, leaving a hand on her head.

"Don't worry, Marte. I never will. Megan, come sit with me a while."

"Yes, Mama."

They went and sat in the hot, dim back room with Lixand. He would throw his head back and forth or fight the covers, drinking the water Ness gave him without opening his eyes. His hair was pasted to his face with sweat.

"Megan, tomorrow you can go back to school as long as you promise not to say anything about me or your papa. We paid for the year and you should miss as little as possible since you're going to need all the schooling you can get."

Megan sat on the edge of Papa's bed and walked her fingers up and down the bedclothes. "Shouldn't I help you, Mama?" Ness poked Megan's cheek with a finger and tried to smile, but Megan didn't; that was Papa's trick. *Little solemn face.*

"You may help, after school. Do you think you can walk all by yourself, to Szyzka Lane? I can't come with you."

Megan nodded vigorously. "I can. I'm big enough to help."

"You can help most by not saying anything, even if

Rosziviy says or does *anything* to you. If her papa finds out we're all still alive he might try to hurt us even more."

I really mustn't. I hate Rosziviy. I hate her papa. I wish the Dark One would take them away into Halya and freeze them in ice and burn them with steam and make all their skin fall off and their eyes boil and have eagles with fire for wings pick them.

"I won't say anything, Mama. I *promise!*"

Ness smiled a little more broadly. "That's my bylashka. Why don't you go play with Rilla some more?"

When Megan turned to go back out to the big room again, Papa started shouting and Ness leaned over him to keep him from flailing his burned arm against the bed. "No! . . . Vyar . . . Ness, get out! Take Megan. I'll . . . ahhh!" She was leaning on him and he was trying to get up, waving his arms. Megan watched, frightened, her stomach twisted, knotted together inside like the snakes and worms in the display case in Sysbat Tenara's museum. *But Mama's all right. And Papa'll get better. The Haian says so and Mama'll make him get better.*

Koru, are you listening? I'm sorry I thought you were a crumbly old statue with bird poop on it. Please help us. Please? You're a powerful Goddess and it wouldn't be hard. Koru? Pretty please? We're all safe, even Brunsc because Sysbat Tenara has him, but can you make there be a home again, please? Amen.

Chapter Four

Sysbat Karlovna stood in front of the class reading a history. Nobody liked to sit close to her, even if she did mumble, because she sprayed everybody in the front with spit. Megan didn't think Sysbat liked reading aloud much, and didn't really listen. Instead she thought about her papa and mama. The Haian had come back a couple of times in the last two days.

". . . the Zak leader, Dayovich, realized that the independent—can you say that word, children?—the independent tribes of the Zak could never win against the Armai, and swore that we would be one nation, one people . . ."

Ness had tried to talk to Papa's friends but had come back both saddened and angry, saying they put her off. "Scared stupid that they'll lose their places if Vyaroslaf ever finds out about it," she'd said. "And all of them thinking the others would help more than they. They gave us money, because they're not *that* scared, but getting them to take legal action with us against a new Guildmaster? Phhaugh!"

She was angry enough that Aunt Marte didn't even say

"I told you so." She'd just watched Ness, like a lizard. Then she said, "The family . . . *we* can't afford an Advocate by ourselves. Besides, Vyaroslaf could out-bribe us now, with the Guild coffers behind him." Mama had stopped and stared at her, then went to look after Papa without answering back.

After the door was closed behind them and Megan held the basin for Papa's bandages, she saw Ness try to hold back her tears. Lixand was often delirious. Megan had gone to play with Rilla as her mother had asked, but heard Mama sobbing into the clean bandages she'd been holding.

Megan curled her toes inside her socks, hoping that what Mama had said—that they'd have a home again once Papa got better—was true. She looked around the other children listening to the history.

Sysbat Karlovna had a thread trailing from the hem of her robe that swayed back and forth as she read. ". . . and when Iyesi was an empire, we were one people again." Sysbat put the book down and told them to stand to recite. *History goes a long way back. Almost all the way back to when the world burned. I like history better than the arithmetic that comes next.*

"First there were Zak. We had a *K'mizariza*, the age of Great Kings. Then came the Republic when the mob ruled. Then came the priests' Seven Hundred Years of Holiness and Corruption. Then came the Years of The Three—Priest, Priest, and War Leader. Then came the generations of the *SmiurgTeik*, our Beloved Dragon Lord, the Woyvode."

Megan scratched her back, telling herself she should pay attention. *I promised the Goddess I'd be good so she'd keep the Dark Lord from taking Papa away.*

Rosziviy smirked at her across the circle and Megan made her face stony. Ursella winked and Megan felt a little better.

The day's heat sat inside the house where the night breeze couldn't touch it, though all the windows were open. The herbs on the ceiling rustled, but the breeze never came down inside. Megan lay on her pallet next to Rilla, watching the light under the door of the spare room, where the Haian was. The door was closed, although the back room was stuffy even with the windows open.

Rilla was asleep. Earlier that evening Aunt Marte had hit her for being bad, though all that she'd done wrong that Megan could see was sing too loud. She had the marks of tears on her face and a bruised cheek. *Mama's been with Papa all day and didn't see and stop Aunt Marte from doing it.*

The dark pressed down on Megan as if it didn't want her to breathe. *Aunt Marte's house doesn't like us either.*

The Haian was doing something that clinked and rattled and made a strong smell as if the still was working. Rilla rolled over in her sleep and whimpered because of her bruises.

Megan looked over to Aunt's wallbed where she was asleep, too. She'd drunk a wine jar empty, staggered around and slammed a few doors, threw up, then went to bed. *Her tunic got vomit on it and she didn't even put it in the bucket with water. It stinks,* she thought, and woke up with a jump from where she'd dozed.

The door clicked under Aunt Marte's snoring. The Haian stood by the table, leaning on it, looking tired. Mama had a whole bundle of bedclothes and there were dark splotches on the white sheets.

The smell wasn't as strong anymore, but it was mixed with another smell like rust or the smell of a skinned knee. Marte's snoring was muffled by the closed doors of the bed.

"I'm sorrie I could do no more," the Haian whispered, glancing over to where the two children were supposed to be sleeping. "He has hees life, and ay femily to care for heem. I weesh I could have done more."

"Thank you," Mama said. "You did the best you could."

"He needs quiet end weeth luck eet will heal up

weethout eenfection. I will kip an eye on heem unteel the stump heals over."

Ness walked the Haian up the steps to the door. "Thank you. I'll walk you to the gate."

"He will be asleep for at leest enother hour. He might wake efter thet and go beck to ay more naturel sleep. The drug for pain is on the table. Eef he develops fever again, call me."

The door shut behind them, and Megan got up and went to see her papa. It was very hot and still in the back room, and he lay on his back, sweat shining on his skin in the candlelight. Megan's shadow flickered across her father, making it hard to see, and the edge of the wallbed made a dark shadow across his burned arm.

She felt better because she could see his chest rising and falling. *He's alive. He looks better. He looks like he'll wake up and be fine.* His left hand lay across his chest.

She put her hand over the wooden sill of the bed before she looked. His shoulder stuck out in a strange way and his chest seemed dented in. *What happened?* Then she saw that it wasn't a dent, it was her papa's shoulder, but his arm wasn't where it was supposed to be. *It isn't there at all.*

Her hand was on the mattress, smooth and cool under her fingers. His shoulder was bandaged white and smooth and round like the eyes in Koru's statues.

"Megan." Mama came up behind Megan and lifted her up, and she hid her face in her mother's neck.

"The Haian took his arm away, Mama. She took it away."

"Yes, Megan-mi. He would have died if she hadn't. She did it to save him."

"Did Papa say he wanted that?"

Mama sighed. "If he wakes up before you have to leave for school, you may sit with him. If not, you can talk to him after school."

"Yes, Mama." Megan yawned. Ness carried her daughter back to bed next to Rilla. *Rilla's sucking her thumb. I'm not a baby to do that.*

Megan hugged Brunsc until his sawdust squeaked, watching her mother's shadow bounce around the room as she tidied up. Ness took the candle back into the spare room, and when she blew the light out it was like a puff of dark.

Megan hugged Brunsc. *He's got teeth. He'll keep me safe from Aunt Marte's house and from Haians who need to take people's arms away.*

Papa's going to be all right. He smiled at me this morning. He'd eaten and sat up in bed and Ness cried happy tears. Those kinds of tears Megan liked. Marte stood in the door and looked at them all, hugging each other. The smile on her face had supposedly been for the family, but Megan suspected that Marte would rather Megan or Ness had been hurt instead of her brother, as if they could have taken his place.

Megan jumped over a puddle as she ran to school. She'd given Brunsc to Rilla because she needed him more. *I'm a big girl with a nice mama and papa and I don't need bears with teeth.* Rilla had cried a long time a couple of days ago, because Aunt Marte hit her again and yelled at her while Ness was at the market. Brunsc would help.

Yim, the Koa Alley baker's boy, had his stand open to sell breakfast; stacks of sticky buns with honey running down them, and loaves steaming in the cool morning. The market-drovers who came in every morning by dark stood between the baker's and the kahfe stall where there was a street lamp still lit—unless the weather was bad, when they stood under the counting-house overhang.

Their horses would pull back their lips from the cold water in the troughs, breath blowing steam in the air, like their masters slurping thick, hot kahfe out of Nanty's chipped mugs. The drovers would laugh loud and wipe honey-covered fingers on their baggy pants. Megan had been afraid of them at first.

Megan wiggled between people's legs, and ran past one of the Honey-Giver's Shrines, whose Bearcub statue

looked like her Brunsc. *Rilla's Brunsc*. She wouldn't have
time to stop at the Shrine and pet Him this morning.
Her books bounced on her back as she ran. She'd started
taking them home with her, because ink and sticky things
had mysteriously kept getting spilled on them while they
were in her box, or they would disappear. Sysbat didn't
even try to do anything about it anymore, acting as if it
were Megan's fault.

Megan tucked her jump rope more firmly in her belt
so as not to lose it, looking forward to mealbreak when
she and Ursella could skip. The Baba doll that Ursella
had given her stood on the shelf over Megan's box, and
no one dared touch her because then both Ursella and
Megan would have been after them.

It was foggy this morning, long fingers trailing along
The Stairs. Up the street the leathermaker's sign creaked
in a slow breeze. Megan dawdled a bit along the Sneykh
and poked in the mud along the banks with a stick. *I
don't ever walk up Szyzka Lane anymore.* She had once,
and saw the black place, a hole with bricks, and grass
growing in it where their house had been, like a rotten
tooth-hole in the ground. The trees were all dead too,
though the Brewery had been rebuilt.

She heard the boom of the Garrison drum up the city
and started to run again. That meant the morning guards
were coming on duty to protect the Woyvode (long life
to him) and if she didn't run, she'd be late.

Ursella wasn't waiting for her at the Student's Gate
the way she usually was. At first Megan thought she was
late, but everyone was still out in the children's hall when
she panted downstairs. *Maybe she's sick today. Maybe
she's late. Maybe she had to help her papa sell bowls in
the shop or unpack things.*

Megan didn't partner with anyone when they were
called to line up, waiting for Ursella, then saw her best
friend and Danacia come out from under the ramp and
line up together. Megan ended up next to fat Piatr, who
nobody liked. *Why didn't she wait for me?*

Ursella was whispering in Danacia's ear and they giggled together. Sysbat Karlovna clapped and they filed into the classroom. *I have a class, in a bit, with Sysbat Tenara in the library. I'm glad I do. I'm glad.*

At the mealbreak, Ursella sat down next to her. "I couldn't pair with you this morning, sorry."

"It's okay," Megan said munching on her piece of sausage. *I don't want to talk to you.*

"I wanted to give you this back." She held out Megan's marble bag and stylus. Megan stared at her, her throat closing thick and tight.

"You don't want to be my best best friend."

Ursella looked down at her boots, picking at the splinters on the bench. "I can't."

"You swore." Megan took a drink of water and dabbled in it with her fingers so she wouldn't have to look at Ursella, looking at the black specks in the bottom of the cup instead.

"Danacia asked me to be *her* best friend, and she's always with Rosziviy who's always fighting with you, and Danacia gave me the blue bead-rings I always liked so much."

Ursella held out her right hand, four blue beads on thin wire, one ring on each finger, with a blue ribbon looping between. Everybody had said they looked good, even if there were ribbons instead of chain, and everybody had wanted ones just like them.

"And I want my Baba doll back."

Megan got it and gave it to her. *Papa would say that they bought her.* Then she stood there holding her cup of water while Ursella looked at the floor and the doll and the rings. "I liked having you as a best best friend," she said at last.

Megan reached out and dumped her water on Ursella's head, and she slapped Megan who hit her back . . .

Everybody else gathered around them in a ring, pushing them closer together, yelling, "Fight! Fight! Fight!" And Sysbat came and pulled them apart, trying to make herself heard. Megan could hear Rosziviy yelling that it was Megan's fault—"*She's always the one fighting . . .*"—as they got taken down to the K'mizar's office, where they both got three swats. When they left, carefully far apart, Megan put her chin up and clenched her teeth. She could feel Ursella's look and walked faster, not listening to Sysbat's lecture. *I don't even* want *to cry. I don't care. Ursella's being dumb. She deserves it more than I do. She's not my friend. She swore. She promised.*

Chapter Five

On the last day of school, Megan hugged Sysbat Tenara good-bye. There was no more money for schooling. Papa had talked Aunt Marte into letting them stay at her house until Megan's year was done, just after she turned five.

Ness had been doing a little lace-work, the kind of thing the Guild wouldn't notice, pieces too small to care about. There wasn't enough of that kind of work to keep them, and Lixand had said that he couldn't rebuild the house because of the high building tax and because the land belonged to the Guild anyway. They had enough to rent some rooms in the River Quarter where other poor people were, and Megan was glad they didn't have to go all the way down to the Lake Quarter. Lixand had to find some work soon.

"You take care, child." Sysbat Tenara almost looked as of she were going to cry. *She never does that, but her blue eyes do look more watery behind her spectacles.* She brushed Megan's hair out of her eyes. "You have a good mind. Don't waste it."

"I won't." Megan looked around the library. It was pretty dark because the sun had gone down, but the kraumak still shone on Tenara's desk and the clock still tocked to itself in the back. She put her waxboard down on the desk with the slate because they weren't hers to borrow any longer.

"Megan, this is for you." Tenara handed her a parcel wrapped in brown paper. "Just a little something to remember us by."

Megan could tell that it was a book through the paper and realized that Tenara didn't want her to open it till later. *She's looking at me as if she'd be mad if I said "No, it cost too much."* "Thank you, Sysbat." Megan looked at the parcel in her hands. "I don't have anything to give you."

"Shush!" Tenara straightened some papers on her desk, not looking at Megan. "I didn't give it to get something! As long as you promise not to forget what you've learned."

"All right." Megan scuffed her foot on the floor, embarrassed. "Bye." She turned away and walked to the door, having left saying good-bye to Tenara till last. *I don't want to be here anymore. I don't. They don't want me here either. I don't want to be here, truly.* She could reach the glass knob easier, and the door wasn't as heavy as it used to be. She closed it carefully behind her.

Faintly, through the closed door, Megan heard Tenara say "Goodbye, Megan."

The hall was cold and the herons on the pillars stared down at her as always, but now it seemed like a friendly stare. At the end of the year Megan had always had to hang around with Fat Piatr and Elixiy, who nobody else in the class liked. *It happened. They were okay. They were just weird. Elixiy's one papa is a cutler, and he told me all sorts of things about knives. His other papa's a bone-carver. And Piatr wasn't really all that fat.*

Rosziviy had passed into next year second highest in the class. That was okay, too, because Megan had been first. She patted the stuffed Ri as she went by, and trotted up the stairs to go out by the Student's Gate. At the front gate, someone had stolen the bellrope for a swing again. When it happened, just after snow-melt, K'mizar had just smiled and said it was almost a tradition. It was dark now so she couldn't see Student's Walk and the patterns in the tile.

She'd promised her Mama that she'd stop at the wood-carver's and ask if they liked the collars Ness had made. That was Ursella's place. *They owe us for the lace-work,* was all Megan thought.

She hugged the book Sysbat Tenara had given her and ran through the park. They would be moving at the end of the week, and there was a lot to do at Aunt Marte's.

"Ness, there has to be more I can do!" Lixand snapped. *They only fight when Aunt Marte's not here.* "Vyaroslaf isn't worried about us any longer. I have the Guild pension, but with your contracts and guild-tokens revoked, you can't work either."

"There's one guild that will take me, unsponsored, that we can afford," Ness said quietly.

"NO!" Lixand shouted. He stood up, rubbing his shoulder where his arm had been. "That's *not* an accept-able choice. We are respectable folk. You are not going to apprentice yourself to the Thieves."

"What are we to do then, Lixand?" Mama got up to face him. "The other skill you have is story-telling, and you'll be paying that Guild anyway. You already know they'll charge you for protection, and that we must! They control the Bedwarmers' Gu—"

"Ness! You wouldn't enjoy it. You'd be competing with people who do and have been training for a while. Damn Marte for suggesting it!"

I hate it when they argue. Megan ran upstairs and outside to play tag with Rilla, but she could still hear their raised voices. *We have to be careful not to step on Aunt's herbs.*

The gate banged and Varik stepped into the garden.

"Hi, short stuff. Your aunt around?" He was wearing plain brown clothes today.

"No, Teik. She'll be back soon though." Rilla acted shy and hid behind Megan.

"Mind if I wait?"

"You'd have to ask my papa. Paaapa!" Megan yelled, and Lixand came up to talk, so the children went down to the shrine to play instead, Megan carefully holding on to her cousin's hand so she wouldn't get lost, Rilla holding Brunsc in her other arm. Megan had told her all about his teeth and how he could help, and ever since he was never out of Rilla's reach.

"You help, Megan," she'd said, and hugged her older cousin and the bear at the same time. "Mama's better now."

"Oh. That's good."

When they got to the shrine they played hide-and-seek around Koru's statue for a while, careful not to step on the offerings, then sat on the back of the bench, pretending they were riding horses. Rilla said, "Megan?"

"Yes."

"You going far away?"

"Not that far."

"Gonna visit me?"

" 'Course I am!" Megan turned around, kicking her legs, pretending to make her horse stop. "It's only the River Quarter." It was a long way away, but Megan wasn't going to say that.

"That's all the way down the Stairs." Rilla cried. She hugged Brunsc hard, on the verge of tears. "I'm too little to visit. Mama won't let me come see you." She threw Brunsc on the ground, crying. "You're going way far away. You're all gonna leave me." She thumped down from the bench and kicked Brunsc. "He can't help. You can't help!"

"Rilla!" Megan cried out. Rilla had never gotten angry before, and it was as startling as having Brunsc bite. "You're kin." Megan got down and tried to hug Rilla, who pushed her away. Megan picked up Brunsc and hugged him instead, not knowing what to do or say. "Rilla. Mama and Papa and I aren't going that far. You'll be big enough to come down to visit by yourself soon. I can come up to get you. I'll look after you. I promise. If you need help, I will. I promise."

Rilla, her face all dirty and teary, stood, hugging herself. "You promise?"

Megan nodded firmly. "Yes. By the Lady, and the Lord's shadow." She swore the highest oath she knew.

Rilla finally hugged Megan and took Brunsc back, brushing at the dirt on his fur. "Forever and ever?"

I don't swear that anymore. Ursella said forever and then went away because someone gave her better presents. "As long as I can."

"Okay." Rilla took Megan's hand and they went to the tap to wash their faces and hands because Marte always got angry if Rilla got the least bit dirty. Megan hated seeing Rilla get hit, so she made sure her face was clean. "I'm gonna miss you Megan," Rilla said.

"So'm I. But I'll come back lots. And I promised."

They moved down to a rooming house, called the Flats by the inhabitants, on Cooper's Lane. As they walked down the lane Megan stared, fascinated. At one end, where they made the wheels, it smelled like wood and scorching and sawdust and hot vinegar; the air full of clamor as the rims were hammered on. Ness had to pull Megan's hand because she'd wanted to stop and watch. At the other end, near the Flats, it just smelled bad and her mama explained that it was because it was a spring heat wave.

In the heat, people leaned out of the windows to catch a breeze. People were picking through the piles of garbage against the walls, scavenging for scraps to sell to the Ragman, Nomo, who lived across the street.

He stacked his wares in front of his door, leaving only enough room for carts to pass one way. When Megan's family came down the lane he was standing, yelling and shaking his fist because a cart had just driven over one of his rag heaps. There was a basket of glass bits by Nomo's door. In school Megan had learned that glass and paper were both expensive because they were imported.

The Flats had once been a manor house for a merchant family before the Middle Quarter shrank away from it. It was a large open square that had had a glassed-over courtyard with three floors below ground. Now it also had four above, the top three added after it was subdivided. The pillars, metal strapping to hold up the glass, and the glass itself had all been salvaged long ago and replaced with wood.

They had a garden below ground, in the center. Mama said it was a natrium. The galleries were all turned into closed hallways with pine boards nailed up for the winter and they hadn't all been taken down. In the gaps Megan could see the strung lines of washing. She peeked through one of the holes in the wall, down into the atrium where puddles of water stood between the turkey and chicken cages three stories down. *Papa says there used to be ven-til-ation.*

A flock of pigeons quarreled with the miniature gulls nesting on the outside of the building, and the inside was brighter than she thought it would be. She looked across the atrium where people had painted the winter walls, bright swirls of color somewhat faded. Someone had painted a blue-skinned face with winking green eyes. There was a sign of a naked woman someone had painted over; the covering paint was peeling. Megan tried to sound out the letters. "The Lussious . . . The Lukious . . . Mama, what does that sign say?"

Ness looked, and sighed. "The Luscious Peach."

"Oh. Is that lady a peach?"

"No, bylashka, a peach is like an apple with fuzz but they taste different. They grow further south, along the river or in Laka."

"Oh."

"Come away now. That side of the building is the business side."

Megan winked at the painted face and pulled her head

back in. Mama and Papa and the landlord were standing in front of a door. Their new home was a room on one below, a good location. Lower down there would have been the dampness and the dark and lack of air, with turkey cages close by, while any floors above ground were rickety and the wood walls were thin. Nobody would mind that in the summer because of the heat, but winter was much longer and more likely to kill you.

Three and four above would be colder yet because they extended above the other buildings and caught the wind. *Papa said that up there, you'd "Freeze your as . . . behind off."* Megan knew she wasn't supposed to hear because Mama had looked at him *that* way when he said it. But then Ness had smiled at him and hugged him as if she were afraid of losing him. *She's been doing that a lot. I'm bigger now and I understand. He could have died.*

The landlord had a scraggly beard and the top of his face was wider than the bottom, and he had three teeth missing from when he'd been the bouncer at the Peach. He smelled of sweat and old beer. His husband kept the turkeys and their wife sold them in the lesser market, Mama said. He showed them the combination to unlock the door, then left.

Inside, the room was painted a dirty brown/pink looking like what Megan imagined the inside of a nose would look like. The kitchen corner had dark purple tiles that were mostly whole, but had smears of hardened food on them. The brazier was missing a leg. It smelled like wet old people and, in the middle of the floor, someone had left a pile of dirt: mud and wood chips, bits of sacking and broom straws and splinters. A squishy green and pink flowered cushion, with white fuzz growing out of the seams lay in the mess.

Ness stood, looking around at the dirt rounding off the edges of the walls. They still had a small kraumak that Papa had retrieved from the ruins of the house, but it gave the room a greenish color. The door stuck in its frame and there was a gap under it big enough for

Megan to push her hand through before Papa stopped
her. There wasn't even proper wallbed but one built of
wood, like a wardrobe standing against the right-hand
wall. It smelled of mice.

"Well." Mama put her bundle down on the cleanest
piece of floor. "A bit of work."

"Hallo, then!" A cheerful voice called behind them. A
woman stood in the door whose tunic was definitely in
bad taste; red and pink stripes that clashed with the pre-
dominant red tint of her hair.

"Welcome to the Flats! My name's Shenanya, called
Stander. Or Wit. Pro'lly Half-Wit behind my back, but I
get on better with half than most folks do with all of
theirs." A door down the hall to the left slammed, point-
edly. Shenanya shrugged and rolled her eyes, accepting
the fact that the neighbors could hear everything. "You
folks need any help, jus' ask away." She winked at Megan
and giggled at Lixand, though she was too old for that
sort of flirting.

"Thank you." Mama smiled at her. "Might I borrow
an extra bucket and broom?"

Shenanya looked at what little they'd brought with
them and Ness's smile went away at that look. All they
owned in the world they'd carried on their backs; it
wasn't enough to need a cart. But Shenanya didn't say
anything except, "Av course, luv. All three of you, come
over to my place. I'll have us a cup of chai ready and
we'll all be back in a flash!" She waved them out into
the hall. "Come on, I'm your neighbor on the right." She
leaned close to Papa. "Watch the old haux on the left.
She's a buzzard with constipation of the brain and runs
of the mouth all at the same time. You'll see. Zazan's *her*
name. My use-name for the bitch is sh—" Mama tsked
but Shenanya didn't stop, though she changed what she
was saying mid-word. "—Shucks-for-brains." The door
down the hall slammed again, harder, and Shen laughed.

She sat them down and gave them a cup of bitter chai
that Megan thought tasted like hot sweat. When no one
was looking, she poured it into the cat's litter-box. "Gotta

keep a cat or ferret or the mice'll eat the hair off'n your head," Shen said.

She told them all about all the neighbors. "Lotta decent men and women at the Peach, like Jerya, well, she's paying to learn to read and figure and support her boy, Dmitrach who's the best on the block, and Kijo, who's saving to go home." She mentioned the neighborhood had gotten better since the people around cleaned out the Dusters, especially from Sour Note Street off Victory Square.

Then she rolled up her sleeves and came to help them clean up and move in. "Little work now, less later! That's my motto! Yup." She said that a lot, but Megan liked her despite it.

They settled in with help from Aunt Marte's friend, Journeyman Varik Borkyovych, a member of the Rivermerchant's Guild. Mama made new sitting cushions, with his help.

Ness went out with Shenanya for a while, and Megan stayed behind to look after Papa. "Papa," she said, twining her fingers in his beard.

"Yes, bylashka." He blinked and looked down at her. *I'm almost too big to climb into his lap anymore.*

"When are you going to be better?" He jumped as if Megan had stuck him with a pin. To Megan's mind her papa had always worked, was always busy. Now he was always home, so he must be sick again. *I thought he was all better. He just sits and looks at the walls. Mama keeps saying, "You're not useless, Lixand. We love you. We need you," but he says, "Yes, yes, I love you, too," like he was asleep.*

"I am well, Megan." He put his arm around her. "My stump healed up long ago."

"Then why is Mama doing everything?" He didn't say anything for such a long time that Megan clung to him, frightened by his silence, not knowing what she'd said wrong. He hadn't even gone on any walks around Cooper's Lane with Megan, so they didn't know where the shrines were, or the parks, or anything. She jumped when a spot of water fell on her head, wiped it off, and looked up.

Lixand was weeping. He held her close with his one arm and turned his face away but couldn't wipe his tears, so Megan reached up and did it with her small fingers. "S'all right, Papa. What's the matter? It's all right. I'm sorry. I'm sorry . . ." He shook his head and cried for such a long time that Megan didn't know what to do. *It's all wrong. The world is all wrong where Papas cry.*

"No. No, bylashka." He wiped his cheek on his shoulder. "I'm all right. I think I'm better now. Yes, I have been sick in a way. I'll be better now."

"Did I . . . did I do anything bad?" She twisted at one of his buttons, and he couldn't put his hand under her chin while he hugged her.

"No. You did something good." He let go of Megan, reached up and poked her gently in the cheek with a finger. "Little solemn face."

She laughed and threw herself on him, tickling. "May we go for a walk? Just us?"

Smiling, he held her away out of tickle range. "Just us. We'll find the nearest Ladyshrine, hmm?" he said, and Megan ran to get his boots. They had worn spots right over the toes and the soles were thin. She could never remember his shoes having been shabby before. Papa said he could get his patched but Megan's feet had growing to do. Megan helped him put them on. "Then tomorrow I'll go talk to Varik. He's been a good friend."

"I like him, Papa." He smiled.

Papa's all right again. Papa's all right again. She sang that phrase over and over as they went up the stairs to the street. *Nothing bad can happen as long as Mama and Papa are all right.*

"Child!" Megan stopped and looked back over her shoulder, stick in hand, which she'd been rattling along the old railings in the wall of the gallery. "Come here this instant!"

It was the lady on the left, Zazan, calling from her door, where she stood holding a long-haired yellow cat with snooty eyes.

She looks like she's sucking on a big pickle. There are wrinkles all around her mouth. "Stop that noise at once! Didn't your parents teach you manners? Well, I suppose you learned what you were showed. From out-city I suppose. Well. You are not to run past my door, you are not to be noisy outside, I won't have it." She petted the cat absently. "Do you understand? Hmm? Well? Do you?"

I'd answer if she gave me time to. "Yes." That's all Megan said at first, because the cat lady was rude. *She's nasty, so I can be rude too. Mama wouldn't like it though.* "Yes, Teik."

"Humph. Go on then." She slammed the door with her foot.

I bet her manrauq is tiny. I bet she's a black witch who doesn't shine. Not like my mama and papa. Mama's a red witch and Papa's red-orange. Mama says that sometimes your gift is bigger the bigger your spirit is.

Megan left her stick and went to one of the open places in the wall, looking over to the bottom. There were more washing lines strung, full of bright clothes. Just down the hall at another opening a man wearing a blue satin loin-cloth hung his washing. He waved. Megan hesitated a minute. Her papa said that the neighbors were all right to talk to, at least during the day. Most people wore loin-cloths in the summer, but she'd never seen somebody in a blue satin one. He worked at the Luscious Peach, Megan guessed.

He pulled a clothes-peg out of his mouth to pin up a green and purple tunic. "Whal, you've met the old drag'n, eh?" he said in an out-city accent, smiling with one corner of his mouth. "Don't worr'ye about the aul biddy. She a dried up aul hoor. Her girl the Madame nu." He tossed his glossy black hair, putting on a careful city accent. "My name is Dmitrach." Then he stuck clothes pins back in his mouth and went back to his washing. Shenanya had said he was all right, he was the healer at the Peach.

"Hi. My name's Megan."

"Phlef chu ..." He pulled the pins back out of his mouth, eyes twinkling. "Pleasured tah meet. Here, you wan talk, hold mah pins."

So Megan ended up helping. *It's not bad, living here. Mama and Papa were talking like we'd be moving out-city or to Halya. There's lots of nice people here.*

When Mama called her in, Dmitrach said thank you just as nicely as a Sysbat, even if he did say it in a rougher accent. "Been a good day, to met you little Teik. Goddess guard." He bowed as if he was a great courtier at the Nest and he and Megan were both Zingas. Megan bowed back and ran down the hall, home.

Over supper Papa said that he'd gotten a job as a storyteller, with his own corner at Zidium Lane. Megan thought Mama would be happy and Papa too, but they didn't talk much about it. *Maybe he'll buy something good to eat tomorrow.* They'd been eating 'maranth tubers and soup without meat, and *zahbeans*.

Megan spooned the beans, thinking that tomorrow she was going to find Zidium Lane. She was big enough to go out by herself. After all, she had when she went to school. Mama would be out looking for work tomorrow and Papa would be at his new spot, so she'd be by herself. *I'm supposed to go to Shenanya, but I'll tell her I'm big enough to go out, because I am.*

Chapter Six

It was late summer by the time they settled in. Megan looked up from her book, the book Sysbat Tenara had given her. Mama and Papa had been helping her with lessons as much as they could, making sure she kept learning. The book was called *Mayshan's Fables*, and Megan was proud that she could read most stories in it by herself. The one she liked best was a cautionary tale about a dog and a bone and a pond.

Her parents couldn't help as much as they wanted to, with her Mama looking for work that was legal. It could be that she would have to try and find someone who would accept an adult as an apprentice.

"Be a good girl today, Megan."

"Yes'm."

When Papa and Megan had gone for their walk a few weeks ago they'd found Victory Square and a Bear cub shrine and a Dark Lord's shrine. Lixand had said that *His* priests could make all *His* shrines shine black with manrauq, but one could see it more if you were powerful yourself. If not, then it was more of a nasty, itchy feeling

71

behind your eyes and you didn't want to be there. *Besides, it's a year of the Dark Lord. He's the Year Kievir.*

"Bye, Mama! Love you!" Ness gave her a kiss and a quick squeeze, making sure Megan remembered what order she had to pull the latch-strings to get back in.

Megan had been going out every day, because it was both stuffy and boring in the room with nothing to do but read the one book. First she'd explored the Flats from the roof down to the bottom of the *atrium. Mama told me I was calling it wrong.* It really stank down there, with the wet and the mud and the turkeys. There were both kinds of turkeys in the cages, those with wings and those with four legs, though both were dumb, in Megan's opinion. The boards in the halls there were all rotten at the bottom, and people from upstairs sometimes threw garbage down, though they weren't supposed to, and the landlady, Teik Erharn, would curse.

Then she'd explored the neighborhood. She'd found Zidium Lane, running between the Stairs and the corner of Victory Square and the Little Market, full of shoemakers and paper-makers. Her papa's mat was on the flagstones under a tall, spindly pine between two shoemakers. Her mama had been angry when she'd found out that Megan was going out in the street by herself, but Papa had sighed and said, "What are we to do? Keep her in the Flats? She found my place and sat beside me, listening." Megan had gotten bored and he couldn't pay her any mind, so she'd come home the long way. There were lots of alleys between Cooper's and Sour Note, between all the *real* streets.

Today she dawdled in the hall, deciding that the first place she'd go was down the alley to Sour Note Street, where all the instrument makers lived, then along Vischy Street to Zidium Lane and see if there were anyone to play with. There were lots of kids along Cooper's Lane and more around Sour Note, but they weren't being friendly. *The kids fight a lot, I think. They yell a lot anyway. They all looked at me and Papa when we went through the first time, and I didn't pay any attention. I learned how to do that in school.*

Megan locked the door behind her and went to say good morning to Shenanya and tell her she was going out, petting her skinny cat, Blue, who was really a bluish-grey, like a shadow on the snow. He only had one ear, was blind in one eye, and one of his fangs was missing because he got beat up a lot by other cats, Shen said. That was because he wasn't a fighter but a wuss who liked having his behind scratched. If you blew on his fur you could see the fleas run.

She climbed the steps, skipping the cracked one third down. Teik Varik was a good friend. Ness had said they could never have gotten such a good room for so little if Varik hadn't spoken to Teik Erharn.

The door to outside had had patterned glass set in the doors at one time, but the spaces were all filled with good thick wood now, except one or two little pieces of glass over the outer door. Megan didn't like it dark and wet, and resolved that when she grew up she was going to live in bright places. Being too low underground was like being buried, the way naZak did their dead. *I wouldn't like that either. I want my name to be called to the Goddess and have the wind and birds take me back to her. Being under all that dirt would be pretty bad.*

The first alleyway had a small opening but widened further in. She wasn't afraid of the rats because when she stomped they ran away. Papa said that was because there were enough people who hunted them to eat, and Megan stuck her tongue out at the idea of having to eat a rat.

Farther down the alley a willow tree grew up beside a building, the wall bulging out from where the roots cracked the bricks. She climbed up because it was easy and at the top it wasn't dark. In the upper branches she was almost as high as the whole world, like being on Papa's shoulders.

She sat, pretending she was a bird sitting in a tree and could fly away if she wanted to. *I wouldn't because Mama and Papa would be sad if I went away.* The Garrison drum boomed the mid-morning guard change. She was hungry but didn't want to go back to Shen since there was only cold rice during the day. Megan climbed down, getting her hands all icky on the bark, snagging her braids.

She could go up the alley behind the Sharpener's shop and hear the grindstone squeal as he sharpened knives and scissors or even a two-fang or a naZak's sword; even if there weren't many naZak left in the City there was always a chance one might be there. That would mean she'd have to walk all the way around Victory Square.

Instead she went past the balika-maker's house at the end of Sour Note, next to the vacant lot. Someone had broken down the board fence, and people used it as a park or slept there in the summer because their rooms were damp and hot and dark and they didn't want their fingernails and toenails to fall off, which is what Sysbat Karlovna said damp and dirt could do.

Her papa was busy with a crowd. She could see his arm waving as he described something. It looked like he was telling "Summer's Ending." That one always made Megan shiver because the Goddess had to ask the Dark Lord's help to find Her son's soul in Halya—and the story "Bargain," where They wandered for three days in frost and fire.

She poked in the mud-puddle under the tap on the corner of Vichy and Zidium streets. The tap at Cooper's Lane was broken, for the third time this week. She watched the mosquito larva whip down to the bottom mud to hide and filled the puddle with a handful of mud before she went to watch the cooper put iron rims on wheels. She stood in the cooper's open door, watching her heat the rim in the fire so it would fit snugly on the wood when it cooled.

From behind her somebody yelled, "Yeah! And you got worms!"

"No, *you* got worms, wigglin' out'cher bum!"

"Don' you spit on me! I'll spit on you!"

"Gotta catch me first! Asshole, asshole, asshole!"

"I spit on you and you catch worms!"

Megan turned to see what was going on. Three kids were chasing each other around out on the street, dodging through the crowd. A big boy with the black hair and narrow face ran up over the tongue of a cart waiting to have the new wheel on, and the oxen stamped and bellowed so the carter yelled at him. The other two kids, a girl with hair almost as light as Sysbat Tenara and another boy who looked like the cat-monkey Megan had seen in the Great Market, chased after him. Watching them run around were a bunch of other kids sitting on the street marker stones, shouting encouragement.

"Run, Jorge!"

"Get'im Eula! Spit on 'im good!"

"Ivar's on Jorge's side! Eula, look out!" The cat-monkey boy climbed over the half-door of the cooper's storage shed and the girl turned around as he was about to jump on her. She spat on him and he fell down, rolling around in the dust holding his stomach.

"Auugh, worms, I got worms," he squealed, pretending he was dying while she ignored him and chased after the other boy, who jumped up on a barrel with a bucket in his hands.

"Spit on me and I douse you! Come on!" He waved the bucket at her and she stopped; spat disgustedly on the ground instead.

"You started it!" she yelled, then grabbed a rotten 'maranth root off a midden heap and pegged it at him. As he ducked, the bucket tilted, showing that it was empty. "Yaahhh!" she yelled, and jumped at him. He rolled off and stood up next to where Megan watched.

"Hey!" He was a lot bigger than Megan and looked at her as if she were a rotten tuber. "Hey, lookit this!"

The other kids came around until the cooper yelled at them to get lost, they were blocking her door.

I think he's the leader. Jorge. He might be way older than me. Maybe even eight.

"Maybe's a baby the Sour Noters' lost," someone said.

"I am not," Megan snapped, answering to Jorge, even though he hadn't said it. "I'm no baby, I'm Megan."

"Ohhhhh! It talks back. A Megan." He sniffed, as if she smelled bad. "Well, I'm Jorge and I'm head of the Cooper's Lane Killers."

"Jorge, you just lukewarm runs who wants ta be real hot shit." It was a girl who had a burn scar on her right cheek. He pulled away from where he'd been leaning over Megan to glare at the other girl instead.

"Marin!"

"You yell 't me, Jorge, and my mama won' give you even a burnt sticky-bun fer a whole year."

He pouted at her. *I don't pout. Much.*

"I live on Cooper's Lane, too," Megan said. "In the Flats."

He ignored her. "Marin, I's just . . ." He looked down at his feet.

"Come on, we're not the Killers an' you know it. We just one squat over from the Sour Noters, is all. Leave the freshie alone."

He looked around, then said, "Stay outta my way freshie, ya got no zight with me. Marin, didjer mam have fresh sticky buns left?"

As Megan stood there, wondering what she should do, they all decided to go visit the bakeshop and started pulling out stuff to trade to the baker, Marin's mother. *I'm hungry too, but they don't like me, just like the kids at school and they don't want me to . . .*

"Hey, freshie! You comin'?" It was the girl with the light hair—Eula.

"Marin's mam'll give you sumin' anyway, 'cause you're new." The others had gone down the street already, leaving Megan and Eula behind. Jorge had a leatherwood stick and pretended to lead a parade. Then Eula yelled, "Follow My Leader!" and climbed the wall to swing from a gargoyle's horns. Megan followed Eula and a lot of the kids came back to play follow-my-leader rather than parade behind Jorge.

*   *   *

Eula told Megan that the vacant lot where everyone played was called the Ground. Crooked Alley and Vischy Street converged there, and Sour Note Street ended at the hole in the board fence, where the two "squats" touched. A squat was the ground a kidpack defended, calling themselves the "mesne" or owners of the squat. At the Ground, the Sour Noters and Cooper's Laners stayed at their own ends.

Megan didn't like it when the other Cooper's Lane kids called her freshie, but she hung around anyway, determined not to be left out. Jorge was loudest of the kids, "all wind and no balls," like Aage the Older, Aage's second papa, said.

Aage had a great scar on his forehead, right where his hair parted over his left eye, from a fight with the Sour Noters. Someone had hit him there with a thrown bit of brick. Aage's blood-papa was a blacksmith, and his second papa was a farrier.

Some of the kids were children of quad marriages, and some like Eula and her brother Egon had just two parents like Megan. Onya and her little brother Yuri only had a mama, and Megan thought that was why Yuri was a scaredy-mouse who whined. Marin's only family was her mother and a big brother too old to run with the kids, choosing to help his mother in the bakery instead. The fire that put the scar on Marin's face had killed everyone else in their family when it burned down their block.

Then there was pretty Tantine, who had two mamas and thought she was so pretty. *She's always there if there're fights. I don't like her.* There were fourteen kids all together, if you counted Megan.

"Joooorge. D'ja like me?" That was Tantine, with a wilting daisy in her curly brown hair.

Jorge, busy tying bits of broken rubber together and winding them tight to make a ball, just said, "Nah, get lost."

"You're mean."

"Nah, you bug me."

She sat down—next to him—pouting.

"Hey! Ev'body! Lookit!" Serkai called from the street. *He wants to be a guardsman someday*. He hurried into the crowd of children, holding a bundle carefully in both hands. "I got two *real* knives!"

"Where'd ja get em?—How'd ja get em?—Serkai, you didn' steal 'em, did you?—Shit, I was going ta get the first knife—How'd ja get 'em?—How?"

Everyone was pushing to see. Megan, who sat on top of a broken bit of wall, could just see over Aage and Lixa's shoulders as Serkai unwrapped his prize, two plain steel knives, double-edged, leaf-shaped, with ridged horn handles, lying on the burlap he'd hidden them in.

"Hey, let the Sour Note kids try something *now*! I'll cut 'em." He picked up one, then the other, and weighed them in his hands, grinning. Up until now, all the kids had been practicing fighting and playing *cniffta*, the knife-juggling game, with knives made out of wood or rubber balls.

"I din't steal them," he said. "Well, not really." He started cleaning them, though they didn't need it. "I's up at the Market and there's a bad challenge at the cniffta circle. Somebody called somebody else a *Kuritz h'Rokatzk*!"

Arvi whistled. " 's bad."

"What does that mean?" Tantine whispered.

"I don' know, but it has sumin' ta do with corpse handlers."

"Eaaeu!"

"Yeah." Serkai stood up to tell his story. *Not as good as Papa but okay*. "Then the one woman *killed* t'other one." Everybody around him sucked a gasp through their teeth, going quiet.

"Really?" Megan didn't see who whispered.

"Really." Serkai nodded, firmly. "I *saw*. She's jumpin' an' then made a gurgly sound an' fell down with a knife in 'er neck right there." He pointed to illustrate. "An' bled like the 'Nest Fountain—pump, pump, pump. Then it stopped and 'er feet kicked. An' I's a knife fetcher.

When she died ev'ybody forgot 'bout the knives an' I scatted 'fore somebody could count 'em all."

"'s good, Serkai," Jorge said, looking at one knife. "You're still seven? Hey, 'f they caught you stealing ja know what'll happen?"

"No."

"Shit, din't anybody say?" Jorge looked around at the other kids, who shook their heads. "My older sister tol' me." He puffed himself up. "'f you get caught stealing an' you're under 'prentice age, your ma or pa gets a hand broke so they can't use it."

"Broke?"

"With a big hammer at the Market block. They hit three times."

Megan remembered something that had happened a while ago, when she and her parents had gone up to Teik Sandar's bathhouse.

They'd been passing a crowd around the Block near the bookseller's and Lixand's face had gone grim. He'd hustled them past, saying that the girl was only eleven and had stolen something to eat and that he wasn't going condone a tyrant's brutality. Ness had hushed him, looking around to see if anyone had overheard. Behind them, muffled by distance, there had been a wet hammering and someone screaming. They'd broken her hand.

"Yeah," Jorge said. "An' when you're older than seven they do it to you."

"Well, I'm not gonna get caught!" Serkai took his new knife back from Jorge. "Now I kin practice cniffta, two knives!" He rolled the knives away in the burlap, then picked up the stick he usually carried. It stood taller than he was and he'd scraped it smooth with a piece of brick. "I could tie one on each end an' make my own two-fang!"

"An' get caught fer sure! Only Dragonguard kin carry two-fangs inna street, turkey-head!"

"Blppppht!" Serkai put his tongue between his lips and blew air through them. "Turkey-head jerself! I got knives 'fore you did, maybe I should be leader."

Jorge leaped on him and they wrestled and the rest of them all yelled, jumping up and down until Serkai, with his face in the dirt and his nose all bloody yelled, "Rhunay! Rhunay! I give!" and Jorge let him up.

It's not fair, Jorge is older and bigger'n Serkai. He's all right though. We don't hurt each other. Well, at least the kids who belong don't hurt each other. I don't belong yet. I'm still the freshie. That's why Serkai didn't cut Jorge. Megan lent Serkai her kerchief, wetted in one of the puddles in the broken flagstones, to clean his face, and he let her see his knives. She cut herself three times trying to flip them like a real cniffta player, but she managed it, finding they were easier to throw than wooden ones.

It hasn't snowed yet but there isn't much day to play in. She was with the rest of the kids, scrounging bits of glass to sell to the glass-blower in the Market. If you collected a whole basket she'd pay a copper Bite. Megan had done that last week, then bet Yuri his Bite against hers on a spider-fight that she won. She'd been so proud to be able to give the whole Fang to her mama who, at first, had been worried where Megan had gotten it. *She was happy I wasn't stealing. I don't really steal.*

Eula had showed Megan a neat trick while they'd been in the Market, hungry, with no copper or anything to trade. She'd said "watch this" and walked over to the apple-sellers, looking back over her shoulder to call back to Megan.

"Eula, watch out!" One of the sellers had just stepped down from his wagon with a box of apples on his shoulder and Eula, not paying attention, bumped into him. He yelled, swayed, and she jumped out of the way as the box fell and broke, scattering apples all over the flagstones.

"I's sorry, Teik," Eula said, almost in tears. "Please, lemme help. I'm sorry. I'm sorry." She'd helped him pick up the apples rolling around and put them in a basket he'd grabbed out of his wagon. Megan made a motion to help, but Eula frowned and shook her head. She apologized so hard the apple-seller just waved his hands and gave her a couple of the more bruised ones. She said thank you and came back to sit on the other side of the square with the rest of the kids listening to Chandro, who had different stories from Megan's papa. In the crowd of kids, she gave Megan two apples.

"But Eula, you said you were hungry too." Megan tried to be fair and give her one back, but Eula shook her head, grinning.

"I have some," she said, showing three more apples hidden inside her shirt where her vest hid the bulges. "I picked 'em up while I was helping."

Megan didn't think Mama would like her doing that, but they still tasted good. Eula said that Nomo the Ragman would pay for all sorts of things and not ask how they were gotten, paying the best for good metal, like buckles or buttons.

After the first snow, Megan started looking forward to *Dagde Vroi*, the Days of Fools, in two more iron-cycles, when the whole city would celebrate. The Sysbaet and the Brown Brothers and the Ladyshrine priests would feed poor people in the River and Lake Quarters a big meal and everybody would get at least a piece of sausage. *We've been eating a lot of 'maranth lately. Maybe the sausage'll be spiced with garlic.*

Everyone would be making their best costume to wear in the streets or planning parties, and the Woyvode might have hot spiced punch given out at the Dragon'sNest Gate as he had in the Lady's Years. *Papa says he doesn't have to in the Dark Lord's Years.*

There was enough snow for the kidpack to make snow-demons with wings and roll snowballs that had bits of leaves and grass stuck to the outside. Megan threw one at Jorge, not meaning to hit him smack in the face, but he didn't duck.

"You . . . you . . ." He came and stood over Megan. "You don' really belong!"

"I do so! I live on Cooper's, just like everybody else!"

He sneered, *"I'm* leader of Cooper's Lane kids an' I say you don' belong!" and pushed her so hard she sat down.

Megan got up, sticking her chin out at him—*all wind and no balls.* "Push me again and I'll bite you!"

He laughed in her face. "See? 'f you were one of us, you wouln't say that! You keep hangin' around with us an' you play with us, butjer not *really* our friend."

"Oh, yeah?"

"Yeah!"

"I'm just as good as you!"

"Are not!"

"Am so!"

"Are not!"

"Am so! I can do anything you can! I can do it better!"

"Yeah?"

"Yeah!"

"I could steal sumin' from the Wizard's House," he said.

"I could too!" As she said it, he grinned.

"I Dare You," he said. Everybody went as quiet as when Serkai had told them about the woman getting killed.

"Jorge, 's not fair," Marin said in the quiet. "You never stole anything from the Wizard."

"I snuck into 'er lean-to though." He swung an arm at Megan, who ducked. "She said she'd do anything better! Well, 'f she wants ta be one of *us,* let 'er prove it!"

"Jorge, she shouldn' have ta," Aage said.

"I said I would," Megan said. *I'll show them. I'll show him.* "Piss on you," she yelled, and kicked him in the shin, connecting solidly because he wasn't expecting it. "I'm goin' now and when it gets dark I'll do it!"

He hopped, holding his leg, and by the time he thought about hitting Megan back she was already on the way to the Wizard's with everyone else following along.

"Meg, you shouldn' have ta do this by yourself. We'll come an' help," Marin said.

"And get caught."

"But . . ." Marin stumbled over explanations. "She's *the Wizard*."

Now Megan was frightened by her rash promise, but she couldn't back down or Jorge would laugh and she'd never be part of the pack. The Wizard's house was built on the north side of Victory Square, the only place that didn't need a high wall because no one would dare offend her. She even had windows on the outside and didn't need to keep dogs. Around the garden there was a border of tied-up rose bushes as high as Megan's waist.

The Wizard lived in the River Quarter because she chose to, and *her* pipes never froze like other people's. It was rumored that she had so much manrauq that she'd lived longer than most Zak, perhaps even longer than a naZak.

The rumors all said she was a witch strong enough to use the colors with no name, beyond violet. *She could turn somebody into a toad.* When she went out with her wing-cat on her shoulder, she went where she would and no one would dare lift a hand against her.

The Honey-Giver's Shrine, where Megan stopped, sweating even in the cold, was already too close to the Wizard's house, just across Chigger Street. There were kraumak on the gate-posts as big as Megan's head, which you didn't see anywhere else but in the First Quarter or the Nest. There was even a night-siren in her garden; black, flat leaves just unfolding in the breeze, the scream of the wind through its branches still eerie and thin this early in the evening.

If I don't go, Jorge'll laugh. He's like Rosziviy.

"Megan, she might turn you into a bird an' put you inna cage," Eula whispered, looking across at the lighted windows.

"If she does," Serkai said stoutly, patting his knives. "We'll come an' rescue you."

"Thanks, Serk." Megan shivered, feeling the snow on

the wind. They sat in the Honey-Giver's Shrine, since it was warmer than out in the square. This shrine was dedicated to the Mama-bear who was only roused to anger if her cubs were hurt. *Koru, Goddess, help me. Mama-bear let me be your cub, at least for now.* The drum from the Nest sounded the third hour of the day, and though it was getting dark no one went home.

Jorge was still right here, wanting her to say she was too scared, a baby.

"You'll be all right," Nikolai said, nodding reassuringly. "You're smallest, 'n you kin get in real tight places." She nodded again, and made the Goddess's sign on Megan's forehead and chin. "She'll never see you."

"You watch," Megan said. "You'll see," she said to Jorge, who looked a little sick because he hadn't thought she'd actually do it. She looked at him, wondering if he were worth being friends with.

Megan said, "Everybody stay here," and walked down to Yalshoi, the other street touching the Wizard's garden. She could hear the night-siren in the front garden wailing up and down with the breeze. If the wind picked up much more the siren would start flaring, sending blue sparks to the ground. It was starting to snow. Megan pulled her threadbare coat tight and looked for a safe way in.

There was a small pine tree poking its branches through the back garden fence. It was darker here because the house on the other side of the street presented a wall covered with dead red-vines to the pavement. The pine trees down the street creaked and whispered and Megan started nervously, thinking they were watching her. She looked at the little pine wondering if it would grow fingers and grab her if she climbed it.

She clenched her hands into fists in her pockets. She'd said she'd do it. In the left pocket she had her rubber ball, almost as big as her fist. She took it out and threw it over the border into the Wizard's yard, holding her breath.

It bounced twice, raising a puff of snow, then rolled to a stop by a statue of a hermaphrodite with glass wings like a fly's. It was carved sitting cross-legged, with closed eyes. *Maybe it's not a statue.* But her ball was right by its knee. If she got caught, she could say she came into the garden to get it back. With her heart hammering, she jumped and climbed over the low fence, using the pine tree.

The garden looked the same on the inside as the outside, with dead grass still poking up through the snow. *Soon it'll be deeper than I am tall.* She ran to get her ball and away, but the statue didn't move. It had snow on its head and face, thick on its closed eyelids. It was snowing so hard that her footprints were already disappearing. She ran across to the wall of the house between two windows and looked back. The statue's eyes were big and yellow, and Megan wondered why she hadn't noticed before.

She thought of going back, but Jorge wouldn't believe that she'd come this far unless she brought proof. So she slid along the wall, to a door in a lean-to, and found it locked.

The lean-to's roof let her get to a window that was open just a crack. It was dark inside, and even though the pane was only open a bit, she was small enough to wiggle through.

She found herself in a warm room that smelled of books. When she peeked from behind the drapes, she saw the full shelves, as many books as the Sysbaet had. Megan wanted to take one, thinking surely the Wizard wouldn't miss just one, then thought better of it. A book was too expensive; all she needed was a little thing.

There were thick rugs and a pile of furs and cushions near a cut stone fireplace. The objects lined up all along the mantelpiece were too high for her to reach. She started as a board creaked outside, and hid behind a globe of the world on a stand taller than she was, but nothing else happened.

To one side the shine of glass drew her eye, and she

tiptoed to look at a low shelf of bottles full of colored liquids. She squinted at one shadowy jar and flinched back when she realized she was staring at the toothed mouth of a pickled lamprey as long as her arm. Next to the bottles was a cat skull, like in the Sysbaet oscasa.

On the shelf above was a bell shining in a ray of light from the window. She picked it up to read the writing on the rim but couldn't make it out. As she lifted it, it rang, and she grabbed the clapper, wrapping her mitten around the bell and stuffing it in her shirt. Jorge'd believe her now. As she turned away from the shelf, something hissed at her from the near corner.

She ran, wiggling out the window but getting stuck half way because of the bell. Frantically she squirmed, trying to worm free. *It'll get me. I don't want to be here ever again even if there are books there are things with yellow eyes in the garden and things that hiss and look like big grey shadows.* She wiggled free just as a light bloomed behind her.

She looked back over her shoulder. The Wizard stood in the door, with a light shining around her hand. Megan almost fell through, and clung to the windowsill roof.

The Wizard, a woman with long, curly black hair and eyes the same yellow as the statue in the garden, wore blue trousers and a shirt gleaming rainbow colors under a black vest. She had a half-smile on her face, more frightening somehow, than a frown. Her hand whipped down, as if throwing something, and Megan ducked, slipping, feeling an ice wind graze her head as she slide down the roof and rolled into the snow. She jumped over the fence and ran and ran and ran. *She'll catch me. She knows who I am.*

"Megan!" somebody called in the dark ahead, and she tried to stop but ran right into Ivar and they both fell. *I got out.* They got up and the whole pack was there, asking questions, but she just shook her head.

They all went back to the Ground where it was safe. *I'm all wet and dirty and I lost my other mitt.*

"So?—Didja get in?—Nah, she couldn't—didn't—didja?—Hey . . . where'sa thing you said yah'd steal?"

Jorge looked down his nose and yelled "QUIEEEETTT!" It took a bit, but everybody shut up. "So?" he asked.

She stared at him a minute, then pulled the bell out of her shirt. He grinned all across his face and whooped, "Ya did it! Ya did it! Hey, Megan, yeah!" He pounded her on the back in congratulation and hugged her. Serkai lifted her up as high as he could, which wasn't very high, and they fell in the snow. She rubbed his face with her wet mitten and laughed.

When they'd all quieted down, Jorge took the bell. He yipped and dropped it as if it had bitten him. It rolled over, ringing, and stopped against Megan's boot—TING. It rang louder than such a small bell should, and everyone held their ears.

When it stopped they waited, standing frozen, for someone to come and yell about the noise, but no one did. Jorge shook his hand and said, "I'm not touching 'at again."

"Wh . . . whad is it?" Egon whispered from where he hid behind Eula.

Megan didn't want to touch it either, but since she already had and it hadn't hurt her, she picked it up. It was cold, but that could be because it had been lying in the snow. "Just a bell, but it was too dark to read the letters on it in her house."

"Shee-it."

"Megan, I don' think the Ragman'll buy *that*," Marin said. "'r you gonna *keep* it?"

Megan didn't want to, but didn't know what else to do and stood there, biting her lip, looking down at the bell.

"Well, you took it. You did sumin' Jorge *Dared* you ta. That's goodnuff ain't it?" Aage said slowly. "I kin take it to my dad's forge and melt it. Yeah kin sell the metal."

"Would you? Please, Aage?" She only had her one mit to wrap it, so they found a scrap of burlap bag instead.

"I'll do it now, then," he said. "Wait an' I'll come back."

He took it and the rest of them all sat in the fort they'd made out of boards with snow for chinking. Every one patted Megan on the back and told her that she belonged. She enjoyed every minute, and though the idea of stealing from the Wizard still made her feel sick, she didn't show it. *I wish I had Rilla with me. She's kin. I don't have to prove anything with Rilla.* Blizzard wind was starting to whip the falling snow by the time Aage came back.

He came back with a worried look on his face, still carrying the wrapped bell. " 'twouldn't melt," was the first thing he said. "I threw it into the forge an' it just lay there. I poked it an' it just lay there. My da's hottest fire." He looked at the bell, polishing it back and forth with the bag. "I showed Da."

"What!"

"Din' say where 'twas from. He told me give it back, get rid of it."

Now everyone was looking at Megan. "I'll find somebody who'll take it," she said defiantly. "Piss, it's just an old bell."

"Yeah, here." He threw it to her and she caught it with her bare hands. *TING.* She put it back in her shirt, and it lay like an ice cube next to her stomach all the way home.

She hid it in the bottom of her bed. *I don't know what I'm going to do. I belong with the Cooper's kids but I've stolen the Wizard's bell.* At night, when she lay down, it made a cold lump against her feet.

Chapter Seven

"Are you feeling all right, bylashka?" Ness felt Megan's forehead a few weeks later. "You might be fevered; and what's wrong with your hair, here?" She pushed Megan's hair back from her temple, exposing the roots. Megan pulled away.

"I'm fine, Mama." Megan had just been thinking about the bell. Her papa had gone to visit Aunt Marte and Rilla to see how they were after the blizzard wind stopped. It was still snowing, filling the streets to the height of second-story windows again. They'd planned on going to Teik Sandar's for a Dagde Vroi party later if the tunnels were open.

Ness appreciated the gap under the door now because it became the draft for the brazier, all along the floor unfortunately, but it was still warmer than not having a fire at all. She could keep the fire burning and it wouldn't use up their air. Candlers made it into the City only rarely once the snow set in, driving up the price of candles so most of the River and Lake Quarters made do with *wadiki* lamps when they didn't drink the fuel rather than burning it for light.

Most people smelled of wadiki in the wintertime—wadiki and sweat. Megan sniffed, looking into the brazier's coals. *Our room still smells a little wet, but not so much. It smells more like home, like us.*

She hadn't been able to sell the bell, though she'd tried. The Ragman had just shook his head, flat no—no bargaining. Next she'd taken it to the Market and somebody told her that only a naZak would buy it because it was too "powerful." The silversmith who couldn't read the words on the bell either, had looked at her and said, "Take it back to whoever owns it, if you know."

She hadn't told her parents about it, or about the Wizard. Her head had been cold at one temple, ever since she'd ducked the Wizard's gesture. *I don't know what to do.* She considered throwing the bell over the fence and leaving it to be found, but the Wizard had seen her steal it. The Wizard knew.

Megan stirred the spoon in the 'maranth porridge, trying to think of anything but the bell. *I used to pretend you made porridge with milk instead of water and there was tree-sugar for it. Mama got a treat a while ago. She bought some raisins.* That had been when she'd been accepted as an apprentice to a jewelry-maker named Yneltzyn, on Teik Varik's recommendation.

It was good there was some money coming in, because Papa didn't make much in the winter and still had to pay to keep his place on the street. He could work as a storyteller at the Rusty Cup on the Stairs if their regular performer, Vilischch, wasn't there, but it wasn't steady. *Mama asked me to do a lot of glass picking before the snow fell.*

Ness looked at her daughter poking at her food, sighed, and said, "Megan." The girl finished eating in a rush, scraping the bowl clean. Papa would be home soon, and if they were lucky all the snow would be packed down when Days of Fools started, tomorrow.

"Get your slate, bylashka," Ness said after they'd cleaned the dishes. This summer, Megan had found a slate tile in the Grounds and brought it home. Now

Mama, when she wasn't working or weaving something
or trying to patch clothes or anything else, was teaching
her Enchian with the slate and a lump of chalk. Lixand
could speak Enchian but not read or write it. Ness had
learned when she was a little girl, and it was because she
could speak to naZak that the jeweller had wanted her.
The Woyvode had announced, through the city's corner-
criers, that naZak would be allowed back into the City
and there would be more business, even if they had to
stay in the naZak enclave in the River Quarter.

Ness and Megan sat down by the kraumak on the
cushions, thinner than the ones lost in the fire because
they couldn't afford as much horsehair or wool to stuff
them. But Mama had gotten bright blue cloth from her
friend Arvi, called Weaver, and the color made the room
brighter. With the fire in the brazier on one side and
Mama sitting hugging her, she was nice and warm.

"*Parald l'Enchais?*" Ness asked. *Do you speak Enchian?*

Megan thought for a bit. "*Putre 'nepu, tipu,*" she
answered. *Only a little, a tiny little.*

"That's good, Megan-mi." Ness hugged her. "Now how
do you say, 'hello'?"

"*Juur!*"

"And good-bye?"

"Ummm, *reyiv?*"

Ness laughed. "Yes, but without the 'ummm'."

"*Tamee, mar!*" That meant, "I love you, Mama," and
Megan hugged her.

"I love you, too." They both turned, startled, as the
door was hit hard enough to jump on its hinges. Ness
sprang up and as she did, the door slammed open so
hard it hit the wall. Lixand stood in the doorway, snow-
covered, holding something cuddled in his arm. He'd
kicked the door open. Megan had never seen him so
angry before; she could see it by the way he moved even
under the layers of wool over his face.

"Lixand, what's happened? What's wrong?" Ness went
to close the door and help him.

"Careful, that's Rilla," he said, handing the bundle to

Ness. His face, as he unwrapped his scarf, was white
with two bright red spots on his cheeks and over his
eyes. "That bitch. That bloody, vicious bitch." He pulled
off his coat. "If she weren't my own sister I'd kill her."
Megan ran to help her mother but Lixand shook his
head, no. "Megan, go hang up my clothes instead."

Mama unfolded the blanket wrapped around Rilla and
made an unhappy sound. "We can't afford a healer,
love."

"I know. Megan, run and get Dmitrach."

"Papa, what's wrong with Rilla?"

He took Megan's hand.

"Your aunt hit her too hard. I took Rilla away from
her for a while. She'll be staying here."

"I'll run."

"That's my girl," he said, letting her go with a pat.

Dmitrach was the healer for the whorehouse, usually
only for little things and birthings, but he might be able
to help.

The hallway was dark except the cracks in the winter
walls, and Megan could see her breath in the needles of
bright shining between the boards as she ran around the
near side to the door at the head of the hall that separated the rented rooms from the Peach.

It was early and Megan didn't want to disturb anyone,
but she knocked anyway because she had to, for Rilla.
Boryis, Dimi's lover, answered the door. She could tell
he and Dmitrach weren't taking customers tonight, resting up for tomorrow, because he wasn't wearing his fancy
clothes.

"Hi, Meg. Problem?" He ran a hand through his
shaggy brown hair and smiled at her.

"Boryis, we need Dimi to help my cousin. 's he here?"

He winked at her and said, "Your cousin, sweets? Is
he good looking?"

"She's littler than I am and we need a healer, not sex,"
she said, and he stopped teasing, his face sobering.

"Sorry." He turned, calling into their rooms, "Dimi!"
The healer came out, pulling his robe on, his hair tied

back and no makeup on his face, but he woke up quickly when Megan explained.

"Dmitrach, Papa says we can't pay you right away . . ."

"Shush on 'at noise, sweets. Ay' cum." He looked plain in a shabby, worn robe out at the elbows, but Megan thought he was one of the most beautiful people she knew right then. He grabbed his kit.

When they came in, Lixand had Rilla in the wallbed and Ness had some chai brewing. Papa didn't look angry any longer, just tired and sad. He called Megan to him while Dimi went to look after Rilla. "Stay out of the way, Megan."

"We're not going to Teik Sandar's party, are we?"

"No, Megan-mi. There'll be other parties." She sat with Papa and they waited, watching Ness and Dimi at the wallbed.

After a while, the healer came over and settled down next to them with a sigh. Lixand handed him a cup. "Ay'm no Haian," Dimi said. "But ay think she be fine. Near ay can tell, t'arm's not broke, just out. I put her shoulder back. 'n the littl'un bruised bad. 'Time worried 'bout's her not wakenen." Megan could tell he was worried because his out-city accent was very strong.

"Her mother shook her hard enough that she was dizzy and vomiting when I came," Lixand offered. "And saw what was going on."

Dimi shook his head. " 's bad, that. Her brain's shook, good." He put the cup down, went back to the bed. Ness held the kraumak closer while Dimi looked in Rilla's eyes one, then the other. "Well, nuh. She wakes up soon, she be fine. Mightbe 'f you call her, 'll help."

When Papa tried to say something about money, Dimi shushed him. "It's a present for the Days, forget it, Lixand."

He's got his city accent on again. Megan went over and climbed in the bed next to Rilla.

"Bedtime, bylashka," Ness said.

"Mama, may I stay, pleeeeese. I promised Rilla, I promised!"

Ness kissed the top of her head and let her hold Rilla's hand. "No hugs, now. That would hurt her, Meg."

"Okay."

Rilla's face had bruises on it, blue and green and some old ones, yellow and faded. Megan lay down and held onto her hand, whispering in her ear that people would be mad if she went away and that Brunsc would be lonely and that she'd think Rilla was a turkey-head if she didn't wake up.

Piss on Aunt Marte. She's what Jorge calls an asshole. She is. She is. You don't hit kin. You don't hurt kin.

Megan roused late that night, when Rilla did. Mama and Papa were smiling and Rilla was acting sleepy and slow but understood that she was supposed to stay awake for a while to make sure she was all right. *I'm sort of dreaming and everything's foggy and my eyes don't want to stay open.* Papa said, "Go back to sleep Megan, we'll look after Rilla." So she did.

Next time she woke up, Ness was in the bed with the two children, which made it a bit crowded. Megan wondered sleepily where her papa was, thinking that maybe he was in her bed, behind the rickety wooden cupboard bed, out of the draft.

Rilla hung onto Ness, who held her cuddled close, with both hands. The wallbed doors were ajar and the cold crept in around the edges, but it was warm and smelled of feathers and wool and her parents. Megan scratched an itch then lay still, thinking that she *had* to get up because she'd dreamed of what to do with the bell. She climbed carefully over Mama's legs, opened one door a crack, then closed it quick behind her so the warmth would inside. She hissed between her teeth as her feet hit the cold stone floor.

The Wizard saw me. She looked right at me and threw something at me. My head still feels cold there. If she wanted to get somebody's hand broken, it would have already happened. So I've got to go give it back. Maybe

I should tell Serkai in case she decides to turn me into a bird and keep me in a cage.

"Megan," Papa whispered from the kitchen corner, where he was cutting bread. "Happy Days of Fools." He'd gotten some proper leavened bread instead of flat bread and it was still warm from the baker's. Megan put out the big plate they still had left from her mother's good set. Though they no longer had separate plates, they still had that. That, and a table because Aunt Marte had given them her old one and Teik Varik had sanded down the burns and scars. Megan didn't like it much, the old stains showing like ghosts as if Marte's presence were haunting them, but it was theirs now, anyway.

Lixand spread the bread with a little nut butter and Megan got a cup of chai with milk and a whole handful of raisins because it was festival. The rest of the First day, everyone would eat only flatbread and drink chai without milk or anything sweet, but first thing in the morning everyone got a treat.

Mama got up and went down the hall to the privy, while Papa put her cup out and Megan plumped her pillow for her.

"Uncle?" Rilla called from the bed. "You said I could stay last night. Can I stay here? Pleeese?"

"You may stay with us for a while, Rilla. I mean to have some words with your mother."

"I'll be good, I promise."

Papa looked unhappy. "You're a good girl, Rilla, I'm sure of that—No, no, don't get up, stay there and I'll see you to the privy in a minute." Then he looked at Megan. "Megan?"

"Yes, Papa?" She looked up from where she was pulling a splinter off the table. He was holding the bell out to her.

"What's this?"

"A bell, Papa."

"I know, Megan." He set it down on the table in front of her where it made no noise at all, not even a click as it was set down. "I want to know where it came from and why it was in the bottom of your bed."

"I . . . borrowed it from the Wizard, because it was pretty. I have to give it back today." *That's what I dreamed. Maybe the bell told me to say that.* "I din't think you'd like me borrowing it so I hid it—" He held up his hand, interrupting.

"All right. All right. You don't have to tell me every detail. As long as it's borrowed and is going back today. Right after breakfast."

"Yes, Papa." Megan ate very slowly.

It was still dark, as it would be almost till the middle of the day. The Days of Fools were the darkest cycle of the year when any light was welcome. Megan hadn't told her parents that she'd lost a mitt, so she pushed her hands into her coat sleeves. It was getting a little colder but she stopped to look at the decorations anyway. Some people had enough power to make little kraumak of various colors that would glow for an hour or two, or even a few days. Those who couldn't afford to buy dreams from more powerful people would cut evergreen branches and hang them over doorways and around windows.

At one door a bunch of fairies with wings sat in the boughs of pine over someone's door, while the house across the street was wreathed in blue and orange flames, without burning. Next door to that was a house that was melting. Megan wondered what kind of people *liked* to live in houses decorated like that.

During the last days of the cycle, people would come out in their personal costumes. *I, I shouldn't dally. Papa said I had to give the bell back this morning. It's still morning.*

She walked past a tree that danced in place, roots making ripples in the ground, branches bending and waving in the still air. Someone had a phoenix as tall as Megan on top of their wall, slowly building its nest, and the whole street around it smelled of camphor and myrrh. Next door someone else built a bear out of snow and ice, with green witch-fire in his eyes. She told herself that she shouldn't stop and look at the decorations. *I have to go to the Wizard's house.* She shivered with cold, all over now, not just the spot on her head.

She walked slowly but still got to Victory Square much too quickly. A bonfire had been built in the middle of the square where people were selling cheap mulled wine and expensive hot chocolate while the poorest got the hot, vinegary cider free. Megan stood in line for a cup, and the scent went up inside her head as she drank it, standing next to the fire where it was warmer, trying not to look across the square at the Wizard's house.

It was well-lit and her main decoration was her garden where the winter had disappeared. Her roses were blooming, the grass and trees were green, and butterflies flew. Her fountains flowed with colored light. And her house door had teeth all the way around.

The bell inside Megan's shirt was cold and she shivered despite the bonfire. Her hands were bluish and there was frost on her eyelashes though it wasn't *that* cold. The cold spread from the spot on her head. She gave the cup back to the cider people and tried to smile at the man who gave it to her. "Happy Year-Turning, Goddess guard," he said.

"May you never be foolish," she answered. *I was foolish. I took a Wizard's bell.* It was worse than the library the first time; that time she hadn't done anything wrong to own up for. She dragged her toes all the way across the square and into the puddle of the light at the gate, wishing for a shadow that she could hide in. She jumped back as the falcon on the left gatepost, under the kraumak, opened yellow eyes and hissed at her. On the right, the sandy-colored cat just watched, tail twitching; just the tip. It blinked and yawned, showing her its teeth. She *had* to give it back. *She had to.* She tried again, and this time the gate animals let her by.

Beyond the gate it was warm, but the path was cooler than the flower borders and the rest of the garden, cool enough that she was glad of her coat.

To knock on the door she'd have to step between the teeth; ivory incisors hanging down almost to the top of her head. The stoop had small pointed teeth set in red gums and the doormat was a tongue. *I don't want to. I don't want to.* The bell TINGED though she'd wrapped it in her shirt to muffle it. She *streeetchhhed* over the little teeth and put her foot on the doormat-tongue. Nothing happened. She hopped a little, getting both feet together.

The doorknocker was like the pink uvula hanging down from the top of a mouth and Megan was glad she couldn't reach it. It looked sticky. *I can hardly breathe. I'm too cold to breathe. Or I'm too hot, I don't know.* She tapped on the door, very quietly, thinking that if nobody heard she could leave the bell on the stoop and go home. She tapped one more time so she could honestly say she tried. *There's nobody home . . .*

The door crashed open all by itself. "Enter." Megan peeked in. If there was someone there, they were invisible. "Enter, I am waiting." She stepped in and stood on the landing. The blackwood stairs reminded her of Papa's old desk. She was shaking and the bell tinged again. "Ahh," the voice said. "Close the door, child."

She does know. Maybe I won't mind being a bird; birds are happy. She closed the door behind her. It had a metal bird painted on the inside. Megan put my hands behind her against the door. "Come downstairs, to the garden," the voice said. Megan was hot but her coat, wrapped around her, made her feel more secure, so she didn't unbutton it as she went down the stairs.

The atrium had a sand garden with cactuses, centered around a pool with a cow's skull next to it in the sand; a purple flower grew out of one eyesocket. The Wizard, dressed in a robe the color of granite, sat on a red cushion. Her face was impassive.

"Come, sit down." She pointed to a spot in the sand before her and Megan walked over and sat down, not knowing what else to do, unbuttoning enough to take the bell out.

"Ididn'tmeantotakeithere," she said all in one breath, putting it down in the sand in front of her where its ring, *TIN—k*, cut off as the edge was buried. Megan didn't look up, feeling the Wizard's eyes on her.

"Didn't you?"

"I had to."

"Did you?"

"WellJorgesaidIdidn'tbelong. AndhecouldandIsaidI-couldn'—"

"He dared you," the Wizard said. Megan nodded, looking up. The Wizard's eyes were plain dark brown, but they were still scary. She looked so young.

A big boy with slanted eyes and yellow skin and hair so black it shone blue, came across the sand carrying a rake.

"This is San. You met him in the garden the other day, wearing his costume."

Megan gulped. "You mean the statue with wings?"

"Yes."

"Hi. I'm Megan." It was the best she could do. *Mama'd want me to be polite.* He nodded at her then gave the Wizard a bedraggled red mitt. She put it on the sand beside her and talked to him in a sing-songy language. He bobbed his head in a half-bow.

"He doesn't understand you, Megan, but I passed on your greeting." She picked up the bell as she got up. San plumped up the cushion and started raking the sand smooth. Megan hesitated, wanting to pick up the mitt but afraid to. The Wizard waited, then pointed. "Take it and come with me," she said, unsmiling.

"Yesteik." They went upstairs to the second floor, Megan following a step behind, over the deep grey carpets in the halls. She walked so soft Megan couldn't hear her at all. She looked to see if the wizard had a shadow. *That's silly, of course she has a shadow. Only demons don't have shadows.*

"Stealing, at your age, usually gets your parents ruined. The loss of a hand is disaster." She opened a door and

Megan followed her into the library where the bell had originally been. Megan was suddenly cold again.

"You should be careful who you steal from, if you're going to do it at all, though I can't fault you for your taste in victims. The current Blue Mage would have had you as one of his gate-posts."

She sat down again and a big black wing-cat flew over to perch on her shoulder. Though Megan had seen pictures, she'd never having seen a live one before; for a moment startled out of her fear, she stared.

"Most people would say, 'Don't steal at all,' though in current times it is often necessary. It will likely become worse before it gets better. Come here." She curled a finger at Megan, who scuffed her feet in the carpet uncertainly, then obeyed, and the Wizard handed her the bell that was suddenly warm in her hands.

"Put it where it belongs, then come back here," she said, and waited until Megan stood before her again. "The words on the bell just say 'Be careful what you wish for.'" The Wizard took Megan's chin in her hand and touched the cold spot at her temple, drawing the chill out.

"If you must steal, don't get caught." She let go, reached up, and scratched the cat under his chin.

"Yes, Teik."

She smiled at Megan, like a cat. "You'll remember, believe me. Look in the mirror over there, then go."

"Thank you, Teik Wizard." Megan went over to the mirror, as tall as she was, real silvered glass, to do as she was told. At her temple the roots of her hair had gone shining white. "Will it stay?" she almost wailed, pulling at the lock hair. *That is what Mama meant.*

The Wizard nodded slowly. "One lock of your hair will grow in white," she said.

Megan wanted to cry, to run, but just walked to the door. *It isn't as bad as getting a spanking or Mama or Papa having a hand broken.*

"Megan." The child turned around in the doorway,

holding onto the frame, sniffing. "Two more pieces of advice. First, don't ever steal from me again."

"No, Teik."

"Second, when you're old enough, get a good teacher of manrauq."

"Yes, Teik. Bye." Megan ran down the stairs, out the door between the teeth, down the path out the gate.

When Megan got home, Rilla was sitting in Papa's lap, in Megan's spot. Megan stopped. She felt bad that her place on her Papa's lap was filled by Rilla and at the same time guilty. Then Papa said, "Bylashka, come in, you're cold. There's only hard bread and chai since it's First day. Your mama will be back in a bit and then we'll celebrate." He held out his arm and Megan cuddled under it, sharing his lap with Rilla, where she told Papa what the Wizard had said about the manrauq, not mentioning anything about stealing, or her hair. He hadn't noticed it yet and Megan guessed it would grow out slowly. *I guess you can hardly see it.* She sniffled and hid her face in his shirt, feeling better.

After a while Mama came in and sat down, and Megan hooded the light so the room went black. Then Papa said, "This is where we came from. From the dark."

Mama answered, "Outside it burns. Inside we are safe."

Then Papa again. "Remember. The world died. The sun was dim and winter ruled for years." Then it was Megan and Rilla's turn.

"We were born in the dark. We are hope." And Mama uncovered the light.

"I love you," Papa said, and Rilla and Megan got hugged between Mama and Papa. Megan didn't like just hard bread and chai, but Lixand told the story of the last days of the Old World before it burned and just after, when hard bread and *maybe* hot chai was all anybody had to eat. Megan nibbled on the bread, glad that when the Days of Fools were over, the world would be safe from the burning for another year.

Rilla stayed till after the year turning, healing; the two children running together, Megan sponsoring Rilla to the rest of the kidpack. They often went sledding with the other kids, on boards that they'd bent back; and made the hill in their squat icy by packing the snow down. At the bottom, everyone had piled up a snow mountain so you could whiz down and go *ker-smack* right into it. They could slide on the Stairs, but people disapproved, so they mostly stayed in the Ground to play.

Ivar had said once that if you were being chased you could get away by sliding, and he'd prigged a buckle that way last iron-cycle. It had been right at the end of the Days when he'd seen someone with metal boot buckles and had cut-'n-grabbed, then slid faster than the guard could run. That had been all the way up in First Quarter, and he'd slid down and hidden in an alley in River.

The Ragman only gave him a half-Bite for it because it wasn't steel, but had said he'd pay a whole Fang for steel buckles and a whole Bite for a button. A Bite was paid for a big basket of glass that could take a Hand and a couple of days to find, while a Fang could buy a whole bag of 'maranth seeds for flour or porridge, or a little bag of barley or a thick sausage.

Ivar had given the half-Bite to his da to help get his little sister Lixa's teeth fixed. She'd had one growing in wrong, in the roof of her mouth.

Serkai and Ivar were always playing real cniffta now, getting their hands cut up when they missed, since Ivar had saved and bought his first knife. Megan had made herself a knife out of wood and practiced with it so when she got a real knife she'd be as good as they were. She almost had enough for her first knife from the cutler's, even though she gave her papa most of her scrounging money. Black-rock had just started costing more and Rilla needed milk while she stayed with them. Milk, and Mama said that they all needed a little fruit or their teeth would fall out and they would get sick.

Rilla and Megan went sliding with the rest of the pack,

then they all had a snowball fight with the Sour Note kids, trying to chase them out of the snow fort they built too close to their squat. *We're the mesne of Cooper's Lane and all the Ground north of the gap in the fence at their street, and they can fight theirselves against the Victory Square kidpack.*

The Cooper's Lane kids never fought with Victory Square because they fought dirty, sneaking up to bash other kids with boards. During the snowball fight with the Sour Noters, Ivar and Megan tried to dig tunnels through to the Sour's wall, but they all caved in. It was fun until one of them put a rock into a snowball and hit Arvi in the head. Megan told Rilla to hide before the fray started.

The Cooper's Laners threw rocks back and there was a lot of yelling and Serkai and Ivar's knives came out; and Eula had Serkai's stick. Arvi had gotten up with a bloody nose and Aage held onto her so she didn't do anything stupid while Jorge challenged their leader, Moden, fists only.

She bloodied his nose and he hit her in the eye so it started to swell up, but then he got her down because he was bigger and sat on her and shoved her face in the snow until she yelled "Rhunay!" and promised to give up the Sour Noter's chunk of the Ground.

They were covered in snow and wet all the way to skin; Arvi and Jorge holding snowballs to their noses till they stopped bleeding, grinning and laughing and pounding each other on the back.

Megan had to go back to find one of her mittens that she'd lost when her tunnel fell in. When she wiggled out, holding the mitten triumphantly, Rilla said, "I'm cold, Meg. Can we go home now?"

When they got back to the Flats, Megan pulled the latch-strings, left, right, up, down, CLUNK and they went in. There wasn't a fire and Megan wasn't supposed to light one, either, until Mama or Papa came home, so the two children took off all their wet clothes, hanging them up on pegs that Teik Varik had put up. He hadn't

been coming around that much lately, saying he had a
voyage to prepare for downriver with his Gospozhyn,
come break-ice. Whenever she hung up her things,
Megan was always reminded of what he said when he
put the pegs up; that wet clothes got to smelling like a
pile of dead fish and you started to smell poor.

Megan didn't want to smell poor. *I bet Rilla wouldn't
like it, either.* She picked up the kraumak and they cuddled up in the wallbed in the blankets, where Megan
told Rilla stories out of her book. Ness had said that if
her Gospozhyn, Yneltzyn, was pleased with the gem she'd
just been working on, he might grant her more copper,
or even silver. She said that he earned steel Claws for
his work, but she could only earn copper as yet. She was
saving for feathers to make a tick that would be warmer,
and Megan would get the extra blanket.

Megan rubbed Rilla's hands and feet and her own,
making sure they were all warm. Somebody started
thumping on the door, but Megan didn't move because
she wasn't to answer unless she recognized who it was.

Marte's voice came drunkenly through the door. "Lix-
and! Lixand, don' you shu . . . shut th' door'n my face!
You answer! You an . . . answer now!"

*I don't want to answer the door. I should, though.
She's . . . she's nasty kin, but she's family.* Megan pulled
her mama's robe around herself and told Rilla, "Hide flat
behind the pillows."

"Op . . . open up. I'm here f'my daughter." Bang-
bang-bangety-bang. Megan opened the door and Marte
half fell into the room, bringing the odor of wine with
her. "Whha?"

"Hi, Aunt Marte. Mama and Papa n' Rilla aren't here."
*I don't want Rilla to go. Papa said that Aunt Marte was
a nalcolic.* "You can come back later."

"Bitch." Aunt Marte scrambled up, hanging onto the
door. "Lil' bitch, jus' like your dam. F'r all you look
like my *brother*!" She shouted, looming over Megan who
backed up, scared, tripped over the hem of her mother's

robe, and fell backward. "Li-AR!" Marte raised a hand up to hit.

"Shenanya!" Megan yelled as loud as she could, squirming backward, hoping the neighbor—someone—would hear. "SHEN!"

Lixand, come home early because of the weather, caught his sister's hand from behind. "Marte." *Papa saved me.* Megan wiggled out of the tangle of robe, leaving it on the floor, and scooted to hold Papa's legs. "You won't raise your hand against my child." Aunt Marte swayed, blinking at him.

"Were's m'daughter, li'l brother?" She waved her free hand vaguely, forgetting all about Megan. "Can' keep'er. Not by law."

Lixand was shaking, he was so angry. "Marte, you are not getting your daughter back until you go to the healers and stop this drinking. You'll ruin your life and hers."

"And hers?" Aunt looked innocent—*like Nikolai when she priggs sweets.* "Why?"

Papa put down the black-rock bag he'd been carrying and told Megan to go keep warm until the fire was going, so she went and pulled the doors closed so Aunt wouldn't see Rilla. She put her eye to the crack between the doors.

Lixand got his sister sitting, with a chai cup in her hand instead of a bottle of wine.

" 'ny beer li'l brother?"

"No, Marte. We can't afford luxuries and won't drink the lamp alcohol." He struck a match to the kindling, stilling the shaking in his hands, the anger in his voice.

Quietly, reasonably, Lixand explained how bad she was being, telling her that she was worse than a snake for hitting children, telling her she'd lose her business. She laughed at that but looked a little sick. "And Rilla is going to stay here, for all we can't afford to keep another child, until you are dry enough to be a decent person, much less a decent mother."

She nodded finally and cried, sniffling and blowing her nose into his handkerchief, then had to go throw up, Lixand supporting her to the jakes down the hall. He came back long enough to tell Megan not to play with the fire, that he was going to walk Aunt home.

At night when Rilla was asleep and Megan was supposed to be, she could hear Mama and Papa talking in the wallbed. Ness and Lixand took time for each other at night, even though Ness fell asleep quickly because of the hard apprentice work. Lixand mostly did the housework, with Megan's help, because Ness was worked so hard.

Papa said, "Ness, what can I do? She's my sister. Rilla is such a good child. Marte . . . I just don't understand anymore. She used to be a better person."

"It'll be all right, love. She'll dry out and Rilla will be able to go home. Then the strain will be off."

Papa sighed. "We'll be in trouble once my pension runs out, and that's too soon. We'll have to put off getting some of the things we need, if we're to save for Megan's apprenticing. Yakob said he'd take her, even if Vyaroslaf didn't like it, but he'd have to charge full stranger-price."

"I'll be a journeyman soon enough, Lixand. We'll manage even if we don't have meat for the soup. We'll make do with the bones."

Rilla turned over and hugged Megan with one arm and Brunsc with the other. Someone walked by outside. There was a mosquito-sized sound; music from across the atrium, from the Peach. *I think I hear Papa crying. I know that mama's asleep because she snores, but why is Papa crying? Mama said we'd be all right.*

Chapter Eight

Megan scratched at a rusty spot on her new knife with one fingernail, spat on the stone, and looked at the edge. She'd bought it from cutler Varclaf's rust-stock, offering to run errands for him for a week to make up the difference between the metal she had and what he wanted for it.

"Who's gonna walk me home?" Tantine said, leaning on one hand rolling the paste marbles with her other fingers. Serkai and Ivar both looked at each other like dogs bristling.

"'s my turn," they said at the same time. "Is not—is so!"

"I like *both* of you," Tantine said, curling a lock of her hair around her finger. Ivar and Serkai were always arguing over who was better, who had more zight, but this time it was worse because of Tantine's pushing. Megan listened with one ear, thinking about her knife.

Varclaf's rust-stock was piled at one side of his biggest grindstone, where he sharpened axe-heads and scythes, collected to sell as scrap to the smiths if they weren't *too* rusty. Nobody could do anything with rust because it just wouldn't melt.

Megan, with Rilla by her, had looked through the pile while he kept an eye on them, haggling with another customer. The one she had picked was as long as her hand, with pimples of rust on it and the tip broken off, but it was the best there. If she could clean it and find enough scraps to leather the handle, it'd be okay. To pay for it she swept out his shop for him and gathered the sweepings for him to sift. Aage's father melted the sweepings so the dirt just burnt off.

Megan stopped sharpening to look over at Rilla, who was playing cniffta-ball with Maya, practicing so she wouldn't cut herself if they played real cniffta.

Rilla had a knife now, too. She'd prigged it while Megan wasn't looking, slipping the knife into her sleeve while Megan bargained with Varclaf. Megan wouldn't have minded if she'd gotten caught because it would have been Aunt Marte who'd get her hand mashed. But she decided that that wouldn't be a good idea because she'd be nastier if that happened.

Inside Rilla's sleeve, it got caught on the wool and made her arm dirty red, but it was worth it. It was sharp only on one side, like Mama's kitchen knife, and when they'd broken off all the crumbly bits it looked almost good as new. Varclaf's watchdog had barked at the metal smell on her, but the merchant called him off because he thought the dog was barking at Megan, a paying customer. Megan tried not to listen to Ivar and Serkai's continuing argument. Tantine said a couple more things. *Why's she being even more of a pisser lately?*

"Well, Iv walked you home last time and he only has one knife and I have two and—"

"Oh, yeah?" Ivar got up, staring down at Serkai. "I can catch my one better than you can your two!"

Megan wiped her rusty fingers off on her trousers, then started guiltily. They were new, just given for her seventh birthday, and they should stay clean as long as possible. They hadn't been going to Teik Sandar's baths much anymore, and it was getting hard to keep themselves clean. Last iron-cycle, lice had spread through the Flats.

Sandar had started saying that her bathhouse wasn't a charity, and she and Ness had fought about it. *Mama and Papa's old friends don't ask us up-city much anymore. I think it's because they think we've lost zight. My papa hasn't. I'm proud of my papa and mama, and if they don't see that we haven't lost anything, then poop on them.*

It was still hard to make ends meet, though Lixand was getting more money now that it was warm enough for him to take his place on Zidium. When the daylight lasted eighteen hours, in the summer white nights, he made much more.

Megan usually practiced cniffta with Serkai, hiding her cniffta cuts from her parents, though sometimes they would frown at her when checking to see if she'd washed her hands before dinner. *Mama said I should be careful and she looked at Papa that way, that means she's afraid I'm learning all sorts of bad things.* That was the reason Megan had brought Eula and little Noran home to meet her parents; Mama had liked them.

She usually played with Serkai because Ivar was being a snot, spending most of his time fighting with Jorge and Eula over who was the leader of the Cooper's Laners.

"I think *you're* just wonderful, Ivar," Tantine said, and offered him the back of her hand for him to escort her, their knuckles touching, just like a Zingas escorting the Woyvodaana to a court dance in the Nest. As she went, she looked over her shoulder and winked at Serkai. *Tomorrow she's going to ignore both of them, I bet, and suck up to Jorge.* Megan spat on her rock and kept sharpening.

"Hey! HEY! Everybody! HEY!" Onya scrambled through the hole in the fence her face covered with tears and dirt. "Where's my little brother? Shit. Shit. The Guard

came and got my mom. My mom hasn't done anything.
Where's Yuri? Where is he? Anybody seen him?"

No one had seen him since he and Lixa went to the
Market to hear Chandro. Maya got Onya to stop yelling
and wait for everyone to get to the Ground. Nikolai got
Marin, and Arvi ran to fetch Aage from the smithy. "My
mom hasn't done anything wrong. She hasn't, she hasn't.
Why'd they . . . oh, shit. Fishguts. Oh, piss."

They gathered and went to the Market to try and find
Yuri or what had happened to their mom. Ivar and
Megan found Lixa hiding at the Card-painter's booth,
scared green.

"They caught him trying to steal a button off this fat
lady in a sling-litter, and her guard came when she
squealed but she hung onto him," she said, shaking.
"They took him away to the guard-post by the block, and
then they went and got his mama."

The block-drum was being pounded to get people's
attention, so Ivar and Megan took Lixa's hands and went
out, though Megan didn't want to. *I think I know what's
going to happen. It's not fair. It's not fair.* Yuri and Onya
helped their mother pay the rent. They never ate well
and Yuri's teeth were falling out. Their papa had been a
guardsman who died in the north war against the Ice
People. He'd gotten cashiered even though he was dead,
so his wife didn't get pension.

Onya's mother stood on the block between two guards,
who held her by the elbows. To one side another guard
held onto Yuri who kicked and yelled, trying to get loose,
but there was only the Guard's armor for him to vent
his anger on, no exposed skin he could bite. The Guard
captain stepped forward, holding up his hands.

"We call thee forth!" *He's calling everybody out to see,
formal, so we have to go.* "We call thee forth! We call
thee forth!"

Onya's mama had been crying but she wasn't now, her
face white. In the crowd of people Megan could see Aage
holding Onya back so she didn't run up to the block.
Many people don't like this. They know the family.

They're her friends. The guards held their two-fangs ready.

"Thievery of a lad under age— One silver button from Zingas Imla. Judged guilty—"

"By whom?" Someone shouted from the crowd but the Guard captain ignored it. "Where's the truth-teller? Did he steal it? Proof! Proof!" The crowd got noisier, shouting, drowning out the captain. The guard pushed people back away from the block, using the shafts of their two-fangs. The captain's voice rose over the noise.

"Punishment is the breaking of the hand of the one who misraised him, by our Serene DragonLord's will. So decreed by the Third of the title; so upheld by the Fifth." Somebody behind Megan said, "Upholding truth with no truth-teller. With more people around there'd be a riot."

The Guard captain held up the fate-coin to show that it was true: white on one side and black on the other. If the white side, Koru's side, showed after he tossed it, they'd crush the hand she used less often. Megan could feel the tension in the air, the crowd's manrauq, combined. *They can't stop it, but they can make it better.*

The captain tossed the coin and everyone watched it spin up in the sun, up, white, black, white, black; and down so it landed by his boot, bounced three times and clicked flat, white showing.

"Koru's mercy," he said. Yuri wasn't kicking anymore, just hanging in the guard's arm, but he watched them take his mama to the hand block where the *K'gebar* stood, holding the wooden mallet capped with black metal on each end. *It depends how hard he hits, and if the hand is flat.* Megan put an arm around Lixa, who was crying, and after a second so did Ivar.

"Koru show you all the mercy you show us," Onya's mama said and put her hand out, but the guards still held onto her and the *K'gebar* raised the hammer.

It came down almost gently, *thump*. Megan couldn't look away, blinking because it seemed so wrong that the arc of the hammer should end where her hand lay. The second swing, *thump*. Megan felt her stomach lurch, tighten, and the taste of bile clutched the back of her throat. Onya's mother wasn't kneeling anymore. She didn't yell, but her head was rolling back and the guards had to hold her up. *Thump.* There were cracking noises mixed into the last. Megan's stomach knotted again a thickness rising up her throat. The guards let go, and Onya's mama slid down as if they'd broken all her bones.

When they let Yuri go he ran to her. Sour saliva gushed into Megan's mouth, and she turned and threw up. Around her the crowd was muttering.

"*Rokatzk,*" someone said. "*h'Rokatzk* DragonLord's answer to thievery."—"Starve us all, that way."—The noise was rising as people got angrier again and started to shout.

"Calm. Everybody calm down. The last riot spawned a sweep through that hurt a lot of innocent folk, calm." One of the Sysbaet, a woman with brown hair, raised a pale, thin hand, holding people back. Nobody pushed against the soldiers anymore, but it wasn't because of the two-fangs but because of the Sysbat. *They aren't supposed to help a criminal.*

In the quiet the Guard marched back to their posts, holding their fangs ready. A man jumped up on the block and picked up Onya's mama. Yuri sniveled, held onto her, and then him too.

"Sysbat, I can't pay hard metal for healing, but I'm willing to work in exchange," he said. *I think he's sweet on Onya's mama.*

"By law, we cannot help," the Sysbat answered him, leaning on the words "by law," and more people spoke up. "I have a Scale or two to spare."—"And I." Others said that they could give a little toward healing though nobody could spare much. The Sysbat looked after the guards, then to where Onya's mama lay in her friend's arms, around at the crowd; then she nodded. People stayed around the block after they took Onya's mama away for healing, whispering.

"Gettin' heavy-handed the old—man is; Dark Lord see him. Chases the Haians out. Raisin' tax on 'maranth and meat-beans. Black-rock's gettin' dear ..." They stayed, talking until the guard, a whole squad, came through again to break up the gathering. The kidpack headed back to the Ground, except Aage who went with Onya to the Sysbat healing hall.

"Come on in, Megan!" Serkai yelled from where he was treading water. The other kids piled their clothes on an old stone block sticking out of the water. It was a hot summer day and the water was warm. She pulled her clothes off, slowly because she didn't know how to swim, but she couldn't sit while everyone else was in the lake. It looked deep, and cold.

She stuck her toe in. It was cold. Megan stood, wishing Rilla were there. Marte had come to take her home again, since Lixand said Marte had dried out. *She didn't look wet. Then he explained that he meant she wasn't drinking. I miss Rilla. It was fun this winter when she was with me.* She waded in, crossing her arms across her chest, yelling and jumping up and down, yelling some more.

"That's not the way to do it," Jorge yelled, running along the high stones, then jumped. "Yaaaaahhhhh!" He curled up like a ball and splashed thu-whu-swish into the lake.

Eula and Jorge had thought that the pack should go swimming because it was so hot. The water side wasn't anybody else's squat, so they wouldn't get into any fights as long as they didn't run off the Stairs between their squat and the lake. *I don't want to swim.* She bobbed and picked up pebbles with her toes.

"Megan's a scaredy mouse! Megan's a whimp-er!" Tantine yelled.

"I am not," Megan yelled back, and splashed her so she squealed. They splashed and shouted and ducked each other for a while. *I'm going to learn how to swim like Jorge. I don't like to swim though. The lake's dark, and when I bob I can think of all sorts of things floating up underneath me. I think of big big mouths full of lots of teeth.* She decided to go sit on the stones.

The lake was bigger this year, with more water being let out of the mines, the catch basins, and temples, with the dam's fourth mark covered with water. The thunder of the waterfall was louder this year, falling a hundred *pyash* straight down.

"Psst. Hey, Megan!" Ivar hissed from the top of the fence. "Hey?"

"Yeah?" She wasn't paying attention to him, concentrating on trying to spin her knife twice and catch it on the back of her hand.

"There are a whole pile of Sour Note kids coming."

"Here?" Megan caught the knife by clapping her hands together flat so it couldn't cut her. "We have to get everybody."

"Yeah. I'm just going to yell for Jorge, but Aage can't come, he's working."

"I'll get Marin if she isn't helping her mama."

"Okay."

Megan ran, and when she and Marin got back almost everyone else was there. Tantine, Eula, Jorge and Ivar were all there. Onya came running with Yuri behind. *Their mama's all right, sort of.* Nikolai, Maya and Serkai sat on top of the fence watching for the Sour Note kids.

"Good, you're back," Jorge said. "Let's go. We don't know where Arvi is, but we can't wait." Serkai lent Jorge one of his knives and the pack ran down to the gap in the fence.

The Sour Note kids were already there, kicking up the dust where they'd promised not to come anymore. There were more of them than of Megan's kidpack, but the Cooper's Laner's had four knives—Serkai's two, Ivar's, and Marin because she'd borrowed her mama's knife without asking. The Sour Noter's leader, Moden, was the only one who had a knife as far as any of the Cooper's pack knew.

She walked out in front of the Sour Note kids and

Jorge went out to stop her coming any further. She glared up at him and yelled, "This here's part of *our* squat, you bedbugs. Get lost! Take a walk in the Dark Lord's Temple!" She held her knife ready, bright, shining new as Serkai's. *She prigged it, I bet. If she sticks Jorge, we'll get her.*

"Your family's raised a liar, *Liar!*" Jorge shouted back. "It's *our* squat! *We're* the mesne of all this Ground, *we're* the pack!" He leaned toward her, almost nose-to-nose because she was nearly as tall as he was. She put her free hand on her hip, shoving her chin out belligerently.

"Leave my family out of it! Your father got you on a corpse handler!"

"You take that back!"

"You're all scum! And we don't want scum on *our* ground!"

Jorge lost his temper and slashed at her. She ducked but not fast enough, got cut across the side of the head and cut back, then they both lost their knives.

She grabbed his hair with both hands, yanking down, and kneed him. Megan heaved a rock at the Sour Note pack who were rushing them, yelling, saw a boy fall holding his head.

For a moment it was all happening in a blur, then went slow and clear. A big boy swung a stick at her head, two-handed. She ducked and laughed as he hit the wall behind with a crack, dropping the stick. She brought her knife up, suddenly knowing she'd use it if he tried to hit her again.

He shook his fist and they yelled back and forth, and when Megan stamped her foot he grabbed at her. She tried to cut him but her knife caught on his sleeve, so she let go and the clarity went away in a cloud of dust as they rolled in the dirt. He held on but she wiggled around, and when he tried to stand up she sat on his head, beating on his back with her fists. She was yelling, "Go away. Go away. We don't want you." He had snot running down his face. "I hate you, I hate you, I hate you!"

Everyone had gone quiet so Megan looked up, the wild feeling gone in an instant. The boy under her bucked. She got off him and he half-crawled, half-ran back toward the rest of his friends. They had retreated to the gap; Jorge had a long cut on his cheek and Eula had their leader's knife stuck into her arm. There was blood dripping all over her hand and on her face.

Megan, breathing hard, felt at the scrapes on her cheeks and hands, the soreness where her hair and ear had been pulled. The Cooper's Laner's threw a couple of cobbles but not hard. She picked up her knife and went to where Eula sat with Ivar and Serkai and Jorge all around her, and the Cooper's pack stared at the Sour Note kids. They stared back and the only one moving now was Tantine, who handed one of the knives to Jorge.

He stood up. "Go away and don't come back or I'll *kill* you." He started walking toward them, most of Cooper's Lane closing behind him. The other kidpack shuffled, backed up one step then two. Jorge had this strange look on his face, like a grownup; like Lixand when he went with Vyaroslaf so his family could get away. They backed up. Moden was limping and her one eye was swelling shut, blood from a cut trailing down her neck. They kept backing up until a couple of the littler kids started crying and ran, then they all ran. Moden spat on the ground by Jorge's foot and followed.

"Ivar, get Nikolai to help you close up the gap in the fence," Jorge said. "They aren't going to come back." He stuck his chin out. "I'm going to help Eula."

They knotted a handkerchief around the knife wound; Eula turning grey, shaking and cold. Then they made a chair of hands and carried her home where Jorge told her mama it was a bad throw in a cniffta game. Eula's mother looked him up and down, taking in the dirt and scratches and the cut on his face, but only said, "Go on. I'll look after her."

Outside Eula's house Megan started realizing how awful she felt. She hurt all over and had a hole in her pants and her braids were all undone.

Back in the Ground, Tantine and Megan redid each other's braids and they all washed their faces, so their mothers wouldn't scold too hard.

It was their squat now, though. *We won.*

Megan told Serkai that she hated swimming and he and Tantine talked to her about it, though Megan wished he hadn't mentioned it to *her*. The two of them took Megan down to the lake and showed her how to swim a little. By the end of the afternoon she could keep her face out, though she needed more practice.

Afterward they sat in the sun to get dry. Her hair was dribbling water down her chest and her stomach felt hollow; the funny kind of hollow you get if you stayed in the water too long. The roar of the waterfall was a thunder in the ground, more felt than heard.

Prafetatla or Middle Quarter kids had towels for swimming all to themselves and they didn't come down to the lake. They went to the bathhouses or had their own. Megan lay on her back on the long mats of grass. There had been houses at one time, but now there was long grass and thick trees in the space between two big old warehouses. *I guess Tantine's not so bad; not when there's only one boy around.* Across the lake the high ridge and the mountain beyond was full of splinters of shadows from the windows cut into it. Over the River's Road in the Lake Quarter, the shadows of the dragons lay, each a carved spout about five hundred paces apart. They were the openings of the catch basins dug into the mountain, holding enough water to flood the City twice over even without the springs that fed the lake. When the seals wore out, the statues rained a spatter of water down the side of the mountain as if they were drooling. Someone had climbed up and tied a red ribbon around one of the fangs of the spout over the lake shore, for a joke.

She shut her eyes, listening to the buzzing hum of flies and bees and locusts in the grass. *I don't have to go home yet. Mama'll be working because her Gospozhyn keeps her late.* She pulled a grass-stem to chew on and was tickling Tantine behind the ear with the fuzzy head when Marin came running, shouting, "Serkaiiiii! Seeeerrrkaiiii!"

"Here! What's happening?" They jumped up, brushing bits of straw off. Marin stopped to gulp air so she could talk.

"You . . . you should . . . get dressed." She swallowed and wiped her face. "Your mama sent me. We're all supposed to go home."

"Why? What's going on?"

"Your mama came back from the Market looking scared. There are riots happening because of the 'maranth tax, she says, and they might spread, so she told me to tell my mama and asked me to get you home. You, too, Megan, Tantine."

"Riots?"

"Yeah." They were already yanking their clothes on, dragging trousers over wet legs. Megan with the sick feeling in the pit of her stomach, remembering the last time. "People are fighting the Guard with rocks and sticks and bricks and they can't close all the streets. If it gets bad the DragonLord might close the bottom door of the dam and let go one of the catch basins to flood out the bottom quarters, my brother says."

Megan looked over her shoulder at the dam, set between the two ridges. If he did that then the lake would rise to the spur, and everyone but the Prafetatla would drown. She imagined the dragons spitting water, each mouth wider than she was tall. Was there more water dripping already? Papa had told her once that the first Dragonlord closed the dam until the City proclaimed her Ruler, but he never said that where anyone but family could hear.

They ran up the Stairs and Megan tried not to think of the lake perhaps getting deeper behind them, following on their heels, going blurp, blurp up the Stairs. *It sounds like there's another waterfall in front of us.*

She yelled good-bye to the others and squeezed sideways into an alley shortcut they were too big for. When she got to Cooper's, the usually crowded street was empty though it was midday. The Ragman's door was shuttered and his piles of stuff were scraped back against the wall. The sound from the Middle Quarter echoed. *What if somebody's locked the door, and I can't get in?*

"Pssst, Megan?" Boryis looked through one of the panes of glass over the Flats front door. "Get in, quick!" He opened the door a crack, then climbed back up the ladder to keep watch, the afternoon sun streaming in around the shadow of his head. Zazan stood just down the way, twisting one of her frizzy curls in her fingers.

"Are Mama and Papa were at work?" Megan asked, and Zazan said, "I think they came in . . ." in a whisper.

Megan ran downstairs and found the door open, her parents there. They hugged her and the three of them sat listening to the reports that Boryis passed through Zazan.

If the riots come here we should maybe try to run, or hide downstairs with the turkeys. I don't want this house to burn, too. I don't want Mama or Papa to get hurt.

"The Guard! The Guard!" The words whispered down the hall, passed from one open door to another, and everyone held their breath. Megan wiggled out of Papa's hand.

"I'll go look," she said, and ran though she heard him shout after her in a whisper:

"Megan!"

She ran up to two above, where Jerya's room was, and she sat on Jerya's lap with her boy Lavi, who was too little to run with the pack. They looked out the tall crack, as wide as Megan's finger, in her summer shutters.

The Guard trotted down the street, boots clack-clacking against the cobbles, filling the street between the walls, dart-throwers shoved in their belts and the dart-buckets thumping on their belts as they ran to secure the Lower Stairs. Their helmets were painted with dragons and phoenixes and some of them were bloody, but it was dim between the houses and Megan couldn't see for sure.

None of them seemed to be hurt, so the blood was likely from the rioters. Lixand had said once that people would be going hungry or starve outright if the tax were raised, but the DragonLord wouldn't listen to commoners, or care if some died. The riots also would give the Woyvode the excuse not to open the common law-courts.

I hope nobody's out. If they catch anyone in the River or Lake Quarter, the Guard can just take them to the dungeon, because they might be rioters or thieves or something. Sometimes it takes a lot of money and a lot of time to get people out once they're in, even if they are citizens.

The street outside was bare again, the Guard having poured through like a long shiny black snake, scouring things clean. There should have been carters and lots of people out this time of day, but there was only the wind and the gutter-mud splashed on the cobbles. A cat ran across.

It felt like the manrauq gone bad as sour milk, like Aunt Marte hitting Rilla. Megan squirmed out of Jerya's lap, blurted her good-bye and ran back down to Papa and Mama. *We're safe. Like Papa's story. We pull our heads in and wait until the riots roll past. We don't have much that the Prafetatla want.* She got hugged between Mama and Papa and they listened, though Boryis didn't pass down any more news. Megan could hear the turkeys downstairs, and Shen's cat meowing to be fed. *The riots will go away again.*

Chapter Nine

The worst of the riots did go away, with the rain and the fall cold coming on, the days so short, but there were little ones here and there once a Hand or so that were put down by the Guard. They either killed the rioters or cleared the street into the dungeons. Most of those prisoners were sent on "reparation" to the salt mines at Talitsa. Then something happened that cooled the whole mood of the City, despite the new tax. The Fifth DragonLord, Piatr III, Woyvode, Defender of the People, finally took the stroke that killed him. There were no contenders for Regency, so there was no further trouble and the Red faction, led by Mikail, stepped in.

The plateau above the city was a holy place, where the Goddess wind blew forever. When someone married they followed the road under the Nest to the plateau and came down in pairs or quads with music. When someone died their kin carried them up and laid them out for the Goddess's birds on the *Proletarion*, the field of bones. When they'd taken Onya's mama up there it had been summer still. Her hand had healed and she had planned to marry her friend, but took summer fever instead and died.

The bone-field was off to one side; the laying out plat-forms, open-spoked wheels were raised up on tall poles, set in holes or cairns, if raised in winter. The ravens wheeled there most of the time, but if a procession came up, they gathered in their hundreds.

Her children and Teik Svarch, her promised husband, laid her on the platform and undressed her. Megan was one of the witnesses.

Onya's mama looked so like herself, but also thin and empty, that Megan thought she would open her eyes and complain about them taking her clothes off in the wind, but she didn't. They laid her down as if she were sleeping and tied her body onto the platform, and then all the friends helped raise the pole.

Megan had tipped her head back and looked up the pole to where the platform rocked a little as it settled, and one of Onya's mama's hands waved back and forth as if she were going to say, "I'm not dead, let me down," but she hadn't done that either.

The other old platforms had bones around their bases and only the young birds waited for people to go away; the old ones were landing and squawking already, and Onya the Elder had a black feather cloak to cover her body, going to the Goddess.

Now, in the fall, the whole city turned out to the laying out of the Woyvode. Megan stood between her parents watching the birds fly around and around over the pla-teau, so far away that they were slate-pencil dots against the clouds.

The three of them wore the grey and red for mourn-ing, in honor of the old DragonLord, as decreed by the Regent Mikail and the Zarizan. The Prafetatla wore the same color as the crowd, but they would not wear plain cloth and leather; they wore grey silk and red fur man-tles. Mama had made the family new mourning clothes, though they weren't warm wool.

"Some people might say he was an evil old man," she'd

said while sewing, touching the streak in Megan's hair that had grown out white. "But someone loved him once." Megan was helping her while Lixand read to them from a book he'd borrowed from the whorehouse library. There were some strange books in there, but good ones, too; the whores who wanted to teach themselves and their children spent money on books, and sometimes, once an iron-cycle or so, a teacher came. They didn't mind Megan's family borrowing because they were careful. Most of the rest of the Flats didn't bother.

"If Koru can love someone like that," Ness had continued, "we can at least mourn his passing." She made the avert sign that means "Dark Lord look away." "Pray Koru that we won't need these for ourselves for many long years."

"Yes, Mama"—"Yes, my love," Megan and Lixand had answered. That had been three days ago. Papa had said most people had their kin lay them out, or if they had no kin then the corpse-handlers. Mama had said "That's why it's so bad to be a h'Rokatzk, you have to touch and lay out strangers: naZak."

Today the city smelled like smoky perfume, pine and cold and wet stone. It had rained all night, and the wind was cold. *We might get first snow today.* Everyone in the crowds held a pine twig, and Ness held Megan's hand so Papa could carry his.

The DragonLord was going in the last procession through the City, carried at the head, wrapped in his phoenix robe. The Zarizan wasn't of age yet and couldn't help carry his father, so he walked before, with the red stripe painted across his eyes. He had a Greathound puppy with him, a white one taller than he was. Mikail was first bearer.

The Guard were all around him, carrying banners, red and gold and silver, the Ruler's Dragon proceeding before him, upside down. The walking drummers came behind, drumming his passing, making Megan's chest under her ribs shiver with the sound.

There was no sound except the drums and the footsteps of the walkers. Being quiet was hard, but they had respect for the dead, and when the procession had gone by the crowd closed in behind.

The DragonLord would go up to the Goddess with only his kin watching, alone, just as everyone else did. The Guard, and the crowd, stopped at the Iron Gate and watched the bier. It was shaped and painted like a metal bird, carried by four, up to where the birds waited.

There were two others to add their voices, calling the former Woyvode's name to the wind with Ranion: the Dark Lord's priest first, because she was the Year Kievir, then the Lady's priest. Megan remembered Onya, standing alone to call her mama's name to the wind.

She had called it long and loud into the wind, and Megan was sure the Goddess heard it, even if there were tears in it, even if she was alone, because only those who could gift the Temple or Temples enough would have a priest there to call as well.

Like then, the priests would go away and leave the Zarizan up there to watch, as Megan and the others left Onya. Yuri had wanted to stay, too, but couldn't; he was youngest and would watch the next year. There were no other kin, so the memorial would stop with his turn, though Teik Svarch might come up the year after Yuri, if he chose to.

Megan was glad she didn't have to do that for her parents, hugging Ness's hand in hers, then taking Lixand's, pine twig and all, as they walked home. The whole city would stay in grey until the Zarizan Ranion became DragonLord or until Regent Mikail said so. The Hammer and the Scythe-blade would sit on the empty Dragonthrone until Ranion picked them up. *I wonder if anyone ever dusts them?*

Megan was getting very big now. *That's good because I can help Mama and Papa more, though I tell them I get lots scavenging,* she thought. She was quickest at prigging buckles in the winter, when sliding was the way to get away from the Watch in First Quarter. You took a board, the way Ivar had, and bent it up on one end. Some kids rubbed the bottoms with wet sand to make the wood smooth. It was fun, and made it easy to get away from the Guard since most of the streets around the Market were steep enough so you could cut a shoe or boot buckle and be gone before anyone could even yell.

It wasn't so good that she was getting big because there was some trouble with her being apprenticed. Papa said she'd have to wait a bit longer. This was bad; she knew she could get too old. For Ness to be apprenticed as an adult had almost been a miracle from Koru.

She was balancing six parcels and a broken basket she'd found that maybe could be fixed and didn't want to drop anything as she tried to open the door. "Hello!" A voice she knew called down the hall. "Hello, Megan!" She couldn't tell who he was though, not through all the scarves and under the fur hat. What was somebody with a fur hat, made out of better fur than catskin, doing in the Flats?

"Here let me help, then." He tugged the hat off and she dropped everything and hugged him, snow and all. It was Teik Varik, gone so long, come home again. She tried to tell him everything all at once, and he laughed and swung her up as high as he had when she'd been a little kid. Her heels almost bumped the outside wall now, and he set her down, puffing. "You've grown some, little Meg." He poked her cheek with a finger, just like her papa did, over her scarf, and she smiled. Mama opened the door to see what the noise was, cried "Varik!" and hugged him, too.

Papa came, and when Mama let go, hugged him and pounded him on the back. "Come in! Come in!" He was smiling more than she'd seen him do in a while as he picked up Varik's ship-kit for him. "You've been gone since before the Esteemed Dragon died! Come in for a cup of chai, at least!"

"Hello! Yeah, 'course I'll come in." He laughed. "Why, did you think I'd come a'visiting to stand in cold hallways?"

"Varik," Mama said, "Lixand, enough teasing, get those wet things off and hung up!"

Megan gathered her parcels and the basket and hung up her things, while Mama and Papa and Varik settled down on the cushions. That was fun because they didn't have a visitor's cushion so Megan got to sit in the wallbed and be higher than everyone.

She went to get a glass of milk first, sniffed the jug by the door. "Mama, the milk's gone."

Ness sighed a little. It meant making more thick-milk to eat, but there was no milk for chai. "Run over to Jerya's and ask if we can borrow some then. I'll be going to market soon and pay her back."

"All right."

When she got back they were being serious. "Lixand, you mean your friend won't take her?" Varik was asking.

Lixand looked angry. "No, he's given me excuse after excuse and his price keeps going up." *They're talking about my apprenticeship.* Papa's friend had been going to take her on a long time before, and hadn't. Her parents had tried to get her in somewhere else, but the City was crowded with Zak coming away from the Thanish border disputes. Guilds were full; they could pick and choose, and Megan was on several waiting lists.

"Hmm." Varik looked at them and sipped his chai, then looked at Papa in that way that meant he'd talk to him later. "Little Meg, you look like a jar full of questions . . ."

"Yes! Where did you go? What did you see? Did you go all the way to Brahvniki? Were there pirates? Were there storms? You're safe home so it can't have been bad. Did you make lots of money?—"

"Megan!" Ness snapped, irritated that her daughter had asked about money so bluntly. Megan put both hands over her mouth, but Teik Varik was laughing and didn't mind.

"Ness, it's all right. Yes, Megan, the trip was—to our advantage, you might say. There were pirates but we outran them—rather we ran them aground on a shoal. And as for the rest . . ."

He pulled his kit around and opened the top tie. "Look." He pulled out a purple scarf fine enough almost to see through, and a shell with spiny bits all over it in a yellow and black wood box that smelled like summer, and an arm ring that looked like red lace but was made out of stone.

"Ooohhh." To Megan it seemed as if he were carrying the whole world in his kit. He'd seen the places the gifts come from.

"For you!" he said, and gave the scarf to Mama and the shell in the box to Megan and the arm ring to Papa. "There. Just a little memento of my stay south."

"Varik, we couldn't . . ."

"Now don't go all proud on me now! What are friends for? I'd give you the same either way, rich or poor." Mama looked a little sad for a minute. Megan guessed she was thinking of all the other people who weren't friends any longer.

Then she smiled and kissed Teik Varik on his beard that covered a new scar. Maybe he'd had to *fight* pirates instead of just run away. *Teik Varik wouldn't run away*, Megan thought. *He's brave.* "Thank you," Mama said. Papa was looking at the arm ring between wrist and elbow.

Megan looked at her box and shell, and sniffed inside. The shell smelled like the box, and of iodine, too—a Haian smell. Then she heard a funny noise, and when she looked at Teik Varik his shirt was moving; it had a bump. Megan stared, and the bump wiggled across his stomach and a wet black nose peeked out of his shirt lacings.

"Varik . . ." Papa just sighed and said thank you, too. Then they all looked at Megan. She kept staring at the bump with a nose in Teik Varik's shirt. He looked down and laughed again.

"This is my friend, Tik-Tik." He unlaced and pulled out an animal that looked as if a ferret and a raccoon had traded pieces. It had a long striped rubbery nose as if someone had grabbed it and stretched it out long as a finger; skinny black hands, and a black mask and furry black rings all the way down its tail. It made a chirping, whirring noise, and its long, long nose bent sideways when it sniffed. Then it sat up on its hind legs on Teik Varik's palms, twisted its fingers together, and bobbed up and down. "T'is little prigger snuck into my quilt bag one night," Teik Varik said, "on a beach in Krim, and tried to make off with my small-clothes, but I caught 'em by one corner and after a bit of a tugging and some talk he allowed they were mine. He's more a friend than a pet and'll steal anything not nailed down."

When Megan reached out to touch him, Tik-Tik squeaked and dove into Teik Varik's shirt again, and the bump he made wiggled around the back.

"Ah, little Meg, he's his own creat'ur and he'll play with you by the by when he gets comforta'l with you." Varik's city accent was softened by strange foreign burrs, as if he were more used to speaking naZak.

She hoped Tik-Tik would like her soon. She looked at her shell and box again, and Mama reminded her what to say.

"Teik Varik, thankyouverymuchfortheshell. When you go sailing next can I come, too?" Then she could get a friend like Tik-Tik and see all those places, and Mama and Papa and she wouldn't have to live in one room that smelled like wet, with a cold draft along the floor.

They all looked at her, biting their lips as they did when they didn't want to laugh. She hated it when they laughed at something dumb she said.

"No, Megan, you're not . . ." Then Teik Varik got a funny look on his face and changed the subject. *I'm not going to feel bad. He was going to say I wasn't apprenticed and I'm almost nine.*

Ness and Lixand told Varik about what he'd missed in the last year, and about the regency and how it was going. Nobody liked the Regent much, but he hadn't done anything *really* wrong yet so there hadn't been riots, and the snow helped keep things quiet. Something might happen in the spring, but there were the wedding plans to distract people. Shortly after Megan's tenth birthday, the City would celebrate the Zarizan's wedding to Mikail's daughter, Avritha. Papa said the whole show was to keep people's minds off what was really going on.

The Ragman and Varclaf had got dragged off to the dungeons a while ago, just for being in the wrong street. The Guard had closed it off and taken everybody, but Ranion and Regent Mikail had had a fight, and on the Zarizan's birthday he'd ordered everyone released, so they'd both got out. The Ragman had been skinny as a stick, but he was better now. Varclaf had had a cough and some sores, but his wives and husband looked after him.

People said that clearing the dungeon was good, but Ness said it was as bad as taking innocent people without trial; she'd rather have the law courts opened again than let the Guard or one of the Prafetatla just say "guilty" and that be the end of it. Sometimes you could get people out if you bribed the Guard with enough money.

That's not fair, Megan thought. *But there's lots of things going on that aren't fair.* She'd heard in the pack that the commoners' truth-teller's school had been closed and the children sent home, which meant that only the Prafetatla would have truth-tellers; none for the ordinary people.

Megan decided to go out away from all the boring adult talk. She could play with Jerya's kid or maybe climb to the roof and see if it was still snowing; if she couldn't play with Tik-Tik, she wanted to do something that wasn't dull.

Blue and Zazan's cat spat and yowled at each other on the stairs and Teik Erharn swatted them apart with the broom. The corridors got very dirty in the winter; snow, carrying soot with it, sifted in from the plank walls and down from the hall, then melted. Dimi's ferret bounced down the hall and the cats chased it until it whipped into a rat-hole where they couldn't follow, so they both sat with their noses pressed almost together, staring. The ferret wasn't dumb; it wouldn't come out there again, but stuck its nose out and screamed at them.

Megan climbed to the top floor where it was cold and windy, because the walls weren't very good. Then she slipped through the crack between where the wood roof was now and where the glass had once been.

When the landlord had closed in the roof, he or she hadn't bothered to dig a big plate of glass out, that had broken in a "v" from two of the supports onto a beam below, for salvage. It was worth almost a month's rent, it was so big, and when she'd found it she realized everyone had forgotten it. At first she tried to break it, because that would be the only way to get it out, but it had just hurt her hand, then when she'd kicked it the roof had shivered too, so she guessed it was partly holding the roof up and stopped trying. That was probably why it was still there. It was her secret place, her secret treasure, and she didn't want anybody to find it.

There was a dark space between the big beams where she could stand up almost straight. One wall was the pane of glass and the floor was the wood ceiling and the other wall was the brick chimney. Someone had covered the hole where the glass had fallen in with more wood so it was like a wood sandwich with a glass "v" in the middle. It was her favorite place in the winter, as if she had a room of her own that she didn't have to pay rent for. It was getting harder and harder to squeeze in, though, as she grew. There was so much snow caught in the gap next to one of the chimneys on top of the outer roof that it was actually warm. If there was a fire below, the bricks heated up and she could even take her coat off.

Only the cats knew about this place, and her. She rubbed her mitt over the cold glass next to her. It had spidery lines where it had cracked. *Like people do, I guess.* If she could somehow get through the glass she would be able to walk the length of the beam at the top of the house, right over the atrium.

She hoped things would get better soon. Mama and

Papa were looking more and more like Zazan, or like Shen when she didn't think anyone was looking. Even Dimi looked like that early in the morning when it was his turn to get water for breakfast—crinkly around the eyes and old.

But perhaps some people didn't crack apart, and she prayed every day that it wouldn't happen to her mama and papa. She couldn't do anything to help them but be the best she could so they wouldn't worry.

I'm already the best cniffta player, she thought, *and that's good, but that won't help Mama and Papa. Maybe Teik Varik'll help. I wish I could go with him. I wish I could see all the warm places he talks about. I want a friend like Tik-Tik.* Teik Varik had been out-river a couple of times and seen beaches of black or pink sand, or sand so white it could blind you like snow. He'd told her about giant cormorants and Haiu Menshir's islands, and Hyerne where the men weren't allowed to fight and Arko where the women weren't. She closed her eyes and pretended, but couldn't smell the flowers even though she could see them in her head. *All I smell is mouse shit and snow and wet.* She was wet through the seat of her pants. *I hope somebody apprentices me soon or I'll be too old.*

She went to play cniffta with Rilla, who was very good at it for one so little. They kept up until Rilla got cut; they'd used the two real knives as well as the wooden ones they'd made, and the steel ones flew differently. Megan helped her wash her hand so that it wouldn't get cut-ill, though it wasn't that bad—a nick that went from the bottom of her thumb to the long line.

"Megan, I don't wanna go home." Megan looked up from where she was dabbing the cut with a corner of her coat. Rilla was frowning as if the cut hurt more than she was saying. *I guess her mam isn't in a good mood lately.*

" 'kay. Let's go to the Market."

Rilla smiled, which Megan liked; she'd been getting quieter lately. They went up to the Market, throwing

snowballs at each other and the signs. Megan mashed
snowballs on a wall; made a face out of them. Rilla
stuffed some snow down Megan's neck and ran away
yelling while Megan chased her with two handfuls, her
hands bigger. Megan washed Rilla's face good, and she
wiggled and swore.

"Pig-kisser! I'll get you! Stopfffth that! Ug, stop, it was
only a little snow! Fish-Face!"

"Say yield! Say you're sorry. Say Rhunay! Say it!"

"I give! Rhunay!" Rilla's face was all red, but she
wasn't really mad, not any madder than Megan. Both
wet, they stopped in the Papa-bear shrine on Na Yehk
Road to get out of the wind. The statue was of the Bear
rearing up on His hind legs, with all His claws out. She
hung her scarf on one of His paws—*I don't think He'd
mind*—and they brushed all the snow out of their collars.
She bowed to the Bear and they both ran their fingers
through the stone bowl in front of Him, having nothing
to give. It felt cold and slippery, as she remembered
good soap being, not like the sand-soap they used now.
She picked up the clapper and tapped the bowl to make
it ring sweet, like the honey He liked. It made her sad
that she had nothing to give Him in winter, but she tried
to make up for it in summer, giving both Koru and the
Bear flowers.

At the Market, they watched the cock-fights; it was too
cold for outdoor spider fights, and the dancers in the
circle and the shadow puppets. The priest came out with
his black and white robes and furs afterwards and blessed
them for watching. As they wandered away, Megan saw
one of the perfume-sellers look around and duck to slip
a fish under another perfume-seller's stand. It was only
a little one.

They went past the food stalls. She wanted a meat pie
but they were expensive, and though she tried not to
smell them, her mouth still watered. *If there were more
of us I'd try prigging a couple. But there's just us two,
and I have to look after Rilla.*

The younger girl dawdled to look at something and

Megan was looking at the toy-seller's stall when somebody behind her yelled, "Stop, thief!"

She looked; you were supposed to help if somebody raised the hue. *If it's somebody I know maybe I can accidentally help them get away.* They'd caught someone around the herbalist's stall . . . *Oh, shit.*

It was Rilla. She wriggled and yelled and the stallkeeper had her by one arm, the hand with a herb bag in it. The Guard was coming. She could hear them, clangety-clank. *What do I do? What can I do? What am I supposed to do?*

A guard had Rilla and was asking her something, shaking her to make her answer. She cried and kicked at his shins. "I'm six! Six!" she yelled. Megan wiggled past grownup to get close.

"Teik Guard!" She didn't want him to notice her, but Rilla was her kin, and in trouble. "Please, she's my little cousin and she's six."

He had a mean, thin stare and she felt smaller than a baby bug about to get stepped on. He'd been eating sausages in garlic sauce; he smelled like that and it was in his moustaches. He squinted at her and gave Rilla another shake. "Your parents' names, brat."

Rilla pressed her lips together. He peeled her mitt open and pulled the bag of herbs out of her hand. "NAME!" he shouted, and she yipped. "Marte, Marte, called Canter."

"And where do you live?" He tightened his hand on her arm, his leather gloves squeaking in the cold.

"Pisnichy Street." Rilla had tears running down her chin and snot all over her lip. Megan wanted to kick him, cut him, make him stop hurting her.

"Valyria!"

"Yessir!" Another of the Watch.

"You heard. Get her. Bring her to the block."

"Yessir!"

The guard half dragged Rilla with him to the block, walking just a little too fast for her to keep up, even if she ran, so she kept falling and being pulled along.

Megan was right behind. Papa was too far away to get. *This isn't supposed to happen. This can't be happening, not to anyone in our family. I can't leave Rilla alone with the Guard.*

She saw Serkai and Noran across the lane of stalls looking over at the commotion, and shouted the pack's yell for help. "Serkai! Dzhai! Dzhai!" *He's got to hear, he's got to hear me call.* "Serkai!" He looked up and then waved. "Run to the Wooden Plate and tell my papa what happened, please?"

He waved a fist, and he and Noran ducked down the alley next to the Deib's Den Inn. Megan found it hard to breathe; it was like breathing a knife as she gasped cold air into her lungs. *Rilla, why'd you get caught? Why?*

The Guard waited on the block and they wouldn't let Megan up with Rilla, so she stood by the stairs looking up at their boots.

"You'd think the River Quarter scum'd be stealing food before anything else," one of the guards said to another. "Zarizan's right when he says they just breed more vermin. Should clean the whole quarter out."

"Shut it, Stavislev, the Comp'ny Small-Stick's listening." The first guard spat into the snow, just by Megan.

A crowd had gathered from the winter Market, so when they brought Aunt Marte, they almost didn't need to call people out. She was yelling, two guards dragging her, but when she saw Rilla on the block she went quiet and pale.

The Guard pronounced sentence just like in the summer on Onya's mama, but the air didn't go as tight and funny as then because Marte wasn't as well liked as Onya the Elder. Megan wasn't surprised but still felt sick. Megan still wished hard when the fate-coin spun. It stuck in the snow on its edge and the Guard captain cursed and scraped the block with the side of his boot before doing it again. Everyone was quiet now. Tick. Black.

"No! You little bitch! Why'd you get caught? I *need*

my hands you . . ." Aunt Marte screamed at Rilla. The Guard dragged her to the hand-block. She didn't want to listen, didn't want to see, but she couldn't look somewhere else.

Marte struggled, almost whining, with her right hand curled into a fist to try and hide it from the hammer. Then she gulped and sobbed, once, looking up at the K'gebar. She shivered all over and forced her hand open. She watched the K'gebar and the hammer, like a mark watching a shell-sharper take his last copper. The wind blew her hair across her face but she didn't even blink. Megan didn't think she could.

The K'gebar raised the hammer and brought it down. Aunt Marte tried to pull away and they held her. She screamed once, then again before he hit the second time—it cut off when she fainted. She didn't feel the third time. Most people didn't.

The guard let Rilla go, but she just stood looking at her mama lying in the snow. Megan climbed on the block, when the Guard had gone away, and held her. Rilla just stood looking. *I'm ashamed. Papa, where are you?*

The crowd was going away, but Megan was high enough to see Papa coming through all the people. Serkai had him by the shirttail to stay with him.

His face was closed. *Koru, how much more is going to happen to us? When is it going to stop?* But it wasn't really them it had happened to this time, but to Aunt Marte and Rilla. Marte had bitten through her tongue and it smelled as if she'd pissed herself. That didn't matter though; they all helped getting Aunt carried to Megan's home, where Lixand laid her in the wallbed. That meant Mama and Papa would share Megan's and she'd sleep with Rilla on a bed made in Mama's box to keep out the draft. It would be crowded but everybody would be warm. Then they asked Dimi to help again.

He didn't like Marte but helped as a favor to them. "He hit pretty hard; must naht been having a good day," Dimi said. "Don't know, Lixand, if she'll get it back.

Mightbe a little. I've given her somethin' to make her sleep."

"Thank you, Dmitrach." Papa gave him the copper he'd made today that was supposed to go to the rent. Maybe Mama had made enough; Megan hoped so.

" 'ixand?" It was Aunt. She couldn't talk straight because of her tongue. "I hur'. She ha'es me. Ro'n kid. Ha'es me." She cried, slowly. "Nobo'y's faul' bu' te 'ragonlor'. Shi' on him, 'n' my poor, bad kid."

"Hush, Marte, you'll be all right." Papa sat on the edge of the wallbed, making it creak. He patted her hand, then moved it to her forehead. Her hair was soaked at the temples from sweat and tears, and her face looked raw and empty. "Hush, sister, shhh, you'll be fine."

Papa sent Megan and Rilla to get bed linens from Aunt's house because they didn't have enough for everyone.

They went up to Middle Quarter and it looked strange to Megan. So much space; space between all the houses and small gardens. She'd forgotten. The pack ran through here to get to the Market, but stuck to the big streets, and she'd spent the rest of the time in alleys in the River Quarter.

Rilla had always met her at Koru's Shrine because Megan didn't want to see Aunt, so she was surprised at the state of the house. It was dirtier than a bottom room of the Flats and *it* didn't have turkeys outside its door. The shutters were broken and rattled, letting the wind in.

She opened her mouth to ask and Rilla interrupted, "We're doing all right." She had the stubborn look on her face that said "Don't ask."

"Okay. It's none of my business. Linens?"

"Spare room, in the walnut box."

"I'll get 'em." *What has Aunt Marte been doing*? She hadn't been cleaning. The still was the only thing not dusty. It smelled worse, nastier than the last time they'd come to visit two years ago. The herbs looked different, too. Megan dug down into the box to get the blankets and her fingers hit something cool and hard, and something that clinked.

There was a whole row of glass bottles, of wine, she thought, some wadiki, and a pouch full of silver. *Silver.* And a whole silver Dragonclaw.

I've got to show Papa, she thought. *There's something wrong here.* Eula had said the Blood-sibs, the "upstart assassins," were trying to get kids to apprentice. And they got paid silver for killing somebody. Eula said that her Gospozhyn had been "talked to," his Guild had him under protection. *Mama wouldn't like it if she knew I was friends with an Other Guild member, somebody training to steal; but I learn all sorts of stuff.* Silver. Was Aunt Marte a Blood-sib? Was she killing people?

Rilla was at the door with a bundle of her mam's things, tears on her face. "Megan." Then she gulped and threw the bundle on the floor and really started sobbing. "I did it. It's my fault. I did it."

Megan went and hugged her. "It's okay, Rilla. She'll be all right. It isn't your fault. It's the DragonLord's fault for a stupid, dumb rule."

"It is! It is! It's all my fault!" She was trying to hammer her hands on Megan's shoulders, and Megan had to hold on tight. "I did it on purpose!"

"What?" She stopped squirming, crying so hard Megan could hardly understand what she was saying.

"I . . . I got caught on purpose before I got too old." She grabbed on to Megan, buried her face in her neck. "I hate her. I hate her but she's my mam. She's my mam and it's bad to hate her but she hits me and . . . and . . . she hates me. She doesn't love me. Why did she have me? If she hates me why did she have me?"

Megan couldn't think of anything to say, wishing her mother were here to explain, but there was just her, and she didn't think Mama would want to hear Rilla say all those things. "We love you. We're your kin." Megan wiped Rilla's face with her sleeve. "Like when you got stuck in the hole in the fence with the big dog chasing us and I came back and got you?"

"Yeah." Rilla sniffled. "You gonna tell?"

"Not if you don't want me to. I promise."

"I love you, *fatrahm*." That meant father's sister's beloved child. Megan had thought Rilla was too little to understand formal speech. Megan hugged her. "I love you too, *patrischana*. We'll stick together, won't we?"

They sat for a bit longer just hugging, then Megan said, "Rillan, what's your mama been doing?"

Rilla looked around the spare room, then at the still. "She's been selling to somebody who pays lots and always comes at night."

"You ever seen him?"

"It's a her and she mumbles, but mam always makes me go to bed early so I don't see her." Rilla twisted the end of her braid. "I don't think you ought to tell. I think it's poisons, or 'Dust. They were fighting about price and the lady said '. . . for that price we can ship 'Dust in!' but I think she paid and mam got drunk again after that."

"She promised not to."

Rilla twisted harder. "She makes sure your da doesn't find out."

"I gotta tell him about the bottles though."

"Okay." They got the bundles, and Megan took the bag with silver to show Papa and tell him some of what Rilla had told her, except the sworn secrets.

Papa's lips thinned and Mama held him. Then they sent Shen and Rilla and Megan out to Market with a silver bit to change into copper and get all the food and black-rock they needed so Aunt could get better.

When they came back with everything, it was like festival. There weren't enough cupboards for everything, and it smelled like home had before, with sausage and leaven bread and soup and an old hen boiling in the pot. Mama and Papa were angry but not at Megan, and Aunt wasn't saying anything, so when they ate it was hard to swallow, like swallowing the anger with the food. So after, Megan and Rilla went to the library, and Megan read to her cousin and started teaching her Enchian. Her mama wasn't spending money on school, so Megan would help.

*   *   *

It was almost spring and Megan enjoyed having Rilla living with them again, though Aunt Marte complained a lot. Marte couldn't afford to keep the house when her hand was broken, so she and Rilla had moved down to the Dogleg, an alley off Cooper's Lane, further south and across the Stairs. Rilla was part of the pack now. Aunt came around too much, but she was behaving and not drinking, and even trying to do business again. *I guess Koru's smiling again, or the Bear swatted some of our bad luck away.*

Mama had been doing well at Gospozhyn Yneltzyn's and she'd been getting quite a few gems to reset. Lixand had a space as an inside storyteller at the Wooden Plate because the owner had built another room on. Megan practiced sneaking around a lot. It was fun, and in the pack she and Tantine were the best at it.

Tantine had gotten to be a better kid lately, because the summer before some of the other kids, mostly Jorge and Moden—the Sour Noters and Victory Square had joined Cooper's Lane so they were one big mesne—had got tired of her being so snarky and causing all the trouble, and ducked her in the lake. She yelled a lot and got a lung full of water, almost drowned without them noticing, so Megan had to yell at them to let her go. They hadn't listened, and Megan had waded in and gotten a lung full of water, and they'd faced Jorge and Moden down together. Since then, Tantine had been Megan's best friend next to Serkai and Ivar.

She and Ivar were kissing sometimes now. She'd thought it was messy at first and they bumped noses a lot, but it got to be fun. Shivery feelings ran through her when they kissed and hugged, but she didn't want any more than that. *I don't want to have sex yet. I'm not old enough and Ivar isn't either, but it's still nice.*

Jorge finally put his foot in it when he and Eula argued over who was leader of Cooper's Lane, and he said she was a half-Zak, Arkan bred. She got so angry that she hit him and they'd fought, seriously. He was stronger but she was quicker, and she'd put him in the midden behind the Deib's Den Inn. It had been good that it was mostly frozen or he could have drowned, but he had got stinking. They were friends again but she was leader.

They'd been playing sneak-on-each-other ever since Dagde Vroi. The game was to sneak up on someone else and touch them before they knew you were there, or take something of theirs without them knowing. If they caught you, you had to do a forfeit. Marin got caught with her hand in Aage's pouch and she had to go three landings up the Stairs yelling "I am a dead horse!" Megan hadn't been caught by anybody yet.

Today was a boring day so she tried to find a new hidey hole in the Flats, wiggling into the space between the inside wall and the outside. There were lots of places in the Flats where the division of the old rooms wasn't very good, so there were crawl spaces, and she was trying to find all of them. They were good for hide 'n seek, too.

She heard Mama and Papa talking. *I think I'll wiggle close*, she thought, *then I'll yell boo and won't they be surprised!*

"Lixand, I don't know what to do. I never thought . . . I can't stop. I'm a Journeyman, earning a real wage rather than just room and table's worth. I can't quit."

"Tell me, Ness, don't just jitter, tell me everything that happened." Megan put her eye to a knot-hole and looked. Papa was holding his arm out for Mama but she was pacing, too upset to keep still.

"A thief came in to sell Gospozhyn Yneltzyn a gem. I wasn't there at the first. Yneltzyn had sent me out to fetch a repaired mould from Evgniy, and when it wasn't ready I came back to the shop early. I went in through the back, instead of the front, because I had to stop at the privy."

She stopped to think. Her hands were shaking and she picked up the kitchen cloth to give them something to do. "I was just setting the piece for Teik Felekof when I heard them in the front of the shop. I thought it was a customer bargaining until the man all but said he'd stolen it from the Nest, and he had to sell it quickly because he might be followed."

She was wiping off the counter, and knocked over a jar of lentils that spilled. She just stood looking down at the mess. "Gospozhyn Yneltzyn bought the gem ... he was familiar with the thief." She started sweeping up with too-vigorous swipes of her hands. "I sneaked out because the thief was going to sneak out the back right past my workbench. What else was I going to do? Call the watch, call the Guard and have them haul us off to the dungeons because there's no courts?" The lentils made a slithery sound going back into the jar. Lixand was so quiet Megan could hear all of it. She held her breath.

"What was I to do? I came in front and told Gospozhyn Yneltzyn the mould wasn't ready. There were a couple of DragonGuard in the street, but I didn't think about it.

"They must have cut off the thief's escape route because he was hiding in my tool cupboard. I didn't know that until later. I drew the half curtain at my bench and tried to work some, but the thief sneaked out and held a knife to me—"

"Ness!" Papa started to get up but Mama's shoulders twitched and she kept on, "—and had me call Yneltzyn into the back because he thought he'd been betrayed, and they argued a moment before Yneltzyn convinced him otherwise. He took the thief up the pulldown ladder and let him onto the roof." Papa put his hand on Mama's shoulder and she held onto it for a minute, then pulled away and started pacing again, stepping around Brunsc, whom Rilla had left behind when she visited last.

"Gospozhyn Yneltzyn came back and looked at me and at the piece I was doing and said, 'you've forgotten, haven't you?'" Ness finally sat down, but on the edge of the open wallbed instead of her cushion next to Lixand. "Of course I said, 'Forgotten what, Gospozhyn?' He nodded and left me to finish. What else was I supposed to do? Lixand, what was I to do?"

They were both quiet, apart in a way she hadn't seen them in a long time; not since the deep of winter when they hadn't had any money at all and Teik Erharn's wife had tried to get them kicked out for not paying the rent. They'd managed then. Jerya had lent them some, but Mama and Papa had done a lot of fighting or holding each other.

If everything was all right it didn't matter how far apart they sat, they'd still be *together*. When they were like this it was as if they were strangers to each other.

Lixand sighed and got up, sat next to Ness, making the wallbed shake. "You did what you had to, love." He looked like he was carrying the Gate-rocks on his back, but still smiled at Ness and put his arm around her. "Hang on. Do the job. I'm sure he isn't trusting you to do anything illegal. When you're another step up, perhaps another jeweller will take you on or perhaps you can hang on till you're a Gospozhyn in your own right."

"That could take years, Lixand." Her voice was thin.

"The, ah, *Re-Distribution* Guild isn't all that bad. Not like the Blood-sibs. You've done nothing wrong, love." Ness smiled at him using the joking name for the Thieves. Megan agreed with him, though.

Ness leaned into his shoulder and he held her for a long time. They felt "together" again. Then he kissed her ear. She put her arm around him and kissed his neck. Megan wiggled backwards quietly because it wasn't polite to watch someone else making love, especially if you weren't supposed to be there in the first place.

"Megan, put that cat down, wash at the tap and come home!" Ness called over the edge of the gallery. "We have to go talk to Varik."

"All right, Mama!" She was playing with Blue and Dimi's ferret, who ran in circles inside her shirt from front to back while Blue tried to catch him from the outside. Now she dug him out of the middle of her back, though he didn't want to come, and got Blue off her legs. Mama had said they were going to talk to Varik's Gospozhyn.

The Middle Quarter had more space than River, but the First Quarter had even more than that. There were manors as big as the Flats, all given over to one family, and they had lawns and walls and gates around them that could have held five or six more houses at least. They had gardens under glass that you could just catch glimpses of through the gates. They even kept horses.

In River where there were cobbles, they were loose and mud squished up between them and they wobbled and slid in the spring. Then there were some streets that just washed away, and couldn't be rebuilt until the rain stopped and the melt was done. On those streets you could sink all the way to your knees. Here there were granite blocks that fit together neatly and were even laid in patterns.

The gate to the River Guild offices had a ship carved on it and the corridors went into the mountain; the stone blocks and wood panels changed to smooth stone and wool tapestries. There was a strong warm breeze blowing in all the corridors against damp. The halls were full of things from foreign lands and there were a few naZak; a man with a towel wrapped around his head and face, making Megan wonder if he were cold even inside, so tall he had to duck his head under the ceilings. Sysbat Tenara hadn't been that tall and Megan had thought she was a giant.

The Gospozhyn's office reminded her of the Wizard's house, full of all sorts of neat things, but unlike the Wizard's house it was a mess. There were piles of papers mixed with books and ledgers, boxes and bags piled in the corners, parchments on the cushions; the *samovar* was almost buried. The cushions were red and black, the carpet white, and the hangings blue. An old yellow dog lay curled up on the cushions, snoring. Varik was already there waiting.

The Gospozhyn wasn't *that* old. He looked a little older than Lixand, but his hair was white and thick instead of thinning in the front, while Lixand's wrinkles had been going further and further up his forehead. Ness and Lixand stood nervously, dressed in their best clothes, trying to hide it.

"Yarishk Yakushevyovych, called Silverhand," Teik Varik said. "Lixand, Storyman, his wife Ness, Gemsetter and their daughter Megan."

"Ah, ah, yes. Do come in. A cup of chai?" Teik Yarishk dug a couple of cushions out from under the old dog and a pile of papers. "Here, do make yourselves comfortable."

They talked very politely about the weather, how things were going in the city and the rumors about the Zarizan and the Regent's fights and the wedding coming up. This reminded Megan of when she'd been put in school, only worse, but Teik Varik was here to speak for her. After they'd shared the salt, she stopped petting the dog and listened.

"Well, she is a bit old . . ." Yarishk said, and Journeyman Varik cleared his throat.

"I mentioned the alternative, Gospozhyn . . ."

"Ah, yes, you did indeed, but these good folk might not be interested."

"Excuse me, Teik Yarishk," Papa said. "Which alternative is this? I understood that my Megan would find a position in the River Guild."

Yarishk got up and paced, and Megan thought he looked like Dimi's ferret. She liked him, but wouldn't have wanted him angry with her. Ferrets bit.

The dog started awake and scrambled up, woofing at Varik, who stood up, putting one hand in his shirt.

"Ow! Little ingrate!" He pulled his hand out and bowed to his Gospozhyn. "If you will excuse me—"

"Varik, how many times have I reminded you not to bring Tik-Tik in here with my Sashi?" He stopped pacing. "Not that I mind the little vermin, but it causes too many interruptions."

"Yes, Gospozhyn." Varik looked sheepish. "I forgot he was there."

"Well, get out, lad. Once you've stowed him, come back."

"Yes, sir." *But Teik Varik's not a lad. He's old*, Megan thought. *Almost five and twenty.*

"Well, please excuse the interruption. As I was going to say, the alternative is to induct your Megan into, well, not the River Guild directly. There is an affiliated Guild, very closely associated with us, that has no age limitations on apprenticeship."

Ness got this funny look on her face. "Teik Yarishk, you mean that Yneltzyn took me on at such a low 'prentice price because he's a Gospozhyn in this Other Guild? Because Varik recommended me?"

Yarishk smiled a little. "Well, in effect, yes. The Guild I'm speaking of has a policy of training 'Gospozhyn' under various other Guilds, mostly with the River Merchants, though we do need jewelers and so forth."

Mama looked down and sighed, and Papa put his arm around her. "I will admit, Teik," he said slowly, "that I don't like the idea of being directly affiliated with the Guild in question—" Mama bit her lip, looked at Papa.

"I can leave you a moment to discuss it," Yarishk said.

"Please," Papa answered. *Why are they so nervous about it? It's just the Other Guild.*

"One final thing," Yarishk said. "The Guild in question does not deal in addictives, unwilling sex, slaves, or contract murders." *They just steal, then, and mostly from people who need to be stolen from.* She already prigged stuff like knives or food. Of course, Mama and Papa didn't know that. *They wouldn't like it*, she thought. *They still think Middle Quarter-like.*

Teik Yarishk went out and Ness looked at her husband. "We're already paying them," she said. "And I'm, all unwitting, affiliated already."

"Ness, we could manag—"

"No, we couldn't." She was almost crying.

"Papa," Megan said, "if I'm good I can learn what I'm supposed to and what Koru wants me to. I'll make lots of money, and when stuff gets easier to get and sell, I can switch to just merchanting."

Papa looked at her sternly, then nodded. "I see I have the both of you against my tender sensibilities."

"Lixand, think of what we must—"

"Don't tell me 'must' again, love. I'm sick to death of having my nose rubbed in how little choice I have." He ran his hand over his face. "All right. I know. We have to. This is probably one of Megan's last chances in the City. I know."

Ness and Megan both hugged him. The dog thumped her tail on the papers behind her and Megan ran to call Gospozhyn Yarishk. Things were settled.

When Gospozhyn Yarishk came back, with the honey pot, as if he went to get it—Megan liked that, it was polite, pretending he'd left for another reason—Papa said, "Our Megan'll be trained as a th—"

"No," Gospozhyn Yarishk interrupted. "She'll be trained as a merchant, Teik, I assure you. We are not what most people believe us to be."

Papa nodded. "She'll be trained as a merchant."

"My word on it. By the Lady's Name and the Lord's Shadow, I swear."

"Our pride isn't that great," Papa said. "If you will take her, Teik, we have the price."

Sashi snuffled over and dropped her head in Megan's lap for her ears to be scratched. *I'm going to be a River Merchant, and a Thief, too, I guess,* she thought. *I don't know if I'm going to like being a thief, but that's better than being 'prenticed to the Red Brotherhood. I'd hate being a Blood-sib, like Aunt.*

I'm going to make lots of money and Papa and Mama'll have their choices again. Lady Goddess hear me, I swear. I going to be good at both merchant and the other. I see already they don't—we don't like being called thieves. I'm going to be the best.

Chapter Ten

He had his head turned away. Megan sneaked her hand toward the pouch hanging on his belt. He coughed and she froze. *Careful*, she thought. When he bent his head to his book and started reading again, she risked moving. Her arm was shaking a little, but she made it be still. *I can't get caught*. The pouch looked heavy and she wondered if it had silver in it. She couldn't just cut it and run because she didn't have a razor, and would have to empty it without him noticing. The edge of the pouch was rough against her finger, some of the leather had gotten wet . . . *I've got it, it's opening just a bit, tease it open a bit more—*

"Hey!" He yelled and grabbed her by the wrist. She pulled back but he had her. She shoved a knuckle into the spot under his thumb, yanked her hand free and ducked under the table, out the other side.

"Well, Megan," Gospozhyn Yarishk said, shaking his hand. "You might have gotten away, but you missed the pouch."

She hung her head. "Yes, Gospozhyn."

"Good enough though. Nal-Gospozhyn Olynkova has you for accounting and history next?"

"Yes, Gospozhyn." Megan petted Sashi instead of looking at her master, and the dog wagged her tail and slopped her tongue all over Megan's hand. *I wish I'd been more careful*.

"Go on then." He picked up the ledger-book again and dug the inkwell from behind a kahfe cup and out from under Megan's scarf that she'd left on his desk when she arrived for her lesson. "Oh, and Megan—" He sniffed and blew his nose into his handkerchief.

"Yes, Gospozhyn?" Megan had gathered up her waxboard and fidgeted from foot to foot, impatiently. If he didn't let her go, she'd be late.

"Don't depend on your size and quickness too much. Sometime you'll be in a place where you can't run or hide."

"Of course, Gospozhyn." She closed the door as he blew his nose again. He always got grumpy when he got a cold, she thought. Almost everyone had caught something because the weather was so wet; the days when even the wind shivered. She sniffed and wiped her nose on her sleeve as she trotted down the hall.

At first, she'd kept getting lost because the River Guild's hall was connected with the Other Guild that was spread throughout the northern slope of the City. She had to go through a couple of doors in the mountain tunnels, behind the bakery oven—that was good on a day like this, warming up the tunnel—then past the Tanner's Apprentice Hall. She could always hear somebody through that wall. *They're boors*, she thought.

Then up a flight of stairs and through the next door that lead into the Minor Merchant's Guild counting house.

I'm only an apprentice now, but that won't be for long, Megan thought. She'd be a Journeyman proper, then a Yolculvik, then a Nal-Gospozhyn, then Gospozhyn. In Enchian one had to specify male or female for anything above "apprentice." Megan snorted. In Tor Ench, the

Masters of guild were all male. They thought that women had to be hidden away in *femkas* in the back rooms of their husband's houses. Megan thought that the Zak idea of Gospozhyn was much better.

The back tunnels were stuffy and plain because, while the River Guild showed off its treasures in its halls, you couldn't really show a counting house's things.

It looked and smelled like a counting house: dull. But it was fascinating because you could keep track of where all the interesting things were.

Columns and rows of numbers were a lot simpler than people because they would do what you made them. *Kids can't tell anybody to do anything except the littler kids and that's not fair.* Megan realized that other things ruled adults, and that wasn't fair either, but if you were a grownup with lots of money no one would boss you around. *I'm going to be rich and Mama and Papa and Rilla and me are going to be comfortable and nobody's going to tell us what to do ever again if we don't want to listen. And maybe Serkai too*, Megan thought, as she ran up to the third floor. Under her soft boots the stairs were worn grey stone, with smooth hollows to the right and left and the lip of each step worn round.

Megan touched the earring Serkai had given her, with a bit of both their hair knotted together. He'd kissed her this morning and promised to marry her when they were both grown up and he was a great warrior to protect her rich ships and they'd be happy. It was possible that Ivar'd be part of their wedding if he found a girl or another boy, and they'd wed as a quad. Serkai had just been taken on by the DragonGuard as a squire. As far as Megan knew, his parents had sold their house to pay his way in, but he would earn enough to buy it back, soon, if he stuck it out. He'd given her the earring for her tenth birthday today.

Mama and Papa had said she was to have a treat today, and there was usually sausage in the soup again.

She knocked on the door, breathing hard. "Ave," called an irritable voice from inside.

Nal-Gospozhyn Olynkova was just a little taller than Ness and had black straight hair like her, but her face was rounder than most Zak, in fact most of the Masters of the River Guild and the other small Guilds allied with it didn't look as purely Zak as most others. *I think that's because our Gospozhyn aren't as snotty as in other Guilds.*

Today she wore a bright yellow Aeniri-style vest over a red wool shirt, and her pants were plain black felt. Her slippers were curl-toed, embroidered in red and yellow. On her wrists she wore heavy silver bracelets and finger-chains with red or yellow stones at each knuckle. Since she usually wore dark blue and black and never wore finger-chains, it must be a very important party she was going to.

"Megan, come in, shut the door. You're a little late, but I expect it was because of Yarishk." Without waiting for Megan to answer, she went on. "T's not your fault. We can't waste much time then, though. History first."

Megan was used to her Nal-Gospozhyn's abrupt manners and already had her waxboard open. Olynkova always rushed on without letting the person she was talking to answer. That wasn't so good for a merchant, Megan thought, but she was a higher rank so she must know what she was doing.

"You were to read the fifth chapter of *Social History* and the Enchian version of *Merchants and Thieves*." She rubbed her hands together, rings chiming, unused to the pinch and scrape of the finger ornaments. "Recite, then."

"Nal-Gospozhyn Olynkova, the *Social History* states that the rumors of the Thieves Guild began about twelve hundred years ago during the years of Holiness and Corruption. Zakrof recounts the quote 'apocryphal creation story of a thieves society' unquote, in the middle of chapter five."

Olynkova held up a hand to stop her. "Don't just quote it word for word, child, I know you've read it. Summarize in your own words."

Megan sat and thought for a moment. "There was a

priest who thought that the poor in the City and in the Zak Empire weren't being looked after, so she set up the Guild so that smart kids could get out and so that people who *should* be helping the poor were made to . . . by people stealing from them."

"What was her rationale—her reasoning?"

"Ummm. I think . . . I think she thought if there were a cheaper way to teach people a trade, 'cause the Guilds were stronger then and were charging more, more people could be helped. Enlightened self-interest."

"Good enough."

They switched to the accounting books. Olynkova had given Megan an imaginary company to keep track of. Megan hated losing money and having to fire people.

Her papa had helped her make a couple of decisions but Nal-Gospozhyn said that was all right because even merchants could ask for advice. Problem is, she said, sometimes they could advise you wrongly.

Last Hand-of-days, Megan had taken a good risk, but today Nal-Gospozhyn said there were rumors of a storm over that part of the River and Megan might have lost ships or would have to pay for damage. Megan hadn't known there were so many ways to lose money and had already been bankrupt once.

Olnykova cut the lesson off early because of her dinner engagement at Kievir Anatoli's. Megan whistled to herself, understanding why Nal-Gospozhyn was so carefully dressed. He was almost as important as Kievir Mikail, controlling the fur trade.

Of the nine main Kievir, Mikail ranked first, but if all the others got together they could push out another Kievir. The only one no one could touch was the DragonLord, because he held the key and the code for the dam and catch basins, but even he wouldn't really want to make all nine angry. Most of the time, though, they spent fighting each other for position. Journeyman Varik said that political faction fighting was a Zak national sport.

Because Megan's family lived in the City, she went

home for the day of rest. Sometimes she felt sorry for Yegor and Tikhiy, who had to stay in the Apprentice quarters because they were from out-city, but they liked it fine. They both said it was better than being at home, herding horses, mucking out stalls. At Chorniy Street, where Krasniy turned into Market, she had to stop and wait for the passage of another herd of cows. They were being driven into the Va Zalstva, the old arena, for the Zarizan's wedding feast; his gift to the whole City—real beef and fine white bread. Not a scrawny old hen or sausage with big chunks of gristle. The Va Zalstva was the only place inside the City walls to keep that many cows.

Yegor had said everyone should get mutton, too, but all the other apprentices sneered at him and called him a Thane. His use-name now was Lambchop or Mint-sauce, and he wished he hadn't opened his mouth.

They wouldn't decorate Market Street for the procession until after all the herds had been moved in and the street cleaned up. *The Dragon's horses aren't going to have to step in cowshit.* Megan stopped to scrape her boots on a curb stone. *They don't care if we do.*

Since the herds were moving through part of the Great Market, many people had moved their stalls into Reyeka Street, so it was more crowded and people almost stepped on each other's toes when they moved to let horse and donkey traffic by. It was so noisy Megan covered her ears with her hands going through the narrow bits that had between-house arches, where the haggling and shouting echoed under the full lines of washing. The Stairs were too busy to set any more booths on.

Megan ducked under Tinker's arm as he waved a pot under a potential customer's nose, and squeezed between two heavy-laden donkeys that idly twitched their ears at her.

The wedding procession would start at the Dragon'sNest, go all around the First Quarter by way of Kharoshya Street, Yekh Road and Na Yekh, where they'd stop to be blessed at the Lady's Shrine. They'd have to turn aside to stop at the Dark Lord's Temple but they would, lest He be offended. Then the procession would wind back the Va Zalstva where Ranion and Avritha would cut bread and meat for the City, and around to the Nest again. Then the pair would have to go up to the plateau to be married.

Megan had heard rumors that a priest of the Bear would be called from Brahvniki to do the ceremony because they'd be neutral. The Benaiat of Saekrberk, Zar Ivahn, would be there through a mind-speaker.

The wedding presents had started arriving, and they would be on display to the City for a whole Hand of days. Gospozhyn Yarishk had said there would be a lot of thief-sniffers around, whose talent was related to truth-telling, though fortunately rarer, among the guards.

Yarishk sometimes gave her the odd coin as spending money, so she bought a sticky-cake, though she shouldn't because it would spoil the dinner Mama and Papa would have for her. *I just won't tell.*

All of the newest apprentices in the River Guild were assigned the task of figuring out where all the wedding gifts came from. Shepilova complained about it, but Megan thought that it would be fun. She sat down and dangled her feet over the edge of the Reyeka bridge, watching drips of water fall down and go plunk in the puddles on the ice as she ate her cake. The loose tooth hurt but it was almost a good pain and she worried at the tooth with her tongue. When it fell out or she managed to wiggle it out, she'd wash it and give it to Mama to keep. She spit out a bit of walnut shell that had gotten baked into the cake.

Even more fun than just figuring out where everything came from would be figuring out how to steal something. That would take a Gospozhyn Rearranger to manage, though. *I bet one of their presents would feed a family for a whole year.*

Below, on the Middle Quarter bank there was an old fire still smoldering, wisps of smoke coiling up. There were only two or three houses burnt out so it hadn't been that bad a fire, probably because they were Middle Quarter enough to have thick fire walls. It was a good thing there wasn't a wind or it would have jumped the water. On the other side of the river it used to be Middle but was River Quarter now, with small wooden houses built between the big stone ones. When a fire took hold, there wasn't much anybody could do except try to keep it from spreading, if that.

The rain knocked down the smoke and most of the people who got burned out were back trying to build again, probably without paying the building fee, but there hadn't been timber brought in for sale because of the wedding. The Regent thought there were other things more important than letting River scum rebuild.

The fire reminded Megan of what was happening to Onya. There hadn't been someone with a Salamander's talent in the City for more than fifty years, Varik had said, because Salamanders tended to set themselves on fire and die when they manifested, if they weren't trained. Once trained, though, they could control fires.

If Onya doesn't kill herself, she might be one. The Guilded Manrauq have taken her in for testing. She was being kept very carefully and if she were a Salamander, then her family could afford to live in the First Quarter.

Varik had been teaching Megan the theories of manrauq and testing her to see if she were going to be powerful someday, when she became a woman. He had tried everything and finally said that maybe she'd have a little manrauq, but the signs weren't showing. He'd even taken her to a Power-Ferret, but couldn't find anything.

Megan had talked to Onya just before she went into the Hall of Light, and had cried over her accounting books that night. Yarishk had found her and reassured her that it was too soon to tell about her lack of manrauq. Later on she'd overheard him yelling at Varik for trying too soon because it might block her.

I don't care if I'm going to be a stinking red witch all my life; means I'll live longer.

Her mama had said that it wasn't as important as some

Zak thought and that she probably won't be "deaf." Ness had said that she herself hadn't manifested until she was fourteen. *I don't care. I'm going to be the best merchant there is, so manrauq doesn't matter.*

Serkai was starting to send sparkles, like fire-flies, and thought it was a turkey kind of manrauq, but Megan thought it would be better than nothing. Shepilova had just found out that she could "pinch" from a couple of feet away, and everyone was miserable for a Hand until she got doused with buckets over doors and had her bed short-sheeted three times. There were other ways than manrauq to get back at people, as house master Zyatki Yarovych said.

It had been useful though, when Nar-Kievir Botek's son rode through in the Market Square. Megan and her friends had thought he was just a Prafetatla of the House because of the colors, but found out later that it was just himself. Megan, Serkai, Shepilova and Tikhiy were in his way and he'd taken his whip to them, calling them gutter-trash and so on. Shepilova "pinched" his horse, and it bolted straight through a cheese-seller's stall and then bucked him off in a garbage pile.

They'd all had a good laugh about that after, though Tikhiy had to have a whip cut on her head looked at. Her hair would cover it mostly, except the tail end that curled around to her cheek, under her right eye; she scarred easily.

Megan licked her fingers and rubbed them together, looking at the coiling fingers of smoke from the ruin. *I'm glad it wasn't summer.* Everything was so dry then that the whole City could burn. In spring the rain wet every-thing down. *I'm glad that I wasn't alive to see the Great Fire the Paladium Dragon year when Papa was sixteen.*

Fires were like monsters sneaking around, licking houses down. It smelled bad; like wood and wool and hair and meat. Like when their house burned, ages and ages ago. She didn't remember much, except the smell and that horses scream like people.

She got up and threw a pebble into the river for luck,

sniffed, and wiped her nose on her sleeve again. She shouldn't have been sitting on the stone because her pants were soaked through.

The drains were plugged here, because somebody shouted down, "Pot!" from four floors up, and everyone hid under the overhangs so as not to get splashed. *Phew, somebody has the shits. Mama would say diarrhoea because that's more polite. Arvi'd say 'the shits' too, but then he's going to be a blacksmith so he doesn't have to watch his tongue as much.*

The Apprentice Hall of the River Guild was near the Main Hall, down the street, on the Middle Quarter side. The apprentice rooms were on the second floor, with four wallbeds per room and a small window, all paneled in dark wood. Megan fluffed her pillow and smiled at the scent of clean linen and feathers.

The gargoyles carved out of chestnut burls along the wooden stairs and the gallery had made her nervous at first, but now they were old friends.

"Megan!" Tikhiy called into the 'prentice rooms where she was making her bed. "It's your sweet boy!" Megan ran out and leaned over the gallery rail. Tikhiy was still standing downstairs by Master Zyatki's office, looking up, so Megan dropped the pillow she was holding on her yelling, "He's just a good friend!" Tikhiy caught the pillow and tried to throw it back, but it fell short and hit Serk in the head.

"Hey!" he sputtered, trying to smooth his hair with one hand, the pillow in the other, while Tikhiy giggled. She was always making gooey eyes at Serk and Ivar when they came to visit.

"What's the matter, Tikhiy? Manifesting?" Master Zyatki stuck his head out of his study and was looking at them *that* way, that meant they were all being too stupid mention. From where she stood, Megan could see Serkai blush. *He's been doing that a lot lately,* she thought.

Tikhiy ducked her head and mumbled something about Megan and the pillow. Serkai was holding it and started to put it behind his back but stopped, embarrassed. "Well, a little less noisily then, hmm?" Master Zyatki nodded at them, looked up, winked at Megan, and went back into his office. He was the sort of person who could quiet a whole room full of rowdy apprentices just by raising an eyebrow; one reason he was the Gospozhyn of the Quarters.

"I've gotta finish here, Serk, then I'll be ready to go." Megan said.

"Okay." He handed Tikhiy the pillow and she ran up the stairs to give it back. Megan saw the twinkle in her eye and caught the pillow when she threw it, the air oofing out of her lungs.

"Ow! You know, I wouldn't do that if you didn't dribble when he or 'Var come visit."

"OOOOh! I do not dribble!" Tikhiy glared at her, then they grinned and hugged each other. Next to Rilla, she was the closest friend Megan had.

Megan went back in to finish making her bed. Shepilova made a slurping, dribbling sound. "Tikhiy's like Sashi, she drools on what she wants to eat!"

"Shut up!" Tikhiy said amiably. "You were the one making cow-eyes at Vladik!"

"I was not!" She and Tikhiy kept trading friendly insults as they tidied up their parts of the room. The boys had already left, but Megan could see the toes of Yegor's socks poking out of his box and Vladik had just thrown his dirty clothes on top of his unmade bed and closed the door. *Master Zyatki'll catch them both for that*. Megan hurried because she'd promised Serk she'd go with him to see the presents, and then they'd meet Mama and Papa and Rilla to eat at the Va Zalstva.

She ran down the stairs and hugged Serk hello, then touched the puffy skin around one of his eyes, gently. "You all right? I didn't give you that black eye with the pillow, did—"

He laughed. "No, Meg, I stepped into something that my arms-teacher didn't pull enough." She had to look up to look into his face now, because he'd started getting his growth around his eleventh birthday. She looked into his eyes, wondering about all the bruises lately, but he always brushed it off saying it was normal for a guard 'prentice. His instructor was one of the toughest women Megan had ever heard about, and by the way he talked about her, she could fight wildcats and give them the first two licks.

Serk said that a lot of the younger apprentices, who were all boys, hated her because she was so tough. The guards picked now were mostly men. Papa said that was a Thanish or Arkan idea. They thought that God was a man and didn't like women to fight. *That's dumb. Koru's the best God there is and she fought for all of us, right at the beginning. She was the best warrior of them all.*

Serk grinned at her. "I'll have to show you the move. It's something you could use in cniffta, you and Rilla."

"Okay." She smiled at his un-swollen eye and put her arm through his. He was wearing his best red tunic and Megan was in her best dark blue, with her hair loose because he thought it was pretty that way. It was long enough now that she could sit on the braids.

Tikhiy leaned around the corner, hanging onto the gargoyle at the top of the stairs as they went out, making kissy noises. Megan leaned back and stuck out her tongue.

It was warm enough that they had their coats slung over their shoulders. *It's funny*, Megan thought. *At the start of the winter, it would have been cold and we'd all be bundling up, but after the winter, when we got used to being a lot colder, this seems really warm*. A blue *Fchera* sat on a bare tree twig, dark blue against a blue sky, singing, "Yes-ter-DAY! Yes-ter-DAY!" Megan tickled Serkai and he chased her down the street. She could have gotten away if she'd wanted, too, 'cause she was sneakier than he was, but that's not what she wanted to do.

It was weird. Serkai was seeing things in straight lines. He wasn't as sneaky as he used to be. *I guess that's what*

*he's learning. Zak are better sneaky. We can't walk up
to just anyone and hit them straight on the head if they're
trying to kill us, we have to whip around and hamstring
them. That's what Yolculvik Varik says, even about business deals.* Gospozhyn had promoted Varik from Journeyman just last iron-cycle.

They dodged back along Chorniy and down Tsviet
Street to the Stairs, because a crowd was already gathered in the square by the Va Zalstva.

They'd figured there wouldn't be many people looking
at the presents since it was the last day, and she'd have
to complete her assignment from what she could see
today.

One could actually see the inner buildings of the Nest
better from further out in the City. There was an outside
wall that ran from one cliff to the other, with pointed
crenels on top, like fangs. Right in the middle was the
Iron Gate that wasn't solid but a metal shell on wood. It
hadn't been closed for two hundred years, and the only
part of it that was kept polished were the hinges, just in
case.

Krasniy Street went through the gate and into the tunnel that could be closed off with three other gates all
along its length before Gorat Road began.

But out this far one could see the buildings inside the
wall. The Sto Solstne window, the height of ten people,
in the Grom Hall was all of glass with an ivory sill, edged
in paper-thin shaved stone. At night the glass and crystal
chandelier shone there, hung by silver-washed chains, lit
with five hundred white wax candles. *The light glows
through,* Megan thought. *It looks like the voice of Koru's
wind, like something sacred.*

All the doors and windows in the Nest were edged in
carved bone or ivory, decreed by a DragonLord, three
generations ago. *Papa says it suits; bones, like a real
dragon's nest.*

The domes of the towers were painted, with copper-
pointed tips, and the red banners flew like long, whippy
tongues licking the sky. The tunnel underneath the Nest

was lit with both kraumaks and reflected light from mirrors.

"I don't usually come in this way," Serkai said. "I hardly ever see the public rooms, 'cause I'm usually in the training halls, over that way." He pointed to the smaller gate that led into the wing that melded into the south ridge of the mountain. The shutters of the mountain rooms were all open to let the fresh, spring air in.

"We should come to visit you, Serk."

"No, no. Don't." He stopped and held her by the arm. "If I get too many friends coming to visit from outside, I'll get too many marks against me and then I'm out on my ass."

"Okay, okay, Serkai. I just thought I'd ask. We'd never do anything to get you to lose your place."

"Well, they try hard to wash us out." His mouth was tight, making him look older. They were harder on the guard apprentices than they had to be. *Mama says that they try their best to break you and build you up again, but different. I wouldn't like that for me, or Serk. He's losing bits of himself. It's like he doesn't dare laugh because he's afraid of stepping out of line. But he doesn't want to talk about it, not today.*

What were called the public halls weren't really public but marked the limit that anybody who wasn't a member of court could go on special days or audience days, but that hadn't been allowed since Ranion's grandfather's time. Now the way in was to bribe or know someone already at court. Megan ran her hand along the stone banister, liking the soapy-smooth feel.

The first gift room was an animal garden, and the air was full of chirps and bleats and whistles and stranger noises.

"Koru, Serk, look at all the cages!" They wandered slowly down the carpet path between the thick, braided ropes. There were guards everywhere to make sure no one would try to step off the path, or touch Ranion and Avritha's precious beasts.

"Yeah." Serk sneezed. "It usually doesn't smell like

this." It wasn't bad, just hot and a little like cat and a little like horse. Megan ran over to a small cage to one side.

"Snowcat kittens!" They rolled and squealed and played pounce in their litter of cotton scraps. Just past them was a cormarenc chick, taller than Serkai, just losing its fluff. It grawked and croaked and stabbed its beak into a barrel with fish in it, splashing water around itself. They stood well out of its reach, holding their noses. It let a big gob of shit go that stank until a slave shoveled it up and carried it away. As the man came in reach, the chick strained against the collar on its long, thin neck, trying to kill him with its beak. "Wouldn't want to have to keep that," Serkai said, a little nasally.

"It wouldn't fit in the house." Megan giggled, and they sidled past it to the small bamboo cages full of singing birds, spotted and striped and tiny, smaller than the cup of Megan's hand. At the opposite side of the room from the cats were horses, a stallion with his nostrils flared and red, and his mare and her foal, from the Aenir. "The foal's cute, but he's just going to grow up to be a *horse!*" Megan said disgustedly. Serkai just rolled his eyes.

"I like the third room best," Serkai said. "I've seen them before, but I like looking again. But I'm not going to tell you why, you'll see." Then he looked around. "Hey, it's Ellach on duty, come on!"

"What? Serk should you . . ."

He whispered to the guard standing there with his one gauntlet on his dart-caster. Megan swallowed and followed. It was going to be hard when Serkai was a guard himself. *Nobody talks to them unless they have to.*

". . . just for a second," Serkai was saying. The guard wasn't as old as Megan had thought he was. *He's trying to grow a mustache and it isn't working.*

The guard cleared his throat, looked around, then said, "As long as no one sees you." He jerked his head at the fuzzy-plumed tail thing. "Go on. You owe me one."

"Come on, Megan," Serkai said, and ducked under the

rope. "This one's real tame and only eats ants anyway. Come on, quick, before anyone else comes through!"

Megan nodded cautiously at the guard, who ignored her, and she followed Serkai, scrambling through to pet the anteater. It was both fuzzy and rough and smelled like a stepped-on ant's nest. *Its tongue* is *sticky.* Megan had to peel it off her wrist as the guard hissed at them to get out of there. The servant who looked after the beast helped her and they ran, giggling. They were on the proper side of rope as a Middle Quarter family came around the end cage that had white-faced monkeys in it.

Right at the door to the second room was a tank full of water with a plant floating in it. It had thin white roots coiled tight in with the green ones. Next to the tank was a bowl with thumb-sized bits of raw meat in it. "Here," said Serkai. "Try this." He picked up a bit of meat and waited until she did too. "Throw it in." As the bloody meat hit the water, the white roots snapped like springs and grabbed.

"Ick," Megan said. "It's like Gospozhyn Farsht's sundew that catches flies." She threw her lump of meat. "It's neat, but still ick. What are Avritha and Ranion going to do with all of this?"

Serkai hissed at her and she shrugged. "The Woyvodaana and the Woyvode, then," she corrected herself.

"I guess they'll make the menagerie bigger," Serkai said. "More space we have to keep guarded."

"Yeah."

The next gift room was down a marble corridor, with mirror sculptures hanging from the ceiling that turned and moved in the kraumak light. "They're like silent wind-chimes," Megan said. "But I think I like windchimes better. They aren't spooky and cold." Serkai looked up at them and shrugged again. Megan stared. Last year *he* would have noticed that they were cold first.

The next room was so bright she almost couldn't see in the light pouring in the windows. It was full of bright things, all carefully displayed.

"That's a Yeoli sword," Serkai said, pointing to a wall

that was bare except for the sword and its fittings in green and blue enamel. "A *kraila*." Nearby was a glass case holding a weapon she'd never heard of. It had a tube on a wooden handle and three brass and paper things next to it, labelled "Shot-Thrower—Nübuah." Megan had never heard of Nübuah before either. "It throws those, farther than an arrow or dart. I never saw it work," he said wistfully. "But I heard about it from our commander, she did."

Megan pulled him past it to look at the wedding bed bigger than Megan's family's room in the Flats, round and carved like a dragon biting its own tail, with red satin curtains embroidered in silver and sable blankets piled high on feather pillows. "I'll bet they didn't want to show the Thanish wool carpets," Megan said. "They're bright, but, well, *I* think they're ugly," she whispered, looking at the wide red and blue stripes. "There's so much stuff. Who dusts it all?"

"Servants. Don't be dumb." She poked him and he glared at her, so she tossed her hair out of her eyes and looked at the mahogany and gold brooms for the bride-pair to sweep out bad luck, instead of at him.

The big wood table next to the bed had shells carved all around the edges, inlaid with real hammered silver. "That's an Enchian-style table," Megan said. On the table stood fancy jars of perfumes and ointments. They were rose quartz and red or blue glass, and one that she thought was a tiny amethyst but couldn't get any closer to see. "Won't the perfumes all dry up before anybody uses them? A person can only wear so much smelly stuff at one time," she said. "Even if they didn't bathe once a day, like they can."

"They'll use them, maybe, and if not, well, they're *wedding* presents. You don't have to use all of them."

"Don't be a jerk, Serk. My folks did."

"Yeah, well, so did mine, but our kin weren't Zingas."

"No shit. My feet are starting to hurt."

Next to the table was a large open space with sculptures in it; one of Ranion and Avritha, him standing and her sitting next to him. Megan plucked at Serkai's elbow, whispering, "I guess the sculptor did that to make Ranion look taller." He poked her back, grinned, then wiped it off his face.

"Avritha's taller than he is, but then she's older. He might have some more growing to do." On pedestals all around there were other sculptures; amber and jade and turquoise. There were paintings that made the bridal pair more beautiful than people could be.

There were rows of mannequins wearing furs and silks and satins to show off the new clothes and bolts of satin embroidered with gold and black and every color of the rainbow. "They could wear something different every hour of the day and never repeat in an iron-cycle, I bet," Megan said.

"Yeah, I didn't think there was that much silk in all the world," he answered. There was a pain under Megan's chestbone and she put her hand up to it. *I guess it's because they're so lovely. I didn't think that something pretty could hurt like that.*

Megan stopped to rub one foot then the other. This was only the second room. After the clothes, came the cases of jewelry. "Those are as big as my fist!" she exclaimed, pointing at the diamonds surrounded by ropes of rubies cut as smooth as eyeballs. *In those cases there's a rosewood and gold mrik set from Laka, and a gold and glass chess set from Arko.* "I won't have time to see it all. I want to. It's all so beautiful."

"Don't stop too long here," Serkai pulled her on. "You stay too long in front of one case and the guards and thief-sniffers get nervous." They stopped in front of a rainbow disk from before the Fire that must have been an ornament; it had a hole in the middle so you could hang it in the light.

Serkai started grinning like a fool again, so Megan turned from the disk and tilted her head questioningly at him. He hid a smirk and pointed, whispering, "Ranion's favorite."

Megan almost fell over laughing when she saw what

was on a table in isolated glory. "It's so ugly," she whispered.

"Shhh. It's his favorite!" he answered, putting one hand up to hide his grin.

The sculpture was solid gold, a man's member as long as Megan's arm, shaped like the marriage blessing cakes except there wasn't a corresponding *yoni*. It had emeralds and sapphires set all over the balls; one diamond at its tip. "No wonder it's all by itself, it might attack something else," Megan whispered to Serkai.

There were three guards around it looking bored and uncomfortable. Serkai giggled and turned it to a cough behind his hand. One of the guards glared at them, but his mouth twitched, too. Serkai grabbed Megan by the arm and dragged her out so they wouldn't embarrass themselves.

Once they were out in the corridor to the next room they howled, leaning on each other so they didn't fall over. Serkai pretended walking as if the gold *lingam* were his own parts, leaning over backward and straddle-legged. Megan pretended to faint at the sight, and both of them laughed so hard they were crying. *He hasn't laughed a lot lately, I think. That gold thing is so big; so ugly. It doesn't look like Papa's or Ivar's or Serkai's.* Serkai said, "If any man had one that big, he'd pass out when he wanted to make love!" And they giggled again.

"Toys!" Megan darted in to the third room. "Toys for the heir when he or she gets born!"

"Shhh!" Serkai caught her and put his finger over her mouth. "The heir *has* to be male! Zarizan says so."

"That's not right!" Megan hissed back indignantly, standing in the midst of a family of stuffed lions. "That's a Thanish idea! Girls can be Woyvode, too!"

"Will you shut up!" Serkai looked honestly scared. "Meg, don't say that here, okay?"

She glared at him as if he could do anything about that. "Okay. But he's *wrong!*"

Serkai walked under the stuffed giraffe, whose stubby horns touched the hall's ceiling. "Yeah, he is, but I'm a guard—I'll be a guard and can't say things like that, or even hear them."

"Okay, Serk. I understand. Look, I'm sorry."

"That's okay. Lets look at the rest of the toys, okay?"

"Yeah."

There were more toys than any ten shops or stalls at the Market all put together: clockwork monkeys and a rocking pony with a red-silk halter and saddle, enameled building blocks and toy swords and little suits of armor and little two-fangs with wooden ends, and more than she could remember, later.

She walked out holding Serkai's hand, feeling as if she'd been asleep and dreaming. When they came out of the tunnel it didn't seem right somehow that the sun should still be shining, that the outside should still be the same. *That's weird. You could forget that outside even existed.* Megan's stomach rumbled, reminding her there would be beef served today, beginning the first day of the wedding feast. She tugged at Serkai's hand saying, "Do they feed you meat in the Guard?"

"Yeah, but usually only pork, let's go!" They ran down Krasniy. *What's behind is a dream, something that's too bright to think about, when I know what's real.* She sniffed the wind blowing from the Va Zalstva that smelled of hot fat, ignoring the odor of horse dung in the street.

They found Mama and Papa and Rilla at the corner of Zalstva Square and Krasniy. *It's a good thing that we had a meeting place set out or we would never have found anybody.*

Megan hugged Papa and Mama first. When she hugged Rilla, her cousin whispered, "Meg, can I talk to you later?"

"Sure, Rilla. Whenever you need to."

"Okay. Thanks."

Her mama and papa both had new tunics, and that made Megan feel good because it meant there was more money to spare. Since Megan was apprenticed, they didn't have to feed and dress her. *I guess that helps,*

Megan thought. *But Rilla stays with them whenever Aunt Marte goes on a binge.*

The Va Zalstva arena could seat forty thousand, dug into the mountain, a high, white stone wall with the entrance gates built around the street side. At one time the stone was cleaned every Hand, but that was when it had been used more often. The feasting would go on all day and night until everyone was fed or the food ran out, which might not be until the wedding a Hand from now. The first DragonLord had tried to hold blood-sport games but someone had finally managed to assassinate her without flooding the City. Bear-baitings were still held, and the rat pits were used for the executions of criminals who didn't deserve beheading or strangling.

Today the pits were covered over with gratings, and though you could sometimes smell the rats, mostly the smell was beef and bread. There were even barrels of butter lined up on platforms on the sand next to the bread. Kievir Anatoli and his family were honoring the people by serving first, a holdover from the time of the Republic. *They don't like it, but it's an old tradition. All the nine Kievir and their families are going to serve. Even Ranion and Avritha are going to serve once.*

Kievira Anatoli was standing by the first spitted cow with a long knife and two-tined fork, her sleeves rolled back and her face red from the heat. There were twenty fire-pits in the sand with cows roasting, and when she finished carving one, a servant would go on to carve the next while they put a fresh one on to roast.

After Kievir Anatoli cut a thick slab of bread and it was buttered by his Heir, Lilovyi, a piece of beef as thick as the first joint of Megan's thumb got put on top of that. The only one who looked as if she enjoyed what she was doing was the family's Heir buttering the bread, so Megan smiled at her and she smiled back.

The juices dribbled on Megan's hands and she juggled it from hand to hand, trying to roll her sleeves out of the way. There was even beer if you brought your own cup, and Mama and Papa had brought one for the three of them to share.

They sat in the spring sunshine on the benches carved into the mountain with everyone else, and ate and talked and toasted the wedding.

"Mikail insisted, the rumor goes," Ness said, biting off another piece of meat. "Ranion didn't want to feed us. If he didn't though, the City'd be up in arms. What luck we've had this last little while would be ruined if that happened." Lixand nodded and handed the children a cloth to wipe their chins. "Avritha apparently supported her father. She might moderate the young Dragon."

"Well, he's young and impulsive; she'll steady him down once they're married."

Ness raised her cup and around them others followed suit. "As long as Mikail doesn't get too used to wielding power just through his daughter," someone muttered. There was a second's silence as everyone got very interested with their meal, then turned the talk to something safer.

Megan told them all about the toys and the *thing* that Ranion liked so much, and Ness and Lixand rolled their eyes at each other while Rilla giggled. Then Serkai and Rilla and Megan all went to the amphitheater because there was a wedding show being put on free, while the adults decided to spend their afternoon just walking.

The show was okay, not bad for something free, but a little dull. Serkai had to be back to his barracks by the late afternoon guard change, so the two girls walked him back to the south gate as the Garrison drums rumbled to life behind the Nest wall.

"Bye, Serk. I'll come drag you out next Hand-ending. We'll watch the procession with the rest of the old pack, okay?" Megan shouted, holding her hands over her ears.

His face was getting longer the closer they got to the barracks. *There's more going on than he'll tell us.* "Okay," he yelled back. "I'd like that. Goddess guard."

"Don't let the Darkness jump on you."

He grinned and went in, waving.

Rilla and Megan walked down to Climbing Road Bridge and sat on the stone railings under the arches. "You wanted to talk?"

The younger girl nodded. "Yeah. I don't want to ask your Ma and Da for any more help, but mam says she still doesn't have enough saved to 'prentice me somewhere. I think she's a liar and your da does, too. Mam wants me to learn how to be a Canter like her. That way she won't have to pay the fee."

"How can I help?" I'll help if I can."

"I've been prigging stuff from her chest when she's too drunk to know—"

"Shit, she's that bad?"

"Yeah. I don't tell your da much. It doesn't do any good, Meg. She cries and gets soppy and gooey-mothery and 'nothing's too good for my baby.' You know—lasts as long as she's sorry; stays dry for a cycle or two, then blows everything."

"Yeah." Rilla was pulling mortar out and dropping it in the water, *plink*. Megan leaned her head back and looked up at the old carvings. Aunt Marte and her drinking made her tired. "Hey, not that I need to know, but does she still try to beat you?"

Rilla didn't answer for a while. The wind blew from the lake and a man down-city somewhere was singing "Young Widow's Ballad."

Rilla sighed and shifted on the railing. The sun was going down red, tinting the clouds pink and purple; purple fading down into the black shadows between buildings.

"Yeah. She still beats me if I don't run first. But I've always gotta go home. 's not so bad as all that." She leaned away, as if from a comforting arm, though Megan hadn't moved. "Last time . . ." Rilla gulped and wiped tears. "Last time she yelled that I'd broken her hand and that she'd fix me. When she grabbed me as I got out the window, I ripped my tunic. When I came back a couple days later, she belted me for ripping it, but that was better than getting my hand mashed."

"Rilla!" Megan hugged her though Rilla didn't want her to at first and pulled away, but that almost pitched them off the bridge rail, so she hugged back. She cried for a while, then made Megan promise not to tell her mama and papa. *I should tell but they'd just talk to Aunt more, and talking doesn't help*. They couldn't take Rilla away, and the only way to help would be to get her apprenticed to someone other than Marte. *Shit*.

"Rilla, how much have you got?"

"Um, well, last time she got drunk I got enough to buy 'maranth and groats and other stuff like that. She spends most of it on wine."

"Oh." Rilla was trying so hard to be tough and just say everything without feeling it. *Mama and Papa are probably helping all they can anyway, without knowing, and I know that Aunt Marte would have to sign any apprentice agreement, even if we got the money. But there's gotta be something I can do*. Perhaps Gospozhyn Yarishk could help somehow.

"Rilla, I'm going to talk to my master. Maybe he can tell us what to do."

"You think so?"

"I think so." Megan nodded firmly and wiped Rilla's face with her hand. "It can't hurt, 'cause he won't tell *her* and something good might come out of it. You feel better for crying?"

She nodded. "Okay. 'm glad you're here, Megan."

" 'love you, coz. I'll have to wait until I go back to the Guildhall next Hand to talk to him, after the wedding."

" 'kay."

Ivar and Arvi and Marin and Serkai and Rilla and Megan were all lined up sitting along the top of Tsik's studio on Market Square. They'd tried to get a seat on the glass-blower's, but that was too far away to see the procession, and the buttery owner had chased them off his roof.

Tsik was an artist who made his money teaching rich kids art, renting studios to other artists, and trying to "capture the spirit of the city" with his brushes. He drank a lot and cried a lot and worked like a fiend sometimes. Whenever he got disgusted with the world, he would chuck his art things out the window and swear he'd go back to something safer, or steadier paying, like masonry, as he was trained. Tsik and his husband sat in the window one floor down with sketch pads.

Earlier this morning it had rained, and might rain again; if it didn't it would be a sticky, cold-muggy spring day that made all the clothes you were wearing feel moldy and cold at the same time. The swallows flicked in and out of their nests under the eaves beneath the children's boots, and the chicks complained every time as if their parents hadn't brought good enough bugs. Megan slapped at an early mosquito on her neck.

Ivar, who was nearest the corner, nudged Marin and she stood up to see. "They're coming!" From Koru's Temple, high on the south cliff, they could see the ribbon of color coming down the road between the crowds lining the way. *Everyone who got fed is happy enough to cheer and sing and throw budding branches down in front of their horses.*

The City banners came first, with the DragonLord's banner taking second place because Ranion hadn't risen to the throne yet. The banner-bearers wore all black armor, shiny and hard like ants. The Zarizan would come before Zingas Avritha because of his higher rank.

After the City and Woyvode's banners came his personal guard. Behind them came two naZak women, tall as the bottom of the banners, both with red hair and black skin, wearing wooden slave-links, leading a pair of snowleopard kittens each.

"He's a giant!" Rilla yelled excitedly, leaning out to point. The slave was twice as tall as the tallest person in the crowd and his skin was so black it shone like ink. *Did he color it? His hair is a green mane. He must have colored it. Did he?"*

Ivar hauled Rilla back. "I couldn't even lift that spear he's carrying, or the shield." The spear had gold ribbons on it and a shield shaped like a lace-shuttle, all fringed in hair or dry grass. "He can't be real," Megan said. "*But there's no wavery edge that would mean he's a manrauq-made image.*" He left footprints and limped. She leaned out, trying to see more clearly, and Serkai caught the back of her tunic so she wouldn't fall. The warrior looked up and smiled. "He can't be real! His teeth are pointed."

After the black man came more guards with their two-fangs canted at a precise angle; some were drummers and some carried small hand bells. At the end the big bells came; tube bells so long that it took two people to sound, one holding the frame while the other walked backward, ringing it with a mallet. The thunder of the big drums and all the bells ringing echoed between the buildings, drowning out people's cheering. Megan covered her ears, feeling the noise tremble in the pit of her stomach.

"There's the Bear priest!" Marin called, pointing to the man, wearing plain red linen, walking alone in the procession, leaning on a carved staff.

"And there's the Bear!" The image, with a honey-pot before it, was carried by twenty people dressed in blue. There was a long gap in the procession and the children ran to the corner of the building to see why, but Tsik yelled from below.

"My plaster's falling, sit down you young halyions!"

Just out of their sight, at a bend in the road, there was a roaring and someone screaming. A giant spotted bear lunged into sight, dragging some of the people who had been trying to lead it. It reared up and swung a couple of people almost off their feet, swatting at them with black, dagger-like claws. Foam splattered its fur, spilling through an iron-strapped muzzle. It smelled like a dropped crate of rotten eggs.

Arvi liked the bunch of balika players and dancers, though both she and Ivar liked the yellow witch walking in front of the Royal household with a ball of light just over his arms and head. "He's holding the sun." On such a dull day it shone very bright.

Regent Mikail came next, riding a grey horse with a red harness. The horse pranced and half-reared while he sat its back like a grey-dressed statue. "The horse doesn't dare disobey him. Nobody does," Megan said. As he passed below them, the lowering clouds started to spit rain.

"Nobody disobeys him," Serkai said quietly. "Except the gods."

Ranion had a white and gold carriage like a boat, drawn by white horses with red eyes. The Zarizan sat surrounded by red flowers, his garland crooked across his forehead, and Megan could see a red wine stain on his wedding tunic. "Do pearls stain?" Megan wondered aloud. "If this were my wedding, I wouldn't look scared or sulky." Arvi laughed.

Ranion's cloak was made out of red and green hummingbird feathers. "He waves like he's wagging a dead fish on the end of his arm," Rilla said, and Megan poked her. The horses rolled their eyes and fidgeted, trying to balk because of the bear smell, but the coachman managed to keep them going, though they snorted and flared bright pink nostrils.

Marin squealed. "Lace! Oh, look, look! A whole bolt of lace."

Twenty bearers on each side carried the unrolled bolt of lace as wide as the street; silver flowers with tiny shells, which shone even on this dull a day. "I hope it doesn't rain harder. That might ruin it," Marin said.

Arvi shrugged. "Sometimes the weather is too heavy even for the most powerful witch."

There were more guards with the Regent's red and silver house banners. Behind them came the bride.

She drove her own hand-polished wood *troikamal*, the three matched chestnuts stepping as high as her father's horse. Her over-tunic, in bride's red, filled the seat; the lace train was edged with tiny diamonds with two children on matching chestnut ponies to bear it, careful not to pull. Her hair was unbound, crowned with roses. "She looks as cold as her father," Megan said, and this time Serkai prodded her though she hadn't said it loudly.

More dancers followed and another powerful witch, a green witch who had images of mother animals with cubs all around to grant the new pair lots of children.

The crowd closed behind the last guards, still singing "Kha'khaya."

"Let's go in. It's really starting to rain," Ivar said. Below, the street looked more grey now that the colors were all gone past. "I hope it isn't too muddy on the plateau for them by the time they get there."

"My papa said the light-sky show might not be held if it rained," Megan said. "I wanted to see that. Mama heard that the Wizard was going to make a sky-dragon with light and pictures of Koru and the Bear and sunbursts and all sorts of things."

They clattered down the skylight ladder, talking. "Maybe it'll stop raining before tonight. Maybe the weather-witches can push it away. I hope so. I like manrauq shows almost better than the toys," Arvi said.

"You bunch of heavy horse-feet! Come down out of the wet and drink some chai," Tsik said.

"Sorry about your plaster, Tsik," Serkai said. "We didn't mean to stomp it down." Megan looked for chunks on the floor but didn't see any.

"Well, I suppose I shouldn't have yelled quite that loudly," he said, closing his skylight.

They sat and drank chai and talked about the procession while the rain beat on the glass skylight. *I don't think I'd like to get married on a wet day.*

Chapter Eleven

Further Income: Fourteen bales of wool through Aenir'sford. Lading and carrying charges: 3 silver Fangs, paid. One crate glass ingots through Brahvniki. Lading and carrying charges: 3 silver Fangs, 2 copper Fangs, paid.

It was high summer and so hot in the Apprentice Hall that trickles of sweat oozed down Megan's back as she bent over her books. She chewed on the end of her pen and considered doing the last of her extra work on the roof where it would be cooler under the potted tree, but shrugged to herself and bent over the book again, deciding to finish here.

Eighteen bags black-rock. Lading and carrying charges, vessel absorbed: paid.

Tax and customs: 1 silver Claw, paid. Seals received.

Profit on original cargo: 1 gold Claw, 6 silver, 5 copper.

She didn't like summer as much when she had extra work and couldn't just go jump in the Lake. Three whole days to Hand-ending. She couldn't wait.

Shareholders demanding payment on delivery, charges: 18%, 10% & 5% of profit, respectively. Captain/shareholder: 67% . . .

"Megan," Master Zyatki said from the door, "your mother sent a message that you're needed at home."

"At home? Why? What's wrong?"

"I don't know, Megan. You have leave to go. I'll pass on your excuses to your teachers."

"Thank you, Master."

"Run along then." Megan slapped the book shut and tossed it on top of the others on her shelf, yanked her sandals on. She pulled on the tie holding her hair back, to tighten it, as she ran down the stairs. There weren't many people around in the mid-afternoon heat. They'd mostly be somewhere cool inside the mountain rooms or under trees or snoozing. A fruit-seller languidly waved a fly-whisk over his baskets of berries, looking up under his hat as she ran by.

It's hot. What's happened? Is it a problem with Marte? Is it Rilla? It's probably that. Koru, Goddess, keep us all safe. Running like this, without knowing exactly what was going on, reminded her of the long-ago run to get Marte's help, even though it was bright midday instead of midnight.

She tried to reassure herself, but if the news were good her mother wouldn't just have sent a note summoning her home. She could hear her steps echo all the way across the bridge.

She ran again, holding her side against the ache of a stitch. A flock of pigeons burst out of her way as she turned into Cooper's Lane. The Flats doors were open to let in all the breeze, all the galleries opened. Everyone from the Peach was out lounging, but she didn't stop to wave. She almost forgot to jump the fifth step down where Blue always slept, stumbled, and he climbed the railing, yowling at her.

"Mama, I'm home, what's wrong?" The door would be open; she'd hear. Shen looked out.

"Megan, good, you're here. Meg, your Papa . . ."

Megan stopped for a second, not wanting to be rude, but she could hear her mama crying, so she squeezed by.

"Megan," Shen said helplessly.

Ness was sitting on her cushion, hands over her face, rocking. Megan knelt next to her, threw her arms around her. *Papa?* "Bylashka, they took him." Ness clutched her daughter. "He was just where he was supposed to be. He had a paid license to tell stories on that spot. Signed. But they just took him."

"Who? Who took him where, Mama?"

"The Guard. They did another sweep and . . . he's in the dungeons, I think. That's all I know. I tried to find out. The Guard wouldn't let me see him, I only had copper bits, not silver. All he would say is that a one-armed man had been brought in with other suspected thieves and riff-raff."

"Oh, Mama. What are we going to do?" Megan choked as she realized. Her father, in the dungeon. Helpless tears welled up. It was hard to get people out of the Nest dungeons once they were in. *What are we going to do?*

Shen hugged them both together. "We'll help you as much as we can, Ness," she said. "I'm sure our friends at the Peach and perhaps your Gospozhyn will help, too. He's a jeweller and should help his apprentice." She nodded at Ness. "If he has any shred of decency in him. Hush, hush now, Ness. You'll find a way to get him out."

Megan's mother dried her tears on her shoulder and hugged Shen with the arm she didn't have around Megan. "Yes. I've been acting without thinking. I've got to find out how much it would cost. If only the courts were open. It used to be that they couldn't just drag you away without evidence of wrongdoing."

"Great Bear grant that Ranion brings justice when he rises." Shen rubbed her hands together. "Well, we'd best get started trying round up some Claws. I have one you can borrow."

Mama looked at her, then down at her hands, then at

Megan, trying not to cry again. This was no time not to accept charity. "Thank you, Shenanya."

"Oh, go on with ya. I'd be a fine friend if I didn't help, now wouldn't I; like those white-nights friends who dumped you when you weren't Middle Quarter enough."

The old gang will help us, Megan thought. Her other friends at the Guild would help, too, and maybe Gospozhyn, but she didn't say any of this to her mother. *She wouldn't like to know where some of the bits are from, even if they do get Papa out.* Megan was fighting tears because that wouldn't help right now.

"I'll have to arrange an appointment with the Guard Commander," Mama said quietly. "Svaslasfyav isn't known to be a fair man."

"Pay him and he's fair enough," Shen said. "He's saving for his days of peace when he's old."

"Mama, should I come with you?" They looked at Megan.

"No, bylashka. No, you do what you can, borrowing."

"All right, Mama, I'll start at the River Guild. I've got friends there. And I'll come back tomorrow, okay?"

"That's my strong girl."

"Would Aunt help?" Shen coughed and Megan glared at her. *Aunt's kin, even if she is a shit.* "I could ask her, instead of you, for Papa." Megan remembered what Aunt said about Mama never to come crawling to her for help. *I can*, she thought. *And I won't be crawling. She better help Papa, we've tried our best to help her. If she doesn't, well, I'll tell Rilla and we'll clean out her silver when she's drunk.*

"My mam doesn't have any silver right now," Rilla said. "She spent it on fixing the still."

"Shit." They had to find some more money. Gospozhyn had looked solemn when she'd told him; said he'd see what he could do, but it was going to be hard to get. He was angry, too. He said, *"Does he think your poor mother is made of money?"*

A gold Claw is what the Guard Commander wanted,

to let Lixand out. A gold Claw. He might as well have asked for a steel Claw, worth twice as much. Most of the River Quarter didn't see silver from one year to another, and he wanted gold. Mama looked upset but determined. She thought that he asked so much because she spoke like Middle Quarter. *Shit on him.*

The Other Guild had been better to the family than anyone else in the City, even more than their own kin. *I wouldn't care if I owed them the bribe price for years and years.*

"Thanks anyway, Rillan." She nodded and fingered through the stuff they had between them on Megan's kerchief. They were sitting in Megan's favorite summer hiding place, an old forgotten roof garden in a partly burned-out building. The two of them had often played here before; for a more serious purpose now. *I don't have time for kid's things anymore.*

The gang got together, and all of the hunting in the Market scraped together a copper Claw's worth of bits. Megan shivered, thinking of her papa in the Nest dungeons.

Koru, be with him, keep him safe. Don't let them hurt him. He never hurt anybody in his life, and if something happened to him it would be even more unfair than everything that has already happened. My papa's better'n most people in this City and Mama loves him and I love him, so please keep him safe.

She felt empty, crazy. The Nest had swallowed up her Papa. She looked up the City to where she could barely see the point and the banner on the highest red dome of the Nest, and wanted to see it burn.

They managed to scrape it together, somehow, half a year's rent; with everyone's help, even Aunt Marte. She'd come, just yesterday, and given them three silver Fangs.

Lixand had paid his license fees to the Other Guild through the River Guild office, so they added in because he was one of theirs. Mama's Gospozhyn had given some and so did people in the Flats, except for Zazan and the landlord and his wife. Rilla and Megan sold their knives back to the cutler.

There would be a birthday celebration for Zingas Avritha tomorrow and the whole City was disrupted for a few days. Shen advised that they should wait and see if they would clear the dungeons as they had on Ranion's birthday, but Ness said that the Guard Commander wanted his money now and that every day she could spare Lixand the dark would be a blessing. Svaslasfyav would get half today, and the other half when he released Lixand.

Megan swept and tidied for when her mother would get back, thinking, *she shouldn't have to worry about anything that I can help with.* Blue came in and sat on Megan while she waited, and she talked to the cat, telling him everything she never told anyone else; not Tikhiy, not Serkai, not Ivar or even Rilla. Sometimes she almost thought he was answering, but Blue understood enough when she worried. *Papa'll be out tomorrow. Then everything will settle down again.* The white-nights were here, and with the galleries and the roof opened the sun still shone though it was almost midnight. She could see the light under the door, but it was shut because they needed the privacy.

Megan set Blue down and he gave her the "I wanted you to do that" look. When Ness came in she was sweaty and looked disturbed. They hadn't had a gold Claw, not quite, so she had to tell him that was all he was going to get because they didn't have another copper flake. Ness undid her hair and pulled off her clothes because they stank of the dungeon.

"He let me see your papa," she said. "He's in a cell with nine other men." They had water from the tap warming at the brazier and she washed herself all over, except her hair. *I guess she wants to scrub the smell off, she's rubbing so hard.* There were bruises on her legs, just coming up red. Megan, holding the towel, looked at them, then at her mother's face, not saying anything. "Thank you, Meg." She pulled on Lixand's old robe, rolled up the sleeves, and sat down with her daughter.

"I gave him a hug from you, and he sent one back." She folded up the collar of Lixand's robe and turned her face into it, rubbing her hands along her cheeks as if it were him touching her.

"We're to be at the Va Zalstva high gate tomorrow. When the celebrations are under way, we'll meet the Guard Commander and pay him and he'll let your papa go then, when no one is likely to notice."

Megan nodded, wanting her father now. She shivered and huddled under her mama's arm, hugging her. They held each other and Ness hummed "Mirror Eyes Lullaby" for her, though she was too old for that kind of thing.

The Va Zalstva was crowded, though not as full as when the wedding feasts were held; here and there were seats or whole sections empty. Megan pushed her face between the wooden bars of one of the high gates and looked down the bowl of seats to the sand. The rat pits, evenly spaced around the circle of the arena, were uncovered, grills pulled back against the wall. Sometimes you could see the rats jump for the edges; big black and brown ones.

The Dragon's box was on the mountain side of the circle, across and down from the gate they were at. It was hung with red satin, Zingas Avritha's favorite color.

Ness fidgeted nervously, trying to hide it, leaning against one side of the gate, looking at the street where the Guard Commander would bring Lixand.

Trumpets and drums sounded and Megan looked back down into the ring as everybody cheered. Avritha was just taking her chair, with her hand on Ranion's arm. He looked thrilled while she just looked calm. There would be a circus after, but Megan didn't care because her papa wasn't there to share it.

Ness started away from the gate and Megan whirled around to face the street. "You have him? Where is he? You promised him to me, here, today."

Commander Svaslasfyav, a very thin man, with a half-smile on his face, said, "You're here for your man then, River-scum?" Ness pressed her lips together but didn't talk back, just nodding, holding on to what scraps of hope she had.

"You won't get another flake until I see my husband."

He snorted. "I couldn't do a thing about it."

"What?" Her voice rose. "You were to free him, where is he!"

He lost his pose of superiority, looking uncomfortable for a second, motioned with his chin over her shoulder. "Down there," he said.

Ness whirled around, looking down into the arena. Megan stared at the Commander in his plain black uniform, then turned to look too. She saw her father in the chain of ten under the Dragon's box. The four chains, each with ten people, stood on the sand, blinking at the light. That was how the freeings had been arranged last time, for Ranion's birthday. A herald in the Dragon's box held up his arms for quiet.

"I didn't have to pay you, then," Ness said. "Or bed you." In the background Megan could hear bits of the herald's speech. ". . . to suffer the fate of all those who would disturb the City's peace . . ." Svaslasfyav stepped closer, grabbed her arm, and yanked her back from the bars. She pulled her knife and Megan wished for hers.

"No. Of course this might not be what you think." He jerked his head at the arena. "The Zarizan and his Zingas decreed this. Think a mere Guard Commander would dare sully the Zingas's birthday?"

". . . to show the swift justice in a ruling hand," the herald was saying. "As well as mercy." The guard were pulling the lines of chained people to their knees and unhooking them, cutting behind their heels and wrists and flinging them one by one into the pits.

Ness screamed, her hand reaching through the bars. Megan's face was pressed between the bars and they wouldn't yield, wouldn't let her through. Papa. Papa. They were going to kill her papa.

The guard took him by the neck ring and his arm and

he stumbled. The yelling of the crowd faded to an insect buzz, muffled and far away. Papa. He looked up and around at all the people as if they were the most precious things in the world; then at the sky and the sand under his feet. They unlocked the collar and the knife flashed in the guard's hand, three times, and the sand soaked redder. Lixand folded back on his legs as if he could stop the cut that was already done, cradling his arm against his chest, and the red soaked into his grey shirt. He had squeezed his eyes shut as they cut, then he opened them again and looked up, around at the high gates. Megan reached, screaming, with both hands as he looked, not knowing if he saw.

They held him upright and Megan thought she could see tears on his face; they pushed and he fell sideways into the pits where the rats were squealing, loud enough to hear, high, high over the noise the crowd made, and blood sprang up, bright drops, just for a second. *Papa. The rats. Papa, no. Please.*

Megan had borrowed Gospozhyn's spare knife without telling him, and got Ivar and Aage to come with her. Svaslasfyav used her mama, and her papa was dead. Ivar and Aage hadn't wanted to come at first, but she'd told them she would do it with or without their help. She hadn't been in the Guildrooms at all the last few Hands, but they thought she'd been staying with her mama the whole time.

It was one of the few dim hours in the summer, when it never got dark, but wasn't daylight either. She lay on the roof of the house in the First Quarter, across from where Svaslasfyav had gone in. Ivar lay flat beside her, and Aage was on the roof across Bolduschchy Street. *My papa's dead.*

They hadn't even had Lixand's body to take up and give to the birds. Ness had cried his name to the wind and cut bits of their hair, but her mama hadn't said anything since then. She would sit and cry, or try to but didn't have any tears left. She would make a hurt sound in her throat, like a moan or a whimper and Shen would hold her hand and wouldn't leave her alone for a minute.

Megan had wanted to get Serkai to help, but he was in guard training and would have to report it and they would have gotten caught.

A light shone in the street as the door opened and Svaslasfyav came out. She'd been following him the last few days. He came here to visit his old father. *His papa*.

He walked down the middle of the street whistling, and the children kept up with him up on either side on the house tops. He'd have to turn down *that* narrow street to get back to the Nest.

He hit the trip cord and tucked and rolled and almost came up standing, except that Aage hit him in the head with a cobble as he came out of the roll. He staggered a step or two with his daggers already out, then fell on his face. The lantern boy was already running, squealing for the watch.

She didn't want to touch him but did want to hurt him. Ivar and Megan slid down, lashed Svaslasfyav's wrists together and Aage threw down a rope. She tied a loop under the commander's armpits while Ivar swarmed up the building and he and Aage hoisted him up. Megan snatched up the trip rope and climbed after. When the Watch came, the street was dark.

They used the ropes to carry him over several roofs and down to an alley in Middle Quarter. Sweat ran into their eyes by the time they got him to down to where no one would bother them, in the River Quarter.

I hate him. The back of his head was sticky where Aage hit him, his hair all clotted together. She pulled his mouth open and grabbed his tongue; cut most of it off, sawing. His tongue was sticky, and when she cut it, it was like dead meat; trying to slide out of her fingers. She turned his head and the blood drooled down his chin so he wouldn't drown.

He tried to scream when he woke, thrashing against the ropes they had him tied with. She gagged him anyway, to soak up the blood.

He pulled at the ropes tying his wrists and ankles, shaking his head, no, no. The pupils of his eyes were different sizes. He choked, coughing against the gag.

"You used my mother even though you couldn't get my father out of the dungeon." He shook his head again, shivering like a wet dog.

"Aage, hold his head still." He did as she told him, looking sick. She put the point of the knife against Svaslasfyav's left eye. He tried to wiggle away, whimpering, but Megan leaned her weight on him and Ivar held his legs. She pushed and his eye popped like a grape. He yanked loose, flopping around, almost biting through the gag, slamming his head into the wall as if that would make it stop hurting, slobbering blood until they caught him and held him still in the mud. He trembled harder, then went limp under their hands.

Her hands were sticky. She thought of the rats and her mother screaming and popped his other eye. Then they waited. It was so late there wasn't anyone out and no one heard the sounds he'd made. *I want to wait until he wakes up.* Ivar pulled in his breath to say something and Megan shook her head at him, glaring. She didn't want to say anything. He'd try to convince her it wasn't a good idea. *My papa felt something like this and he died.* His guard had killed Papa for Avritha and Ranion to watch. *My papa who never hurt anybody.* She had tears on her face, but her mouth tasted like blood where she'd bitten through the inside of her lip. It stank in the alley because of the garbage against the walls and the smell from the guard captain as he pissed himself.

Wake up, you, so you can feel more of what Papa felt, what Mama felt.

She cut his hamstrings and the strings on the backs of his thumbs so he'd never be able to hold anything again; Serkai said something about it once. Every time he woke up it was with a shake, as if he were fighting not to, whining. Aage threw up into the dirt. Svaslasfyav wouldn't die, but someone would have to look after him the rest of his life. He was alive, which was more than her papa. It wasn't enough. It wouldn't bring Papa back. It wouldn't make Mama feel better. *He isn't hurting enough. He can't. I can't make him hurt as much as we do.* She looked down at him, tied and his face bloody, his hands clawed, his toes trying to curl up to his shins, bleeding strings of black in the dim alley, wanting to throw back her head and scream and stamp on him, but it still wouldn't be enough.

She whipped the knife into the dirt and pounded on the garbage with her fists, somehow on her knees . . . *my teeth are going to break I cant make any noise IcantIcant-Icant . . .*

Ivar and Aage held her, one on each side. "Your mama needs you," Aage said in her ear, his breath smelling of bile. She shivered, wanting to throw up, still wanting to make everybody whoever hurt them feel as much hurt. *I'm not sorry. I'll never be sorry.* She got up and the two boys let go of her. "Come on," she said. "Let's finish it." She smashed his balls with a brick.

They untied the Guard Commander, grey and cold with shock, and dragged him out to a road where someone would find him, then went down to the river to wash. They picked their way to the water from the dried mud on the edges. Megan looked down into the water under the bridge, listened to the cold gurgle, feeling watery inside, sweat pouring tracks down the blood on her face. She could feel it all over her, drying on her hands and cheeks, sticking her clothes to her body.

She pulled off her shirt and pants, shoved them in the water, feeling the blood yank on her hair and skin, watching the dark stain float out of the blue cloth, get whisked away by the current. The water was cool, raising goosebumps even in the heat, the stones in the mud sharp. She lay flat, holding onto a rock; ducked under, hearing Ivar and Aage's voices cut off, the thumping gurgle of the water running over the rocks midstream just an arm's reach away, letting the water wash the blood and hate off her.

She didn't feel anything now. Ivar looked at her as if

she'd gone crazy as they pulled their damp clothes on. She expected to feel sick sometime, but not now. Now she was going home to look after her mother. Koru . . .

No, I'm not going to pray. I prayed before and my papa died. If there is a Goddess, she doesn't give a damn about us. We have to look after things like revenge. There probably isn't a Goddess. She looked down at a blood smear on a stone near her foot and scraped mud over it with her boot. *No, I don't think there is.*

Chapter Twelve

"Mama, you have to eat something." Megan smoothed her mother's hair back away from her face and put the bowl down on the floor.

"I'm just not hungry, Megan-mi." Ness turned away, rubbing her hands up and down her arms as if she were cold. Her hair was dirty, hanging around her face, and her eyes red-rimmed. She'd started getting dressed again, even going to work, but her Gospozhyn wasn't happy with her any longer. She was doing simple polishing but no cutting because she didn't care enough anymore.

In the summer, Megan had seen to paying back everyone who had lent them money to get Lixand out of the dungeon; had seen how little was left. She hadn't been staying at the Guild Apprentice Hall at first, because of her mother, but she still was there for lessons, and used the Guild baths.

Their room smelled musty and close, the autumn rains having started early this year. Ness pushed her spoon through the barley stew, not interested.

"Mama, if you don't eat, you'll get sick."

Ness sat and listened for a moment, as if that's exactly what she wanted, then jumped and looked at her daughter, instead of through her. "Megan, love ..." She stopped as if the words were too big for her throat, the easy tears welling up.

"Mama."

Ness held out her arms and they held onto each other. "It'll be all right. It'll be all right. It's got to get better." Megan didn't know how, but saying the words somehow helped.

Her mother nodded. "I suppose I should do something, shouldn't I?"

"Un-huh."

For the first time since the summer heat, Ness looked more like herself. "Don't grunt," she said. "It'll give people the wrong impression."

Megan's smile started slowly. It had been too long since her mother had bothered to correct her in any way. "Yes, Mama."

Ness got up from her cushion and wandered the room, picking things up and idly putting them down again. Shenanya knocked on the open door. "Ness? I've got to deliver a bit of lace to a lady on Bolduschchy Lane. Would you want to come with me then, for the walk? We could stop at the baths first—my copper."

Ness stopped, blinked. "Hello, Shen. I . . . that sounds nice. Thank you."

Megan threw Shenanya a grateful look as she helped her mother on with her coat. That afternoon Megan had come home from the Guildhall to find the lamp dry, the wick burned away into a sooty smear, their kraumak only lighting the darkest corner. Her mama didn't mind sitting in the dark anymore. Maybe that was why she'd been having all the little accidents that left bruised shins or arms, tiny cuts or burns on her fingers.

Ness often sat, turning an old shirt of Lixand's over and over in her hands as if she were looking for tears to mend. She was always getting his things out, as if he would be coming home soon and would need them.

When Megan asked, she would only say, "They remind me of him," and go back to looking at the shirt or the trousers or his best fringed belt.

Shen took Ness's arm companionably. "We'll have a nice talk on the way. The sun's come out for a bit."

Megan stood by the door, watching them walk away down the gallery where Pol, the landlord's middle boy was nailing up the winter walls. She closed the door behind her and stood in the middle of the room, looking at everything that needed doing; the full bowl of stew Ness had left starting to dry around the edges, the breakfast dishes, the wallbed standing open with the feather tick hanging out, the floor needing sweeping.

The room was full of silence and she found herself listening for her father's humming to himself as he used to, marking a waxboard with notes for a story. His cushion lay by the table as if he'd just gotten up to go to the jakes. She found herself straining her ears as if she could hear him if she tried hard enough.

She gulped, swallowed tears, bent to pick up the shirt her mother had been turning over in her hands, and stood holding it as if she'd forgotten where it should go. She buried her face in it. It still smelled faintly like her papa and soap. That brought the tears. She moved blindly over to where his pillow was, now just for guests, burying her face in it as if it were his shoulder. There wasn't anybody to cry on, not anymore. *Mama needs me. I can't cry on her shoulder. It wouldn't be fair. Nothing's fair. It was wrong. All wrong and it's Ranion and Avritha's fault. They're supposed to make it better and they killed my papa who never did anything wrong.* She sobbed until her eyes were red and dry and her nose felt swollen and hot and the silence was there, would always be there, because it was the silence waiting to be broken by Lixand's voice.

She lay still for a bit, then she got up and started cleaning. There was too much to do that Mama couldn't, and there was the schooling to do as well.

Her hands were wet with the washing up when someone tapped on the door. "Hello?"

It was Pol, nervously twisting his hands together as he stood in the hall. "Hi. Umm. Well, me mam sent me down ... I hate asking but she said I should." He coughed. "Mam said you'd been good tenants but, well ..."

"What, Pol?"

He blushed and Megan thought that he'd never make a good landlord. "It's the cycle's rent ... it's only a bit overdue."

"Mama paid that, didn't she?" Megan's voice sounded thin in her own ears. *Mama forgot? Mama never forgot, not once she told Shen that she could manage, and that was two months ago.*

"Well, mam said not." He looked down at Blue who wove around their ankles, purring. " 's long as ye know."

"Thank you, Pol. She must have forgot. If you wait, I'll get it." Megan scooped up the cat. No, if her mother had just forgotten, then it was in the box. Blue squirmed and jumped down. She went to her parents' cupboard box and hesitated. It was her mama's business, something that Mama and P—that Mama was supposed to look after. *But if Mama can't, I have to.* Feeling worse than a thief, she opened it and searched for the rent pouch under their papers. She weighed it in her hand, wondering. Ever since she'd been helping with her Bits, Papa had let her help keep track and the pouch felt too light. "Hold on a second, Pol," she called over her shoulder, and counted out the coins. It was short. Not much but still short. *If it's short and we don't pay, we'll be in the street soon with nowhere to go.*

She counted it out to Pol. "It's mostly there. I think Mama has the rest"—*I hope she has the rest. She has to*—"and she'll be around today, I think." *I hate lying. I don't know. It's not a lie, really, I just don't know for sure.*

Pol grinned and nodded. "Okay, 's fine. Mam said yah'd likely forgot, what with all—uhm, well, *that.*" He blushed again, suddenly interested in the wood grain at his toes. "Sorry," he stammered. "Din't mean tah remind ya."

"It's okay, Pol."

"Right then, Goddess guard."

"Yeah, thanks." *Like She guarded my papa? There isn't a Goddess.* "You too."

She sat down and thought about the money, wondering what her mother might have done with it. There wasn't that much food; a little flour, a crock of peas and beans. There wasn't any fruit, or bread—not even stale—no meat or even any milk.

She started counting up the things that had to be paid for aside from food. Clothes . . . Mama hadn't spent anything on clothes since the summer, except for new boots. A new coat? No. There were Guild fees that her Gospozhyn mostly took out of her pay; tax, always too much tax. Lamp oil? No matter how she tried to balance the money, it always came up short.

Maybe she had lent some to Shen for some reason. That was probably it. *Should I ask her? Am I supposed to ask her? I can't, Mama's always been on time with the rent. She'd never forget—but she did.* It made Megan feel like a coal had just kindled in her chest. If her mother could be unreliable . . . *I have to keep an eye on things. I have to worry about it or she might forget again and we'll lose our room.* She felt helpless and small, fighting huge darknesses she couldn't see; the whole world, it seemed. Everything.

"Hi, Rilla." Megan hugged her cousin, who met her at the Apprentice Hall gate. It was growing dark, lamps being lit and kraumak lanterns unhooded in the dusk like a carpet of fire-fleas glowing on the walls of the city.

"Hi, Meg." Rilla squeezed back then tickled under Megan's ribs. Megan squealed and tried to wiggle free. "Feel better?"

" 'f you stop, Koru, stop that!—eek, I'll—stop—tan

your ass—'f you don't—" Panting, she wiggled loose, tickling back.

"No fair!—hey!—I'm littler!"

"Why'd you start, half-bite?"

They played tag through a couple of streets, then ran down to Megan's hiding place. The cracked mosaic was still warm from the sun, though the air was cold; winter was coming fast. Megan was glad that her mother had straightened out the difference in the rent when she and Shen had gotten back. It would be suicide to be out on the street in winter.

Megan sniffed. "It's gonna rain. T'night or t'morrow, then."

Rilla giggled. "You're starting to sound like Dimi when he forgets to 'talk up'." Megan bristled.

"I do not. I don't! Yer wro—" Then she stopped, listening to herself. "I suppose ye—your right. I'm starting to sound River-like."

"So, 'zat so bad? Nohow like out-city, that'd be a prigging, that."

Megan wrinkled her nose, thinking. Her Gospozhyn at the Guild had been coaching her in other dialects and turns of phrase, but she'd never thought to listen to her own speech patterns. When she spoke, it was more carefully than usual. "That's funny, hearing you talk like that Rilla, but we have to be careful to sound like Middle, at least."

"Whyza—Why is that?" Rilla pulled the words apart with difficulty.

"We're not here forever. I mean, we started better and if we want to be better we have to sound like it, or everybody'll laugh at us behind our backs when we get enough money to get out of River. Nobody'll respect us."

Rilla thought about that, dropping pebbles onto the cracked tile from a height. "I suppose." She sounded doubtful. "You're more Middle than we are—mam and I."

"Bullshit!" Megan said firmly, grimaced, then changed it to, "That's . . . um . . . nonsense!"

Rilla tossed the pebble into one of the holes in the tile; they listened to it hit one of the old beams a floor down, then the couple of seconds later it hit a puddle in the bottom, *plink*. "Y-yes," Megan continued. "We're family, kin, and if I'm Middle Quarter, so are you."

"Okay." Rilla thought a bit longer. "Mam's with your mama. One of our neighbors said something about her being *slough-kin* who didn't care about her own, and mam got offended. She said she'd show high-snot idiots that she was as good as any of them and could look after her kin as well as any."

"Mama won't like Aunt being there all the time."

"I guess not. I wouldn't, though my mam's been getting better. She's been dry after she blew it all getting drunk when Uncle Lixand died."

Megan swallowed the hurt feeling, waiting for it to go away as it always did now; it was getting easier. What she tried to hold on to was her anger, which was hard but getting easier, too.

Megan, arms full of clean laundry, walked carefully through the doorway and put it down on the chest. Tikhiy had helped her, so the washing had only taken half the time it normally would and the sun was still out. She didn't see Ness right away. Her mother sat with her back to the wallbed in the corner where Megan's bed had been. She held the kitchen knife in her right hand, making a pattern of small cuts on the left, smiling.

Megan stood, staring. *It wasn't accidents. She was doing it herself*. Anyone in the City knew what that meant; especially mixed with the faint, sweet smell of the DreamDust in the room.

DreamDust turned the pain you felt into pleasure. A Haian would use it only for the dying, if they used it at all. In a weaker form it was sometimes used to blunt grief. Once or twice, even a little more, was safe enough, but more grabbed you by the throat.

"Mama!" Megan was too shocked to do more than exclaim.

"Bylashka . . ." Ness smiled dreamily at her daughter, then down at her hands. "It doesn't hurt anymore. Not now. Isn't this interesting?" She held up her hand, where the faint cuts bled. "Look." She brought up the knife and laid another across her palm, cutting head, heart, and life lines.

"NO!" Megan pulled the knife away from her mother, who didn't resist, only blinked at the seeping cut. "That's where the money's been going. That's why you haven't been eating. Mama, you'll die. You can't keep doing this."

"Oh." Ness blinked as Megan salved the cuts, scolding. Then she just sat and watched Megan search the bed and the room, finding one other packet of Dust.

"Mama, you're going to bed and sleep it off."

Ness got up at Megan's insistent pull on her arm, turned as if she were in a dream and, laughing, slapped Megan across the face.

Megan stared, her hand covering her cheek. *She hit me.* The words floated through her mind like a bubble in syrup. *She hit me and laughed.*

Ness grabbed the hand Megan had folded around the packet of Dust and pried her fingers open. "Give it. After all I've been through I deserve a little pleasure." She stopped and looked at Megan. "I'm not addicted. I can stop any time I want to, I just don't want to."

"Mama . . ." Megan whispered. "Don't, please. Please don't. It'll hurt you—"

"No, it won't!" Ness cried. "This is the best it gets for now, forever!" She shook the fist in Megan's face, clutching the packet so hard that the stitches tore. She stopped, looked at the powder on her fingers, sticking to the salve, and slow as a nightmare, reached up to put her fingers in her mouth.

Megan, forgotten, backed away from her mother. She dodged around Ness and ran for the door, taking the knife with her.

She ran for her hiding spot and sat for a long while, hugging her knees. Then she got up to go to Marte, though she didn't want to. Shen, Dimi or Varik were good friends, but only kin could really help . . . if you could persuade them to.

She walked down to her aunt's rooms, torn between getting help and the fear that Marte would laugh in her face. *It's Mama who needs help and Aunt said "Don't come crawling to me." But it's me asking, not Mama. And there was the neighbor who made her feel bad about being slough-kin.*

She turned down Dogleg Alley, her steps slowing in the mud. The alley was far enough down the rift that it was almost Lake Quarter, with the street cobbles hidden under inches of mud washing down from farther up the City. On top of that lay garbage; more than around the Flats. Only the center of the street was hard packed, the piles of refuse on both sides rising almost hip high. Underneath, on both sides, you could hear a muffled rustling as rats burrowed in relative safety from the city's cats, or beetles spun webs of tunnels, chewing. In the spring rain these loosely packed ridges sometimes washed away, leaving the path in the middle of the street raised.

Doorways were, often as not, dug down below the level of the street, steps cut into the muck that dried rock hard in summer. In winter it froze, but people had to be careful in spring and fall.

Aunt makes more money than we do. Why does she live in this mess? Her steps slowed further. *Aunt spends a lot of money on wine and wadiki. And Dust is more expensive . . .* She stopped, staring at a Duster lying sprawled out of door well, half across the street. She'd never looked at them, lying in the gutters or under bridges, sitting in the shadows of the Market, staring and laughing at nothing. It had never been important before.

The man stank of urine and shit, horribly cut by the smell of newly baked bread—the smell of someone starving to death. He was a naked rack of bones, great oozing patches all over his body, hiding some of the self-inflicted scars. Some of his fingers were missing. He was awake, eyes open, breathing rattling and wet, his lips and gums greenish blue. He smiled at nothing, flies busy around and in his open mouth. He giggled and occasionally coughed, but the only part of him that moved was his chest as he breathed. *That's what Dust does. That's what could happen . . . is happening to my mama.*

Megan gagged, backed up and fled. *No. No it's not. Not to my mama. She might not care anymore, but I do and I'll make Aunt care. I'll make her care.*

She ran, panting in the cold, fetid air between the narrow houses as if she could run from the memory of the Duster lying in the alley, until she stood gasping for air in front of the building where her aunt's rooms were.

She hesitated another minute, waiting till she wasn't panting any longer. *I'm always coming to Aunt, running. I won't anymore. It's not right. She'll always think I want something and, well, I'm going to stop it.* She walked down the steps to the door, trying to feel something more than afraid.

The inside the house it was almost as odorous as the outside. Musty wood, mud; a faint greenish almond smell that prickled the insides of her nose drifted down the hall from her aunt's rooms, from the drug still. Megan blinked back tears. It was like the smell of the Dust on her mother's fingers.

Marte hadn't yet taken down the summer curtain that was the door and it moved a little in the dim light. From inside there was the clink of clay bottles, the low almost tuneless hum, a mannerism very close to Lixand's, as Marte worked.

"Aunt?"

"Hey? Oh, come in." Megan pushed the curtain aside and stepped in, stopping because it was even darker inside than out, the only light a shaded kraumak over the table. The light glinted off the glaze of bottles on the shelves like beetle's eyes in the dark, ceiling a green fuzz of drying herbs, like in the old house but much closer overhead. It was warm and humid because of the still. Marte sat cross-legged at the low table, sorting bottles into a box rack at her elbow.

"Megan. Hello." Marte sounded sour. "Rilla's not here. She's hanging about somewhere, I don't doubt."

"Hello, Aunt. I didn't come to see Rilla; I came to talk to you."

"Oh?" Marte's voice went from merely sour to cold. "Another problem?"

"Yes. I thought you were the best person to ask because you're a Canter." Marte looked up, silent, curious but waiting for Megan to go on. "I need to know how to get off Dust."

"What!" Marte got up suddenly, unfolding herself quickly enough that the bottles rattled. "What would your father have thought?" Megan backed up but stopped when Marte just stood in front of her, squinting. "Come into the light." She pulled Megan forward by one shoulder. With cold fingers she tilted Megan's head back, peered into her eyes, sniffed at her breath. "It's not you that's on it," she said finally.

"No, but I still need to know."

Marte let go of Megan so quickly she staggered. "There's nothing to give anyone on Dust. They either stop or they don't. Mostly they don't; they just die."

"Can you help them stop?"

Marte looked at her from under lowered brows and finally said, "Sit down. You're going to tell me what's going on." For a second Marte looked like her brother, in the tilt of her head, as she bruskly pushed Megan onto the visitor's cushion and put a cup of chai into her hands. Megan felt something inside her crack and she started to cry, though she'd sworn she never would in front of Marte.

Her aunt stood a little awkwardly, patted her shoulder with bony fingers, then moved out of reach and let Megan cry herself out into her chai. "That woman," she snapped. "It's that woman, isn't it?"

"My mama," Megan said, gulped, and wiped her face with her hands. "It's because of Papa, I think."

"Well, she's just going to have to snap out of it!" Marte

slammed the lid of the box rack shut and latched it. "I can't do anything!"

"You won't even try?" Megan looked at her, put the empty cup down. "All right. I thought I could ask for Papa's sake."

Marte glared at her, her lips tight. "Don't. Don't you dare use that to force me to help your mother. If she'd tried harder to get Lixand out, my brother wouldn't have died."

"That's not fair!" Megan stood up. "We did our best for you, and now you aren't doing anything!"

"You're sounding more like an up-country, out-city bitch every day, brat." Marte's voice was flat. She stood up and slid the box onto its place on the shelf, her hands shaking. Megan stared at her aunt's back, whipped the door curtain aside. *I had to ask. I had to. She's a ... I don't have any words nasty enough, even the swear words. Piss, she saw me cry.*

"Megan!" Marte called from her doorway. "You wait right there. I have to lock up." She pulled the door to behind her and came after. "I didn't say I wouldn't," she snapped, stepping over the Duster in the street without a second look.

They didn't say anything to each other all the way up to the Flats, walled off from each other. Megan glanced up at Marte's face. *You're afraid*, she thought suddenly, as if a door had opened in her head. *I don't know what you're afraid of, but you are!*

The room was a disaster, worse than Megan had left. One of the cushions was ripped open, the laundry scattered around the room. One of the sheets had fallen into the lamp, but mercifully snuffed it rather than catching fire. Ness, half-undressed so the extent of her self-inflicted bruises showed, half-sat half-lay in the empty wallbed, the tick and the pillow tossed into the middle of the laundry. The water jar was broken, everything on the floor damp.

Marte clicked her tongue impatiently. "Well, start

cleaning up the mess. Dusters are destructive, when they're still well enough to be."

"Mama's not a Duster, she's just hooked on it for now," Megan said, ignoring the look Marte gave her.

Marte got the bed made and Ness undressed and into it as Megan cleaned. Under everything she found the arm ring that Varik had given Lixand, broken into three pieces. She looked over to the wallbed and clenched her teeth. *I don't understand.* She wrapped the pieces carefully and put them in her pouch.

It was Megan who got fresh water from down the street, after borrowing a spare jar from Shen, but it was Marte who had the strength to hold Ness down. "I need it. I need it," Ness cried, alternately clinging to Megan and Marte or struggling to get away from them as she sweated most of the Dust out of her system. Finally, like a collapsing puppet, she fell asleep, leaving Marte and Megan to clean up the soaked sheets.

"How long has she been Dusting?" Marte looked haggard as she sat over a bowl of porridge, after. "Do you know?"

"I thought the cuts and stuff were accidents. Maybe an iron-cycle?" Megan hugged her knees and shivered. *Was that too long? Was Mama going to be a Duster? She can't. She mustn't.*

"Well, she has a chance. The stuff can't have settled into her that deeply. If she's lucid when she wakes up and realizes, then she'll help us more as she comes off."

"Oh." Megan opened her mouth but Marte cut her off.

"And no there isn't anything else I can do, or give her. It'll be a couple of Hands before we can leave her alone. If she slides back then . . ." She shrugged. "I'll stay with her during the day, when you're at the Hall." She put the bowl down and ran her hands through her hair. "Whether she comes off, or not, we're quits as kin. I don't owe you or Lixand or anyone anything after this. Don't even bother asking."

Megan looked at her across the table, where she sat

on Papa's cushion, rinsing her mouth with chai. She didn't look like Lixand at all.

Why are you so? Are you still afraid of something? Why? Isn't there anything in you to give? She nodded to herself. That must be it. Marte had only so much to give and it was already gone. With some people being generous was always strong, but some people just cut that gift off at the roots and it died.

Megan gathered up the dishes and set about washing them. She had to tell Yneltzyn that her mother was sick and couldn't come in to work. She hated to lie, but Ness would be mortified if her Gospozhyn found out why. Megan would have to pretend that everything was fine, except that her mama was sick. *I'll have to get my books so I can study here, if I can.*

The first snow of the year tapped against her master's glass window, blowing white out of the dark afternoon. Yarishk folded his hands together with a sigh. "Megan. I know you've been through a great deal with your father's death and your mother being ill so often after, and I sympathize, but choosing to take on more when the house master tells me you've been staying up far too late at night to keep up your work, isn't a good idea."

"Gospozhyn, I need to learn as much as I can, as fast as I can. That way I'll be a journeyman faster and . . ."

He was shaking his head. "It's not that simple, Megan. You'll make yourself sick or your work will slip. It's more than book knowledge that makes a merchant, or anything else."

She bit her lip. She didn't want to say that she didn't want to go home, and felt guilty about it. Ness was off the Dust, but it was as bad as the summer just after her father died. Her mother kept trying to get more Dust or was sick with one thing after another, getting thinner, her eyes bright and feverish.

Yarishk looked at her as she sat on her cushion petting Sashi, and frowned. He wanted to help, but she wore pride like a coat and if a person didn't offer, one didn't pry. "Megan, why don't I see if we can arrange your cousin's lessons? The Other Guild understands some parent's whims in not wanting to apprentice their children and sometimes has to deal with them. Why don't you see if you can come up with the fee, using your latest lessons? I will teach her without formal permission, and you will have the extra work you want."

Megan smiled at him, her hands tightening so Sashi grunted and nudged into her armpit with a damp nose in protest. "I'll do it, Gospozhyn!"

"Nah, nah, softly. You go home to your mother the rest of the day and start worrying about this tomorrow." Megan's face fell a little, but it felt as if he understood, though she couldn't bring herself to tell him anything about what was happening at home. *I'll go scrounging with Tikhiy in the market after we eat, before I have to ... before I go home.* The snow was melting into rain. There wouldn't be many people out so it would be riskier, but with the wind up people didn't notice right away that their purses were gone.

That evening she headed home with a few coppers in her pouch and a string bag with vegetables. Maybe Mama would eat something tonight.

She trudged down the Stairs, feeling lower and lower. The cold rain had soaked through her cloak, first through the patches, then through the thin wool. She stepped around the streams of water running down the Stairs, but her boots were still wet. Her mood had started falling the moment she left Tikhiy. She'd wanted to see Serkai, but if she was "practicing" he didn't want to know. He was a squire now, with leather armor, starting to sound more and more like the DragonGuard, except when his voice cracked. When he kissed her, he was sometimes a little rough but always stopped when she complained. A few times they'd taken off all their clothes and stroked each other. That made Serkai shiver and moan and his member had just started to stand up when she touched it, hot and smooth, like a grown man's. He had a thin patch of black hair all around it and was starting to grow a thick line down his chest and back. She smiled to herself, thinking about it. He'd be starting a beard soon.

When he touched her, it sent sparks all up and down her back, a warm glow in the pit of her belly. The exciting ache between her legs, where she was just starting to sprout hair, was new, and she shivered just thinking about it. It was shiny and precious, something to share with your favorite person, the way Mama and Papa had always shared with each other; kissing and touching and holding each other close. She stopped outside the tenement, sniffing, wiping her runny nose.

With Serkai, she didn't have to worry. With him, everything was all right. She wanted to see him, but he would be in the Nest barracks now, probably eating. And she had to go in.

The smell of the turkeys in the bottom of the Flats rose thickly to cling inside her nose, pushed up from below by more stink and mud and noise. She hugged the string bag to her, peeking through the cracks in the winter walls, where the rain dripped through the atrium ceiling. *I don't want to go home. Mama'll just sit and stare or moan to herself, shivering. Or she'll be in a screaming mood, and stomp around looking for something, anything to do that her shaking hands won't ruin.* She'd broken her lace-frame in a rage the other day. She wanted Dust, but Marte was there or Dimi, so she couldn't get any.

Aunt Marte had said she was ready to give up because Ness had to decide not to Dust herself. She already called Ness a Duster behind her back.

The odor of cooking made her mouth water and she felt lonelier than ever. Ness used to cook like that. Megan cooked for them now, but Ness most often just pushed the food around the bowl. They couldn't afford anything to tempt her appetite, not even apples. For weeks Megan had been dreaming of the taste of oranges, waking up as she was biting into it, leaving her with the dry air of her wallbed filling her mouth.

Megan pulled the latch, opened the door, and stood

blinking on the threshold. The room was clean. There was nothing broken and the only person there was her mother. The kraumak shone on the counter where Ness was cutting—*cutting!*—tubers to roast. Her mother's hair was clean, pulled back away from her gaunt face. Her hands shook as she cut, bony wrists poking out of neatly tied sleeves, but she was being very careful not to cut herself. There was milk warming on the brazier and salt-beef simmering.

"Mmm—ama?" Megan wasn't sure whether she wasn't dreaming. Ness carefully put the knife down before turning, wiping her hands on the cloth.

"Bylashka." Her smile was painful but determined. "I . . ." Her voice broke and she looked away, ashamed in front of her daughter. Megan walked in, still not believing that her mother was back in spirit.

"'salright. There's some greens I brought." She held them out, arm's length, not trusting yet.

She saw the tears come up in Ness's eyes, but her mother didn't say anything except, "That was thoughtful, thank you." She took the bag, as offered, gently as if it were full of glass.

Megan watched her, throat choked with hope and fear, finally turning away to do her old job of setting the table; Mama's cushion, Meg's cushion. It was almost too frightening, this sudden return to normalcy.

Supper was full of careful words, Megan watching every mouthful that her mother ate. Ness ate slowly, steadily, as if trying to make up for the last cycles' neglect, though she didn't seem to want to eat.

"I convinced your aunt that it was all right to leave me alone," Ness said, putting down her eating pick. "I . . . I realized . . ." She twisted her napkin in her hands, a tear splashing down to make a small, dark round spot on the red cloth. She looked up.

"I want Dust but I refuse to need it. It isn't going to kill me, or keep hurting you. I've learned bad habits and it's going to take some determination to get rid of them, but I will. I swear off the DreamDust. By Koru, Goddess, Lady and Lord, hear me, bylashka."

Through the whole speech, Megan had held herself still, suddenly feeling older than the world, older even than her mother. It made her dizzy, that her mother should apologize.

"I—Mama, I can't make you keep that promise." Megan gulped and shrank away. Ness closed her eyes as if against a sudden pain.

"I know, Megan. I know. I have to keep that promise to myself." She sat still, like a Goddess image, her face full of pain, hands clenched, not reaching for Megan, letting her choose.

"Oh, Mama!" Megan flung herself into her mother's lap, banging her hip into the corner of the table as she reached out, hearing the dishes rattle, feeling familiar hands and arms hold her close. "Mama, I love you! I love you! It was like you went away. Don't ever go away like that again. I missed you."

Chapter Thirteen

Midwinter, Ness's fever struck after she'd gone out too soon with a bad cough, back to work. It settled in her lungs, clogging them so she couldn't breathe.

She smiled at Megan, who sat on the edge of the bed, holding her hands. "Bylashka . . ." Her voice was a cracked wheeze. She sat up, straining to look better than she was, to reassure her daughter. "It's all right. I've had a few illnesses this winter. This is just another."

"Mama, I might be able to get some oranges . . ."

Ness coughed, gasped a breath, coughed again. "No, love, they're too expensive." She eased back against the pillows, propped high to help her breathing. "I'm not that hungry, Meg."

Megan laid a hand on her mother's forehead. Her skin felt papery and hot, her lips cracked. Dimi had said he'd be back to check if the fever had broken—*it has to break, soon*—later on that night.

"All right, Mama." The water was low again, though Rilla had brought some in before she left as the wind came up, the ominous whistle that meant another blizzard blowing in; a night to stay inside.

Megan checked the bag of black-rock with her eyes as she sat, wondering whether there was enough to keep the room warm. *Water, the brazier has to stay lit, so that Mama doesn't have to be bundled up ... Dimi says no blankets until the fever breaks.* There would be enough, at least until Rilla came back. Her cousin had made excuses for Marte, saying that she was busy, but Megan knew better.

Ness's fingers trembled in Megan's smaller hands, the dampened cloths Megan had wrapped around her legs already dry. Her eyes flickered closed, then open, gaze wandering around the room as if it were full of mist and there was nothing solid to catch her eye.

The brazier hissed as Ness struggled for breath, her thin fingers picking at the sheet, and Megan tried to get her to drink, laving her face.

Shen looked in later, waving a hand at Megan as she put a basket of black-rock down by the door. "Here, I'll get you some more water, luv," she whispered.

"Thank you." The blizzard howled outside, bad enough that Megan could hear the Flats creak and shift under the force of the wind and snow, even one floor down.

In the middle of the night, as Megan wrung out another cloth, dripping the water back into the bowl, Ness opened unclouded eyes.

"Bylashka ... love ..." She stopped as if it were too much strain to speak, one hand fluttering on the mattress as if she were trying to lift it. She blinked and fell silent then, Megan hoping she'd sleep.

Then her breathing stopped, her hands going slack. Megan flinched away as if death were a presence she could run from, heart pounding, then she sat still, holding her mother's hands as if that would hold her to life. "Mama, no. No. Please, no. Koru, Goddess, Lady of Mercy, don't let my mother die. No. No."

Megan whispered that litany long after Ness's fingers were growing cool in hers. Then she sat listening to the lonely sound of her own breath in the room.

When Dimi looked in, Megan still sat holding onto her

mother. She looked at him dry-eyed and said, "My mama's died. I didn't come to get you because there wasn't anything to do."

Megan stood on the plateau in the freezing wind, ignoring the snow blowing in her face. Her hands wrapped her mother's cloak secure around her, holding it tucked close like an impossible hug. Though it was too big, it was warm around her mourning grey.

All through she hadn't cried. It was too much to cry for. She stood looking at the platform, listening to the ravens yawping. The wind whipped through the funeral poles, and an old raven hopped closer, impatiently cocking its head sideways.

"Get away! Get away!" Megan lunged at the bird a step or two, fists raised, cold wind sweeping into her clothing as she let go the cloak. "You can't have her yet!" It blundered into the air with a papery thrashing of wings.

Yarishk, standing behind her and next to Rilla, made to lay a hand on her shoulder, hesitated. Behind them, politely out of earshot, stood the handlers of the dead, waiting to raise the funerary platform up on its pole. Marte wasn't there, though Shenanya, Dmitrach and Boryis, Jerya and Yneltzyn were. The snow fell thicker, clinging to Megan's face and eyelashes, melting like the tears she couldn't shed as she knelt down by the platform. As she had so often through the early part of the winter, every time Ness had been ill, she put out a hand and smoothed the hair off her mother's forehead. Only this time it was cool, not hot. Ness's eyelids stayed shut.

I prayed again, when Mama kept getting sick all the time. I said I'd believe again if she were all right. That didn't happen. If there's a God, then it's the Dark Lord, because the world is all snow and bones.

Now on the plateau, Megan clung to her mother's corpse still, in the wind and snow, wanting to die too. Perhaps it had been her fault. Perhaps if she'd tried harder to get her to eat. Perhaps if she'd noticed sooner about the Dust, she wouldn't have weakened so. *Mama, I need you. What am I going to do? You're with Papa but you've left me behind. If I don't cry your name, some part of you has to stay with me.*

That evil little thought cracked the ice in her and she finally started to cry. She let go and got up, stepping back, the hot tears mixing with the cold melting snowflakes on her face. *I can't do that. That wouldn't be right.* She sobbed, standing straight next to the funeral platform, threw her head back, and screamed her mother's name into the wind.

"NEEESSSS, Weaaaveerrr!" The names echoed, flapping their way free, like the ravens roused by her scream. "Daughter of Anayita and Tomas of Raeschku Village!" With each word the body on the platform seemed less and less like someone she knew. "Lixand Weaver's wife . . ." She stepped back, whispering, "and my mother."

Rilla hugged her and Gospozhyn Yarishk stood by them as the handlers of the dead raised the platform, the pole grinding into the cairn of rocks, swaying with the weight. *Goodbye, Mama.*

Megan stood in the doorway looking at the empty room that had been home for seven years. Shenanya had tried to help, but Marte had come and said that she'd see to things, and since she had kin-claim no one said anything when the feather tick and the pillows were sold, the table and what few clothes Ness had had. Megan had bundled a shirt of her father's and her mother's cloak into her own things, so they might not be sold off with all the rest. Marte took the knife and Ness's good platter. The room was stripped.

"You obviously can't live here by yourself, or even at the Apprentice Hall," Marte had said firmly. "You'll have your place in my home." And that had been that. Marte had kin-right and was adult, her decisions final.

Megan looked at the bare room that she'd swept out as carefully as if her mother had told her to, for the next tenant, and wondered if she were dreaming.

She shook herself, hugging the bundle of her things to her chest. She'd hidden her best things at the Guild-hall, and would stay there mostly, despite what Aunt said. Rilla had been learning without being apprenticed for-mally and Megan had kept up her own 'prentice fees. *I'll make a merchant that Mama and Papa'd be proud of.* That set her tears off again as she closed the door behind her and set off down to the Dogleg, to Marte and Rilla's room. *I'm never going to call that place home, even for Rilla's sake. It's not my home and never will be.*

Marte had insisted she turn out the bundle when she got there and picked over every piece with pinching, disapproving sniffs.

"No wonder there was nothing left," she sniffed. "Too much spent on fancy things you'd just outgrow." Megan bit her lip, outraged. Her mother had embroidered the cuffs of their shirts when she'd had time. Marte lifted Lixand's old shirt and looked at Megan consideringly. *Don't take it . . . Just don't take it.*

Marte sniffed again and swept everything together into Megan's arms. "Your bed's over that side. Don't know what you've been taught but you'll keep it clean." She nodded at a spot under the shelves, where a pallet lay. Megan swallowed. *I know I'm dreaming now. A night-mare. Mama, I'd like to wake up now.*

Megan folded her clothes carefully, stacking them next the pillow of the strange bed that was now supposed to be hers.

"Here, brat! I won't have you being too sullen, you'll give me more grey hairs than you've got." Marte tapped Megan on the side of the head where the white streak grew, sharp fingers almost too hard.

"No, Aunt," Megan whispered.

"Right then. I'm going out. Stay, or go, as you please but don't touch anything of mine."

"No, Aunt." Megan had clenched her hands as Marte left, blowing out the candle, leaving only the kraumak that used to be Lixand and Ness's glowing in the dark.

She'd run all the way up to the Nest and asked to speak to Serkai.

"Megan." Serkai smiled at her as she met him at the gate.

"Hi, Serk." Megan hadn't wanted to go out, but Marte's room had been worse. "Serk . . ." Megan looked into his smile, not knowing what to say, full of words that couldn't fight their way out of her somehow. He lost the grin and patted her shoulder.

"Meg . . . look, it's cold out here. I could buy you a hot drink or something at the Cup."

She gulped and tried to nod, but the tears came back and he pulled her close to let her cry, stepping back into one of the niches in the wall by the gate. She knotted one hand in his long hair that he wouldn't cut until he was a full guard, crying into his chest.

"Sa . . . Megan. It'll be all right. It'll be all right. Cry. I don't mind. Here." He handed her his handkerchief. "My mama always said that if someone dies you cry for being left behind. Twice a day—once for you and once for them."

She snuggled close to him, feeling real for the first time since the funeral. Her life felt broken, like an iron wheel with three-quarters of the circle perfect but the fourth hammered flat, grinding on cobbles, pulling the rest of the wheel out of shape. The wind blew in on them, smelling of snow and smoke.

"Serkai, I don't know what to do."

He nodded, his chin nudging the top of her head. "Come on in. I'll sneak you in and we can talk. It's an emergency. Besides, most of the older apprentices are celebrating the end of testing."

It wasn't far, through two small courtyards and then into the squire's barracks. Once inside, at his motion, she pulled off her boots and carried them. He left his standing below his peg before they tiptoed in.

They scuttled under an open window into the corridor, where Megan could hear the scratching of a quill and the rustle of paper. They turned the corner and leaned against the wall for a second, getting back the breaths they'd held too long, and Serkai winked at her.

"That's the worst," he whispered in her ear. "Sergeant Tuqashevsky's easier to sneak by on the way out." He led her to a small wallbed and hid her boots in a cupboard under it. In the distance she could hear balika music and stamping and it made her feel more alone.

In the dark of the shut wallbed that almost smelled more of soap and leathersoap than Serkai, she cried herself out.

"They're gone, Ma . . . Ma and Pa . . . Pa and I have to stay with h . . . er!" The straw mattress rustled as he shifted so her head was on his shoulder.

"You'll be all right, Megan. I'm thirteen now, you're almost twelve, and that's only four years till you can marry me. I'll be a full guard, with a full guard's pay. I'll be assigned to guard some posh Zingas, or even the Zarizan's apartments—he'll be Woyvode by then—and we'll be fine."

She shifted, sniffed, and wiped her nose. "You're right. It's not all horrible. I have you as a friend, and Gospozhyn. There's Varik, and I bet Shen and Dimi and everyone at the Flats won't stop being my friend, even if I do have to live with Aunt."

"She's an asshole."

Megan shivered, wanting to see Serkai's face. She'd never heard him that angry, that hard before. "She's . . . she's my kin," she said, though she agreed with him.

His arm around her tightened. "Yeah, right. Sorry."

They lay together in the warm, stuffy dark without saying anything for a long time. *I'm never going to be able to talk to him about the Other Guild. He'd be duty bound to arrest me*, she thought. Then Serkai touched her face, stroking, feather-light down her neck.

"I love you. I want to marry you," he said.

She tried to smile. "We're too young, Serkai. It sounds silly when you say you love me." She hesitated. "I guess I love you too, I think."

"Do you want to make love?" he asked, his voice cracking in the dark. Megan nodded against his shoulder, and they squirmed out of the rest of their clothes, tangling trousers and shirtsleeves and long hair in the crowded space. "We have to be quiet, though," he whispered. "You aren't supposed to be here, and if we get caught my sergeant'll have the skin off my back and her tongue is almost as sharp as the whip."

"Okay."

Before, when they'd explored each other's bodies, it had been more giggly, sillier. Now Megan touched him almost solemnly, hearing his sigh, feeling him tremble when she took hold of him. He was careful, holding her like she was breakable when he kissed her. They'd talked about him getting inside her, but decided that they were too young and she'd probably hurt too much.

"Megan?"

"Yeah?"

"Do you like this?" He kissed her mouth, then her neck, then her navel and blew gently between her legs. She almost squealed, clapped a hand over her mouth.

"Th . . . that's nice." She caught her tongue in her teeth as he kissed between her legs, which he'd never done before. This time, the sparks glowing up and down her back seemed to rise higher and higher toward her head, flow down her legs and to the ends of her fingers, as if all her hair could stand on end until she gasped and clutched his head close, wanting to cry out.

Like a sheet of lightning from his mouth she climaxed for the first time, and when tears came again after, it was because she felt so good. *I shouldn't, I shouldn't . . . Mama and Papa are dead and I shouldn't . . . but I want to.* She felt tired, floating and suddenly not like a child any longer, almost as old as the world and as if she knew everything. Then she cried for herself, slow tears flowing down her face that she wiped away, not saying anything to Serkai.

"You taste funny," he teased, but she could feel him smiling against the skin of her thigh. When she pulled his hair he added, "But good!"

He slid up to hold her, but she wiggled down and said, "Fair's fair. Do men like that, too?"

She'd seen him climax before, when she put her hand on him. This time she kissed him there. He smelled strong and musky, groaned, and pulled her close, hands opening and closing as all his attention narrowed to what she was doing. She took him in her mouth and he came right then. He was salty and his member jumped against her tongue as she tasted him. *He tastes warm.*

The next few weeks were quiet. Marte had pulled Megan out of all but the basic classes, unwilling to pay for anything extra and since, as she explained, the child had a home in-city, it made little sense that the full apprentice fee be levied. Master Yarishk had to agree and return part of the fee. That meant that Megan could no longer stay in the Apprentice Hall or be fed there, and Marte had come with her to clear out her box.

"Aunt?" Megan asked as they walked down Chashiy Street.

"What is it?" Marte sidestepped a crowd around a street juggler who was calling people to toss snowballs into the things he held spinning overhead with only physical skill, not using manrauq.

"Wouldn't it have been cheaper for you to let me stay at the Hall, rather than at your house?"

Marte grunted. "I make enough money. It's a form of charity we don't need."

Megan looked down at the box she was carrying. *It doesn't make sense to me. It's not charity at all. You just wanted the money.*

After that Tikhiy met her at the gate every day and they walked to first classes together. Gospozhyn Edischch, Tikhiy's great-master had, just this iron-cycle, started giving her the separate lessons Megan had already been learning from her Gospozhyn. Megan's friend was better at geography and plain bookkeeping, and they still teased each other about Serkai and Ivar.

"Megan," Tikhiy said one morning, "do you think Ivar likes me?"

"Yeah, why? You planning to ask him to lose his virginity with you?" Megan answered almost automatically, then looked at her friend. She hadn't asked in a joking tone.

"Yes."

Megan stopped right there on the steps and hugged her.

"I'm so glad," she said in Tikhiy's ear. "He was asking and asking whether you liked him or Serkai!" Megan smiled, slowly, then more broadly. "Tikhiy's sweet on Ivar! Tikhiy's sweet on—mmph!"

Tikhiy took her hand away. "You shut your mouth!" She settled her book and slate more firmly on her hip. "That's nice. Maybe we'll be a quad when we're old enough." She leaned sideways and giggled as Megan dug a finger under her ribs. "Ow! What was that for?"

"For being a *bayishka*, arranging marriages at your age!" Megan laughed as Tikhiy just sniffed disdainfully. "I'll see you after my class with Yolculvik Varik."

"Okay."

That day was special, a type of warm glowing day that Megan had forgotten existed; a day when everything went right. It carried her through the silent dinner at Aunt Marte's, and the pallet almost felt like hers.

Marte had been morose for the last few Hands and the housekeeping got bad, so Megan and Rilla tidied after their schooling. Rilla was getting the lessons that Megan was struggling to pay for, prigging—*no*, she thought, *stealing. Gospozhyn said it wasn't right to pretty up something by calling it something else. Call a goat a goat and not high quality mutton*—stealing purses in the market, risking her hands every time.

Rilla put the scrub brush down one day and said, "Megan you ought to stop paying for my lessons with the Other Guild and use the money for yourself. If you get promoted fast, then you can look out for me better."

Megan put the broom down and, after thinking about it for a minute, said no.

"It won't help you learn things you need to know now, when you're younger. And it won't make me a grownup and able to dictate for the family in the courts any faster—if Regent Mikail is ever going to open the courts to the people again—so you'd better learn all you can now."

It was Rilla's turn to think as she aired out the cupboard under Marte's wallbed in the back room, Megan going back to sweeping around the table.

"All right. I guess it makes sense." Outside there was a faint thump, a staggering step or two, then another thump. Rilla straightened abruptly, her mouth going tight as she turned to the door. "Meg, is there wine or beer in the house?"

"No, but . . ." Megan stood still, broom in hand, as Rilla swore and dived for their gloves and coats by the door.

"Here, if you can get out for a couple of hours, maybe the rest of the day . . . she's gone and gotten d—"

BANG. Marte hit or fell against the door, groping at the latch. Megan turned startled eyes to Rilla, who understood what was going on.

Marte fumbled the door open and stood there, swaying. "Hey brat! Or is it brats, now? Yeah. Two of you. Whatcha doin'?" Her tone was a mixture of innocent curiosity and anger. Rilla and Megan stood speechless as she staggered in a step and swigged out of a flask she carried in one hand.

"Shit-it . . . 's empty," Marte said owlishly and dropped the jar, shattering it on the floor. "You, *whore'sbrat*! Cleanin' fer me are you? Not good enough, 'm I—"

"I'm no—"

"Shut UP!" Marte lunged for Megan, Rilla diving out of the way, under the table. Megan jumped sideways— *no room*—and was trapped by the wall and the broom she still held. Marte grabbed her by the ear and one arm, kicked over the pile of Megan's things in her way, and dragged her over to where the broken bits of jar lay on the dirt floor. "Clean it up," she snarled, shaking Megan hard enough to rattle her teeth together, then flung her at the mess.

Megan fell, holding onto the broom as if it could somehow protect her, sprawling over the clay pieces, felt one slice into her wrist, and cried out. *This can't be happening. This can't be real. Nothing like this could happen to me. She's my aunt. She's kin* ... She rolled to one side, dropping the broom, trying to crawl backward toward the door, Marte not giving her a chance to get up.

Megan saw her hand go back, the beginning of the swing, her head snapped back hitting the floor, the end of the full-armed slap a black-edged shattering in her head.

"Clean it up! Clean it UP," Marte shouted through clenched teeth. "Not good enough ... I'll show you, brat ..."

Marte's face was all Megan could see; familiar, inhuman. The flash of another slap, and another—whipping her head around, hair in her eyes, cold grit on hands, sharp pain in one leg. *She kicked me, help me, someone, anyone.* The last swing, a bunched fist, thundering down the dark.

She woke up a moment later. Marte had left the door swinging open, letting in colder air and the smell of sour cabbage from down the hall. Rilla sat, holding Megan's head on her lap and all she could muzzily think was *why?*

Why? And the answer. *She hates me.*

"Megan? You okay? You'll be okay. She's not usually this bad." Rilla stroked Megan's hair out of her face, then helped her up to the pallet.

"When ..." Megan started to cry then, and Rilla held her.

"When is she like this?" the younger girl asked. Megan nodded, throat closed by tears. "Whenever mam's hitting the sauce again, she gets like that. After one flask she gets ugly, and after two she gets too soused to aim prop-

erly. After three she passes out and it's all right, an ava-
lanche couldn't wake her."

Megan huddled on her pallet with the two blankets
pulled around her, her face and head and leg hurting,
holding onto Rilla. All she could think was, *Oh. That
makes sense*. The bruises were coming up and her wrist
stung where the cut had clotted. She sniffled, wiped her
nose carefully on the blanket because her handkerchief
was in the pile Marte had kicked over.

"Is she going to be back?" Megan asked, dizzy, the
idea frightening enough to make her sick.

"It's okay, it's okay, Megan, she'll be too drunk to hit
by then." Rilla grimaced. "And tomorrow she'll be sugary
sorry and apologize all over you and be so nice you'll
want to barf because you know she'll just do it again."
She got up to close the creaking door.

"Okay." Megan limped over to the water basin and
washed her wrist and face, then came back to the pallet
and started carefully folding her things together again.
"Do you have room in your box for my things?"

"Un-hunh, I think so," Rilla said, leaning over to help.

"Thanks, Rilla." The cousins worked together in the
quiet for a bit before Megan said, "We just have to make
sure there's always two jugs of wine in the house."

"Megan!" Rilla whispered urgently, from up over the
apothecary's shop, stopping her cousin as she was about
to turn into the Dogleg. "Don't go home yet. Can we
stay at the Guild for a bit?"

Megan peered up into the dark. At this corner the
buildings' overhangs leaned close as foundations rotted,
braced apart at the top by a couple of beams, cutting off
what little moonlight might have found its way to the
street. Rilla leaned out on the wooden bracers of the
second floor, over the window full of jars of leeches and
the chest with the thousands of tiny drawers. "Hsst, up
here!"

"Rilla? She's drunk again, right?" From the almshouse
next door, voices were raised, arguing. Her feet, in their

worn boots, were cold and wet. "It may be too late to get into the 'Prentice Hall, the gates are probably—" In the distance the garrison drum boomed, faint and echoing this far down in the city. "There, they'll be locked. Gospozhyn will have gone home."

"Won't Master Zyatki let us in?"

"He might."

"She's not drunk enough and I don't have any money for more wine or wadiki." Rilla slid down the remnants of an old, torn awning that crackled frozenly.

"Okay." Megan could have cried, her hopes of getting dry and warm going as cold as her feet.

They stopped under a torch bracket by Eksoticum, one of the unlicensed naZak whorehouses and taverns on this part of the Stairs. Rilla changed the one mitten she wore from one hand to the other, tucking the other in the armpit. "I lost one and now isn't the time to tell mam about it," she said when Megan looked.

"Yeah, don't give her an excuse."

Rilla looked down at their shadows, flickering against the snow. "She doesn't need excuses," she whispered.

Megan closed her mouth, her lips thinning. "She usually doesn't take out her hangover on you, but you can never trust it," Rilla continued.

"Rilla . . ."

"You didn't know. You just never knew how bad it gets." Rilla wiped her eyes clear of the snow that started falling around them, looking at the tall muffled forms of naZak passing by. "Now you do."

Megan stood in the torchlight that was dimming in the snow, the torch hissing as it bled hot pinetar. The world was shrinking around her, the dark pressing in. She shook her head stubbornly. *The world isn't this horrible. I know better.*

"Come on, I'll see if we can get into the Hall." Megan took a deep breath. "If worst comes to worst, I can try to pick the lock," she said, feeling in her belt for the finger-long bit of twisted wire she'd copied from Varik. "If I'm not good at it, yet, I guess I will be." She flung an arm around Rilla's shoulders. "We need to get more money somewhere, for the wine."

"Yeah," Rilla said, a little muffledly. "It'll be easier with you around, Meg."

"Sure, coz. And spring is almost here. Come on, my feet are turning into solid cobblestones on the ends of my legs." They started across the City, back to the River Guild.

"Oh, piss!" Megan swore as the third snowball she'd thrown up at the window burst with a muffled thump, bringing no response from Tikhiy. The sprays of snow shone against the shutters and stone wall. She stamped her feet, blowing on her hands. Rilla shivered.

"Meg, it's getting cold real fast and you've tried three times. Can you try the door? Please?"

The snow was slushy during the day and when the sun went down at night it froze into sharp ridges and hollows that during the coldest part of the night could cut through worn felt or thin leather. Megan's boots had started out soaked, now they crackled and she couldn't feel her toes.

"All right." She blew through the wool of her mittens again, feeling the damp warmth of her breath cool much too fast.

The smaller doors had leather and wood latches, and she knew the sequences would have been changed since Marte took her out of the Apprentice Hall, but she tried them anyway. Only the main door had a wood and metal latch with a key, that Master Zyatki kept once the Hall was locked for the night. She longed to have the manrauq to lift the key from its peg in his office, between the door and the stairs. Even if she'd had as much manrauq as her mother, she would only have been able to pull it loose to clatter onto the stone floor.

The latch was the beard of an ornately carved demon's head surrounded by oak-leaves, painted here and there with copper paint. The copper was covered with frost, as was the demon's keyhole mouth, and Megan was careful not to touch the metal with her bare fingers as she pulled the bit of wire out of her coat where she'd kept it warm.

"Pray the Watch doesn't come," she said to Rilla. "We can't douse the torches."

"Okay." Rilla's teeth were chattering, whether from cold or fear, Megan didn't know. "We can't go back now. If she isn't drunk enough, she'll beat us for being so late."

"Yeah." Megan threaded the wire into the keyhole, following the worn spot on the left. "Shut up for a bit." She felt as if there were a hundred eyes watching her, waiting till the door opened before crying THIEF! She swallowed, reminding herself that it was dark, and late, and Rilla was watching out for her.

She had two of the weights shifted and the third one refused to move. Sudden sweat trailed down her back and she felt it cool in the breeze that stuck icy fingers up her sleeves. She wanted to shiver, but if her hands shook she'd lose the tumbler. There was nowhere else for them to go this late. She considered trying to huddle with Rilla in one of the burned-out buildings and dismissed the idea. Even if it weren't the time of year for *graukalm*, the grievous-wind off the steppe, they'd still probably freeze to death. *Would the Sysbaet take us in? No, because we have a home and an adult relative ... piss on this lock ...* It clicked as the tumbler moved and she eased the bolt back. The door squeaked open a fraction, letting out a draft of warm, and someone said:

"Very well done, Whitlock. I trust there is some *good* reason for such a skill to be practiced this late?" Master Zyatki stood, with a very neutral expression on his face, leaning one shoulder against the inside lintel of the door, arms crossed.

Megan and Rilla stood frozen for a long moment. "Master ... ah ... yes ... well ... there is," Megan stammered, floundering for some plausible reason. Before she could think of anything, he frowned.

"You're both so cold you're blue! In, in, explain in my office next the fire." He shooed them in, and shut the main gate behind them with a boom, locking it again with the key. He herded the two into his office, supervised them sweeping snow off their shoulders and legs, pulling stiff boots and socks off, and had them next to the brazier warming their hands on mugs of chai all before Megan could think of anything.

Rilla clung to her cousin, silent. Master Zyatki had met her once or twice before but she didn't know him well. Megan, in the familiar office that smelled of chalk, paper and damp wool mittens, sipped at her chai and felt sudden tears welling that she hid by blowing her nose in her kerchief. *He's being so nice when he could be yelling at us.* What was she to say? That they hadn't gone home because their kin would beat them? It was private. It was something that kin didn't do, and if some did, well, it was their shame.

"Well?" he said, looked at Megan. One of the Hall ferrets rolled on his lap, chewing at his fingers.

"Mastery Zyatki, there . . . well, it's . . . uhm . . . like this . . . I . . . we . . ."

He cut her stammer off. "How old are you, Whitlock. Eleven?" She nodded. "Certainly old enough to give a straightforward answer to a question."

She blushed, looking down at her chai, wanting to melt into the floor like the puddles dribbling off her boots that stood by the door. She cleared her throat. "Master Zyatki, we had to come in to the Hall because my aunt, Rilla's mother, is . . . uhm . . . indisposed." She couldn't think of any other polite way of saying it. He looked a bit alarmed.

"Indisposed? Is she ill? Then why . . . ?" He raised an eyebrow at her.

Rilla blurted out, "Teik, she's drunk."

For a moment after the only sound in the office was the ferret, scrambling under some papers on the desk, and the crumbly sound of coals settling in the brazier.

"She's not at the passing out stage yet and we can't go home until then . . . we *can't*," Rilla plunged on. For a moment Megan had a wild hope that he might actually help them, get them out of Marte's hands as she saw anger flicker across his face, but then the hope withered. The only thing in his face was understanding and a shadow of helplessness.

"You can spend the night, you two." He sighed, looking older, rubbed his eyes. "This doesn't mean I can give you free room and board. The Guild isn't the Sysbaet."

"No, Master Zyatki, I know." Megan looked down at her chai, feeling Rilla leaning on her other side. *He can only do what he's allowed to, by law.* She didn't know what she was feeling . . . grateful that she was warm, that they had a place to stay, at least tonight. Angry, but she didn't know at whom. It was more than anger that she felt toward Marte, it was bigger than that, older. *Nothing's fair. No matter how hard you try, something or someone kicks you in the teeth when you fall if you're poor.*

"I know the way up to the rooms, Master." She put her cup down, trying to smile thank you at him.

"I'll have Lida show you up. You're officially guests." He patted them both on the shoulder, turning them toward the door of his office. *I know you're helping but that just makes me feel more like a stranger here, in my own Guild.* She fingered the picklock in her belt. *Crying hasn't helped me, or being nice. Nothing's fair. Make them give you what you need.* She held her head up as she followed Lida up the stairs.

"Good night, you two," he said from below.

"Sleep you sound, Master Zyatki," she said. Rilla took her hand.

Chapter Fourteen

Varik looked up from an accounting book at the Greeters desk as Megan tapped on the door frame. "Megan, yes. Yarishk isn't back from a meeting yet, but you're to go on in to wait."

"Thanks, Yolculvik."

He winked at her. "Examinations and reports are always hard to take, 'prentice. I remember."

Megan nodded and went past him down the hall to Gospozhyn's office. She didn't want to hear the report her masters had made, but it was the half-year.

She and Rilla hadn't had to take refuge in the Apprentice Hall more than once since the winter, and that time they'd managed to get Tikhiy to let them in and spent the night secretly, giggly and crowded in her wallbed.

Marte had sobered up more as the days started getting longer which in one sense was better because the money stopped disappearing and in others worse since she began paying more attention to what they were doing. Megan was glad, though, that they hadn't had to practice picking Marte's pocket for food money every time a customer paid her.

Rilla was taking more classes, clandestinely, and was a good unofficial apprentice, Gospozhyn said. Megan opened the office door and settled down on a cushion, looking around the room.

He needs to let someone in to clean up, she thought. *But he never thinks of it.* Rather than sitting and fretting, she got up and started hunting out all the old chai cups and piling them by the door for someone to take downstairs, and added more water and chai to the samovar hissing to itself in the corner. Then she gathered the papers where they had fallen out of piles, re-piled, exposing more of the mismatching colors of the thick rugs. *He could get rugs and wall hangings that matched if he really wanted to, cushions too. Olnykova laughs and says he pretends to have no taste.* She straightened the shade on the kraumak, gathered up three mittens, a scarf, one green sock and a headband. The next piece of clothing she picked up gave her a bit of a pause; someone's pink loincloth. She shrugged and added it to the pile. *None of my business.*

The knitted blanket for the nights he worked late and decided to sleep there was folded and put in its cupboard. *Why is it,* Megan wondered, *that most of everyone's life is cleaning up messes?* She went back to her cushion to wait, which she wasn't very good at, fidgeted a bit, then went and got a book from his shelf—the only thing he kept immaculate in the whole room.

She was puzzling over a translation—is that *"evaluation" or "enigma"?*—when she heard Sashi's claws clicking on the tile outside. The dog's nose poked the door open and she panted over and flopped down, her head on Megan's lap, burrowing under the book. Gospozhyn came in behind her, saying over his shoulder, "If the negotiations are stalled, then we'll stop talking takeback mortgage and discuss post-closing adjustments." He stopped in the door. "If all that fails we can move to part payment in escrow. You worry too much, 'Dela ... Oh, and about the new City tariff, we can't lobby for anything at the moment, Mikail—" He broke off, realizing that rather than finishing up he was continuing the discussion. "I'll talk later, over dinner perhaps? Goddess guard."

She heard Nal-Gospozhyn Tydela's muffled good-bye receding down the corridor. Megan got up as Yarishk came in, earning a whine from Sashi as her lap disappeared.

"Well, you're on time and I'm late. My apologies, Apprentice."

"Certainly, Gospozhyn."

"Well . . ." He looked around the room. "Bored? Ah, me, the silent reproach of someone tidier." He smiled at her. "Thank you." She nodded, half smiling, not wanting to say anything.

He sat down, pulled the lapdesk onto his crossed legs, and unearthed two folders as Megan settled down. In the silence, while Yarishk looked through the reports, Sashi lay down next her master with a contented grunt. "Megan, have a cup, if you like. I'll be a moment or two longer."

She poured herself chai and one for him, then sat down again while he stared into space over his steepled fingers. This office was one of the safest places in the world, Megan thought. When everything else went down, the Guild held steady. *They have enough money to weather storms.* He touched a finger to his cup, so she was free to drink hers. *Manners. Good manners. He noticed, even when he was thinking about something else. I'm going to be like that someday.*

"Megan."

"Yessir." She looked up from her cup, glad the waiting was over.

"I only have one question for my examination."

"Yessir." She twisted her hands together behind her back.

"Tell me the difference between a Guild captain and a freelance captain."

She blinked, startled because it seemed an easy question. Then she realized that it was straight out of advanced lessons.

"A Guild captain is subject to Guild controls. That

means that while prices are controlled, the quality of goods is controlled on Guild ships. It also protects those dealing with the Guild because if there is a problem, they can appeal to the Guild, even if the town, or city's courts cannot or will not deal with the dispute." He nodded, but didn't say anything so she went on.

"The UnGuilded deal in things that Guild captains won't touch, things on the edge of legal. Also, the merchants dealing through the Guilded are guaranteed either delivery, explanation, or compensation." She stopped, sipped nervously at her chai. *That was a bit disorganized. I'll have to do better next time.*

"Good enough," he said. "Your report from the River Guild is very good, though your attention to mathematics should be more careful. Your accounting skills are adequate but not the best."

"Yes, Gospozhyn."

"Since you seem to be approaching fluency in Zak dialects and Enchian and are adequate in Thanish and Rand, I suggest you expand your language studies to include at least the theory of Arkan."

"Gospozhyn." Megan interrupted him.

"Yes, child."

She put her cup down. "Isn't the Arkan Empire a little far away to worry about being able to speak to them?"

He nodded again, thoughtfully. "Many people think so, but it never hurts to know something of the Empire, since it dominates the Mitvald Sea and the land north almost to the ice. You will likely have to deal with them at some point if you trade through Brahvniki."

"I understand. If I study Arkan, could I pick Lakan or Schvait or Yeoli for the next language after?"

"You may. We'll see how your new courses settle first." He sipped his cooling chai, grimaced and put the cup on the floor for Sashi. "Your courses in history, geography and cartography are acceptable, though you seem to be shirking politics." He looked at her sternly.

"If they're all like the Nest, I don't want to know about them," Megan said stubbornly. "Gospozhyn."

"Well, they aren't. If you don't have a grounding in your own culture, you have nothing to properly compare once other systems are introduced to you. Which they will be, shortly."

"Yes, Gospozhyn." She felt her face get red, ducked to sip more chai. Sashi, finished with Yarishk's cup, ambled over to poke a hopeful nose into Megan's hand. The girl petted her then pushed her away.

"The more practical aspects of river trading we'll deal with when you're sixteen and we'll be able to send you on various ships to learn that trade, since you seem to lean toward owner/captain, though . . ." He held up a finger. "Not all merchants are lucky enough to gain more than shareholder status, mind."

He picked up the other file, flipped through it, then thoughtfully tapped one corner on the desk. "The report from your other Masters . . ." He smiled. "Master Zyatki mentioned that he caught you practicing—"

"I had to, that time!" Megan subsided abruptly at his raised hand.

"So he gave me to understand. You are progressing very rapidly due to the extra work you do. I will admit, you were right there." She nodded, but that was all. He raised an eyebrow at that, flipped the folder closed. "An examination is due then, for that," he said. Megan sat up abruptly, startled.

"I want you to pick the hardest target in the City that you think you could successfully get into and out of. I want a full and detailed report on how it would be done and the specific thing you mean to steal."

Megan blinked at him and didn't stop Sashi from lapping in her chai cup. This was the bluntest he'd ever stated an assignment for the Other Guild. He tilted his head at her and she shook herself. *Of course, he just wants the report.*

"Here, you, get out of there!" She turned her attention to the dog, snatching the now-empty cup away.

"You understand, Megan?" he asked quietly.

"Yes, Gospozhyn."

"I want to have that report in one Hand."

"Yes, Gospozhyn."

He smiled. "Other than that, so far, your marks are good enough, for all that you are doing. If you dropped one scholastic, I think I could have rated you top marks."

She smiled back, shaking her head a little abstractly, her mind all ready on the assignment.

"Kievir Vaizal?" Yarishk said a Hand later. "Her golden roses, she commissioned from the Karoshayie?" He looked at Megan over the paper he held. "Don't you think that's a bit ambitious?"

She shook her head. "No, Gospozhyn."

"She's involved with the Talistsa mines, no?"

"Yes, Gospozhyn."

"Any reason you chose her?"

Megan looked at him blankly, shook her head. "No, Gospozhyn. I just thought of her. The whole City was talking about her roses."

He gazed at her a minute longer. "You have this committed to memory?" he asked, gesturing with the piece of paper. She nodded. "Good," he said, and held it in the candle flame. "Go do it."

Of all the dumb things I could do, she thought. *Why did I have to pick this one?* The rain was a steady drizzle making the rock where she clung slipperier and colder.

She rested her arms, trusting all her weight for a moment on the climbing claws on her left boot. She was on the ridge near Sobota Gate, a good long fall away from the street. Vaizal Marteshkya's manor was at the end of Ulitsu Lane, at least the gardens were, the terraces and walls rising to the facades set into the ridge, one of the old manors with rooms deep in the rock. Megan, in the rain, both cursed it and was thankful. Few people stuck their noses out in the wet and it made a dark night dimmer.

She climbed carefully past the last wall fringed with wooden spines, each tipped in painted iron. She'd gotten

Varik to help her plot the possible manrauq traps, because she still wasn't manifesting. He'd told her where they were likely to be that he could see, or had heard of. She bit her lip as she climbed, remembering his impatient click of tongue against teeth. *He expected me to manifest long before.* She headed for the window farthest from the wall, the one least likely to be protected, hanging on to rock that leaned out over the garden with hands that ached and trembled inside the climbing gloves. *Anyone heavier wouldn't have made it. I'm glad I don't have to try it even a few months from now. The roses. I would have to pick something that expensive and recognizable. I'm risking strangulation, not just having my hands broken.* The latter punishment was only for petty theft.

She reached the window, rested the toe of one boot against the sill, and waited. There was a flicker and the glass window bulged, reaching with clear paws. Megan flinched and they swung toward her. She froze—*I am a shadow, not a person. I'm not here.*—and they withered into the rain and washed away. The window smoothed out. Megan shifted a bit more weight onto the sill, watched the same thing happen, freezing again until the illusion faded.

Good image. If Varik hadn't told me, I would have tried to get away and started believing it. It would have gotten me. The third time the glass only seemed to ripple before it subsided. *Vaizal paid someone top price for that trap. Too bad.* She put both feet on the sill.

Nothing happened. It was a half-second's work to open the simple latch. *Depending too much on manrauq, tsk.* A soft step down behind heavy curtains onto thick carpets. It was like the Wizard's library, the same sort of feeling, though more dangerous than it was then. She knelt and eeled under the heavy curtain, into the dressing room of what should be a guest suite. *If I do this ... never mind, keep your mind on what you're doing when you're doing it. Think about after, after.* It was dark, except for the dim glow of the brazier set into a carved alabaster screening bowl, but she stopped a minute straining to see. This room was supposed to be empty, and was. It was bigger than the two rooms on the Dogleg; twice as big, and it was only the bedroom. There were faintly glittering tapestries keeping the damp of the walls out.

The inner door wasn't locked. Dressing room. Guest's servant's room. Sitting room. Another sitting room. Each one was a different color, she'd heard, but they all felt the same; thick silk and spider-wool carpets, silk hangings to warm the stone behind. Even though there wasn't a guest in them, all three rooms were kept fresh. She could smell fresh flowers, when outside not even the snowdrops had bloomed yet.

She was dry enough now that she didn't drip anymore and she paused at what had to be the hallway door, listening, then eased the door open a crack—*metal hinges*.

The hallway, with a spindly Enchian chair and a heavy sideboard, was full of space and the odor of beeswax, lemon, cinnamon wood, the wooden floor elaborately inlaid.

From downstairs, the strains of music drifted up with the scents of spicy food and mulled wine, the sounds of Vaizal's dinner party. Gospozhyn had been invited and the Kievir would be showing off her roses. He wouldn't expect Megan to have sneaked in tonight. In the dim hall, she grinned to herself. On the stairs, a board creaked and a light grew. She backed up a step or two toward the door she'd come out of, realized she wouldn't make it, dived for the sideboard.

There was only a double handspan of space and she wiggled frantically under it. *My hips, shit I'm stuck with my legs out, shit, don't panic, SQUIRM!!* The sideboard rocked a bit, her hips slid past the skirt, and she pulled her legs in just as a servant, humming bits of popular songs to himself, mounted the last step. He carried a candlestick in one hand, a bundle of linen in the other, and noticed the vase rocking on the sideboard. Megan held her breath, watching his feet in painted silk house-sandals walk toward her hiding place and pause as he steadied the vase. He called, "Puss, puss?"

When no cat appeared, he shrugged and continued into the guest room Megan had entered from. Megan waited until she thought she'd die if she had to wait one second more.

It'd almost be easier to get out and give myself up to him. She squashed the thought. *Dumb. Dumb. Dumb. Just wait . . . until they spring-clean you out if they have to.*

Finally he came out and went back downstairs. She slid out, more carefully than she'd gone in, and padded after him, staying just outside the ring of light the candle cast.

Down one floor to a main corridor, carpeted with jewel-colored rugs. All the candle-sconces were silver statues of women, their hair and hands outstretched to hold the colored wax tapers that matched the green silk on the walls between honey oakwood panels.

Megan slipped into the shadow of a Rand vase twice as tall as she was at the main staircase as the servant went on down to the back stairs. The vase stood by the bannister covered by a long-haired northern giraffe hide hung over it. Below was Vaizal's Great Hall, done in green and gold. Chandeliers that were hundreds of teardrop-cut quartz kraumak gave a yellow/green light. The Enchian style glass doors on the left led to the glassed-in garden/dining hall, where she could see the guests, still seated. From her studying, she knew that the heavy ticking was another fancy clock, in Vaizal's study just behind her, with its famous stained glass windows.

She settled down to wait, hidden by the vase and the fur, watching. After dinner, the guests would likely promenade through to the main salon across the hall and servants would be in to clear the dining things. Then, if she were lucky, she'd have a few minutes to sneak in, snip a rose—*maybe two*—before the room was locked. She'd have to be out before the dogs were let loose in the halls for the night.

It wasn't dusty, though she'd somehow expected it to be. *Stupid, Vaizal has almost seventy people for this manor alone. They wouldn't dare let it get dusty.* She half smiled to herself, trying to imagine beating the dust out of a fur this size, and waited. Thinking of dust made her want to sneeze.

Her legs were cramped before the servants opened the salon doors and the musicians, playing foreign instruments, began a passacaglia. Even so, the guests waited for Vaizal and her escort to lead and it took some time for them all to cross the parquetry, the back of each pair's hands touching, elegantly raised to shoulder height. The women's finger chains flashed gold and silver, gems matching their vested skirts and their makeup.

Gospozhyn looks gorgeous! He's wearing the best I've ever seen. He usually looks a bit mussed and lost. He and his wife wore matching dark purple, with black satin trim. Among the guests were the famous soprano and tenor pair Lilya, called the Diva and Zima, called the True, Baron and Baroness Iyetska, and Zingas Avritha wearing red and gold, though her husband or father weren't there to escort her.

Vaizal herself wore all red and white. A white silk shirt, a white vest, with ermine trim, woven white-on-white and embroidered with a delicate red vine pattern over red pants and boots. Her eye-paint fanned out to form a delicate butterfly on her cheeks, rubies and diamonds glittering on her hands and against her dark hair falling in loose waves to her waist.

One of those stones would keep a marriage of six and all their children fed and housed for a year.

The Grand Salon doors were shut behind the guests by two footman so no one would have to watch the servants clear up. She crawled along just under the edge of the fur, with it tickling her nose, till she was almost at the head of the great stairs.

She peeked over the edge; the green marble steps seeming to flow away from her like a waterfall, ducked back as the butler, chatelaine and footmen and women came in to carry away the leftover food and the plates.

The great platter took six people to carry, even carved over, a small stag, gilded antlers lying askew in the gravy, herb garlands wilted and torn. Bowls and bowls of vegetables—potatoes yellow with butter—platters of breads and cakes, half-emptied bottles of wine and Saekrberk and brandy. Megan had eaten cold maranth porridge that morning, and day-old bread mid-afternoon washed down with chai. She watched the food be taken by almost underneath her, her mouth watering, pressing a hand against her middle, afraid someone would hear her stomach growling.

One footman carried the metal underplates while another carried the scraped glass liners. Three people carried away the goblets, another the silver eating picks and knives. They came back once more, to polish the lacquer table and arrange the cushions around it, carry away the bucket for plate scrapings—*I'd even eat that*—and sweep the floor, dim the lights. The chatelaine surveyed the garden room, nodded at the butler, and closed the doors. Then there was only the empty hall and the faint sound of dance music through the wooden salon doors.

Megan ghosted down the stairs past the life-sized crystal panthers at the bottom, eased the garden door open and closed behind her. She stood with her back to the wall so no one would see her through the doors, just breathing in the strange odor of the room. It was warm and moist air moved along her skin from unseen vents. The room was full of flowers—roses, lilies, tiny potted flowering cherry trees brought from the main greenhouse, orchids. Hummingbirds hovered, red and green and purple. Tall palm trees, imported from the Mitvald Islands, grew in the corners. It smelled earthy as well, as if summer had climbed into Megan's lungs. *The roses are in here, somewhere. Probably near the table.* Very faintly she could hear one of Vaizal's guests singing. *The Diva.*

The lacquer dining table sat in a lake of black polished slate, with soft chamois leather cushions around it, one perfect red bowl by Tze Finiz gracing its center. A wall of climbing yellow roses framed the head cushion. Megan looked for the vase or tray that would display the roses sculpted out of soft gold, but couldn't see anything like that anywhere. *Is it here? It's supposed to be.* The air whispered through palm leaves, a soft, alien sound, rustled lower bushes and made the blossoms nod.

Where is it? I can't have gotten this far and fail because she's had the sculpture moved. I can't, I can't. Her hands clenched with frustration and she could have cried. *I could take something else, but I said I was going to get the roses.* It had gone so perfectly till now and somewhere in her a small voice whispered "Hurry! hurry!" tugging at her muscles with the will to do something, anything. She wiped a stray wisp of hair out of her eyes. *I have to think—that breeze is nice, but I don't have time . . .* Her jaw dropped. The breeze was moving all the leaves at that end of the room, except the climbing roses.

She cast a glance over her shoulder to where the light came through the doors from the Great Hall and tiptoed over to the wall behind the head of the table. The roses gleamed in the faint light, glossy leaves showing dimly against the black marble wall. She reached out a gloved finger to touch one flower. The gold was almost soft enough, pure enough, to dent with the fingers, the leaves carved of green tourmaline, malachite and jade, even the pale green thorns. They looked real enough that she was tempted to smell them. She shook herself, pulled the box out of her belt.

They were set into the stone with gold pins that sheared off easily with her knife. *One, two, three. Don't be greedy.* She laid the heavy flowers in the padded box and strapped it shut. *Done. Now all I have to do is get out. It'll be easier now that my scent is mixed with all the other guests, it'll confuse the dogs.*

She made it out to the stairs before her luck went bad.

A servant, carrying a tray of sweetmeats to the salon saw her and yelled. She bolted up the stairs. *Shit. Oh, piss.* Behind her the noise grew as the salon doors where thrown open. "An assassin or thief in my *home*?" Vaizal. Megan darted down the long, straight hall. *Hide. I have to hide, Goddess help me. I have to get out. They'll break my hands, my legs, then strangle me. Throw me to the rats.* She lunged at the nearest door that might lead to an outside room.

Study. Clock. Windows . . . sealed oh shit oh shit . . . The crash of glass.

When the Vaizal's guard plunged into the room it was empty, one of the windows smashed, strands of leading twisted outward, rain blowing in.

"On the wall," Vaizal snapped, leaning through, careful of the broken glass. "Check the gardens, go! Retrieve that chair and get those dogs out of here!" The gardens were flooded with witch-light flares, burning eye-hurting white every hundred feet along the wall, throwing light so nothing could have moved without being seen; dogs running, dragging handlers on leashes to begin quartering the ground below.

Vaizal turned to the crowd of nobles standing clustered in the doorway, chatting as if this were all part of the evening's entertainment and raised her hands in dismissive waves. "No need to get excited. It's all right. My people will surely catch whoever it is. Why don't we go down again and let them work? I'm sure we can find something amusing to occupy our time until the miscreant is caught." Her voice was almost more amused than angry or upset.

"My father is right about the City riff-raff," Avritha said as she turned away, her hand on Yarishk's arm. "If they're this bold, one must be harder on them."

As the nobles moved back downstairs, laughing, Vaizal turned to her chatelaine. "See that this is cleared up in the morning. Have someone block that window so nothing else is damaged."

"Yes, Kievir." The chatelaine bowed.

Squeezed inside the cabinet of the clock, Megan could barely hear what was happening, the TICK/clack, TICK/clack clipping bits out of everyone's words, the pendulum swing just brushing her hair as she sat in the bottom, crouched with her face on her knees. She was shaking, trying to be as still as possible, biting the cloth of her pant leg. *It's dumb to cry, now. They haven't found me. I'm safe, for now. It's dumb to cry. Be still, be quiet.*

The box with the roses in it gouged into her ribs and one of the weights brushing her shoulder gradually got heavier and heavier as the clock wound down, but she didn't dare move for fear that the door would burst open.

TICK/clack, TICK/clack, TICK/clack. She tried counting ticks, lost count after six hundred or so. By then, her shivering had stopped.

The weight slipped off her shoulder to thump against the wood. She waited for someone to open the door and drag her out. When no one did, she pushed the door open a crack. No one was there. The mess was cleared and the window boarded. She fell out onto the rug, the clock jangling faintly. She was so cramped that she couldn't uncurl at first but just lay there.

Out. I have to get out. The study door was half open so she shook her arms and legs, wobbled out of the room and behind a hall tapestry. She sat there for a time, with her face in her hands. *I have to get out, now.* It took her twice as long to get up to the hall where she'd gotten in, holding herself back from running, jumping at shadows.

In the guest hall she paused by the sideboard, flinched, and nearly screamed as something brushed her ankle.

"Meoow." The cat stropped against her again. She caught her breath, leaning against the wall.

"I get scared one more time and I'm going to die," she whispered to the cat, stroked it, and nipped into the guest suite she'd come in by, closing the door so the cat couldn't follow.

Standing at the window she saw that the weather had turned freezing again, the rain icing on the rock. *Oh, joy. Thief's weather because only a thief would be out in it.* She fought down the irrational urge to giggle. *You're not out yet.* She had to wait until they doused the witch-lights. She stood in the warmth, heavy velvet curtains resting against her back like a congratulatory hand.

As she stood and waited, she cursed suddenly and turned back into the room. *I worked hard to get in here, why am I wasting it?* There was still room in her pouch, aside from the box and she'd never be able to sell the roses, they'd have to be held for "reclamation." A small gold candlestick was what she grabbed; all she could carry.

When the lights died, she pulled on her climbing gloves and slipped out the window into air icy on her skin. From a window below she could hear the party music and people laughing. Soaked through in an instant, she took a couple of deep breaths and forced herself to climb slowly down the way she'd come, slowly so she wouldn't slip.

Yarishk, when he went to unlock his office next morning, paused with one hand on the door. He nodded to himself and turned the key. His wards had been disturbed, but he knew the by the feel who it was.

Inside he stood looking down at Megan, asleep on his cushions, with the knit blanket pulled up around her chin. Her hair had dried in draggled wisps across her cheek and her clothes were hung here and there around the room to dry.

He started the samovar boiling, dropped in a handful of leaves. She blinked awake at the smell of steam, yawned and stretched. "Good morning, Gospozhyn. I'm sorry I borrowed your office."

"As you should be. Goddess morning to you, too. I have some idea why you might have gotten in here." His face was stern. "That's why I left *my* protections mostly down this Hand. If they weren't down, they might have killed you. Don't do it again."

Megan looked down at her hands. "No, Gospozhyn."

"Well, I'll send Barela down for some breakfast."

"Yes, Gospozhyn." When he went down the hall, she scrabbled her clothes together and darted down the hall to the jakes.

When she got back he was waiting for her, desk on his lap.

"Well?"

Without saying anything she pulled out the carry box and the candlestick, put them on the desk. He lifted the candlestick first, then unstrapped the box and laid the three roses—click, click, click—out on the wood and gently smoothed one petal with a fingertip. "Hmm," was all he said.

He lifted the desk off his lap and paced slowly around the room. "You returned Varik's climbing claws and equipment to him?"

She nodded. *What is he thinking? I did what I said I would. I did it.* "Good. The Other Guild claims two of the Roses, since you are apprentice. We will accept the danger, if caught with them. The value of the third rose and the candlestick I will hold in trust for you till you are of age, since you have no safe place to keep them and don't want kin to know of your possession."

Yeah, Marte isn't going to know that I have money of my own, even if she pulls my toenails out. Then an awful thought struck her.

"Gospozhyn, will they be broken up?" That hurt, though she told herself that she didn't care.

Yarishk looked at her, his back to the window where she couldn't see his face. "Do you care?" he rumbled. He walked back to the desk, swept up one of the roses roughly, and she cried, "No, don't!" She closed her mouth, then said, more calmly, "I thought you were going to break it, Gospozhyn."

"Their value is more than what they're made of. We'll keep them . . . perhaps even sell them back to Vaizal . . . if she thinks to ask. I suspect she will pay the 'reclamation' fee."

Megan breathed a relieved sigh. They were too beautiful to destroy.

"You think you're an accomplished little thief, then," Yarishk said. She blinked, puzzled. "Broke into one of the Prafetatla's manors and got away clean as a Goddess offering?"

She shook her head. *I'm not, until he says I am.*

"I have another assignment for you." He was packing the roses away and putting everything out of sight. "After you eat," he waved a hand at the reading alcove. "In there, out of the way, there is a file on a house I want you to report on, on Sto Bumaga Lane, Lake Quarter. Tell me what you mean to take and how you will get in."

"Yes, Gospozhyn," Megan said, though she wondered what could be worth stealing in the Lake Quarter.

The house was a hovel; a muddy, collapsing hole in the ground propped up with scavenged boards nailed over with other short bits here and there to hold it all together. The door had finger-wide gaps stuffed with rags. One good storm and the mud and trash would shift and fill it.

Megan walked by once, to find it, then again. *Steal from them?* The lane was a dead end street, blocked by a rotten wooden building that had fallen, garbage mounding it higher. A path had been beaten over it, around one end where it was lowest. Megan passed other homes dug out of the dirt.

This is where the unclean live, the h'Rokatski, the corpse handlers. The stink of dung and people and mud was almost overpowered by the smell of the nearby tannery. Someone was rendering down bones and fat, too. Megan put her hand over her nose and mouth, wanting to throw up. She found a niche in the crumbled building, where no one would see her easily, to watch the house.

A family of eight. Two men/women pairs, one man/man pair, two children, with one of the kids, sick. She watched. They were worse off than Megan was, ever. They begged for their living, one pair trying to tend house, hauling water from the lake three roads away. That one kid cried constantly but sounded sicker every day.

The first night she went back to her aunt's and lay on the pallet in the front room, not able to sleep. Though it had been cold she'd washed in the lake, but she couldn't wash the memory away. *Gospozhyn wants me to say what I could steal from them. It's an assignment. There isn't anything to steal but the begging money. I'll tell him that and it will be all right. He wouldn't tell me to steal from them. I know him better.*

"Do it," he said. Megan sat looking at him as he burned the report, just as he had the first time, sick to her stomach. She sat as if he'd turned into Marte and hit her. Then she got up and started for the door, still without saying anything.

"Apprentice, don't be rude."

She paused at the door. "No, Gospozhyn, my apology. I understand," she said tonelessly and left.

I have to. It's part of what's kept me and Rilla going. They're bad off. The kid'll die. They don't have enough money even six begging. I . . . I. She tried running, up and down the Stairs and through the Market until she was too winded to run any more, and it still wouldn't go away. She couldn't talk to Serkai. She couldn't talk to Rilla, not to anybody.

If she failed this, would Gospozhyn let her continue lessons to be a merchant? If she screwed up, would he stop teaching Rilla? *If I can't learn, I'll be like them. I have to. I have to.*

She climbed to the rock spur by the waterfall, staring down into the thunder of the falls as they spouted out of the gates and down to the Brezhan, wanting to go away down the river, to be anywhere but there, to have any decision but that. She delayed, and delayed until her Gospozhyn called her in, the last day before Hand'send.

"Well?" His face was stern. "You were quick enough with the other."

Megan felt her face and hands go light and numb. She opened her mouth to try and explain, but all that came out was, "I can't."

"Eh? Your report was clear enough. The assignment is simple." He raised a lip in a sneer. "Aren't you good enough?"

She clenched her fists. "I *w* . . . *won't*."

He pursed his lips and, narrowing his eyes at her, asked softly, "Even if it means losing something you've gained?" She nodded, eyes clenched shut against what was coming. Suddenly, she was afraid of him, too. This wasn't *him*. She opened her eyes and stared at him, getting cold inside; cold and hard where no one would touch her.

She swallowed. "They're too poor. I don't need their money—they need their money. It doesn't make sense. It's not worth it. We don't need to steal from people poorer than we are.

"If I can steal from Prafetatla it's worth it. This is wrong! Set me on somebody worth it." She clipped off the torrent of words, shaking.

"Well, well," he said coldly. "An ethical thief."

She looked down at her open hands. She wasn't clenching her fists any longer because there was nothing left to fight. But she knew she could steal from very rich people—in some other city, she thought bitterly, and got up to go.

"No, Megan, come with me." He rose, Sashi at his heels. *Is this important enough for him to kick me out himself?* She pulled away from the hand he would have put on her shoulder.

He didn't turn to the outside corridor but the inside one. "Come along." Megan followed him numbly.

He tapped on Nal-Gospozhyn Zeyvoydna, the Guild healer's door, and Megan starting to wonder what was going on. Yarishk wasn't smiling but . . .

That was what I thought he was like—nice. He's not.

"In, go on." He waved her in and followed. "Hello, Zey-voydna, as I warned you earlier, here we are."

"Sit down, on that stool, there," he said to her. This time Megan didn't pull away, puzzled. "Take your shirt off, Megan."

"Gospoz—"

"Shush, child." He turned to Zeyvoydna who was laying out a tattooing needle, swabbing at Megan's shoulder with a bit of lint soaked in alcohol. "I will witness." He smiled. "One—discreet—Journeyman's tattoo." He winked at Megan, who was clutching the table not to slide onto the floor, mouth hanging open.

"An ethical thief, indeed," he said.

Chapter Fifteen

"Rilla, psst, Rilla wake up!" Megan jumped back as Rilla, waking up, struck out.

"Huh? What? Wh . . . oh, sorry." She rubbed the sleep out of her eyes. "What's going on?"

Megan pulled her tunic off, proudly displaying the small, open-spiral double diamond tattooed onto her shoulder. It was bright, sore around the edges.

"That's pretty. Where did you get the money?" Rilla lay down again pulling the blanket up because the room was cold.

"I didn't. It's a mark from the Other Guild." Megan grinned. "I made Journeyman!"

"What?" Rilla's whisper threatened to spiral up into a shriek but she clapped a hand to her mouth, glancing at the door of Marte's room, dreading to see light around its edges. "What?" she repeated more quietly.

Megan poked her in the ribs. "You heard. I made Journeyman. Lie down before you catch a chill. Do you mind if I slide in with you? My bed's cold."

"I don't mind. Journeyman. Like Varik was. Eula will just bite her tongue if you tell her."

Megan wiggled in beside Rilla. "I don't think I will. Besides, am I going to go around shouting, 'I just made Journeyman in the THIEVES GUILD?'"

Rilla snickered. "No, ow, you're cold. Can I put my head on your shoulder?"

"Sure, Rillan, as long as it's the *other* shoulder. Go back to sleep, I'll tell you all about it in the morning."

They both froze when the wallbed in the other room creaked, relaxed when no other sounds came. "All right," Rilla whispered, then yawned into Megan's neck. "Sleep you sound."

"And you."

Hand'send morning. Megan was just grinding one of the last dried onions for stew when Rilla came home with the bread and milk and a marrow bone. "I couldn't get more than that," she said.

"We'll make do. Someone just ordered something from Marte."

"That's good." Rilla put the bread away in the box and began rinsing out the milk jug. "Where is she?"

"Not up yet. I think she wants to take advantage that it's Hand'send and nurse her head . . . oh, there." From the inner room faint rustlings got louder. A bang as the wallbed door was flung back, a staggering step or two, then retching noises. "I hope she didn't miss the bucket."

"Yeah." Rilla poured chai for her mother, thinned it down with milk. She set it down on the table, turned to the wall of glass vials, picked one and shook the creamy-colored powder into a measuring spoon. She set it next a cup of water near the chai. "She has to make some more pain-soother; she's almost out."

Megan shrugged. "We can go get willow twigs together. There's at least one tree in an alley that I know hasn't been scavenged bare."

"Okay." The inner door creaked open and Marte stumbled out to slump on her pillow. She picked up the chai cup with both shaking hands.

"'morning."

"Goddess morning," Megan and Rilla answered automatically. Marte stirred the pain-soother into the water and drank it down fast, grimacing. Megan sliced the bread and slathered the pieces generously from the fat jar. Marte had felt rich a Hand ago and bought bacon and some beef so the drippings were good.

"Good God, no, I won't eat that." Marte ran a hand through her hair, shuddering. "I'll eat later." They sat together, Megan and Rilla eating, Marte sitting with her forehead held in her hand, staring into the dregs of her chai. When she put her cup down sharply, both children flinched though they tried not to. Marte looked at the bruise on Rilla's face. "Hit someone, did I, last night? Humph, well." Her eyes narrowed. "What did you do?"

Megan cut in. "Nothing, Aunt."

Marte looked at her, shifting her attention and foul mood to her niece. "That's a lie, brat. I only hit you when you deserve it."

Megan pressed her lips together, not saying anything.

"And *don't* give me any of your dumb insolence!" She slammed a fist on the table and winced, holding her head. "I don't need that shit from a twelve-year-old." She sat a while longer, pushed up from the table and wobbled out the door, heading for the tap to rinse her head.

Rilla looked at Megan, who started clearing the table. "Right, let's go."

When they came back later carrying the bundle of willow twigs between them, Marte was back, her hair braided, measuring from the piles of crushed herbs on the table in front of her, face still pinched with pain and irritation. She flickered a look at them as they came in, jerked her head at the corner by the door. "There."

"Yes, mam."

They tiptoed around and spooned themselves some stew. Megan looked for the heel of bread but it was gone. In silence, not wanting to disturb Marte, they sat at the opposite corner of the table to eat. That was like many evenings, though. They'd sit and the only sounds would be the clink and clatter of spoons or bowls, muted; kept to a minimum so as not to irritate Marte. Tonight the sound from her end of the table was a steady grinding as she turned dried Bluehood into power with the mortar and pestle. The still in the back room smelled sweet and sticky, like almost burned sugar. "Rilla, fetch me the Halyabore and the Colshchizn seeds."

"Yes, mam."

Megan gathered up the empty bowls and filled them with water to soak, her back to the room.

"I want you to go to First Quarter with this," Marte said. "It's to go to the cook at Windwood Manor." The crackle of brown paper as Rilla tucked the packet into her belt.

"All right."

Megan rinsed the picks. "You'll be getting silver for this," Marte said. Megan stopped scrubbing for a second. *Silver for herbs? To a cook?* "It's been bargained already," Marte continued.

"Okay." A bang as the door closed behind Rilla. Megan wrung out the cloth and hung it on its hook, turned around just in time to see Marte set down a flask of wine next to her as she settled back down to the table. *Oh, shit.* Marte didn't usually drink on top of a hangover. *I have to get out of here.*

"Come sit here," Marte said, a little uncomfortably, nodding at a spot near her elbow. Megan hesitated but pulled her cushion around and sat down.

"You're almost old enough to talk sense to," the woman continued. "Never could understand kids anyway." She used the spatula to scrape the pestle into a small glass jar, carefully using a squirrel's hair brush to gather up the last crumbs. *Maybe if I talked to her, she'll be nice. Maybe I just never knew how to talk to her. She can't be all bad.* "What's that for?" Megan asked, pointing.

"Don't touch!" Marte flared, blocking her finger. "It's dangerous and can seep through your skin! Bluehood, you know." She seemed surprised when Megan nodded, then more enthusiastic. "Wolfbane it's called, or love poison," she continued, capped the jar, and sealed it with a pouring of wax. "For liniment, or to induce sweating and . . . other things."

"Like Beautiful Lady," Megan said, and got another surprised look from her aunt. "I read it somewhere."

"Yes." Marte uncorked the wine flask expertly and raised it, paused and set it on the table, looking thoughtful. "Get a couple of cups, will you?" She packed away the tools, and the herbs. "Go ahead and pour, brat."

She's being nice. Not syrupy like she usually is. What's going on? Megan felt nervous, fluttery as if a bear had walked up to her and licked her face rather than tearing her head off. "Drink up, brother's daughter. Drink with your old aunt."

The wine was sour red but warming. Megan puckered her face as Marte drained her cup. "Good for hangovers," the woman said, and poured herself another. "You know, when you look like that, kid, you look less like your bitch mother."

"My mama wa—" Megan ducked as Marte raised a hand, waving her silent.

"No, don't say it, and I won't have to belt you." She burped gently. "No, you look more like my little brother when you're not crossing me." She drank the second cup down. "When you look at me like that . . . like him. Only thing in the world worth *shit*. My brother. Never did listen to me, and damn lucky apprenticed already. I only had the best of intentions after the rest of the family . . . Family was just us two."

Papa told me about Great-Gran Diezhdi, Grandmama and Grandpapa and Grandpa. They were a trey that had four children, Aunt Beda and Uncle Noltzha along with Papa and Aunt Marte. All but Lixand and Marte had died in The Great Fire. She sipped the wine and listened. Marte was crying, stony-faced as she drank. "Li'l brother . . . Start the family again, my Solntze died, too . . ." She drank a third cup, put her head down on the table. Megan, sipping at her wine, reached out and awkwardly patted her shoulder. "Lixand, shit, why'd you die on me, brother? You too? You too?" Marte snapped up a hand and caught Megan's in a crushing grip, lifted her head and glared. Megan pulled back but couldn't get away. "Family ... 'n he had to marry *her!* Out-city trash despised me from the start ..."

"Have another drink, Aunt," Megan said frantically, knowing she couldn't pull away. "For Papa's memory."

Marte stared at her for a long minute, still. "Yeah. I need something stronger than this shit." She got up and got a small glass bottle, the size of her palm. "Brewed this myself. Something really good, something Zingas pay in gold for. Nah, you don't get. It's powerful stuff, green like Saekrberk ... Wormwood."

As far as Megan saw it was green as poison, thick and oily as Marte poured it, the smell of bitter licorice faint. She set a jug of water on the table and mixed the worm-wood oil with it, watched it turn milky. She drank the cup down, shuddered and grabbed the water jug, drank straight water. Then she mixed another. "To ... my ... li-tt-le brother!" she enunciated carefully and drank. Megan drank a sip of wine too, not quite daring to say anything. A few minutes they sat in silence. Marte drank a second cup. After a while she started smiling, a slow, blissful smile.

She looked around, her movements slowing, shook her head. "One ... more 'n I'm here f'r t'e night. Don' help!" She set her palms flat on the table, levered herself upright and grabbed the bottle of wormwood oil, the water jug and the cup hooked on her thumb, already staggering as she went into the back room to the wallbed, bumping gently against the door frame twice before she made it through.

Megan sat, shaking, the wine left in her cup splashing on her hands. She watched Marte close the door behind her, muffling the hissing of the still.

Marte didn't get *that* drunk that night, or if she did, didn't come out of the room to vent it on them. Rilla came back with the silver and locked it away in the box.

Next day, Marte didn't say two words to either of them and they stayed out of the house. Megan lingered very late with Tikhiy after they finished studying, and they talked about Serkai and Ivar and Master Zyatki and his wife's new baby girl.

Rilla and Megan haunted the edges of Marte's house, feeling the storm brewing though there was nothing they could do. Marte made herself the pain-soother, then didn't get drunk at all for two Hands.

Megan came back from the Hall after studying ship types with Tikhiy and Yegor, and she and Rilla carried water for the laundry next day. They borrowed three buckets from the neighbors so they could both carry and make half as many trips. Carrying the heavy swinging buckets on the yokes they'd improvised without spilling was tricky, and they made a contest of measuring who got back with more water.

"I made almost two full buckets," Rilla boasted when they met at the tap. "I'm littler than you and I got more waaa-ter!" she singsonged. Megan, holding the filling bucket looked at her. "I, got-more-wa—spliffth!" Rilla spluttered at the face-full of water and retaliated with a handful from one of her buckets. Seconds later the buckets were empty and the two girls were soaked, standing on the muddy cobbles around the tap.

"Well!" Megan said, grinning. "You certainly *did* get more water! Here, why don't you head back and I'll finish filling this. We ought to have enough now for one wash and rinse."

"Okay, General All-Wet-Behind-the-Ears! Sir!" Rilla ducked another handful of water and trotted carefully up the street, buckets swinging.

Megan followed a minute later, stopping to adjust the set of the pole on her shoulders. When she came in, she heard something—a jar smash. She put the buckets down and ran.

She burst in the door in time to see Marte drag Rilla up off the floor by the upper arm, start hitting her with the other hand. ". . . filthy chi'd! Lo—ok at you! Dirt. Wet. I . . ."

"Aunt!" Marte looked up, Rilla hung crying, holding up her free hand as if to stop the next blow. "It's my fault. I got her wet."

"Shut up!" Marte shook Rilla again. "She broke my flask."

". . . dn't," Rilla blubbered. Marte swung again, her face purpling. "Don' talk back! Insol't 'n' dirty! Evil girl! You . . ." Her fist bunched.

"NO!" Megan flung herself at Marte, hanging off the upraised arm, kicking. "You bitch! You vicious bitch! She's kin!"

Marte flung Rilla aside and seized Megan by both shoulders, lifting her up and shaking her with every word. "You called me a bitch," she said clearly. "You ungrateful child."

Beyond scared, Megan yelled, "My father said so! He said so! You're a viper! He said so!"

For an instant Marte held her by the shoulders, Rilla disappeared into the cupboard under the bed in the back room. The only sound was a shout down the hall—"will you keep it down for once, woman!"—and a dog barking outside on the street. Megan braced herself as best she could, Marte staring at her.

"Your father said so," Marte repeated in a drunken monotone. "Your father."

She dropped Megan suddenly as if burned, stamped over and rummaged in the money box, cursed it being empty, and stormed out.

Megan lay on the floor where she'd been dropped. "Megan?" Rilla crawled out from under her mother's bed. "Megan are you all right?"

"Yeah," Megan said shakily. "Maybe we'd better get out for a while. Do you have the coppers from the money box?"

Rilla nodded. "Thanks, Meg."

Megan shrugged. "I couldn't let her just hit you." But her hands were shaking. Rilla hugged her, wet as she was.

"Come on, big coz," the younger girl said. "We'll get another two flasks and we'll be fine."

"We ought to get into dry clothes at least," Megan said. "And get the borrowed buckets back."

"Okay." They had just changed when Marte came back.

"Megan. Come, come on." She stood in the door, swaying, the wine soured on her breath. Megan hesitated wanting to run out into the city but couldn't get by.

"'ll no' hit yeah, but 'll drag. Come on!" Marte advanced a step into the room and reached for Megan, who dodged around the table, trying to get away from her.

"No."

Marte reached, snatched up the broom. "Don' say no, brat." Rilla tried to get back into the back room. Her mother swung around as she moved, caught her across the back, the handle making the air buzz like a fist-size bee. Rilla was jolted forward and fell, her arms curled protectively around her head. Megan, half out the door, hesitated. *I can't. She'll kill her.* She turned and darted back, grabbed the straw of the broom and yanked. Marte let go and Megan, staggering back, cracked her hip against the table and fell.

Marte pounced on her. "Thought I's stupid, din't yeah," she growled, and hauled Megan up by the wrist. When Megan tried using the thumb jab, Marte pulled her hand higher and dragged her out the door, yelling, "Yeah better be here when I get back, brat," over her shoulder at Rilla.

"'nuff of 't, vicious brat, t'ink I don' know that trick? Stop it and come on quiet or 'll belt 'cha." She walked down the alley, too fast for Megan to keep up without running.

The girl tried to dig her heels in and get away, was dragged around in front of Marte and cuffed in the head,

her wrist held in a vicious grip. "Look, brat." Marte
jerked on the captive arm. "We can't live like 'is. Time
you went onna river journey—heh? 'N we won' say stupi'
th—things t'each other. Be good fer you. Yeah." She
turned east on the Stairs, pulling Megan with her into
the crowds on the street; no one looked at them twice.

Megan tried to break in, but Marte wasn't listening.
"Aunt, Marte—"

"Shut up." Marte just plowed on, through the naZak,
like a lurcher in among wolf-hounds, her greying brown
hair uncoiling from its bun to bounce on her back. Megan's right hand was going numb in Marte's grip, the wool
of her sleeve pulled tight from her shoulder. *Where are
we going? River journey? What's she talking about? At
least she isn't hitting me.* She hoped Rilla had the sense
to put the broom and the wooden spoons away before
they got back.

"Aunt you don't have to hang on so hard." She couldn't
feel her fingers. "Aunt, please answer me. Where are we
going? Aunt? Aunt, please?" Marte's only answer was to
drag her on faster till Megan didn't have the breath for
questions, a stitch growing in her side.

They turned off the Stairs at Yok Oblach Street, joining
the traffic for Vikhad Gate. This half of the city was
already dark, but the setting sun was still high enough
that it gilded the other ridge and the underside of the
storm blowing in from the north. The guards at the gate
weren't slowing the line, practically waving people through
the narrow corridor. The temperature was falling and
Marte blew on her free hand to warm it up, since she'd
rushed them out without their coats.

Megan blinked at the stab of sun as they came through
the gate and plunged back into the shadow of Docking
Cavern Road. *A river journey? What's going on? My
Gospozhyn should know ...* She squirmed harder and
got Marte's fist across the side of her head for her pains,
dazing her.

The road led into the docking cavern, where the waterfall's thunder echoed against walls and ceiling and the

eddies from the water flowed around the spur of rock that separated wild water from the calm. The water still kept the ships tied up to the stone docks moving, rubbing against the rope bumpers. Megan's head had cleared and she almost forgot her numb hand as she looked around. She'd been here so seldom it was almost a different world.

A dhow. *An arrowship. Racks of canoes for going north where the big ships can't go. A merchanter.* In the outer harbor the bigger ships, with masts still stepped, turned slowly at anchor. The strongest smells were tar and paint at first.

"Damn narrow walkways, can't they build—" "—pay taxes like this—" "Vilsh chavrash? Eilier!" "—watch where you're stepping, you—" The bits of sentences that Megan could catch, mostly in Zak and Enchian, seemed to bounce off the ceiling with the echoing water.

Marte shouted a question at a woman down in a jolly boat but all Megan caught was "—leaving?" The woman pointed out two ships in the outer harbor.

"Where's the jolly boat berth for the *Dulshe Vi* then?" Marte called. Her answer was a wave back through the crowds to the other side of the wharf. "And the other? The *Zingas Brezhani*, the River Lady?"

"Oh, right there." Another sweep of hand, indicating the next quay over. "Hei, ask for Atatra—Atraha—shit, ask fer Goldhair—Sarngeld—he know nobo'y ken say 's damn name! 'E's captain/owner!"

"Thanks!" Marte shouted back and pulled Megan over to the next stone pier, elbowing their way through the crowds. "Should bui'd mor blashted dockin'," she snarled as someone jostled them and almost knocked them both into the water. In here, out of the wind, it was warm with body heat and smelled—of rotten fish and unwashed wool and bodies, of burning grease as block and tackles hoisted cargo, of garbage washed in, a dead rat floating against the pier where a duck scavenged, adding its dung. Megan only faintly heard the rumble of thunder but could see the distant flash of lightning outside the cavern.

Marte hesitated a second, looking down at her niece, but her face hardened at some thought and she pushed on.

"I'm Atzathratzas Joannen," the man rumbled, straightening from where he'd sat on a crate, watching his crew load the boats. "Owner." He paused and looked Marte over slowly. "Teik." He was a large naZak, an Arkan of about forty, muscled and scarred, a broad leather belt holding in the beginnings of a belly. His blond hair was long and straight to his waist at the back, the strands of white in it not showing yet, his forehead rising bald to the line of his ears.

"You take on River-Guild apprentices?" Marte asked. That drew another look and his attention shifted to Megan. *Gospozhyn should be arranging . . . this isn't right. This isn't right.* She tried to pry her hand free and Marte took her attention away from the Arkan long enough to shake Megan hard. "Stop that, brat." She didn't, and got clouted again. She was starting to feel sick, starting to realize . . .

He watched. "What terms?" he asked, more interested now. "You selling her . . . ah . . . bond?" He used the term for "guild-bond," meaning the agreement between parent and guild. Marte hesitated again. "Well, woman?" His tone made it an insult. "Do you want to bargain?" He stepped close and put a hand under Megan's chin, tipping her face up to where he could see it more clearly.

"Yeh," Marte said shortly. "In metal, not goods."

"Aunt, shouldn't Gospoz—"

"Shush, child, it's for your good." Marte's attention went back to Sarngeld who was considering, one scarred thumb rubbing thoughtfully over his lower lip.

"A gold Claw," he said. "Unlimited, no haggling." He turned away to let Marte think about it.

Unlimited? But that's illegal, except for criminals, and never to foreigners, but if I get away, where do I go— Gospozhyn, he'll save me. "Aunt—don't do this, Aunt—"

Marte called him back. "Done! Though you're offering less than you should."

"Do you think I care? Here." He rummaged in his pouch and came up with several bits of metal, three small gold Fangs, six silver Claws, and counted them into Marte's hand.

"Go with him, Megan, he's your new ma—Gospozhyn," Marte said and pulled Megan forward. The girl struggled frantically.

"No, Aunt. Don't do this, you're kin, help me, don't, for Papa's sake—pleees—" Her voice was cut off as Sarngeld put his hand over her mouth and lifted her down to the jolly boat as if she were a doll, his hands clamped on her tightly.

He sat down between two burlap bags that smelled of flour as the boat was pushed off, giving his orders in Arkan. Megan had only enough of the language to catch "—wait . . . cabin, leaving tonight." Her heart was pounding, hands sweaty. *Koru . . . I'm afraid. Unlimited bond?*

The jolly boat pulled out into the outer harbor, bobbing in the choppy waves. The wind was coming up and the cold was a shock as they left the warmth of the cavern—*Freeze tonight for sure*—the sailors avoided looking at their captain or her. He put her down and she considered trying to jump out and swim, but the waterfall would have made it dangerous even for a good swimmer, which she wasn't.

She looked ahead to where the river ship swung at anchor. She was an old merchanter, maybe a hundred tons, with the paint peeling off the name *Zingas Brezhani* and the figurehead. The blades of the single rank of shipped oars were like teeth, but missing two or three. Megan wrinkled her nose as they got close. The bilges stank.

She was passed up like a bundle onto a deck where the caulking bulged between the boards. "Come on, kid," one of the crew said, a slight-built young Zak, with a wavy black hair and a mustache narrow enough to almost have been inked on. "You're down for his cabin where you're to wait." He looked away and led her toward the stern, stepping around an uncoiled rope on the deck.

Is everyone on holiday? Megan thought. *I thought ropes were supposed to be out of the way and a furled sail was supposed to be better tied than that.*

"Okay," she said, following along. "My name's Megan, called Weaver's Daughter." She offered her hand, palm out. He looked uncomfortable, touched her hand for a second as if he didn't want to.

"Piatr, called Quick. Come on."

She followed him down the deck and the short ladder under the poop. There were only two doors there, and he opened the one on the left.

"Thank you," she said.

She waited by the portholes, watching the storm blow in, hearing the various thumps and bangs as things were loaded. With a groaning rattle the anchor was drawn up, the clatter as the oars were unshipped to walk the ship out of the harbor. *He must want to make the great rock at least before it rains.* The room was low, cramped and dark, a rope-slung bed filled one end of the room—*big because he's naZak.* She smiled to herself, a little nervously. *He wouldn't want his legs to hang out of bed.* There was a table and chair and a chest pushed under the bed, an unlit lamp swinging gently from the beam over the table.

There's nothing here that tells me what he's like. She sat down on the chair and waited. Thunder rumbled. More bumpings and banging outside, the squeal of a block and tackle. A heavy tread came down the companionway ladder and a board squeeked outside the door.

Sarngeld opened the door, stooping so he didn't hit his head against the beams, and locked it behind him. Megan's heart jumped into almost a painful pounding in her chest.

"Gospozhyn?" she whispered, hoping that she was wrong, hoping that the world was better than she feared.

He looked at her, pulled off his gloves and his belt. "Enough of that babble," he said almost amiably. "You're mine and you'll speak a civilized tongue to me."

Megan slid off the chair and backed up a step, switching to Enchian. "Yours? I'm your apprentice—"

"No. You don't understand do you?" He pulled his tunic off, rubbed a hand over his shaved chest. "Come here." He grabbed for her. She dived under the table, tried to keep it between him and her, but he reached over it and grabbed her by the hair as she tried to dodge again.

"You're learning," he said. "Come to father now . . ." He dragged her over to the bed and held her between his knees as he pulled the rest of her clothes off. She bit him and he hit her hard enough that the room spun.

Chapter Sixteen

It was a nightmare, it had to be. Then, *No, this is the way things are and will be. There isn't anything else.* Megan shifted her weight, squeezing her eyes shut as pain shot through her groin. Thunder faded away southward, the sound of pain. The rain was freezing, now; on the rigging, on the spiny coils of the rope under her hands, on the deck around her. Tears of ice clicked on her eyelashes, though she refused to cry. *If I cry, I'll break, shatter like the ice forming on the wood.* She was crouched in the port rope-well, too cold to shiver. The oak slave-links he'd locked onto her, from one wrist to the collar on her neck, clattered.

He'd done that and shorn her hair close, though he hadn't shaved her head. The stubble stood almost straight up, icy. The *Brezhani* was anchored in the lee of the rock, with oaks and pines leaning out over the gorge. The trees were shining with ice, cracking and groaning from the weight, the rock black with it.

If I wanted to die, I wouldn't have to do anything but sit here. The air will fill me full of ice. Like he did. The only warmth was the bleeding from between her legs, but that cooled fast, too. The water below was like pupils of the Dark Lord's eyes. The Arkan had let her run— crawl—away because he knew he could catch her, but all she needed to do was go over the side. She couldn't swim well. *I want to die.* She leaned, letting go the rope.

Sarngeld's gloved hand darted down and grabbed the wooden chain. "Come here." He pulled her up to the deck. *I'm bleeding all down my legs.* She almost fell and he gathered her up in his arms as if to protect her. *He smells like blood and like his sweat and my fear.* She hung in his hands, not fighting anymore. His chest was red where she'd scratched and bitten him.

He carried her below and patted her dry, his hands gentle now. "There, there, my little girl. There, there." He wanted her again, and pulled her head down. *I could bite him—it would be worse—* She bit him, and didn't see his hand move, only the dark and red, the sound of thunder. *If I pretend hard enough, think hard enough, I won't be here. I can make it not real. I'm not here.*

"Hush, child, it's all right." Megan thrashed, clawing at the voice and the hands, felt her wrists caught, blinked awake to see a woman's face.

She was a round-faced girl—no, a woman, with long brown braids woven with blue ribbon and Aeniri hair bells. "You'll be all right. I'm ship's healer, Katrana called Healheart." She smoothed back the stubbly hair on Megan's head. "You're in the officer's quarters—my clinic— for now. That's across from his cabin." She tucked the feather quilt around Megan's shoulders, sighed and looked away from the girl, grimacing. "I can't tell you he won't do it again. But next time it won't hurt so much."

"Why?" Megan's voice was a husky whisper, throat sore.

"He's Arkan and likes children." Katrana finished mixing something in a cup, the glass rod clinking. "Drink this down now. I've told him you've had more than enough. He's satisfied for a day or two at least."

The cup was bitter and tasted of valerian and fennel. "Thank you," Megan said, and winced as Katrana laid a warm compress on the insides of her thighs where she was raw. "I . . . I don't know what to do."

The healer pressed her lips together. "Wait him out. You're his slave. Until your hair grows back and he lets you out of the chains, you'll be brought back to him. He's a captain/owner who can keep slaves, and people will believe his word first in all open courts. Berths are too scarce for an able-bodied sailor to witness for you, they can't risk losing their livelihoods, and he's usually more discreet than this. The last boy had to wait three years but managed it . . . he was old enough that Sarngeld didn't care much about chasing him down."

Megan stared at her. *Three years.* Then she turned her face to the wall and lay still, thinking it couldn't take very long to die if she never moved again.

Katrana insisted that she get up, that she eat. F'trovanemi she saw through the porthole; the fortress rock guarding F'talezon. The Rock was slick with cold and blowing rain, fortifications like a gate, shutting home away from her. She crawled back into the blankets, feeling burned inside.

As much as she didn't want to, she healed, being young, and over the next few days she found out one important thing that all her books hadn't mentioned. There was little room aboard a ship, no privacy and more importantly no place to hide. He always knew where she was and most of the crew, aside from the most casual of words, ignored her as the *Brezhani* worked her way down the river, whether out of shame or just indifference, she didn't know.

Some, like Katrana and Piatr were as nice as they could be. Some laughed and called her Captain's Toy. She stopped looking after herself, hoping he'd be disgusted. Instead he called her a slut and beat her. She found herself wishing he'd hit too hard, that she wouldn't wake up again. It was too much. Her family was dead. Marte had sold her. She couldn't make herself believe that Rilla would miss her.

She was sitting in the rope-well again, the most private place on the ship, listlessly staring at the water, her hands idly pulling at her greasy hair. *If I die, he'll win. Everyone who hates poor will win. Papa and Mama will have died with no one to remember them and the City won't care. If I die, they'll all win. But it would be so nice not to care.*

Katrana slid down beside her and started whittling at a stick she carried. "It'd be easier if you cried when he wanted tears, Meg."

"I won't cry for him. Not for him, not for anybody." Katrana tugged thoughtfully at her braids with her knife hand, studying the piece of wood in her hand, hair bells chiming.

"You could pretend," she said and spat into the water. "You got anyone to get back for? Anyone, even friends?" Pale yellow slivers of wood curled away from her knife to drift down into the brown water.

Megan nodded reluctantly, then shrugged. "My cousin, I suppose. She's still with ... her mother." *Dark Lord be damned if I ever acknowledge her as my kin again.*

"Ah. Kin still to live for. You don't know how much she needs you."

"She probably doesn't." Megan pulled another strand of hair out and dropped it in the river.

"Ach, did she need you before?"

Megan lifted one shoulder in a half shrug. "I suppose."

"Then you can't just abandon her, can you? You aren't slough-kin, as far as I can see."

Megan hardly looked up. Katrana gestured with the knife. "You know how to use these a bit, hmm?" At Megan's nod, she smiled. "As a healer I've stitched people up often enough. I could give you a few pointers how to slice them, as long as *he* doesn't find out. Piatr'd show you a trick or two if you asked nicely, and the quartermaster, Zaftra, is a teacher in knives—and manrauq, once you manifest." Megan nodded, head still hanging. "Hey!"

The girl looked up, startled. "And if you ever decide to cry, let me know. I'll lend you my shoulder." Katrana's stick snapped and she tossed it into the river, where the pieces bobbed beside the ship, drifting toward shore.

Cheboks was a small wooden town with a chalk cliff behind. The Lion of Cheboks, turf cut away from the chalk, showed for miles down river. The festival to clean the image was just beginning when they docked, and Megan saw the spring green just misting the ground, turning winter grey and brown into something alive again—just when she felt dead.

"I call thee forth!" The first mate, Hanald the Thane, a bandage around his shoulder, bellowed from the poop. "Listen to the wise judgement of our captain, owner of this ship. Zhena, able crew, did rashly raise her hand against a deck officer, for no just cause!"

Standing with the crew on the deck, Megan could feel the anger glowing among the Zak. Sarngeld couldn't quite get along on the river without hiring women, much as he disliked it, Arkans thinking that women were both stupid and lazy.

The first mate had wanted Zhena in his bed. Although he reminded her of the glut of able crewfolk on the river and that if she didn't sleep with him she could lose her place, she told him to suck sheep. Then he'd tried to force her, physically, and she'd stuck her knife in him.

"Captain calls judgement!" Hanald bellowed smugly. "Twenty lashes and revocation of her status!" They'd strung her up and stripped her, but she still spat on the deck by his foot.

"What?" The voice came from on deck. "That's . . ." The voice was lost in an angry growl. If her status was revoked then she was landed; no one would hire her on without her papers. The other deck officers stood by, armed.

Sarngeld stood to one side, arms crossed, his long

Arkan sword at his belt. "Silence! Silence, you dogs!" He stepped forward. "Who spoke? I'll have him on shore so fast he won't have time to spit! Be silent and watch justice!" He waited until they stopped muttering and stepped back, signing with this head to Thoman, the bosun, who acted as K'gebar. At the first stroke, everyone went silent. Megan felt something tingle behind her eyes and all along her skin. She shook her head, thinking for a minute that she'd seen a blue lake shimmer where the crowd stood.

In the midst of daylight it was hard to see, but light glowed over the Zak in the crowd and Thoman, a naZak, suddenly flung the whip away screaming that it had bitten him.

"STOP IT! Cease or I'll burn her as a witch!" Sarngeld shouted. "She'll burn and I'll drop anyone else I think is a witch in the river, weighted with rocks." The tense feeling of manrauq in the air dissolved into ordinary hate as he stood glowering down at his crew. The naZak crew shifted nervously in amongst the Zak, but most didn't move away from them, united for once. The bosun gingerly picked up the whip again.

"We can't stop it," someone near Megan whispered. "Not now."

Maybe later. The idea of being alive and present when Sarngeld finally pushed the crew too far, gave Megan a toe-hold on life again. She went away thinking of how she might help that day along.

She borrowed a comb from Kat and started washing again. She made friends with Piatr and his net-mate Reghina—at least cool friends, afraid to open up to anyone. She started hiding what she though behind a smooth, expressionless face. Sarngeld was an older man and didn't want her more than perhaps twice in a Hand, often less.

Late one night, Katrana jerked awake in the dark. "Who's there?" There was no answer but a sniffle and a muffled sob as if someone stifled the sound with the bedclothes. "Meg?"

Megan clambered up and lay with her head on Katrana's shoulder. The healer gathered her in close, pulling up the covers over both of them and Megan cried, finally starting to heal inside. She cried until her head was aching and sore and she fell asleep cuddled between the healer and the bulkhead of the ship that whispered and hissed to itself as the current pulled them further south.

Aenir'sford, on the split island, was full of half-timbered houses and noisy Aenir. The metal dragons arcing over the harbor mouth, were a wonder of the world, eight hundred paces high, five hundred long.

"Megan?" Piatr called her away from the rail where she watched the jolly boat take Sarngeld into the city, away from her.

"Yes?" She was being very careful of how she spoke now. The more the captain called her a whore and a slut, the more care she took with her language, even the Arkan.

"Watch," Piatr grinned, and started juggling a potato, a belaying pin, and a boot—all three at once. She watched intently, glad he was being so nice. "Smile, child," he called, and she drew back.

"I'm not a child anymore, no matter how young I am," she said. He caught the things he was juggling and watched her walk away.

The *Zingas Brezhani* chased the summer, warmer and warmer the further south they went. Rand was a city of islands, with bridges and cliffs. The fringes of dragons carved on every roof had bulging eyes and coiled red-painted tongues that spat rain; so different from the DragonLord's symbol. The people watched with their blank-faced, polite superiority in stiff, embroidered silks. That was where Megan clambered out of the worst of the dark and started fighting back. *He* wanted her docile, ignorant, helpless.

"Zaftra?" Megan came over to where the quartermaster and the cabin-kid were peeling tubers. The old man looked up, nodded at her. "I'd help," she said, "but *he*'s ordered anything sharp out of my—"

"I know. Thank you for offering." He was a withered wisp of a man, bald with age, liver spots showing on his head, but his eyes were bright and lively. "Can I help you with something?"

Megan sat down on an upturned bucket. "You can. The more important question, I think, is 'May you help me.'" He tilted his head at her.

"Come help me sift through the meal, then," he said. "Sonduk, keep on till these are done."

"Yessir." The youth bent his head over the job.

Megan followed the quartermaster to the bow where he measured out the meal from one of the barrels, and then to the tiny galley. "Look at this mess," Zaftra exclaimed disgustedly as he shoveled meal into the sieve. "Beetles, moths . . ." He snorted. "Rats and mice, despite the cat."

"Katrana said that you might be able to help me." Megan concentrated on sifting for a minute. "I know how to do some of the stuff Piatr does . . . like the tumbling. I learned that playing cniffta—that and juggling knives— and a friend of mine in the guard was teaching me things."

"In the City Guard?"

"Only a squire." Megan had thought about that, trying to get a letter to Serkai, but wasn't allowed even that. She inserted a finger under the slave collar to ease its chaffing, links clicking.

"Ah," was all he said, as he poured the sifted meal into the measure.

"Anyway, I didn't try too hard at that because I didn't think I'd need it much. I've changed my mind."

"And want help."

"I don't have anything else to do that I like—I haven't manifested yet—and it'll keep me from brooding over *him*."

"A sensible course." He added water to the bowl. "Of course, you realize that I haven't taught anyone in years, much less on *his* ship, and if he catches me teaching you I'll be worse off than poor Zhena?"

Megan lifted her chin a little. "Yes. That's why you can say no, as long as you say it to my face." She put her hands flat on the table. "I know more about ships and shipping than he does. I was River Guild—still am because my Gospozhyn never released me. *He's* going to choke on—" she hesitated "—a crew . . . some time when he gets too greedy and I want to know enough to fight him, to be there at least when he dies."

She felt as cold as when she cut up Svaslasfyav. *If you don't help me, I'll help myself, somehow.* Zaftra narrowed his eyes thoughtfully at the batter he was mixing, then reached one hand and touched her between the eyes with his fingertips; she jerked back startled, then held still. He got the distracted look on his face and Megan thought she saw a flicker of color in his eyes. When he dropped his hand he had pensive sort of look on his face and concentrated on adding the soured dough to the mix, then looked at her from under thin grey eyebrows.

"Yes, I'll teach you."

Out on the sea, in sight of the Pirate Islands. The sea was like the rolling grass of the steppe, but deep as thought and blue-indigo, waves rubbing against each other like crowds in a city, going this way and that, all at the same time. She spent hours staring at the sea, getting to know her; could float like a chip, forever timeless.

It was so timeless she almost missed her birthday. "Megan," Piatr said as he paused swabbing the deck. "Before he calls you down to his cabin, come up to the galley tonight."

"Why?"

"New Year."

"Already?" She shook herself. *Of course I haven't been counting days. I was waiting for it to get cold.* "Okay."

When she came, the other Zak were in the bow where

they were partly shielded from the rest of the crew by the bales of cotton stowed midships. When the moon rose and Shamballah shone bright in the sky they stood together, looking north to where the bright star hung low on the horizon.

Though it was in summer heat and the damp in the air was thick, when the highest power witch spoke it was like a breath of cold and silence; every Zak alive was sharing this night in enclaves all up and down the river, around the shores of the Mitvald Sea, wherever they'd been scattered from the river basin.

"One such night was when the world died. We were out in the snow, and on the horizon, the Great Phoenix reached its beak out of the world and then even the snow burned."

The other Zak answered in a whisper, *"We live."*

"Once the Dark Lord decreed that all should starve, saying we were an evil empire and a million deaths were nothing to him."

"We still live."

"Though the world died . . ."

"We live." The Zak raised their hands and light bloomed on their palms, mostly shades of red, but with one yellow glow. Megan felt the shiver before the light appeared and the cool blue undertones were like the taste of ice. She reached for the hands of the people beside her and they shared their light with her, accepting her. They were her family. She wasn't the captain's toy, but a Zak, Megan, herself.

I'm alive. I will live. I will. She smiled in the glow of light. *Rilla, I'm going to come home.*

They were docked at the third of the Aavrit cities, under the soaring limestone blocks of Nuogamesh-gir, the smells of dust and desert rolling offshore, camels and people in the heat that sucked at the damp of the sea; dry as Marte's heart. Megan had felt strange all day, bloated, and had cramps as if she'd eaten too much fruit.

When she felt a trickle between her legs, she went straight to Katrana.

"I'm bleeding," she said.

"Has he been hard on you again?" Katrana asked resignedly. Megan shook her head.

"He hasn't touched me in a couple of weeks," she explained. The healer raised an eyebrow.

"How old are you?"

"A bit over thirteen." Then Megan understood. "It's my cycle bleeding, isn't it?"

Katrana nodded and gave her a couple of sponges to use. "I'm glad I don't have to explain." She reached and touched Megan formally on the top of the head, then the chin, then hugged her. "You're a woman now. Welcome. I wish it could be better."

"It will get better, once he's d—" Megan closed her mouth. Katrana nodded.

"I won't say anything. I'm not that particular about him anyway." *For you that means you can't stand his guts. Sometimes Kat, you're too easy on people.*

That night she was crouched, watching a dice game, when Sarngeld called her, waving from where he stood by the mast. The dicers paused, watching. Mateus, able crew apprenticed to Kat, had just picked up the leather cup.

"It's my bleeding time," she said quietly, in properly submissive lower-to-upper caste Arkan. She watched the spasm of disgust cross his face.

"I didn't think you were that old." He headed for the gangplank. "Don't come near me till you're done."

"No, I won't." And when his back was turned, she smiled. Tachka, one of the deck crew, reached over and pushed gently at her shoulder, a supporting touch. He was a young sailor, just out of Guildschool.

"Roll! Up!" Zaftra's voice was a snap. Megan finished the move, came up to one knee with her hand holding the practice knife over her head, extended. "Hold it there. Don't move." Both of them were stripped to the waist in the dry heat, partly shaded by the city wall.

She held the pose, sweat trickling down her face and neck, tickling itches rolling down her chest and back and into her eyes, straining to hear his steps on the deck behind her. "We only have a little time when all the deck officers are off this ship. Use it. Treasure it. If we're caught, I'm landed and you're flogged. If you don't listen, you are wasting precious time. Up!" She sprang up into the first position, eyes calm, breathing already controlled. "Sparring, with me. Face!"

She spun, aware of the barrels and boxes to her right, just behind, the rail to her left. Zaftra held a long, thin rod in his hand and stood with one foot slightly advanced. "You'll usually be facing someone else with longer weapons. It's time you learned to deal with them." He let her stand a moment longer. "Stevan, call it."

The crewmember, sitting cross-legged on a hogshead, watching, grinned. "Ready!" he called, but instead of "Iya!" the second call, he said, "Begin!"

Zaftra lunged forward, Megan spun aside, the strike missing. She couldn't get close to him; he chased her all around the small open patch of deck, touching her here, there, but only light touches as she was moving away. *He's playing with me. In a real fight, I'd be dead.* The thought slowed her a fraction; he caught her a solid tap on her knife arm. "Wound!" Stevan called. "Drop it!"

She did, caught the practice knife with the other hand and instead of running, turned sideways, stepped in, and slashed at the wrist of his sword hand. "Wound!" cried Stevan, startled. Zaftra dropped the sword and Megan pinned the "sword" to the deck with her foot.

"Hold." Zaftra nodded. "Good." His head and chest gleamed with sweat. "You did well, but you didn't finish me when you had the advantage."

Megan stepped back. "Yes, master." *Why am I so slow?*

"They're coming back!" The call was relayed from forward and Zaftra jerked his head at Megan.

"Go sluice down."

She put the practice knife down by his shirt and trotted forward to drop a bucket over the side, feeling the heat glowing on her face and chest. *Why can't I learn faster? All I had to do was one more move and I could have finished it.*

The cool water made her feel better and she rubbed a scrap of toweling over her arms and chest. *Well, last time he chased me through the stowed cargo and I beat him there.* That had been in the dark of the hold, with no lights, only sounds to guide them, and her small size against his knowledge of how the hold was laid out. *That was fun.* She trotted back toward the ropewell to be out of Sarngeld's sight as much as possible, clambered down, resting her feet on the breast-fast that held them broadside to the wharf, luxuriating in all the space available with the rope payed out. She leaned her head back against the wood, listening to the conversations of the off-duty officers in their quarters just through the thin wall.

". . . a student in years, Zaftra." Katrana said. "Why are you now? You could set up a zahl and teach Prafetatla for far more than a sailor ever earns."

"Ah, Kat, I have m' reasons. I've still got an itchy foot. And I'd miss students like her."

"She's that good? I thought you agreed to teach her because you were sorry for her."

"No. No, I teach no one out of pity, Kat, and I'm sorry you would think that." His voice was stiff.

"Zaftra, I'm sorry, I meant nothing by it."

"Accepted. But to answer your question, yes, she is that good. One of my better students. Did you see the chase she just led me? She already has the important thing—spirit. Now all she needs to work on is her feeling of self and her own zight."

They're talking about me. She pulled her head away, leaned forward with her elbows on her knees and looked down into the dust and a dead leaf or two swirl in an eddy between ships. *My feeling of self? Why doesn't he tell me these things?* She spat wind-blown grit out into the water. *I suppose he will, in good time. But I can work on them myself.* She leaned her head back to listen more, but they were talking about Zaftra's health and the rest of the crew.

Niah-lur-ana, the trade isles, where the dark-skinned people came out in long canoes painted like sharks and single-person boards with sails mounted on them, the men and women both clad only in knee-lengths of bright printed cotton. Megan looked out over the islands, playing with the chain that marked her a slave, and smiled a little at the irony that paradise and halya could be close enough that a person could look from one to the other, only a few feet away.

Sarngeld would often just hold her in the night, having dreams of old battle-fields and the one that ruined him as a *solas*, a soldier.

In the dark he'd sweat and toss, mumbling, clinging to Megan, and she'd lie still listening to his nightmares, hating him, hating herself.

Esaria, in Sria, south of Tebrias which the Srians held, for now; square mud brick buildings thatched with grass, the central fortress a pyramid. All the Srians were black-rock black, and Megan found out that the giant given to Ranion for his wedding was real; they were all, even the shortest of them, almost twice as tall as most Zak.

The mainsail tore right in half, in a stiff following breeze, the upper half flapping from the lateen-yard with fluttering, whip-like cracks, and they'd limped in on one sail. Sarngeld never paid out metal until he had to, and when the sail-makers told him it would never hold a patch, he paid for a new one and was in a vicious mood for a day after. Megan stayed out of his way and out of the first mate's as well.

Hanald despised Zak and had taken to calling her Captain's Slut, as if she wanted it, as if she were at fault for what Sarngeld did.

*   *   *

Kreyen; open buildings with red painted pillars. The people there were not as dark as the a-Niah, their skin shining with the oil of the olives they grew.

She'd gotten used to bleeding every month, to being free for at least a Hand and two days. She wished that he wouldn't look at her, or be attracted to what he saw; she threw wishing stones into the water, daydreamed that he found her ugly. When she slept she dreamed that he never wanted to touch her again, the icy blue feeling of manrauq tingeing these dreams unnoticed, but Sarngeld looked at her less often. The chain came off, though he left the collar and the wrist manacle on and she was still forbidden to leave the ship.

"You're growing up," Katrana said. "He'll leave you alone more and more that you look like a grown woman." That was true, though he still wanted her in his bed, whether he used her or not. *I'll have a bed of my own again, someday, and I'll sleep in it alone. It will smell of me and not him.* He liked to sleep holding her spooned against him, her head on his shoulder, his arm across her body, his other hand holding onto her wrist. *Like a stuffed toy.*

"He's leaving you alone more often, isn't he?" Zaftra said one day. Megan looked up from where she was trying to do the front split stretch. It irked her that she was still a good hand-breadth off the deck.

"Yes, he is."

"I think you're manifesting." Zaftra sat in a cross-legged pose, face turned to the sun as they bobbed on the ocean, becalmed.

Megan slid her legs around to the front and sat down with a bump. "I *am?*"

"Yes, and as far as I can see you're gaining unconscious control. We'll begin on your conscious control tomorrow."

"How do you know? How can you tell? How powerful am I—will I be?"

"It's my gift. I can see it. You're holding yourself back so you're barely a red witch ..." He paused for a moment thinking, the gulls wheeling and crying around the ship. From the stern came the sound of Tachka's pipes winding around the mewing cries. "As for how powerful you'll be . . . that depends on you and circumstance."

Megan calmed herself, wiping sweat off her face with her hands. *That's what he's saying in case I don't get powerful; it'll be my fault if I don't. I know how to do other things than be a witch.*

"Make your mind still. Calm yourself. Make yourself as still as water in a bowl." Zaftra's voice was distant. They sat in the shade of the water barrels the next day, still becalmed. "Don't think! Feel." Megan tried to ignore the sweat on her skin, tickling, itching, running down her face, tried to stare, unfocused at the horizon. "Good," the old man said softly. "Now close your eyes and see it without looking."

She tried, but the sight went away into black again and again until her hands were clenched in frustration and spots danced in front of her eyes, she was squeezing them shut so hard. *Varik said I'd probably never be powerful.*

"Enough. Haul up a bucket and douse your head, get a drink of water, then come back." She shook her head and got up, frowning at him; he frowned back. "You said you wanted my teaching. Learn the manrauq as fast as you've been with the knives and you will be good. Don't fight yourself so hard." She stared at him, wondering why he was so adamant about it when it was obvious that she couldn't do better no matter how hard she tried. She shrugged and did what he said.

"Cooler head now?" he asked when she settled down again.

"Not really. I'd rather learn something more practical."

He sighed. "This is one of the most practical things you can learn, for a Zak. Try again, but not so hard."

Not as hard? She shrugged and looked at the horizon, watched a gull drift, float on the wind up out of the blue; blue, blue as sky, as deep ice, as water . . . she realized that her eyes were closed, his hand covering them gently, and she could still see blue. It didn't seem important.

His voice came, distant, cool. "See your name."

Megan, she thought and watched a red spark dance in the midst of the blue.

"That's you, what every other Zak will see in this place in their minds. We are all here. Think my name."

Zaftra was a yellowish spark that twinkled like an eight-point star, very close.

"Come out."

With a start she realized that she'd done it, jolted her eyes open, and squinted them shut against the sunlight that was painfully bright.

"Good. You're holding back, but these things change. For now you'll learn red-witch things and borderline orange, just in case." He leaned back further into the shade, a contented smile on his face. "You'll have a bit of a headache if you do anything too much, it strains you. And if you overstrain yourself, your lungs and heart might give out, so we'll be careful."

"Zaftra, does it really matter? I mean, you say I'm getting good enough with a knife." She massaged her temples. "It seems like a lot of work for little gain."

"It matters." His thoughtful old eyes twinkled. "I can tell. It matters. Enough lazing about!" he snapped suddenly. "Show me the second position, from sitting, half-speed! Move!"

Then she missed a cycle bleeding. And another. Again she went to Katrana.

"You're pregnant."

Kat's words slipped through Megan's mind like an oiled snake. *I thought she said I was pregnant. That's impossible. I . . .* She felt sick, sudden nausea clutching at the bottom of her throat and she lunged for the covered bucket in the corner, bile spilling into her mouth as she wrenched the lid off. "I don't want it. It's part his, it's like he's growing in me. Kat, cut it out like a tumor, get rid of it. Dark Lord, it'll eat me alive . . ."

"Shush, hush, Meg. It's a baby not a tumor. It will be what you want it to be. It can be yours or his. I'll try to get rid of it for you, with herbs, though Zhena could have laid hands on you, that was her gift . . ." She sighed. "No use wishing for Shamballah. Hush, Meg." Katrana took her in her arms where she clung, shivering.

Tor Ench, where the women were kept in femkas or swathed in lace veils when they went out, the men in fur collars and straight, blunt cut hair.

Nothing Katrana gave Megan helped. The last thing she tried was a decoction of juniper and tansy, and Megan was sick for a Hand after but didn't abort.

"No more, Meg. The baby wants to cling to life. I won't endanger you like that again."

"But, Kat—"

"No 'but Kats.' I won't kill you trying to get rid of it. It will be your baby if you decide it is. Your baby, not his."

"I'm not ready, I'm not old enough."

"Meg, you'll have to be."

My baby. My kin. My baby. That was what she kept repeating to herself, in the dark, with the weight of his arms and leg on her. That weight while he slept was so much less than when he held her pinned to make her panic, make her struggle so she wiggled against him; exciting him. *My baby.*

Yeola-e where everyone had curly hair, waving arms with every word and smiles that seemed very free, as if they'd never tasted slavery, distant mountains floating like clouds. Another year end and she turned fourteen, just starting to show her pregnancy.

She could still climb in the rigging, learning, and knew that she was keeping better accounts than he was. She pretended it was an exercise given her by Gospozhyn, the way he had so long ago in school. The money was always short because he spent it on himself. Hriis Trade Town—no name but that—more sand.

"You know," Megan said to Mateus once, leaning on the rail, "if he trained and paid his own pilot, he wouldn't have to pay the harbor fees."

"He'd still have to pay."

"But less. Look . . ." She started to explain and he listened for a minute.

"You lost me there. That harbor fee is less than the retaining fee of a pilot.

"It seems so, but there are hidden taxes, don't you see?"

Mateus shrugged, spreading his hands. "If you say so. I know navigating and some healing from Kat. This is beyond me."

"Oh. All right." *But it's so simple.*

Sinapland, full of orange robed priests who bought Nellas cheese and Kreyen olive oil. *He could have sold them flawed topaz from the City states as "Toad's Eyes."*

She noticed that if Zaftra could convince Sarngeld to rearrange the hold, the *Brezhani* could ship perhaps another quarter-tonne. He shrugged and tried it. Sarngeld didn't even notice.

Berjus. Selov. Baku. Mahachkala. They were starting to blur together in her mind, so she started writing them down. The names, what they looked like, what they sold.

She watched the dolphins skip in the bow wave when they had a stiff following breeze, trying to see them both with her eyes and hear them. She thought she was starting to hear whispers, inside her ears, of their thoughts. *goodlifefish femalemalesexfeelwaterflow funbreathsun.* "Yes, child," Zaftra said. "You aren't imagining it."

She amused herself trying to out-guess Hanald, or the other deck-officer's calls to the crew; trying to find for herself the best way into and out of the harbors, watching the hired pilots or the row-tugs.

Brahvniki again, the onion domes like a welcoming hand drawing them in through the jostling small-boats, cascades of flowers spilling everywhere over balconies and windows.

"Kat," Megan asked one day as she helped fold blankets.

"Dah, Meg?"

"What happens to his babies? Or his bed partners when they bear children?"

Katrana pursed her lips. "I don't know, Meg. It's never happened before that I know of—he's had mostly boys. You should sit down for a while."

"Yes, healer," Megan said with mock submission.

"Oh, go on with you!"

Later that night Megan stood just inside the door of his cabin, her hands clasped protectively around herself. "Get out, slut, you've gotten ugly. You disgust me." Sarngeld threw a blanket at her and she caught it close around her, wanting to smile. *I get to sleep by myself—and my baby. Koru, I haven't prayed to you for a while. I haven't believed in you. But You're a Mother, so you might have time for me again. Thank You for the baby. Thank You for the shape of a grown woman, that disgusts him so.*

That night she slept in the galley under the table, content enough to fall asleep almost the moment she lay down, cradling her bulging stomach. *Kat's worried about the size of the baby. What happens, happens.*

North again to Bjornholm, just up the Vechaslaf River, west of where it met the Brezhan; chasing winter up the river this time, bringing spring with them.

"Koruuuu! Help me. Kat, it hurts. It hurts. Its clawing its way out of me . . . it's a monster . . ."

"It's all right Megan, here, it's just a baby being born. Hold onto Mateus's wrists."

"The whole world's splitting me apart. Mother Bear help me, helpmehelpme . . ."

"Meg, drink this. No, don't argue, drink it even if it tastes bad, come on." The world went strange and distant, wavering in and out like waves on the sea, but the sea was far away, too ... *I must be dreaming. Kat's arguing with someone—Him—about me, about the baby. Arguing with Him and threatening to leave ... He doesn't want that. Why? Oh, more thunder coming, I can feel it ...* She clung to Mateus's wrists, feeling his gift wash over her, helping Katrana's drug, vaguely irritated at whoever was shrieking like a night-siren.

A Haian voice. Why? Papa's arm's already gone. She tried to twist away from the rubber and cold smelling mask someone pressed over her face. "Breathe in, Meg, don't fight ..." She followed the voice down into the dark.

When she woke up, she was still floating in the dark it seemed, her body wrapped tightly in bandages. *To keep my guts in.* She giggled, or tried to, but all that came out was a whimper. She couldn't make her eyes work and complained.

"Shh, Meg. You'll be all right ..." The healer hesitated, then went on. "Are you thirsty?" Katrana held a straw to her lips and she drank thirstily, clearing the dry scummy feeling out of her mouth. The room stank of Haian medication.

"The baby?" she whispered. Kat's face swam out of the dimness again.

"A healthy boy, born with a head of dark hair." She held a blanket wrapped bundle that Megan tried to reach for. "He has all the necessary bits like fingers, toes, nose, penis ..." Kat smiled and laid the baby in the cradle of Megan's arm.

"My son. Whitlock's son. Lixand," she whispered, touching the fuzz on the baby's head, feeling a rush of joy that was almost as sharp as pain. *Did Mama feel like this when I was born?* "Just like your grandfather."

His eyes were pressed shut and his face was wrinkled in on itself as if he could squeeze the world away from him.

"They're blue," Kat said. "But then all babies have blue eyes."

"I don't care. He's healthy. He's my son." Sleepily,

sorely, she tried to lift him toward Kat as if the healer hadn't seen him before. "See my beautiful baby?"

When Megan was stronger, Katrana helped her walk the companionway, one hand under her elbow. She'd made the deck for the first time since Lixand had been born, and Katrana sat with her.

"Meg . . ." Kat hesitated again.

Megan shifted the baby from one breast to the other, felt his lips tug and the soreness fade. She looked up at the Aenir woman.

"You've been hiding something from me, Kat, about me." Her hand moved steadily, patting Lixand's back as he nursed. "I'm not going to break."

The healer took a breath. "To save your life . . . and his . . . well . . ."

"He was too big for me," Megan said calmly. "Do I still have a womb?"

Katrana stopped, startled. "Oh, Meg. Not one that will bear another child—but I didn't want to be so harsh telling you. You are scarred too badly."

Megan smoothed the baby's curls, wiped the trickle of milk from her breast where Lixand's lips had relaxed as he slept again. "I have a son. So be it."

It was only later that the tears came, as she healed and could bear them.

Chapter Seventeen

"Lixande-mi! Ba-ba-baby!" Megan dangled a rattle in front of Lixand who grabbed at it and tried to stuff it in his mouth. She stroked his fine blond hair and smiled. "You're a strange changeling baby, my child." His dark birth hair had fallen out and come in again bright, bright blond and his eyes had darkened to the color of hers. They were tucked into a niche between two of Zaftra's barrels on deck, enjoying the clear weather. *We should head south soon if we want to escape the winter.*

Sarngeld hadn't touched her since before Lixand was born, and Megan thanked the Goddess every day for that. The baby crawled over to her and she picked him up, cuddling, a solid weight with strong hands that tangled in her hair and tried to stuff it in his mouth. He nuzzled against her.

"Hai, my little piggy child. Wait, wait . . ." She pulled up her blouse and wiped herself before she let him nurse; not as often now that she was weaning him. She rocked him and hummed a lullaby that her mother had sung to her. "Ow, don't bite your mother even if teeth are new to you, all three of them!"

He burped and fell asleep in her arms, one fist still clutching her blouse. She braced her knees under him so her arms wouldn't fall asleep and leaned her head back against the barrel behind her. *Since he's left me alone, life has been calm, at least.* She watched the gulls wheeling over the ship, heart-holdingly white against a deep blue.

"Megan!" Sashe, a middle-aged, cat-nimble man who mostly worked the foredeck, called. "Captain wants you . . ." He went on reluctantly, "In his cabin, now." The afternoon's peace froze in her and Lixand whimpered in his sleep as her hands tightened on him. Every step back toward his cabin was like wading through air filled with the glittering splinters that she was breathing. *Maybe if I take the baby he'll forget about wanting me.*

His door was open, swinging a little in the gentle motion of the river. "Why'd you bring the brat?" he growled at her. "Get rid of it, slut, or I'll drown it."

She backed out and carefully left Lixand swaddled and still asleep on Kat's empty bed, telling Piatr where the baby was.

"I'll keep an eye on him, then."

"Thank you." Then she went back to *him.*

Stretch. She could do the full front splits again, turned her head sideways on her knee to keep an eye on the baby, asleep on an old bit of toweling, sucking his toes.

"Megan! Oh, sorry, I don't want to wake the baby." Sashe settled down nearby. Megan changed from left stretch to center stretch.

"That's all right, Sash, he was fussy all morning and it would take one of *his* bellows to wake him."

"Good. Look, Meg, do you think I could make quarterdeck-crew rating in the River Guild? If I studied?"

"You mean officer? Ocean or river?" Megan shifted to full splits the other way, smooth as water flowing.

"Ocean." Sashe looked down at his hands. "I thought I'd ask, since you're Guild-trained."

"Yes," Megan said promptly, not seeing anything

strange about a middle-aged man asking a sixteen year old for advice. "In my opinion you'd be not much good on a river, no feel for snags or bars." His face fell a little. "But," she continued, "you don't deal well with the confinement and like lots of room and have a feel for deep water. Storm-sense, too, that isn't just manrauq."

She straightened up, wiping sweat off her face with the other bit of towel. "No reason why you shouldn't try for bosun papers at the very least."

He grinned. "I will! Next time I'm home, I will! Thank you!" He got up and sauntered forward, whistling.

"It'll get you away from *him*," Megan muttered to herself. Sarngeld didn't need more officers and hated anyone with any ambition. Sashe would find a place on another ship. The shortage of berths was for able crew, not anything higher.

"There's not an officer we can trust," Megan said thoughtfully. Katrana, Piatr and Mateus nodded. They were sitting in fo'c'sle, the storm rolling the ship, even at anchor, water leaking in around the foremast collar. Most of the rest of the crew and all officers but the first mate were in the town, in dry inns. There was a knock and Megan repressed a start. "Zaftra?"

"Aye." The four of them relaxed, letting out the breaths they'd been holding. None of them had said the word mutiny, though they had been talking for a few weeks. Mutiny was punishable by impalement. To falsify Guild seals meant having one's entrails pulled out and burned, as well. Megan joggled the baby on her knee, sniffed, and pulled out the back of his diaper. He fussed as she laid him down to change him.

"Hush, baby mine."

Zaftra ducked his head under the lintel, nodded at the other conspirators.

"I just checked to see no one was listening." He shook out his blanket cloak and ran a hand over his wet hair and scalp. "It's raining pitchforks out there."

"Yah."

"You know," Megan said thoughtfully. "All of what we've been discussing is 'just in case.'"

Zaftra laughed. "We can say so in front of any truth-teller in the land. Just be glad that Arkan truth-drug is so expensive."

"Uhm. Well. Tachka, Sashe . . . he might not be here if he's going into the Guild."

"A good thing, to be able to use Guild seals." Kat shuddered. "I saw a mutiny trial about ten years ago in Brahvniki."

"We just have to make sure we aren't caught, if it should come to that," Megan said firmly. "Besides, no one but me would risk it. I'm Guilded, if not properly accredited."

She put the baby down on the floor. "Piatr, Thoman is usually with the foredeck crew, so if anything should happen . . ."

"I can deal with him. He's better as a K'gebar wielding a whip than a knife."

She looked at him in the tossing light of the lamp hung from the ceiling. He shrugged.

"I've killed before. Reghina's in."

"Then if you come aft, I'll know you're heading for the weapons locker with Thoman's keys." She nodded decisively. "I want Sarngeld . . . *At-za-tt-ratzas*, Solas . . ." She pronounced his real name carefully, as if pronouncing a curse. "He is mine to kill." *I maimed a man when I was ten. I should be able to kill one.* She smiled at Lixand who was chewing on his fist. "We'll keep recruiting people, carefully, or we'll all be sprouting another leg." Their faces, in the shifting light, were grim.

She watched the baby walk, holding onto the galley table, babbling to himself. Zaftra smiled and moved his measuring spoons away from the edge. Lixand smiled back at him, showing six teeth now, squealed, and tod-dled over to Megan, half running, flinging himself on his mother. She caught him, buried her face in his tummy, flapping her lips to make him giggle.

They were docked at Naryshkiv village, stout wooden walls blocking the view of the fields and manors beyond. It was market day. The barking of sheep dogs, the bleating of Thanish flocks drifted in the distance; music, the reedy sound of an *ahkordi* squeezing out a waltz, the mutter of Sarngeld's Arkan friend on deck.

Lixand ran to Zaftra, grabbing onto his trouser leg then back to Megan, sitting down abruptly on his bottom, considering whether he ought to cry or not. He decided against it and crawled over to grab at the rattle Megan still held. "Ma-ma! No! Ma-ma. No!"

"His favorite words," Megan said to Zaftra.

Lixand recognized Sarngeld's step already and knew enough to hide from it. He dropped the rattle and hid behind Megan as the Arkan came in.

"Come, girl." He gestured with his head. *He always gets very careful about waving his hands around when other Arkans visit. I wonder what he wants me for, now.* Lixand wouldn't let go of her, so she hoisted him on her arm where he threw his arms around her neck.

Sarngeld led them past the other Arkan, a lean man in pale gloves, into his cabin. There he took her by the other shoulder and dragged her over to the metal staple in the floor where the slave-links were bolted.

"Sarngeld, what are you doing?" She started to struggle, Lixand clinging, howling. He locked her wrists in and tried to pull Lixand away from her. *Koru, Goddess, he's threatened to drown him before* . . . She clung to the baby with all her strength. Sarngeld, irritated, backhanded her across the face to make her let go.

"No! Nonono! Baaaa-aad!" Lixand squealed, and then just shrieked as Sarngeld untangled him.

"Sarngeld, master, leave me my baby, please don't drown him. Please, he's your son, don't kill him. Please, he's only a baby. Don't, please, master." Megan crawled to the end of the chains, on her knees, on her face. "Master! Master! Don't take him . . ."

"Drown it?" Sarngeld laughed, stepping back out of

reach of her pleading hand. "It's too valuable for that. I'm short of money."

"No, please! Lixand! Lixand!" She lunged against the chain as if she could tear free. "Lixannnnnd!" The door closed on Sarngeld, muffling the baby's wailing as he was carried away. She screamed, clawing at the oak links, at the metal holding her to the floor, tearing the skin of her hands. "Lixand!" She screamed his name as if the sound of her voice could hold him somehow, until she was hoarse and exhausted, lying flat on the floor, stretched toward the door, whispering her son's name.

The splinter of light through the portholes faded, leaving her in the dark with nothing but the chains to fight, her nose full of the smell of the dry-rot in the boards. "Lixand . . ."

Above, she could hear his boots on the deck, feel the shift and scrape change as they undocked and caught the current south, leaving Naryshkiv behind. *Lixand.*

It was just rising dawn when the door opened quietly and Katrana slipped in.

"Meg?" There was no answer. "Megan?"

"Go away."

"I've got his keys."

Megan sat up, aching, stiff in all her joints. "His keys?"

She caught the shine of the white of one of Kat's eyes in the dimness, the rising sun throwing a splinter of light through the porthole. "And my knives if you want to borrow them."

"It's now, Kat. Get everyone together. It's now."

Megan crept up the companionway ladder, hugging the shadow. *I'm going to kill him.* There was a subdued rustle in the bow; Piatr sauntered by her as if she weren't there, going below. *To the weapons locker. He got the bosun. A muffled splash up forward.* She'd told Mat to set an anchor or they'd all end up aground before everything was over. A shout from the poop as the ship started to swing around.

Sarngeld was over by the port side, shouting for Thoman. Megan swung up over the edge of the poop. The helm yelled as she gained her feet and Sarngeld turned toward her.

Knife flip back over my shoulder—just like in cniffta— throw HARD. The dagger spun once and buried itself just over his groin. He folded forward, a stunned look on his face, gloves stained dark as he clutched his abdomen. She jumped high, landed on his bowed shoulders, driving him down to the deck. One of his hands came up, caught her by the ankle, dragged her down. *I can't see, my hair . . .* She landed hard on the deck, air pressed out of her lungs, but she slashed backhand, something snicked and parted under the blade—*hamstrung*—scrambled up as he fell sideways and drove the knife into his back.

Die, damn you die. Stop squealing and die. Sticky-hot blood fountained across her face as she wrenched the knife loose and drove it in again, and again, the hilt slipping greasily; blood and more blood, feeling the blade twist and catch on ribs. *Die.* She stabbed until he stopped moving, looked up to find herself in the middle of a blood-splashed circle with the rest of the crew, armed, standing watching her. She crawled to her feet, suddenly aware of every ache, every pain, favoring the ankle he'd grabbed, realizing she was coated head to foot in his blood. She spat to clear her mouth, panting.

"We're going back to Naryshkiv, to get my son."

"Who are you to say?" Hanald stood behind the wheel, boot-knives raised, holding off Mateus who held belaying pins. "I'm first mate. I have more right to this ship than you do, murderer."

"Mat, get back. We can always fish him out of there with a boathook."

Hanald laughed. "Listening to women and children, Mateus? Zak have no balls anyway." The ship creaked as she swung, dragging the single anchor, bow-on to the stream. The rest of the crew shifted their grips on what weapons they had, looking for a decision from someone.

"You fight for it, Thane?" Megan asked quietly.

"Meg, no! He'll kill you," Katrana called from the main deck.

"He'll feed the river gar."

Hanald laughed and stepped out. "Fight you, little toy? Captain's slut? A disease-riddled child whore—what fifteen, sixteen—captaining a ship? I'll spank you and set you off at the next town south!" He walked forward as if to grab her, jumping back as she slashed.

"Don't talk, fight." She held herself low, the lessons by Zaftra coming without thinking. He circled right, trying to push her back against Sarngeld's corpse, lunged. She stepped inside his thrust, grabbed his wrist—*flash of pain, shoulder and back, other knife*—and slashed twice across his belly, let go. He stumbled forward with a surprised look as his hands went numb, his knives clattering as he fell to his knees, trying to hold his guts in. She pulled his head back by the hair, cut his throat, watching the spray of crimson splatter the nearer crew.

Cold. I'm cold. She wanted to vomit at the stink of blood and shit on the deck, crushing it down into a knot in the pit of her stomach. *Killed two men in less than an hour. Lixand.*

"We're going north, back to Naryshkiv." Her voice was cool and dry. She wiped the knife on a clear spot on her sleeve. "Anyone else have a problem with that?"

Silence. "I have the most official training to be an owner/captain from the Guild, and they'll back me once I get a message to my Gospozhyn." They waited, listening as if they judged her. "I'll pay out the back-pay *he* was holding and release anyone who won't obey me." A swift mutter around the deck as she stood, feeling the drying blood pull at her skin and hair, wanting to push the crew who hadn't been approached by the conspirators, knowing that she couldn't.

Mateus slotted the pins back in the rack. "Aye, Teik. We ... none of us would try to use a Master's token, not with the Guild watching ... Captain."

Megan nodded, putting the knife away. *Captain.* "Mat, you're second mate. You see that this mess gets cleaned up." She scanned the rest of the crew standing, waiting for orders and her eye fell on one of the half-Zak—a tall, square man, with brown hair and violet eyes, Tze Riverson, whose Zak heritage only showed in his uncanny ability to read the river. He was competent. She decided. "Tze, you're first mate. I want this ship in Naryshkiv by tomorrow."

"Aye, Captain," he answered, not hesitating over the title, and she thought that her troubles would be over if everyone adjusted so quickly. She called Garhert, ship's carpenter, to bring a pry bar below to the cabin—*my cabin, for now.*

No one is ever going to own me again. No one is ever going to rule me like that again. She watched him pry the metal staple out of the wood with a dry *skreek*, carried it and the oak chain on deck herself, and flung it in the river, watching it sink, uncaring that she could sell the metal. *That's my slavery sinking. Lixand, my son. I'm coming to get you. I'll get you back, baby mine. I'm strong enough to now. I'm of age and anyone who tries to hurt me can go fik. I'm free.* In the lamplight, he sawed the wooden collar off her neck and wrist, careful of her skin. For a moment she felt almost dizzy and too light; her balance shifted, as they came off. She went down to her cabin to wash the blood off her skin and out of her hair.

With a careful hand she copied Sarngeld's signature on the document, the bill of sale that proclaimed her the *Zingas Brezhani*'s new owner/captain, assuming all unfulfilled contracts. Sarngeld's seals were in the trunk under the bunk, and she used the ring taken from his hand before they threw the corpse in the river weighted with rocks.

From below a steady hammering sounded. The old *Brezhani* had sprung a board and the bilges had started filling faster than they could be pumped out. They were cobbling a patch but couldn't fix the ship while she was under way.

Megan cursed steadily under her breath but forced her hands steady as she signed her own name. . . . *called Whitlock. No personal seal. I'll have to get one.* A steady scrape from above, where the holystone was being pulled across the bloodstain. They couldn't erase it but could make it seem old. While they were laid up to stop the leak, there was more cleaning being done than for the last few weeks all together, people finding work to hide their tension, coiling ropes, polishing brass long tarnished green, scraping and painting as if they couldn't worry while their hands did the work. They were glad enough to have her take the risk of docking and customs at Naryshkiv.

There. She waited for the wax to cool. The money in the box, *Lixand's price*—she bit her lip at the thought—was just enough to cover the back wages owed the crew and another docking fee. She didn't want to pay them with the money she might need to get Lixand back, but she had to. She needed their goodwill as much as they needed her.

It will have to do.

The customs clerk barely glanced at the bill of sale, affixed his stamp and took the fee. "Good day to you, Teik Captain."

"And to you. Teik Clerk, is the town's record hall open this late?" She kept her tone light, not letting the urgency show.

He considered a moment, checked the height of the sun over the port rail, considered longer while she seethed, pretending calm. The patch had taken a full three days to do properly, dry-rot crumbling the hole bigger. They'd had to ground the *Brezhani* and replace whole boards.

"Nyata, it's too late today." He nodded over at the cluster of stolid red-brick showing over the wooden ware-houses. " 'ts Next to the Guildsquare."

"Thank you."

       o   o   o

Megan ran a hand through the white lock in her hair, forcing calm. The Naryshkiv market clerk was hardly at fault, even if he was the giver of bad news.

"The Arkan trader . . . ah . . . hmm . . . his name . . . Anetenkas Grias, Okas, as far as I know. Dealing with a Thane for exotic goods to go into the Empire, I believe."

"When did he leave?" The clerk looked up at her, a little taken aback at her vehemence.

"Why . . . four, five days ago I believe, in the afternoon, by barge up the Oestschpaz, I think."

Four, five days ago. Four or five days.

"Thank you, Teik Clerk, you've been most helpful." Megan stepped outside trying to feel like an owner/captain.

She stopped in the shadow of the porch, looking out at the muddy, half-cobbled square where the market was just packing up for the night.

I either give up the ship and what friends—family—I have and try to catch Lixand. On foot by myself, or hope I can track him by proxy. Five days . . . There was no money to buy a horse or passage on a barge, no extra at all. Tze and Mat were waiting for her. They were good at following orders, but at commanding? There was a cargo of leather on the *Brezhani*, promised to a merchant in Rand. If she left them, it would be as bad as Marte getting rid of her because she was too much trouble.

She put her face in her hands. *Lixand.* The roiling in her guts settled. *I'm already too late, but I'll find you, wherever you are. I'll get the gold I need to find you. I have a gold candlestick waiting at home to start.*

She threw back her shoulders and strode out into the square.

Chapter Eighteen

The Randish merchant accepted the leather with only the barest flicker of surprise that the Arkan had sold out to a woman. Megan bowed over her cup of Randish tea and waited for him to begin negotiations for the next cargo. This Rand, a coral button Fifth rank, preferred to deal with freelance rather than Guild captains; willing to trade off risk for immediate gain.

They sat in a dark, stone room. At least it was lit with sweet-scent candles. *He's trying to impress the ignorant foreigner*, Megan thought, settling herself to wait as long as necessary. *Nal-Gospozhyn Eyvan always had me play the Randish games of zight until I was ready to scream.* She thought she saw a flicker of emotion across that smooth, creamy-skinned face. *Impressed with my patience? Or intrigued with my youth?* She dismissed the idea.

"Honorable Servant of the Sky Dragon, these mean eyes delight in the lush and elegant surroundings this humble one finds herself, and is grateful that the noble and magnificent host has chosen to honor her with such loveliness." She turned her tea cup the requisite three times, signifying delight and admiration, thinking, *a shoddy copy of Second Dynasty porcelain*.

"Ahh." He put the tips of his fingers together as he bowed at her compliment. "This poor and unworthy host is grateful that the enlightened guest praises him with her regard and elegant taste." *Finally*, she thought. *He's warming up. Enlightened, hmmm? I guess Sarngeld dealt with him his own way.*

"Oh, the lightning intelligence of my gracious host overwhelms this ignorant *jahnin*." *Lay it on thick as a new-rich's buttered roll. Fifth rank need all the buttering they can get. He'll appreciate me calling myself a foreign devil.* "It truly enlightens and enlarges one in the august presence."

He ran a smoothing hand over his red skull-cap, preening, though no expression showed on his face.

"Permit this crude and unlearned host to approach my distinguished guest with a small proposal."

"This lowly one hangs on every precious word." *Bullcrap. You have another load of half-split leather that you want to go north to Aenir's-ford because the fall market there will be good.*

"If the magnificent mind of my guest will deign to dwell on the possibility that her elegantly appointed vessel would bear my dirty, ill-cured wares north to the bluff, crude market. For an exchange of, please forgive the haste and crudity of my language, cash."

"This lowly one is astonished at the largess of her host, whose words are both elegant and stately." *And overblown as all Halya, but he does seem to be in a hurry.*

"The brilliance of my guest overwhelms me." It went on like that for a good hour or so, compliments smeared thick as honey on burnt bread, but they arrived at a deal.

She paused at the tunnel into the open air of the third west island to let her eyes adjust to the brightness. It was quieter than the more important islands of Rand, but during their harvest festival that was not peaceful. Fireworks exploded all around the caldera, streamers floated from the heights to be swept away by the river or caught by the docks clustered around the steep islands. Dragons with hundreds of Rand underneath danced through the upper streets, a few even daring spider-slender bridges swaying in the breeze. The crowd swirling around her was almost as uniformly short as a Zak crowd, but yellow-skinned, dressed in heavily embroidered robes of nobles or would-be nobles, or plain blue tunic and pants of the common, and all as haughty of any non-Rand as the Zak could be of naZak.

Megan was conscious of the weight at her belt. The letters of payment drawn up, cash drafts payable only on delivery— She caught the wrist of a child too poor to own a razor, who was trying to pick the purse, blocking the thumb-jab. "Nyata," she said softly into frightened brown eyes then switched to Rand. "First trick, no cash. Learn more." That about exhausted her fund of Rand. "Go." The child disappeared into the crowd like a freed bird.

Was I ever that young? Megan thought. *I want to get back to my ship and out of this noise.*

The weather on their trip north was rain, freezing rain, sleet and finally snow, the wind blowing fitfully and with little force so they had to row most of the way. After the third day of pulling, Megan called a halt at Beigen, a tiny cluster of buildings with two docks and a half-silted harbor.

"Tze, we'll lay up here for tomorrow. If the snow stops and we get a wind, we'll gain by the wait. Everyone won't be too tired to handle sail."

"Aye, Captain."

"Mateus, set the wards on the ship."

"Aye, Captain." He winked at her before his face took on the unfocused look. She smiled at him, though he couldn't see, his eyes looking into the manrauq rather than into the world. She chewed a flake of skin off her bottom lip, leaned over the poop rail.

"Zaftra!"

"Yes, Captain?"

"Break out the barrel of red wine and mull it for the crew tonight. They've been breaking their backs against the current."

"Certainly, Captain." They were all so careful, so formal. Were they so used to showing their bellies to Sarngeld that they did to her, out of habit?

The deck crew were just changing shift in the white and grey twilight, and Megan turned to head down to the cabin. "Oh, and Tze, crew leave is lots of six."

"Aye, there's not much that'll draw them but the one tavern and an unlicensed whorehouse."

"Well, I'll tell Kat to keep an eye out for cases of the drip."

He grinned at her, and turned to pass on the orders.

At the knock, Megan looked up from the books. "Ave," she said somewhat irritably.

"Lessons, still, Captain." Zaftra nudged the door shut behind him, cutting off the cold draft, and set the dinner tray on her desk, effectively stopping her from working.

"Zaftra! The ink!" She reached for the tray, stopped and sighed. "You're right, I'll just peel it loose when it's dry."

"You should eat first. Then you should make time to practice your skills before you go back to ship books."

Megan looked at him and down at the dinner tray, resenting anything that might slow her down, realizing that taking some time to eat and look after herself wasn't *really* slowing her, it just felt like it.

He smiled when he saw her lift the cover off the soup. "Borshch. With sour cream. When you've eaten, I'll be back to help you with the lesson." He nodded at her and limped to the door, cold making his joints stiffen terribly. He reached for the latch, turned back. "The mulled wine was appreciated by the crew. I thought I should mention it."

"Thank you, Zaftra." She tore the small loaf of bread in half, spread it with soft cheese and sopped one corner in the soup, suddenly ravenous now that she'd let herself think of food.

Next evening the last of the leave-crews wobbled their way back to the *Zingas Brezhani*, leaning on each other, dangerously close to overbalancing into the freezing, muddy water.

Megan watched impatiently as they made their precarious way onboard and the plank drawn in. The wind had come up as the weather cleared and she had decided to take advantage. *At least they'll sleep it off and be out of the way* . . . Her head snapped around as she realized that one of the men, Yneltzin, rather than making his way down to his hammock was trying to take a place among the deck-watch, as the *Brezhani* oar-walked out of the harbor.

"Bosun!" Her voice was high enough to cut through noise of an un-oiled oarlock.

"Aye, Captain!"

"What is Yneltzin doing on deck while drunk?"

"Captain, he's on watch!" Oblaka answered civilly enough, but with a carelessness that set her teeth on edge.

"Bring him away, before he gets into the rigging. To me, move!"

"Aye." The woman called forward and Yneltzin came back, as the oars were brought inboard, clattering. He stumbled over one, jostled the oar-crew on the other, and when they complained, buffeted one companionably on the shoulder as if he'd made a joke, getting in their way. Megan set her teeth.

"Aye . . . Captain." He paused long enough to make it an insult as he stood, thumbs hooked in his belt, rocking gently back and forth on his heels; the arrogant pose ruined every once in a while as he lost his balance. *A nervous habit of his*, she thought. *It's the drink bringing out the idiot in him.* She leaned on the poop rail, frowning down at him.

"Who authorized your leave, just before your watch?"

"It'ss a fa-favor ta me . . . Cap–t–ain." She ground her teeth. Behind her, Tze bellowed and the boom swung. The ship was underway. Slowly, sails bellied out in the steady wind that gave her enough headway against the current.

"You're docked a week's pay. Get below and wake your next shift. You're trading off-duty times."

He wobbled back, caught himself by stepping back, blinked and said, clearly and loudly, "I don' have ta take orders from a SLUT!"

The quiet was sudden and pronounced, except for the ship's sound—creaking timbers, the squeak of rope. Megan could see Oblaka's throat move as she swallowed.

"Mateus. Oblaka." Megan nodded at the bosun and the second mate, suddenly cold. They took hold of the man who twitched, as if he'd pull away, realizing there was nowhere to go but over the side. "Yneltzin, you're under punishment. Ten lashes."

The off-duty crew was called on deck.

"I call thee forth." Megan pitched her voice to carry. Before, no one had cared to challenge her zight and now she knew she had to assert it. "I call thee forth."

The setting sun cast a glow over everything, painting it the color of thinned blood. Megan put one hand on the brace of throwing daggers she carried on her belt, raised the other formally. "I call thee forth."

The crew quieted and she stepped forward. Mateus cuffed Yneltzin as he tied him to the main-mast to make him stop trying to pull away. "For refusing to obey a direct order, and failing respect, Yneltzin called Fisher, is under punishment. Ten lashes."

There was a mutter, but no tightening in the air. Oblaka swung the whip. CRACK. Yneltzin stiffened, yelping. CRACK. "Shit, I only—" CRACK.

"Shut up, Fish," Oblaka hissed through her teeth. CRACK. "Don't make it worse." CRACK.

"Shhhiiii—" CRACK. He held his silence then. CRACK. CRACK. CRACK. CRACK.

"Ten, Captain."

"Good." Oblaka turned to cut Yneltzin down. "Bosun. You made up the leave-schedule."

The woman turned to Megan, who waited. "Yes, Captain."

"Were you also aware that Yneltzin was immediately on watch after that leave?" She was refusing to look at Megan, coiling the single-strand whip in her hands very carefully and methodically.

"Yes, Captain."

"You saw his condition when he came on board?"

"It's been all right before, Captain, he's managed—"

"Be *silent*," Megan snapped, putting all her will into that. Oblaka opened her mouth, then closed it.

"For negligence. Bosun Oblaka, sentence of five lashes. I'll not have a drunkard killing himself or anyone else on board this ship."

"But—"

"One more word," Megan said icily, "and I'll double it." She let the silence stand long enough for it to make her point, then said, "Mateus, take the whip. Kat, look after Yneltzin. I'll speak to him when he's sober."

Megan stood and watched as Mateus administered five quick stripes to Oblaka and cut her loose. Then she went into the cabin and sat in the dark for a while until her shaking stopped.

If I turn him off the ship, he'd have reason to call an investigation on me and the rest of the crew over Sarngeld's "sale," she thought, running her hands over her arms, as if she were cold. *I'd be a fool if I didn't think he'd think of that, but he isn't mean unless he's drunk and he's not vindictive enough to risk hanging himself to hang me.*

She called him into her office next day.

"Yneltzin, if you were in my place, what would you say to me?"

He looked startled, then nervous, rocking. "I, ah, Captain . . . I . . ."

"Here," she said and got up. "Sit down in my chair

and be me." *A Yeoli's idea.* He coughed nervously, then sat down when she motioned him to.

"I . . . ah, I'd give you a warning?"

"That's a good start." He looked down at the desk, at the papers he couldn't read.

"I'd . . . ah, insist on an apology." She waited. "I'm sorry, I called you that. Truly, Captain."

"Accepted." She waited. "Is there more?" As a Guild captain, holding the papers, she had the right to land him and name him blacklisted in every Hall up and down the river. When they'd sworn to obey her, they'd sworn to that.

"I'd tell you that you weren't blacklisted, that your papers were still valid, that you weren't going to get busted to lander." He said all of that in a rush. She nodded thoughtfully.

"I'd like my chair back, Yneltzin." He scrambled out of it as if it were hot. "Your attempt to stop me from finding out about Oblaka's disobedience is noted. If you ever disobey me or show disrespect again, I won't stop at a flogging, clear?" He nodded, hands behind his back. "You have to prove yourself to me, though. Dismissed."

Snow swirled thick and heavy now almost every day, but it was warm enough that the river hadn't frozen more than at the edges, small chunks of ice floating from further north. *If I'm lucky we can make it home before freeze-up. Perhaps even sail out again before hard freeze.* She couldn't go after Lixand, and crushed the nagging thought that she was relieved that he was gone. *No,* she told herself. He was *her* son and none of Sarngeld's. She couldn't go after him. He was too far out of her reach. She couldn't. But the nagging guilt stayed. Perhaps she could have gone after him, but then she would have abandoned the ship and her crew, her family. *No, stop this,* she thought. *I decided. I can't change it, right or wrong.*

She whirled, pacing. If she couldn't free Lixand immediately, then she'd go after Rilla. *Do you need me still, coz? Or have you grown like your mother in these last years?*

She heard a soft step on the gangway and turned to see Katrana beckon.

"Captain, may I have a word with you?"

"Certainly. I'll be down in a moment."

When the door of the cabin closed behind them, Katrana sat down on the bunk and looked concernedly at Megan who sat down at her desk. The girl was thin to the point of gauntness, eyes shadowed.

"Your homecoming isn't going to be easy, is it, Meg?" Katrana said softly. Megan's face closed as she unlaced her cloak, throwing it off her shoulders over the back of her chair.

"You might say so. Why do you ask?" she said, voice cool, hands drumming nervously on her knees.

"I'm concerned, both as ship's healer and as a friend."

"Thank you, but I don't need help." Megan crossed her arms as if to block out Katrana's interference more than to stop the restless motion of her fingers.

"You should at least look after yourself a bit more," the healer said. "Megan, of all people I should know how much you want your son but . . ." She waved a hand at Megan's threadbare cloak and dark tunic that was patched at both elbows and shoulders. "You have to spend some money on yourself occasionally." She raised the hand sharply as Megan tried to cut her off. "I know you're saving it for finding him, but the ship will suffer as you do. I'm saying this as healer. You haven't been sleeping well enough and you've been eating next to nothing, exercising too hard. You'll kill yourself if you keep up, and then no one will rescue your son."

"Well, I will deal with it, Kat." Megan's hand slapped the desk as if closing a book, but Katrana ignored the hint.

"I know you'll deal with it, Meg." The healer sighed and got up to leave. "But killing yourself isn't going to free Lixand."

Megan stared at the closed door, no answer on her tongue except, *You're right.*

Chapter Nineteen

"Zaftra, I can't *do* anything more than that!" Megan let the light spell snap, the dull reddish glow vanishing, leaving her with a headache that pushed at the back of her eyeballs.

"Sh, Meg, it's all right. You'll do the best you can. You can set wards, you can make a light and small illusions."

"And move grains of salt!" she snapped. "What use is all this work?!" She paced back and forth in the cabin, pushing the heels of her hands into her eyesockets as if to relieve the pressure.

"It helps you with your knife throwing," he said mildly. "You're good, but with the talent helping you, however uncontrolled, you are excellent."

She sighed. "Fine. All right. I know the most I'm going to, and I think I'd like to stop with these lessons for now."

"All right, Meg." He patted the cushion next to him. "Want to talk about your worries?"

"My worries are none—" She closed her mouth, putting the tip of her tongue between her teeth. "Sorry.

Zaftra, I'm just trying so damn hard to get enough to get Lixand back. The ship is costing me too much. At this rate I'll never make any money. He'll be in the Empire, a slave for the rest of his life, and if anyone with more money than me decides to kick me or mine in the teeth, I won't be able to kick back." She stopped pacing, looking at the dull grey light shining through the porthole. The ship complained as she broke through the thin crust of ice on the river. "Other than that, nothing's bothering me in the slightest." He shook his head at the bitterness in her voice.

"You'll make more money once you speak to your Gospozhyn and work through the Guild rather than continuing Sarngeld's freelance business."

She nodded, head down. "People pay more for consistent quality," she said quietly. "I know all that. But I don't know if my Gospozhyn will accredit me. I'm not Master rank, yet, and if he jumped me to Master then there would be jealousy and bad feeling. And the idea of an Apprentice, even a Journeyman, owning a ship—that's impossible by current Guild rules."

"You'll convince him when you talk to him face-to-face. That's why you haven't written, isn't it?"

"Yes."

"You're afraid to."

"No, I'm not! That's—" He held up a hand.

"Now, your old teacher isn't accusing you of anything and your zight is safe with me. I respect the person you are, and will be." She finally sat down, looking at him, for once like the child she still was.

"I'm sorry. Yes, you're right. I'm afraid to."

"Be honest with yourself, at least, Meg, it'll be easier to be honest with other people that way." She looked away, twisting the corners of the cushion in her fingers. "If you don't mind a bit of nosy, unasked for advice . . ." He smiled at her look. "You don't have to threaten to swat me, Megan, I'll go on." He shook his bony finger at her. "If you do well, that's the important thing. No matter what you do, if you do it well, it will help your standing; tangible or intangible."

There was a moment of quiet, when the only sound was a call from the deck-crew, the boom of the sails, then she smiled again, and flung her arms around him in a quick, startling hug. "Thank you Zaftra!" Then realizing, she blushed to the roots of her hair and grabbed her cloak. "I need . . . need to check the watch, close the door after you."

"Child . . ." His word fell on a closed door and he looked after the tap of her retreating footsteps. "Child, still. Koru keep you."

The *Zingas Brezhani* worked her way upstream, ice on her heels and Megan paced in the cabin, from the desk to the bunk and back, reining in her frustration. *Never enough. It'll take me years to save enough this way.* She clenched her fists behind her back as she paced. The shadow of the Great Rock loomed in the porthole and was gone, slowly falling behind as they tacked upriver.

That meant they were a long day from F'talezon, unless she ordered the oars broken out. *The* River Lady's *a tub. She's a good old ship but she's still a tub and a royal bitch to row. I can't break everyone's back rowing if it's not necessary.*

The ice floes whirling south were big enough to stove them in if one hit them squarely, but Mateus had a feel for this sort of thing, and he and Tze kept them both safe and on course.

Megan paced, shaking her head against the thought of it being too late for Rilla. *A long time to be away.* This close to F'talezon she felt unsettled, fearful in a way she'd refused to let herself be since Sarngeld died.

She strode out of the cabin to stand by the helm, watching as they came closer and closer to home, wrapped in her thoughts as tightly as the wool of her cloak.

The deck of the *Brezhani* looked much better than when she'd first come onboard; ropes neatly coiled and ready to hand, the brasses polished, the oak deck holy-stoned almost white except the old stains near the rail and down where the water barrels stood. Even the old sails had been patched neatly and the new one shone white in the pale spring sun.

The wind swung around by late afternoon, a solid souther that took them against the current briskly enough that the ship plunged in a jerky up and down motion like a horse pulling at the bit.

"Run with the wind, Tze," Megan called when the wind steadied. "We might as well take advantage." She felt split in two, standing on the deck. Part of her knew that she was good at commanding, doing what she'd been taught, doing what she'd dreamed of, but still she despised herself for enjoying it while Lixand was gone.

"Aye, Captain." He relayed the order and the motion of the ship changed as the lateen sails bellied out. Megan raised an eyebrow appreciatively at the smooth manoeuvre. *It's amazing what crew will do for a captain they like . . . but that's to their credit, not mine. I want to re-rig so we can butterfly, get a bit more speed, but that'll take time and training.*

Megan paced back and forth in the cold wind, shivering but ignoring the feeling, looking ahead to Yneltzin on bow-watch. Ever since the one incident, he'd been solid. One hand on the wheel, she looked ahead to the distant mountain that was home.

The jolly boat ride into the docking cavern was almost a mirror of the way she'd left. The *Brezhani* was moored in a similar spot in the outer harbor, the crowds along the piers, the noise . . . The differences were enough to keep her throat from closing; her hands stayed steady.

She stood for a moment at the top of the ladder, her feet in the worn hollows of the stone, tried to feel as if she were home, shrugged, and moved out of the way of her crew. *It's just another docking, and a late one at that.*

The kraumak had been unhooded, but there were only two or three of those. They had been made at public expense during the years of the Republic and the Other Guild held it gauche to think of stealing them, but they'd been fading one by one, replaced with the cheaper torches that filled the docking cavern ceiling with a hanging layer of smoke.

She walked through the throng heading for the Gate before it closed for the night; sailors on leave ready to spend their pay on the licensed Bedwarmers, or on wadiki and a bed big enough to stretch out on, fishmongers carrying heavy buckets full of the final catch, silvery and squirming, or bakers with sold-empty baskets dumping crumbs into the water before joining the throng on the Gate road.

Megan went up past Vikhad Gate to the Main Gate before entering the City, feeling the dampness on her face as it started to rain lightly, the torches hissing. *Gospozhyn is likely still working late at his office, unless something's changed.* She felt cold, and it wasn't merely because her cloak was worn thin.

At the Main Gate steps where they joined the Stairs she paused, looking out over the City that was already dark; a pattern of lights shining out of windows, the red of firelight or the green or blue of kraumak, peculiarly Zak in a way that none of the enclaves along the river were. The rain was heavier, full of the drowned-worm smell of spring. On the Stairs a door slammed, someone laughed and wished someone else a "Good Blossoming." The odor of maranth bread and spiced barley soup drifted over her, and Megan clenched her teeth against sudden, surprising tears, shook herself mentally and strode toward the Guildhall on the other side of the City, wrapping her cloak around her against the wet.

His habits had changed and he'd moved his office to his manor off Greyvra Park. There, she gave her name to the door-ward and waited, watching the trickles of water find their way into the dry cracks of the flagstones.

It was pouring now, wind driving the rain against the porch wall behind her with a crackle like frying bacon.

"If you will come in, Teik, the Master is in the dining room, entertaining." The door-ward bowed her in with a sweep of her hand. "He said you were to await him in the study."

"Thank you."

The servant showed her into the room that at one point had been immaculate because Yarishk's wife had the keeping of it. Now that it was his office it was crammed with bookshelves and piles of pillows and stacks of paper over layers of mismatching rugs, very much like the old office. Megan stopped in the door, looking at an odd sock lying in the middle of the floor.

She felt the impulse to tidy for him while she was waiting, restrained it and sat down on the guest cushion holding her nervousness inside. *Things have changed.*

When Yarishk opened the door, Sashi pattered in, sniffed and lay down under the window with a grunt. *Then again, some things, like Sashi, never change.* Megan rose to greet her Gospozhyn, who looked her up and down, then smiled.

"Megan! It is you," he said, offering her his hands. She nodded a trifle jerkily, nervous. His face didn't change but she knew he'd noticed.

"I'm very, very glad to see you. Sit down, please."

"Thank you, Gospozhyn." The word felt strange on her tongue, as if it were a language she once knew but had forgotten.

"I . . . we worried about you. I had reports of you from one or two places up and down the river, nothing reliable, and your kin refused to say. What happened?" He settled down without pulling his lapdesk between them.

"Have we . . . shared salt then?" she asked. His chin came up and the worry lines in his face grew deeper. She could almost hear him thinking *so distant, so formal,* but he said nothing.

"Of course, if you want it that way . . ."

"Marte sold me off to an owner/captain by the use-name of Sarngeld," she said bluntly. Yarishk raised steepled fingers to his mouth, nodding.

"I've heard of him. Nothing good, I'm afraid."

"Yes. I found out about him, too. Nothing good."

"Ahh." The sudden tension in the way he held himself, the very calm way in which he said it showed her his feelings. *He's furious,* Megan thought, wonderingly. *A few years ago I wouldn't have known how to read that. I can do that now.* "My sympathy," he said solemnly. She shrugged, looking away.

"It happened." He didn't say anything.

She waited, and when he still didn't say anything to that, went on. "I have a bit of a problem, though. Sarngeld, ah, sold me the ship ... because of a health problem."

"Oh?" This time she couldn't read his face or tone.

Suddenly, she felt like a young apprentice again, during an examination, at a loss for words. She flattened her hands on her knees and bridled her rising resentment. *He ... doesn't deserve my anger. He's done me only good. He's a friend as well as a teacher.* She raised one eyebrow at him, face cold.

"It is difficult to be healthy at the bottom of the river weighted with rocks."

He nodded, sagely. "With numerous ... *disconnections* in various bodily tissues rendered by small, sharp, street-trained blades."

At one time that would have made her smile, but now she just looked at him and nodded back. "Yes." She held out her ship papers.

"Did you kill anyone else?" His face was suddenly as cold as hers, as he took the parchments from her.

"The crew killed the bosun, a naZak, name of Thoman, out of Brahvniki—he's not a Guild member—and I fought and killed the first mate, a Thane by the name of Hanald, after Sarngeld." She paused a moment then continued, "I don't think he was a Guild member either."

"I see." He was frowning now. "Who have you learned from, girl, who taught you to speak of killing so lightly?

I never had a hot-spur for a student and never want one." She looked at him, shocked at the ice in his tone. "I . . ." Her chin came up. "I didn't take it lightly, Gospozhyn. You . . ." Her voice faltered a bit then she went on determinedly. "You judge me too harshly. I'm no hot-spur."

He stared at her, then nodded once, sharply, got up and pulled out a copy of the Guild roll. "A Thane? Unlikely but I should still . . . ah, no. Good, that makes things a *bit* easier. What about the rest of the crew, why have you had no trouble with them?"

Still like an exam . . . "The deck officers are my friends and, well, to be blunt, there wasn't anyone else on board who had any training in trade or the inclination to initiative. Sarngeld didn't hire any like that."

He looked at the forged papers and handed them back. "Good enough. I suppose that most customs clerks just assume that the first one checked, making them official by assumption." She nodded.

He got up and paced. "You understand that you've presented me with a problem for which there is no precedent. You are still just an Apprentice and if I jump you to Master, then . . . well, there are those older and more senior to you who will be very displeased. And the Other Guild . . ."

"I didn't try to make any connections with either Guild when I was further south because I thought I should speak to you first!"

"Good. That's politic. But you still see my problem. If I don't accredit you, then you are going to keep your ship anyway, am I right?"

"Yes. I need to make a great deal of money and it's either with the ship or other ways."

He stopped pacing and looked down at her where she sat on the guest cushion. "A great deal of money? Why? Well . . ." He waved away his own question. "We all need to make a great deal of money, don't we? Your intention doesn't show the deepest loyalty."

Stung, she answered anyway. "I came to you first. And

I need to get enough gold to get into the Arkan Empire, to get my son back!"

His back was to the kraumak, shadowing his face. "Son?"

"Lixand. *My* son by Sarngeld."

"You come arguing your case," Yarishk said, severely, "and you only tell me half the story. Perhaps there is something in it that will have some weight with me, hmm?"

She clenched her hands. "I bore him two years ago, and when he was weaned Sarngeld took him and sold him off to an Arkan trader dealing in exotics going into the Empire. When I got loose, I killed Sarngeld, and then had to kill Hanald and take the ship because if *he'd* taken over he would have put me off on shore right then. I would have been walking, days south of where Lixand had been sold. I was still too late. By then I'd taken the responsibility of running this ship, paying the crew . . . I couldn't just leave it lie. They are my family now. There wasn't anything else I could do but try coming home."

She rose, staring up into his face. "He's my son. I could have seen him as Sarngeld's and made his birth and my life Halya, but the healer told me I could make him mine, see him as only mine. He was only a baby and it wasn't his fault who his father was. He's the only child I'll ever have and I *won't* be a slough-kin." Her chin came up. "And if that's not loyalty enough for you, or the Guild—" she hesitated half a heartbeat "—then that's just tough sailing." She clenched her teeth. If he was already considering not accrediting her status, she had nothing to lose. *I'll get Rilla out and we'll go south somewhere.*

Gospozhyn Yarishk turned away from her, clasping his hands behind his back. She stayed standing, watching him, listening to Sashi's tail thump every time he came near the dog. She swallowed once, then again, breathing hard as if she were in a fight, hands shaking enough that she crossed her arms to give herself something to hang on to. She had to *make* him give her what she needed.

Finally, he spoke. "Megan, I will tell you exactly what I am thinking. You are hardly more than a child. And a child who has suffered terrible and unjust things. Such children, if they have gift and will such as you have, go either very good . . . or very bad.

"I am concerned, not only for you, but for all those around you, over which way you turn. Should I cast you out, I suspect I would be thrusting you towards the dark. In that sense, I do not want to lose you.

"You carry a great deal of anger that you turn into drive, which isn't necessarily a bad thing." He ran a hand through his thinning hair. "It can be good, or bad. You must know it and learn to deal with it, learn to turn it to good. It's the same with pride, which you have plenty of, too. But who will teach you these things? Not your aunt, certainly. Not your crew, even if they are older, if they are not the sort to talk back. Perhaps you've grown hard and brash enough that you think no one can teach you, that you need no Gospozhyn."

His honesty, when she tried to force help out of him, was like pushing with all her strength against someone who wasn't resisting. She blinked, tried to stop the warmth glowing from her neck and ears. "Umm." Painfully reminded of her mother's admonition not to grunt, she cleared her throat instead, as if that could budge the lump she had there. "I never said that. That's why I came back." She looked down at the brazier's fire-screen, as if it had words for her to use. "I . . . I'd rather be an apprentice and have . . . *some* . . . people tell me what to do, but I *can't*, Gospozhyn. I've already had to wait iron-cycles doing nothing while Lixand gets further and further away from me . . ." She drew a sobbing breath to control her tears. "I can't do it by myself, but I don't know how to ask for help anymore."

He looked at her quietly and the coals in the brazier settled. Sashi waddled over and thrust a cold nose into her hand, whining. "You do know how to ask, Megan. You are now." He put out a hand, laid it on her shoulder.

She turned away from him, from the hand she wanted

so much, picked up her books and held them out to him. "Here are my records."

He took them, put them on his desk. "What was the ship's name again?"

"The *Zingas Brezhani*." Megan sat down and petted the dog as if that were the most important thing to do, burying her face in Sashi's ruff. "Anchored in the outer harbor," she said, voice muffled by the dog's fur.

"I'll see what I can do. Stay overnight. You're welcome to and we'll work something out tomorrow or the day after. I never said it was impossible that you keep both your ship and your Guild status." He quirked an eyebrow at her. "I suspect you won't want to retrieve your cousin until your future is more assured."

Next day he sent his apologies for letting her break her fast alone. She stared around at the grey-green tapestries of the morning room with a fresh cup of chai in her hand and tried to keep from worrying. Then she stayed in the library, trying to read, pulling books down from the shelves, putting them back, reading lines over and over without understanding, till early evening when he called her into his study.

He sat reading when she came in, his lapdesk set on the rug to one side; on it was a stack of steel and gold coins as high as a candlestick. He looked up and waved her to a cushion with a smile.

"I'm sorry it's taken so long, but there were a few other things to do as well."

She bit the inside of her lip, not wanting to raise hope, and sat down quietly. *I've been dealing with Rand, why can't I see what I need in his face?*

"In looking over your books, I can see you've been doing well enough that I can justifiably count your experiences as your Journeyman's work. The ship herself is hardly going to make anyone jealous though she's still valuable—please don't take offence, child but I, if no one else, should be blunt about such things—and I can set you a masterwork on her, under my orders. On paper

she must be *my* ship, at least for now, held in trust for
you till you become a Master. That should placate the
older deadheads." She smiled, thinking of other deadheads, half-sunken logs that had almost holed the *Brezhani* and sunk her and he smiled back as he continued.
"As a Journeyman you must journey. Here, you might
have to have it sized." He held out his hand and dropped
the thin silver and copper ring of a Rivermerchant Journeyman into her hand. She closed her cold fingers on it,
shivering. She swallowed.

He nodded at the stack of coin. "Those are the pro-
ceeds from Vaizal's gold candlestick I was holding for
you. I'll allow you that, to clip as you need, because your
Brezhani needs a lot of work or she'll sink midstream
one day. The rose—you might recall I had it in trust?
Vaizal is refusing to pay to get the three back, and they
are far too valuable to break up, so I will continue to
hold yours. You'll have to trade hard this next season or
two—I won't make it too easy for you."

"No, Gospozhyn. I understand." *I did it. I did it,
Lixand-mi. I did it.* She wanted to dance, sing, do silly,
goosey things. *I did it. She's mine—when I make Nal-
Gospozhyn, she's mine.* She put the ring on, finding that
it fit her second finger. "I'll make you proud of me, I
will, I swear."

He shook his head fondly. "I am already, but don't let
that swell your sails too much, Megan. You have to bring
the ship back next season, with a clear profit to make
Yolculvik. If it's enough of a profit, you'll be Nal-Gospozhyn. Even lesser masters own ships in their own right."

"I understand, Gospozhyn. Thank you." She shivered
again, but more from excitement.

"You are welcome. Now, it's never too soon to start
developing contacts of your own, child. You'll have the
opportunity at my dinner tonight. You have something
better to wear? . . . I suspect you've waited long enough
to rescue your cousin and see to your—" he smiled "—
my ship." He lost his smile. "Can you deal with your
aunt?"

Megan looked up from the Journeyman's ring on her finger. "Yes, Gospozhyn. I don't need help there." He nodded.

She stopped by the apothecary shop and looked in the rain-streaked window. The dust was still thick on the inside of the glass, but the jar of leeches was the same as ever, full of red-brown suckers moving as if the water were at a slow boil. *Have I dreamt being away?* She tugged her new black cloak over the dark velvet outfit she'd bought for the Guild dinner.

She turned down the lane, her steps coming slower and slower. The rain was shifting the loose garbage so she had to pick her way into the building carefully, something else that brought back the feeling of never having left; the feeling of being helpless. The stale odor of cooked cabbage filled the hall inside and she found herself clasping one manacle-scarred wrist with the other hand, rubbing slowly at the blemished skin. *Oh, yes, I've been away*.

She walked down the corridor, hearing the bed creak in the room near the door as the neighbors made love. Further on she heard a mucus-filled snore. She padded farther down, pausing at the last door before Marte's.

She hoped that Rilla would be there, that they could just bundle her things together and leave without ever having seen Marte. *I don't care if I never see her again.*

The door opened with the same old squeak and she stopped, letting her eyes adjust to the dark, listening for Rilla's breathing. It was still, the air full of the odor of burnt pennyroyal, making Megan stifle a sneeze.

"Rilla?" she whispered. "Rilla?" No answer. Megan reached for the hood of the kraumak by the door. Rilla's pallet was empty, rigidly well made. The herbs still hung from the ceiling, the dishes stacked to dry, the wooden table scarred and burned and stained. There was a faint, irregular ticking from the other room as the still cooled.

Megan picked up the kraumak and walked to the inner door, her mouth dry, and pushed it open. Her nose wrin-

kled at the odor; sour wine, wormwood, sweat and
unwashed clothing, scorched pennyroyal where the glass
in the still had broken. *I won't pick up fleas or lice with
that stench around at any rate.* The wallbed doors stood
open and Marte lay half out of it, face down. The wine-
skin below her hand had leaked onto the floor where
she'd dropped it.

The light in Megan's hand wavered a moment and she
clenched her fist around it; stepped forward around the
puddle of wine. "Marte," she snapped.

"Hmmm," was the only answer, that and the sound of
swallowing.

"Marte!" Almost a shout.

"Whaaa—?" Marte blearily raised her head. "Go-way.
See'n thin's. No' guil-ty. Couldn' ge' you back ..." Her
voice faded towards a snore as her head went down.
". . . brat."

"Marte, wake up!" Megan grabbed Marte's shoulder
and shook her roughly. "Rouse your wine-sodden carcass
up and listen to me."

This time there was more understanding in the older
woman's eyes, but not much. "Meg'n. Home ... early
... cleanup yer messn go t' bed ..."

Disgusted, Megan slammed the kraumak down on the
bedside table, grabbed Marte's shoulders and dragged
her out of the bed, wrestling with her sodden weight.
She shook Marte so her head snapped back and forth a
few times before letting her sprawl onto the floor. "You
have to be sober enough to hear this," Megan snarled.
"I'm taking Rilla away, hear me?"

Marte pushed herself up on her arms, used the wallbed to pull herself to her feet, staggering. "Oh, shit,"
she said quite clearly. Then she whipped up one hand,
staggered a step toward Megan, finger held waveringly
in front of her. "Yo-u!" she squalled. "You're GONE!
Go—wan, ge' LOST!" She swiped at Megan as if to
brush away a hallucination, stood gazing stupidly as
Megan blocked, grabbing her wrist.

The younger woman looked at her own hand wonderingly for an instant where it held Marte's wrist fast. It had been such a small motion that stopped Marte from hitting her. *I don't have to take this shit anymore.*

Megan looked into Marte's bloodshot eyes before spinning her around and pushing her away, wiping her hand clean on her trousers.

"Yes. Me. And Rilla is—"

"Hey!" An angry voice from the door. "Who'r you? What'r . . ."

Megan turned around defensively, not recognizing the young woman in the door at first. *She's about my height.* The light from the kraumak on the table lit her face clearly. Medium long brown hair, buttery hazel eyes, a thin, unhappy face, high cheekbones—

"Rilla?"

She stepped toward the girl as Marte struggled to get out of the wallbed where Megan's push had sent her.

"Megan?" Rilla's hand, still raised, reached out to touch Megan's face, her fingertip resting lightly on the skin as if she didn't believe what she was feeling, seeing. They caught each other in a hug. "MEGAN! I thought you were gone forever! I thought . . . she said she'd gotten rid of you . . . Goddess, I'm glad you're back . . ."

Marte untangled herself from the last of the bedclothes, snarling, "Rillahhh . . . ahhh . . . mmmph . . . ! Ril-llahh . . . hhh . . ." The woman finally staggered upright and lunged, flailing, at Rilla, who dodged, letting Megan go. *She's still taller than I am,* Megan thought as she grabbed Marte again. The girl hovered near the door, her face showing both hope and fear.

Marte bunched her fists, focused on her daughter, shouting ugly, drunken things, almost pulling Megan off her feet. Panting, Megan braced herself, yanked one of her aunt's arms up behind her back between the shoulder blades and looked at Rilla.

"Go . . . get your things . . . Rilla," she said over Marte's shrieks, gritting her teeth and holding on as if to a sail flapping in the wind. "We're—we're leaving." Her hands burned as Marte twisted in her grip. "I'm your guardian, legally. Let's get out of here!"

"SLUT!" Marte screamed at her daughter. Rilla cringed back, hesitated between listening to Megan or her mother, then stopped herself. She swallowed and her chin came up. "Malkin!" Marte yelled. "You ... you're never going to be worth anything! NO GOOD, filthy drab!"

Rilla's expression went slowly livid and her face hardened from fear and uncertainty to resolve. For a long moment she stood clenching her fists, then stepped forward and swung, a whole-hearted slap that whipped Marte's head around. Everything stopped suddenly, Marte's scream cut off as if a razor had cut her throat, mouth working, eyes round and appalled. Rilla stared, both delighted and terrified at her daring.

Marte slowly raised one hand to her cheek, gaping as Rilla turned on her heel and walked out to the front room. For a second there was only the odor of pennyroyal and the sound of Marte's hoarse breathing as she stared after Rilla, frozen.

Megan let go and stepped away, pausing in the doorway. Rilla looked up from where she had her things tossed into a blanket. "I'm ready."

"Let's go then," Megan said, and looked back at Marte who still stood frozen, hand on her cheek. "If my father had known, he'd have done the same. I disown all knowledge of you, slough-kin. You are no kin of mine. Live and die alone."

She knocked the dust of the house off her boots against the doorframe, threw her arm comfortably around Rilla's shoulders, and they walked away from the silence behind them.

Glossary

A-niah—plural of Niah
Aavrit Cities—coalition of cities on the Mitvald
Aenir—country south of F'talezon, another enemy of the Thanes
Aeniri—a native of that country
Aenir'sford—a city on the Brezhan
Arkan—citizen of Arko
Arko—the Empire far to the south and west of Zakos
Armai—Zak, an ancient enemy of the Zak

Baba—Zak, Grandmother
Baku—a Mitvald port city
balika—a Zak stringed instrument
bayishka—Zak, a marriage broker
Benai—Brahvnikian, Abbey
Benaiat—Brahvnikian, Abbot
Beigen—a small town on the river Brezhan
Berjus—a Mitvald port city
Bjornholm—a city on the Brezhan
Blutrosh—Zak, Blood-roses, large with dark nectar

317

Borschch—Zak, beet soup

Brahvniki—free-port at the mouth of the Brezhan

Brezhan—the main river F'talezon is the navigation head for

Brunsc—Megan's stuffed bear

Byeliey—tributary flowing into Chas lake from the Ladyshrine

bylashka—Zak, meaning little one, or little princess

Chas Lake—Lake at the bottom of the City, feeding the Brezhan

Cheboks—a small town on the Brezhan

Clawprince—Zak and Brahvnikian, merchant prince

cniffta—Zak, a knife throwing game

colschizn—Zak, a herb

cormarenc—a giant version of cormorants

Dagde Vroi—month-long year-end (solstice) festival, Days of Fools

Dark Lord—patron god of F'talezon, god of death and winter

Deib's Den Inn—a F'talezon inn

Dragon Bite—Zak coinage, round coin stamped with a triangle

Dragon Fang—Zak coinage, triangular coin stamped with a circle

Dragon Scale—Zak coinage, a half-circle stamped with a triangle

Dragonclaw—Zak, a six-sided coin, steel, gold, silver, or copper

DragonLord—ruler of F'talezon, see Woyvode

Dragon'sNest—the palace, seat of royal power in F'talezon

DreamDust—a highly addictive drug, that re-routes pain to the pleasure centers of the brain, ultimately causing a breakdown of the immune system

Drip, the—Zak slang for gonorrhea

Duster—one hooked on DreamDust

Dzhai—Zak slang, Cooper's Lane kidpack cry for help

Eksoticum—an unlicensed, naZak whorehouse
Esaria—Srian port town

fatrahm—Zak, father's sister's beloved child
Fchera—a type of bird
femka—Enchian, women's quarters
F'talezon—the capital of Zakos
F'trovanemi—a Zak fortification

Gazhtinizia Gardens—a playhouse in the City
Gospozhyn—Zak, Great Master
Graukalm—'grievous wind,' monster wind that can freeze a living thing in seconds
Great Bitch, The—inn in Aenir'sford
Ground, The—a bit of vacant land near the Flats

Haian—a citizen of the healers' archipelago, Haiu Menshir
Hall of Light, The—manrauq training hall
Hand—five work days, plus one
Hand'send—the day of rest
Halya—Zak, hell
Halyabore—a herb
Halyions—Zak, hellions
Honey-Giver—one of the City gods, The Great Bear
Hriis—a religious sect, also their trade towns
Hyerne—a matriarchal sea-coast country

Iya—Zak, second call in sparring

jahnin—Rand, foreign devil

Kahfe—coffee grown in the Mitvald Islands
Kha'khaya—a wedding song
K'gebar—Zak, executioner, lit. "one who carries justice"
K'mizar—Zak, supervisor
K'mizariza—Zak, lit. "those who rule or guide"
Kievir—Zak, equivalent to baron
Kievira—Zak, baronness

Koru—the City's patron Goddess, god of life and summer

Kraila—a Yeoli sword

kraumak—Zak, lit. "glow-stone." A heatless light source

Kreyen—large island in the Mitvald, also capital city

Krim—a sea-coast country

Krminsk—a town on the Brezhan

Kuritz h'Rokatzk—Zak curse, handler of the dead with implications of disease and necrophilia (you were conceived by a death-handler on a leperous corpse)

Laka—a country south-east of the Arkan empire

lingam—male genitalia

Luscious Peach, The—licensed whorehouse sharing the Flats

Mahachkala—a Mitvald country

malkin—Zak slang, dirty one, diseased one, useless

manrauq—Zak, power of mind, psionics

'maranth—genetically altered plant derived from amaranth

Mitvald—Zak name for the greater ocean, of which Svartsee is a part

mrik—Lakan, a board game

Nal-Gospozhyn—Zak, lesser master

Nar-Kievior—Zak title of nobility, viscount

Naryshkiv—a town on the Brezhan

naZak—Zak, lit. non Zak, foreigner

Nellas—a Mitvald island country

Niah—a native of Niah-lur-ana

Niah-lur-ana—an archipelago in the Mitvald, south east of Haiu Menshir

night-siren—a created plant, to concentrate iron on the surface

Nübuah—a colony city of Fehinna, an empire across the Lannic

Nuogamesh-gir—an Aavrit port city where sea and desert meet

Nuov-Kievir—a Zak title of nobility, equivalent to marquis
nyata—Zak, no

Oestschpaz—a river flowing into the Brezhan
okas—an Arkan caste, just above slaves
oscasa—Zak, bone museum

Piatyacha Tower—a folly built near the Great Market
Pirate Isles—in the Mitvald sea
Prafetatla—the Zak "beau ton," the ruling classes
Proletarion—Zak, field of bones, funeral place
pyash—Zak, a measurement of distance, a bit more than a metre

Raeschku—Ness's home village, destroyed by Thanes
Rand—a city-state on the Brezhan, also a native of that city
Red Briar, The—an inn in Aenir'sford
Rhunay—Zak slang, the children's cry for "I give up!", "Uncle!"
roheji—Perogy-like pastries

Saekrberk—main abbey of the Bear in Brahvniki, and the liquor distilled there
samovar—vessel for boiling tea
Selov—a Mitvald port city
Shamballah—a bright star visible in certain latitudes that moves contrary to regular star motion, said to be a machine built before the fire
-shkya—Zak, feminine suffix, "daughter of"
Sinapland—a Mitvald country
Smiurgteik—Zak, lit. Citizen Dragon, see ZingasSmiurg
Sneyekh—tributary flowing into Chas Lake from the Dark Temple
Sobota Gate—a lesser gate into the City
Solas—an Arkan caste, warrior, second highest after noble
Soltshiy—birds

Sria—desert country with some sea ports

Sto Solstne—the great window in the Dragon'sNest

Sysbaet—Zak, Grey Brotherhood, a healing teaching order affiliated with the orders of the Bear

Sysbat—a sibling of the Sysbaet order

Talitsa—the town north, around the salt mines

Tebrias—capital of Sria

Teik—Zak, sir, mister or mistress, citizen

Thanes—natives of Thaneland, enemy to Zakos

Third Charm Inn—an inn in Aenir'sford

Tor Ench—a country bordering Laka and Yeola-e

troikamal—an arrangement where three horses draw a carriage or sleigh

Two-fang—A four foot staff with a blade at each end

Tukan Islands—in the Mitvald

Tuzgolu—a Mitvald island port

Va Zalstva—Zak, the old arena

Veysnyas—Zak, silverwings. Like fuzzy, coppery-rose butterflies

Vikhad Gate—a lesser gate of the City

-vych—Zak, masculine suffix, "son of"

Wadiki—maranth vodka

Wooden Plate—a F'talezon restaurant

Wormwood—an anti-depressant, non-addictive, toxic

Woyvode—DragonLord, ruler of F'talezon and the remnants of Zakos, Smiurgteik

Woyvodaana—DragonLady, the ruler's marriage partner(s)

Year Kievir—priest/advisor to the Woyvode, chosen between the priests of the Lady and the Dark Lord

Yeola-e—a country east of the empire of Arko

Yeoli—a native of the country Yeola-e

Yoni—female genitalia

zahbeans—Zak, a protein substitute like tofu

zahl—Zak, sword training hall

Zar—Brahvnikian title for the Benaiat

Zarizan—Zak, Heir

zight—Zak, pride or face

Zingas—Zak, Lord or Lady

ZingasSmiurg—Zak, Lord/Lady Dragon

Zingas Brezhani—River Lady, Sarngeld's ship

S.M. STIRLING

and

THE DOMINATION OF THE DRAKA

In 1782 the Loyalists fled the American Revolution to settle in a new land: South Africa, Drake's Land. They found a new home, and built a new nation: The Domination of the Draka, an empire of cruelty and beauty, a warrior people, possessed by a wolfish will to power. This is alternate history at its best.

"A tour de force." —David Drake

"It's an exciting, evocative, thought-provoking—but of course horrifying—read." —Poul Anderson

MARCHING THROUGH GEORGIA
Six generations of his family had made war for the Domination of the Draka. Eric von Shrakenberg wanted to make peace—but to succeed he would have to be a better killer than any of them.

UNDER THE YOKE
In *Marching Through Georgia* we saw the Draka's "good" side, as they fought and beat that more obvious horror, the Nazis. Now, with a conquered Europe supine beneath them, we see them as they truly are; for conquest is only the *beginning* of their plans ... All races are created equal—as slaves of the Draka.

THE STONE DOGS
The cold war between the Alliance of North America and the Domination is heating up. The Alliance, using its superiority in computer technologies, is preparing a master stroke of electronic warfare. But the Draka, supreme in the ruthless manipulation of life's genetic code, have a secret weapon of their own. . . .

BUILDING A NEW FANTASY TRADITION

The Unlikely Ones by Mary Brown

Anne McCaffrey raved over *The Unlikely Ones*: "What a splendid, unusual and intriguing fantasy quest! You've got a winner here...." Marion Zimmer Bradley called it "Really wonderful ... I shall read and re-read this one." A traditional quest fantasy with quite an unconventional twist, we think you'll like it just as much as Anne McCaffrey and Marion Zimmer Bradley did.

Knight of Ghosts and Shadows
by Mercedes Lackey & Ellen Guon

Elves in L.A.? It would explain a lot, wouldn't it? In fact, half a millennium ago, when the elves were driven from Europe they came to—where else? —Southern California. Happy at first, they fell on hard times after one of their number tried to force the rest to be his vassals. Now it's up to one poor human to save them if he can. A knight in shining armor he's not, but he's one hell of a bard!

The Interior Life by Katherine Blake

Sue had three kids, one husband, a lovely home and a boring life. Sometimes, she just wanted to escape, to get out of her mundane world and *live* a little. So she did. And discovered that an active fantasy life can be a very dangerous thing—and very real.... Poul Anderson thought *The Interior Life* was "a breath of fresh air, bearing originality, exciting narrative, vividly realized characters— everything we have been waiting for for too long."

The Shadow Gate by Margaret Ball

The only good elf is a dead elf—or so the militant order of Durandine monks thought. And they planned on making sure that all the elves in their world (where an elvish Eleanor of Aquitaine ruled in Southern France) were very, very good. The elves of Three Realms have one last spell to bring help ... and received it: in the form of the staff of the new Age Psychic Research Center of Austin, Texas. ...

Hawk's Flight by Carol Chase
Taverik, a young merchant, just wanted to be left alone to make an honest living. Small chance of that though: after their caravan is ambushed Taverik discovers that his best friend Marko is the last living descendant of the ancient Vos dynasty. The man who murdered Marko's parents still wants to wipe the slate clean—with Marko's blood. They try running away, but Taverik and Marko realize that there is a fate worse than death . . . That sooner or later, you have to stand and fight.

A Bad Spell in Yurt by C. Dale Brittain
As a student in the wizards' college, young Daimbert had shown a distinct flair for getting himself in trouble. Now the newly appointed Royal Wizard to the backwater Kingdom of Yurt learns that his employer has been put under a fatal spell. Daimbert begins to realize that finding out who is responsible may require all the magic he'd never quite learned properly in the first place—with the kingdom's welfare and his life the price of failure. Good thing Daimbert knows how to improvise!

PRAISE FOR
LOIS MCMASTER BUJOLD

What the critics say:

The Warrior's Apprentice: "Now here's a fun romp through the spaceways—not so much a space opera as space ballet.... it has all the 'right stuff.' A lot of thought and thoughtfulness stand behind the all-too-human characters. Enjoy this one, and look forward to the next."   —Dean Lambe, *SF Reviews*

"The pace is breathless, the characterization thoughtful and emotionally powerful, and the author's narrative technique and command of language compelling. Highly recommended."   —*Booklist*

Brothers in Arms: "... she gives it a geniune depth of character, while reveling in the wild turnings of her tale. ... Bujold is as audacious as her favorite hero, and as brilliantly (if sneakily) successful."   —*Locus*

"Miles Vorkosigan is such a great character that I'll read anything Lois wants to write about him. ... a book to re-read on cold rainy days."   —Robert Coulson, *Comics Buyer's Guide*

Borders of Infinity: "Bujold's series hero Miles Vorkosigan may be a lord by birth and an admiral by rank, but a bone disease that has left him hobbled and in frequent pain has sensitized him to the suffering of outcasts in his very hierarchical era.... Playing off Miles's reserve and cleverness, Bujold draws outrageous and outlandish foils to color her high-minded adventures."   —*Publishers Weekly*

Falling Free: "In *Falling Free* Lois McMaster Bujold has written her fourth straight superb novel. ... How to break down a talent like Bujold's into analyzable components? Best not to try. Best to say 'Read, or you will be missing something extraordinary.'"   —Roland Green, *Chicago Sun-Times*

The Vor Game: "The chronicles of Miles Vorkosigan are far too witty to be literary junk food, but they rouse the kind of craving that makes popcorn magically vanish during a double feature."   —Faren Miller, *Locus*

MORE PRAISE FOR LOIS MCMASTER BUJOLD

What the readers say:

"My copy of *Shards of Honor* is falling apart I've reread it so often.... I'll read whatever you write. You've certainly proved yourself a grand storyteller."
—Liesl Kolbe, Colorado Springs, CO

"I experience the stories of Miles Vorkosigan as almost viscerally uplifting.... But certainly, even the weightiest theme would have less impact than a cinder on snow were it not for a rousing good story, and good storytelling with it. This is the second thing I want to thank you for.... I suppose if you boiled down all I've said to its simplest expression, it would be that I immensely enjoy and admire your work. I submit that, as literature, your work raises the overall level of the science fiction genre, and spiritually, your work cannot avoid positively influencing all who read it."
—Glen Stonebraker, Gaithersburg, MD

" 'The Mountains of Mourning' [in *Borders of Infinity*] was one of the best-crafted, and simply best, works I'd ever read. When I finished it, I immediately turned back to the beginning and read it again, and I can't remember the last time I did that." —Betsy Bizot, Lisle, IL

"I can only hope that you will continue to write, so that I can continue to read (and of course buy) your books, for they make me laugh and cry and think ... rare indeed." —Steven Knott, Major, USAF

What do you say?

Send me these books!

Shards of Honor • 72087-2 • $4.99 _____
The Warrior's Apprentice • 72066-X • $4.50 _____
Ethan of Athos • 65604-X • $2.95 _____
Falling Free • 65398-9 • $4.99 _____
Brothers in Arms • 69799-4 • $3.95 _____
Borders of Infinity • 69841-9 • $4.99 _____
The Vor Game • 72014-7 • $4.50 _____
Barrayar • 72083-X • $4.99 _____

Lois McMaster Bujold:
Only from Baen Books

If these books are not available at your local bookstore, just check your choices above, fill out this coupon and send a check or money order for the cover price to Baen Books, Dept. BA, P.O. Box 1403, Riverdale, NY 10471.

NAME: _____

ADDRESS: _____

_____

I have enclosed a check or money order in the amount of $ _____.